OXFORD ENGLISH NOVELS
General Editor: JAMES KINSLEY

THE LIFE
AND ADVENTURES OF
PETER WILKINS

Tab. IV.

Boitard Fecit

The Use of ꝩᵉ Back flap, when ꝩ Glumm flyes.

ROBERT PALTOCK

THE
LIFE AND ADVENTURES
OF
PETER WILKINS

Edited with an Introduction by

CHRISTOPHER BENTLEY

LONDON
OXFORD UNIVERSITY PRESS
NEW YORK   TORONTO
1973

Oxford University Press, Ely House, London W.1

GLASGOW   NEW YORK   TORONTO   MELBOURNE   WELLINGTON
CAPE TOWN   IBADAN   NAIROBI   DAR ES SALAAM   LUSAKA   ADDIS ABABA
DELHI   BOMBAY   CALCUTTA   MADRAS   KARACHI   LAHORE   DACCA
KUALA LUMPUR   SINGAPORE   HONG KONG   TOKYO

ISBN 0 19 255329 1

Introduction, Notes, Bibliography, and Chronology
© Oxford University Press 1973

Printed in Great Britain
at the University Press, Oxford
by Vivian Ridler
Printer to the University

CONTENTS

LIST OF ILLUSTRATIONS

INTRODUCTION

'PETER WILKINS', remarks Coleridge, 'is to my mind a work of uncommon beauty.' 'It would require a very peculiar genius to add another tale, *ejusdem generis*, to Robinson Crusoe and Peter Wilkins'; 'I would try the marvellous line of Peter Wilkins, if I attempted it, rather than the *real* fiction of Robinson Crusoe.'[1] Coleridge is one among several authors of the Romantic period who admired *Peter Wilkins*. Charles Lamb recalls it as one of the 'classics' of his schooldays;[2] Shelley read it as a child and again with Mary Shelley in 1815;[3] Southey records Scott's high opinion of the novel and describes it as 'a work of great genius';[4] and Leigh Hunt twice published, with appreciative introductions, extracts from 'this curious invention'.[5] Numerous editions of the work in the earlier decades of the nineteenth century suggest a popularity not confined to men of letters, even though Southey considers it to be a 'neglected story'; and later in the century Dickens, Disraeli, and Thackeray all refer to *Peter Wilkins* as an apparently well-known tale.[6]

At its first appearance an anonymous reviewer greeted *Peter Wilkins* with less enthusiasm:

Here is a very strange performance indeed. It seems to be the illegitimate offspring of no very natural conjunction betwixt

[1] *Specimens of the Table Talk* (1835), ii. 337–9, under date of 5 July 1834.

[2] 'Christ's Hospital Five and Thirty Years Ago', *Essays of Elia*, ed. Birrell (1906), p. 21.

[3] Thomas Medwin, *The Life of Percy Bysshe Shelley* (1913), p. 24; Mrs. Julian Marshall, *The Life and Letters of Mary Wollstonecraft Shelley* (1889), i. 123.

[4] *Poetical Works* (1837–8), viii. 231. Scott mentions Peter Wilkins in *The Antiquary*, ch. xi.

[5] 'Peter Wilkins and the Flying Women', *London Journal*, No. 32 (reprinted in *The Seer*, No. 31); 'Peter Wilkins's Discovery of the Flying Woman', *A Book for a Corner* (1851), i. 68–92.

[6] *Martin Chuzzlewit*, ch. xxi; *Sybil*, ch. iii; *Pendennis*, ch. ii, and *Henry Esmond*, bk. III, ch. iv.

Gulliver's travels and *Robinson Crusoe*; but much inferior to the meaner of these two performances, either as to entertainment or utility. It has all that is impossible in the one, or improbable in the other, without the wit and spirit of the first, or the just strokes of nature and useful lessons of morality of the second. There are likewise many things in this work which appear to be derived from hints drawn from the *Arabian* nights entertainment. However, if the invention of wings for mankind to fly with, is a sufficient amends for all the dulness and unmeaning extravagancies of this author, we are willing to allow that his book has some merit; and that he deserves encouragement at least as an able mechanic, if not as a good writer.[1]

Certainly, Paltock has always been overshadowed by his two great predecessors in the genre of the imaginary voyage, but the debt to Defoe is substantial only in the earlier chapters of *Peter Wilkins*. Here we find such familiar material as the wayward youth determined to go to sea, capture by pirates, escape, encounters with savage beasts, storms, shipwreck, privations, moralizings and self-reproaches, and a solitary castaway with few resources developing a personal technology in order to master an unfamiliar environment. Once Wilkins discovers the flying men and women (or Glumms and Gawreys, as Paltock infelicitously calls them) the novel acquires an independent vitality. Wilkins assumes powers and responsibilities that are far more complex and demanding than Crusoe's monarchy of one small island, while the relationship between the hero and his Gawrey wife Youwarkee is developed with a subtlety and wit beyond Defoe. Paltock's colloquial diction and knowledgeable use of seafaring terms are in the tradition of *Robinson Crusoe*.

Swift may have provided the important example of an English sailor's voyage to a community of strange beings; but Paltock's flying creatures stem from a long literary tradition reflecting man's wish for the power of flight, and are portrayed with an energy and imaginative detail equal to any of the inventions in *Gulliver's Travels*. The king of the Glumms

---

[1] *Monthly Review*, iv (December 1750), 157.

and Gawreys is suggestively named Georigetti, and after talking privately with him on religion and politics Wilkins admits
that 'I could not help reflecting with myself, how nearly this
distant Prince, and his State, copied some of my Neighbours
in *Europe*'.[1] The account of court life and political intrigues
may, therefore, possibly contain some covert allusions to con-
temporary Europe; but Paltock is interested in his creations
for themselves, not as vehicles of satire, and Swift's major
purpose is scarcely discernible here.

In structure *Peter Wilkins* is closer to the continuous narrative of *Robinson Crusoe* than to the quadripartite form of
Gulliver's Travels. Paltock has improved on his model by
contriving a less ragged ending and by creating an inter-
mediary narrator, the 'Passenger in the *Hector*' identified only
by the initials R. P. (but no doubt a *persona* of Paltock himself) who rescues Wilkins—first from the sea and then from
the uncharitable ship's captain—and receives as a reward the
story of his adventures 'from his own Mouth'. The death of
the aged Wilkins on the night of the ship's arrival in England
places R. P. in the position of literary executor, and makes the
truth of the narrative, in one very real sense, unquestionable.[2]
Verisimilitude of a kind is also established by the skilful
gradation of incidents throughout the novel, progressing from
the familiar and probable (childhood, schooling, and marriage
in England) to the less familiar but by no means unlikely
(adventures at sea and in Africa), then to the utterly strange
and improbable (a mysterious, hitherto undiscovered land
peopled by a race of flying beings). Paltock takes his time in
bringing us to this land, but Wilkins's experiences in England
and Africa during the earlier part of his life are well integrated

[1] p. 269.

[2] The author remained concealed behind the initials R. P. until a pseudonymous
contributor to the *Monthly Magazine; or British Register*, xiv (1802), 379, identified
him. In 1835 the original agreement for the sale of the manuscript, giving Paltock's
full name and address, was discovered, as first announced in the advertisement to
Smith's Standard Library edition (1839), and restated with fuller details by Jas.
Crossley, *Notes and Queries*, x (1854), 212-13. However, E. Phillips Poole, *Times
Literary Supplement*, 4 October 1928, p. 711, cites evidence that the authorship was
known by at least one of Paltock's contemporaries.

into the story. He acquires the fortitude and resourcefulness that will enable him to survive first as a castaway, and then as a wingless stranger among the Glumms and Gawreys, while at the same time we become acquainted with him. When this English traveller comes to the strangest part of his story, he is a familiar and even predictable character whose very presence in it gives stability to his exotic tale.

Like Defoe and Swift, Paltock shows an acquaintance with the literature of travel and exploration, and perhaps with scientific writings. He owned a copy of Thomas Astley's large compilation, *A New General Collection of Voyages and Travels* (1745–7), which contains narratives scarcely less strange than some of Wilkins's adventures, and apparently drew on it for the African episodes in *Peter Wilkins*. It has been suggested, with a fancifulness worthy of Paltock himself, that his hero is named after the mathematician and philologist John Wilkins, Bishop of Chester, who in the previous century had published speculations on the possibility of human flight;[1] but if Paltock knew any of John Wilkins's writings, it is more likely to have been his treatise on a 'Philosophical' or ideal language, which may have inspired the invention of a language for the Glumms and Gawreys (though, again, hints are not wanting in Swift and Defoe). We are told that their language has 'the most musical Tone', but this is hardly true of the vocabulary sample provided, and Paltock's ingenuity is perhaps misplaced here.

Though *Peter Wilkins* could scarcely have been written in anything like its present form without the examples provided by Defoe and Swift, it is no mere imitation. Paltock has selected and adapted: he employs Defoe's meticulous realism but only to launch his own story, and Swift's inventiveness is present without the satiric assault. Indeed, Paltock has been influenced by all the major novelists of his age. The earlier episodes in the story, such as Wilkins's affair with Patty, the servant-maid at his school, and the loss of his inheritance to the scheming Mr. G., recall the picaresque world of *Roderick*

[1] A. H. Bullen, preface to *The Life and Adventures of Peter Wilkins* (1884), I. xvii.

Random, if not Smollett's callousness; Youwarkee, the hero's second wife, for all her strange properties, is rather like a Fielding heroine with wings; while their courtship, and in particular the wedding night, is imbued with something of Richardson's erotic sentimentality. But these influences have been successfully absorbed and controlled. When the limits of its literary indebtedness are recognized, *Peter Wilkins* emerges as a mature and confident work of fantasy.

In 1823 another anonymous critic dissented from the verdict reached by his predecessor in 1750 and found *Peter Wilkins* to be 'a story of infinite merit'. In a long review and partial résumé of this 'work of so much imagination, and, at the same time, of a character so simple and unpretending' he reproves 'the critical discernment of the times, which allowed a book, of such great and peculiar excellence, to fall still-born from the press':

Considered as a work of imagination, it appeared at a season, either too late or too early, to captivate the fancies or strike deep root in the minds of men. At that particular period, when the gross realities of life had superseded the creations of fancy, and the imagination, lying as it were torpid, awaited the moment when it should be again called into life and action, a work, applying itself chiefly to that faculty of the mind, was likely to be coldly received, and unduly appreciated. . . .

But there was another and more fatal course militating against its popularity, and that was the absolute incapacity of the age, to relish any work of that modest and unostentatious beauty which it exhibits.[1]

It is not hard to see why *Peter Wilkins* was neglected by Paltock's contemporaries, lacking as it does both the satiric content of *Gulliver's Travels* and the sustained realism of most eighteenth-century fiction. Readers whose tastes had been formed by the major novelists of the period were predisposed to dismiss the 'marvellous line'—in Coleridge's phrase—when they found it being pursued largely for its own sake. A generation later, the Gothic novelists and the Romantic

[1] *Retrospective Review*, vii (1823), i. 122-4.

poets had transformed literary values, and *Peter Wilkins* was discovered.

More recent criticism, such as it is, confirms both the work's merit and the fact of its continued neglect. Rowland E. Prothero agrees with the 1823 reviewer in believing that '*Peter Wilkins* appeared too soon', for 'it appeals to the sense of wonder and curiosity which characterized the romantic movement';[1] while, in similar terms, Oliver Edwards says that Paltock's 'descriptions of scenes and events have a sense of wonder and a delicacy allied to their matter-of-factness which weaves an enchantment all his own'; unlike Defoe, 'Paltock had a poet's imagination'.[2] The question of indebtedness is considered by Walter de la Mare, who finds Paltock's hero 'the better company for owing so much to Defoe'.[3] *Peter Wilkins* is mentioned, usually in brief and sometimes in dismissive terms, in many histories of English literature and of the English novel—'a minor classic', 'graceful', 'rather a charming book', 'homely yet sensitive and graphic style', and 'an eccentric but rather charming effect'.[4] More perceptive critics have recognized Paltock's sensitivity to the intellectual movements of his age. *The Times Literary Supplement*, reviewing a new edition, regrets that *Peter Wilkins* 'has never taken its deserved place in the lists of popular literature', for 'to the definite merit of the story may be added the interest of the light it throws on the views of the author, which reflected the moving thought of his day';[5] an observation echoed by Edith J. Morley: 'It is difficult to understand why the book has not been more widely known in recent years, particularly to those interested in the movement of thought in the eighteenth century.'[6]

[1] *The Light Reading of Our Ancestors* [1927], pp. 283-4.
[2] *The Times*, 21 July 1955, p. 11 (reprinted in *Talking of Books*, 1957, pp. 37–40).
[3] *Desert Islands and Robinson Crusoe* (1930), p. 67.
[4] Edmund Gosse, *English Literature: An Illustrated Record*, iii (1903), 327; Sir Walter Raleigh, *The English Novel* [1894], p. 219; George Saintsbury, *The English Novel* (1913), p. 145; Ernest A. Baker, *The History of the English Novel*, v (1929), 44; Lionel Stevenson, *The English Novel* (1960), p. 110.
[5] *TLS*, 7 May 1925, p. 312.
[6] *The Year's Work in English Studies 1925*, vi (1927), 224.

This 'movement of thought' dominates the latter part of the novel, which is largely an account of the 'Laws, Customs, and Manners' of the Glumms and Gawreys, and of the extraordinary changes in their society resulting from the arrival of Wilkins armed with the skills and philosophies of Europe. 'When Peter Wilkins leaves his solitary home to live among the winged people,' writes A. H. Bullen, 'the interest of the story, it must be confessed, is somewhat diminished';[1] but modern readers are likely to disagree, and perhaps to find among these later chapters some of the most interesting episodes in the novel. The title-page promises 'remarkable Transactions' at this stage of the narrative, and we are not disappointed.

Like Pizarro he finds his newly-discovered people demoralized by civil war, and like Cortés he is fortunate enough to find his way prepared by the mythology of the race; but unlike these empire-builders, Wilkins is a philanthropist who comes, as he assures King Georigetti, not 'to possess, but redress a Kingdom'—his conquest is an intellectual one and is attended with the minimum of bloodshed. Many years before Wilkins's arrival a holy man of the Glumms and Gawreys, after vainly attempting to abolish image-worship, had conveniently prophesied the coming of a man

with Hair round his Head, swimming and flying without the Graundee; who, with unknown Fire and Smoak, shall destroy the Traitor of the West, settle the ancient Limits of the Monarchy, by common Consent establish what I would have taught you, change the Name of this Country, introduce new Laws and Arts, add Kingdoms to this State, and force Tributes from the Bowels of the Earth, of such things as this Kingdom shall not know till then, and shall never afterwards want.[2]

Though Wilkins at first gives little credit to the prophecy, it is sufficient sanction for him to loose his reformist zeal on the nation. Gunpowder and the science of European warfare are introduced; a rebellion is quelled and a conspiracy frustrated;

---

[1] *The Life and Adventures of Peter Wilkins* (1884), I. xvi.
[2] p. 243.

colonies are established; slavery is abolished; mines and manu-
factures are developed; and various arts, including writing,
are taught to the people. These policies show Wilkins to be
both the heir of the Enlightenment and an apostle of more
revolutionary doctrines; even the terms in which some of his
achievements are noted recall the rhetoric of eighteenth-
century political reform, for we are told that he *makes Laws
with the Consent of the People* and *opens a free Trade*.[1]

But closest to Wilkins's heart is the purpose that had first
persuaded him to attempt the hazardous flight to the country
of the Glumms and Gawreys; and even before political
stability has been established their easygoing monotheistic
paganism is painlessly superseded by an equally easygoing
Christianity that is perhaps not too far removed from deism.
His reflections on this missionary task are entirely charac-
teristic of the man:

> Having now fully entred into the Spirit of the Business with my
> own good Liking, I was determined to push it vigorously, or
> perish in the Attempt. Have I, says I, so large a Field before me
> now to manifest my Maker in to a whole Nation, and under his
> own Call, and to fullfil their own Prediction too; and shall I shrink
> at the possible Danger? Or may there not rather be no probability
> of Danger in it? The Nation is in distress, the readier therefore to
> try any Remedy for help: . . . Therefore let me consider in a
> prudential way how to proceed to the Execution of what I am to
> set about; and guide me, Providence! I beseech you, to the End.[2]

Courage, opportunism, practicality, and the frightening belief
that Providence operates through Peter Wilkins, are the
qualities that sustain him. Apart from a natural desire to see
his children well placed in life, he is indifferent to personal
aggrandizement. Though his influence over King Georigetti
(who, to judge from his sceptical discourse on religion, was
already a potential philosopher-king) makes Wilkins the virtual
ruler of the country, he is content to remain a power behind
the throne. The government he establishes savours more of
enlightened despotism than of democracy, and the result of

[1] pp. 330, 364.   [2] pp. 269-70.

his labours is a rapid transformation of the society into a progressive Europeanized state.

At no time in the course of this civilizing mission does
Wilkins stop to consider that he may be destroying a culture.
The Glumms and Gawreys are not exactly noble savages, for
they are scarcely primitive enough; but they have some of the
innocence and much of the dignity of natural man. Wilkins,
a well-meaning serpent in this second Eden, brings them
dangerous knowledge. His self-confidence and energy, laud-
able when he was merely an unlucky sailor, or a husband and
father struggling to provide for his family (even his smugness
is comic and forgivable in these circumstances), are dangerous
when he becomes the arbiter of an entire people. In the midst
of so much change Wilkins himself remains apparently
immutable; his social circumstances improve as he advances
from a deferential dependant of his father-in-law to a trusted
and almost indispensable adviser of royalty, but he is unable
to absorb any influence from the society around him. His
instinct is always to reshape whatever he finds into some acceptable European pattern. When the death of his wife removes the
only real contact he has with this society, his reaction is first
to withdraw from public life and then to leave the country;
which he does without any regret, perhaps because he appears
to have run out of reforming schemes.

Only once does the aged Wilkins seem to realize what he
may have done to the Glumms and Gawreys. When he first
encountered them, he recalls, 'all the Riches they possessed
were only Food and Slaves; and, as I found afterwards when
amongst them, they know the want of nothing else: But, I am
afraid, I have put them upon another way of thinking, tho'
I aimed at what we call civilizing of them'.[1] Significantly, this
damning admission occurs before the account of Wilkins's
reforming work among the Glumms and Gawreys, and inevit-
ably makes his achievements seem very dubious. Paltock does
not permit himself explicit authorial comment (indeed, the
mechanism of his story precludes it), but here we can perhaps

[1] p. 215.

B

discover his own opinion of the progressive ideas that his hero embraces. Some of the social and political theories becoming fashionable in Paltock's England are tested in a fictional society. The results are inconclusive, though we may share Wilkins's fear that the Glumms and Gawreys are worse off for his efforts. Little is known of Paltock's life, but his novel, in its modest way, is an intellectual biography, and shows him to be an astute, reflective man, aware of the limitations and dangers in the 'new Philosophy' of his day. A generation before the British began to build a second empire following the loss of America, many of the values and assumptions on which this new empire was to be based are being intelligently questioned through the medium of an imaginary voyage.

NOTE ON THE TEXT

PALTOCK assigned the copyright of *Peter Wilkins* to Jacob Robinson and Robert Dodsley on 11 January 1749 for a consideration of twenty-one pounds and twelve printed copies in sheets, with 'the cuts of the first impression'. The book, listed in the *Gentleman's Magazine*, xx (November 1750), 528, was published in London on 3 December 1750 (Ralph Straus, *Robert Dodsley*, 1910, p. 340) in two duodecimo volumes dated 1751. Six engravings by Louis Pierre Boitard are placed at the end of the second volume, and the work sold for six shillings. George Faulkner's Dublin edition of the same date is a crowded reprint of the London text. A French translation appeared in 1763 and a German abridgement in 1767, but no further English edition was published until 1783, when *Peter Wilkins* was included in the *Novelist's Magazine*, vol. xii.

The present text is printed from the Bodleian Library copy of the first edition. Obvious errors of the press have been silently corrected, and the long 's' has been eliminated. The many and sometimes striking inconsistencies in spelling and italicization, particularly of proper nouns both real and imaginary, have been preserved in a work that purports to originate in a manuscript written from dictation.

SELECT BIBLIOGRAPHY

The Life and Adventures of Peter Wilkins was frequently reprinted in Britain and America during the nineteenth century, sometimes in altered and abridged versions. A. H. Bullen's edition (Reeves & Turner, 1884) contains an introductory essay, and reproduces Boitard's engravings from the first edition. More recent editions include: 1914 (Everyman's Library, with Bullen's introduction); 1925 (Dulau, with a brief biographical note and Boitard's engravings); 1928 (Dent, with Bullen's introduction and illustrations by Edward Bawden).

BIBLIOGRAPHY. Philip Babcock Gove, *The Imaginary Voyage in Prose Fiction* (1941; Columbia University Studies in English and Comparative Literature, no. 152; reprinted 1961) contains a full list of editions and criticism of *Peter Wilkins* (pp. 320-7), and a valuable discussion of the genre.

BIOGRAPHY AND CRITICISM. The entry in the *Dictionary of National Biography* is supplemented by William E. A. Axon, *Notes and Queries*, 10S., xii (1909), 286; and by A. J. P. Skinner, *Times Literary Supplement*, 14 May 1925, p. 335. Studies of Paltock's influence include Harold Leroy Hoffman, *An Odyssey of the Soul: Shelley's Alastor* (1933), pp. 78-83; and John Robert Moore, 'Coleridge's Indebtedness to Paltock's *Peter Wilkins*', *Modern Philology*, xxxi (1933-4), 79-83. *Peter Wilkins* is treated briefly by Oliver Elton, *A Survey of English Literature 1730-1780* (1928), i. 233-5; J. O. Bailey, *Pilgrims through Space and Time: Trends and Patterns in Scientific and Utopian Fiction* (1947), pp. 14, 191; and more thoroughly by Marjorie Hope Nicolson, *Voyages to the Moon* (1948), pp. 136-43.

A CHRONOLOGY OF
ROBERT PALTOCK

THE

LIFE *and* ADVENTURES

OF

PETER WILKINS,

A *Cornish* Man:

Relating particularly,

His Shipwreck near the South Pole; his wonderful Passage
thro' a subterraneous Cavern into a kind of new World;
his there meeting with a Gawry or flying Woman,
whose Life he preserv'd, and afterwards married her;
his extraordinary Conveyance to the Country of Glums
and Gawrys, or Men and Women that fly. Likewise
a Description of this strange Country, with the Laws,
Customs, and Manners of its Inhabitants, and the
Author's remarkable Transactions among them.

Taken from his own Mouth, in his Passage to *England*,
from off *Cape Horn* in *America*, in the Ship *Hector*.

With an INTRODUCTION, giving an Account of the
surprizing Manner of his coming on board that Vessel,
and his Death on his landing at *Plymouth* in the Year
1739.

Illustrated with several CUTS, clearly and distinctly
representing the Structure and Mechanism of the
Wings of the Glums and Gawrys, and the Manner in
which they use them either to swim or fly.

By R. S. *a Passenger in the* Hector.

To the RIGHT HONOURABLE

ELIZABETH,

Countess of *Northumberland*

MADAM,

FEW Authors, I believe, who write in my Way, (whatever
View they may set out with) can, in the Prosecution of their
Work, forbear to dress their fictitious Characters, in the real
Ornaments themselves have been most delighted with.

This, I confess, hath been my Case, in the Person of
Youwarkee, in the following Sheets; for having formed her
Body, I found myself at an inexpressible Loss how to adorn
her Mind in the masterly Sentiments I coveted to endue her
with; 'till I recollected the most aimable Pattern in your
Ladyship; a single View of which, at a Time of the utmost
Fatigue to his Lordship, hath charmed my Imagination ever
since.

If a Participater of the Cares of Life in general, alleviates
the Concerns of Man; what an invaluable Blessing must that
Lady prove, to the Softness of whose Sex Nature hath con-
joined an Aptitude for Council, an Application, Zeal and
Dispatch, but too rarely found in his own?

Had my Situation in Life been so happy as to have presented me with Opportunities of more frequent and minuter
Remarks upon your Ladyship's Conduct, I might have
defy'd the whole *British* Fair to have outshone my southern
Gawry: For if, to a majestick Form and extensive Capacity,
I had been qualified to have copied that natural Sweetness
of Disposition, that maternal Tenderness, that Chearfulness, that Complacency, Condescension, Affability, and un-
affected Benevolence, which so apparently distinguish the

Countess of *Northumberland*; I had exhibited in my *You-warkee*, a Standard for future Generations.

Madam, I am the more sensible of my Speaking but the Truth, from the late Instance of your Benignity, which intitles me to the Honour of subscribing myself,

Madam,

Your Ladyship's

most obliged and

most obedient Servant

R. P.

THE

INTRODUCTION

I T might be looked upon as impertinent in me, who am about
to give the Life of another, to trouble the Reader with any
of my own Concerns, or the Affairs that led me into the *South-
Seas*. Therefore, I shall only acquaint him, that in my Return
on board the *Hector*, as a Passenger, round *Cape Horn*, for
England, full late in the Season, the Wind and Currents
setting strong against us, our Ship drove more southerly by
several Degrees than the usual Course, even to the Latitude
of 75 or 76; when, the Wind chopping about, we began to
resume our intended Way. It was about the Middle of *June*,
when the Days are there at the shortest, on a very starry and
Moon-light Night, that we observed at some Distance a very
black Cloud, but seemingly of no extraordinary Size or Height,
moving very fast towards us, and seeming to follow the Ship,
which then made great Way. Every one on Deck was very
curious in observing its Motions; and perceiving it frequently
to divide, and presently to close again, and not to continue
long in any determined Shape, our Captain, who had never
before been so far to the Southward as he then found himself,
had many Conjectures what this Phenomenon might portend;
and every one offering his own Opinion, it seemed at last to be
generally agreed, that there might possibly be a Storm gathering in the Air, of which this was the Prognostick; and by its
following, and nearly keeping Pace with us, we were in great
Fear lest it should break upon and overwhelm us, if not carefully avoided. Our Commander therefore, as it approached
nearer and nearer, ordered one of the Ship's Guns to be fired,
to try if the Percussion of the Air would disperse it. This was

no sooner done, than we heard a prodigious Flounce[1] in the
Water, at but a small Distance from the Ship, on the Weather
Quarter; and after a violent Noise, or Cry in the Air, the
Cloud, that upon our firing dissipated, seemed to return again,
but by Degrees disappeared. Whilst we were all very much
surprized at this unexpected Accident, I, being naturally very
curious, and inquisitive into the Causes of all unusual
Incidents, begged the Captain to send the Boat, to see, if
possible, what it was that had fallen from the Cloud, and
offered myself to make one in her. He was much against this
at first, as it would retard his Voyage, now we were going so
smoothly before the Wind. But in the Midst of our Debate,
we plainly heard a Voice calling out for Help, in our own
Tongue, like a Person in great Distress. I then insisted on
going, and not suffering a Fellow-Creature to perish for the
Sake of a trifling Delay. In compliance with my resolute
Demand, he slackened Sail; and hoisting out the Boat, myself and seven others made to the Cry; and soon found it to
come from an elderly Man, labouring for Life, with his Arms
across several long Poles, of equal Size at both Ends, very
light, and tied to each other in a very odd Manner. The Sailors
at first were very fearful of assisting, or coming near him; crying to each other, he must be a Monster, and perhaps might
overset the Boat and destroy them; but hearing him speak
English, I was very angry with them for their foolish Apprehensions, and caused them to clap their Oars under him; and
at length we got him into the Boat. He had an extravagant
Beard, and also long blackish Hair upon his Head. As soon
as he could speak (for he was almost spent) he very familiarly
took me by the Hand, I having set myself close by him to
observe him, and squeezing it, thanked me very kindly for
my Civility to him, and likewise thanked all the Sailors. I then
asked him by what possible Accident he came there; but he
shook his Head, declining to satisfy my Curiosity. Hereupon
reflecting, that it might just then be troublesome for him to
speak, and that we should have Leisure enough in our Voyage
for him to relate, and me to hear, his Story, (which, from the

surprizing Manner of his falling amongst us, I could not but believe would contain something very remarkable) I waved any further Speech with him at that Time.

We had him to the Ship, and taking off his wet Clothes, put him to Bed in my Cabbin; and I having a large Provision of Stores on board, and no Concern in the Ship, grew very fond of him, and supplied him with every thing he wanted. In our frequent Discourses together he had several Times dropped loose Hints of his past Transactions, which but the more inflamed me with Impatience to hear the Whole of them. About this Time, having just begun to double the Cape, our Captain thought of watering at the first convenient Place; and finding the Stranger had no Money to pay his Passage, and that he had been from *England* no less than thirty-five Years,[1] despairing of his Reward for conducting him thither, he intimated to him, that he must expect to be put on shore, to shift for himself, when we put in for Water. This intirely sunk the Stranger's Spirits, and gave me great Concern; insomuch that I fully resolved, if the Captain should really prove such a Brute, to take the Payment of his Passage on myself.

As we came nearer to the destined Watering, the Captain spoke the plainer of his Intentions (for I had not yet hinted my Design to him, or any one else;) and one Morning the Stranger came into my Cabbin, with Tears in his Eyes, telling me, he verily believed the Captain would be as good as his Word, and set him on shore, which he very much dreaded. I did not chuse to tell him immediately what I designed in his Favour, but asked him if he could think of no Way of satisfying the Captain, or any one else who might thereupon be induced to engage for him; and further, how he expected to live when he should get to *England*, a Man quite forgotten and penny-less? Hereupon he told me, he had ever since his being on board, considering his destitute Condition, entertained a Thought of having his Adventures written; which, as there was something so uncommon in them, he was sure the World would be glad to know; and he had flattered himself with Hopes of raising somewhat by the Sale of them to put him in a Way of Living: But, as it was plain now, he should never see *England* without my Assistance; if I would answer for his Passage, and write his Life, he would communicate to me a faithful Narrative thereof, which he believed would pay me to the full, any Charge I might be at on his Account. I was very well pleased with this Overture; not from the Prospect of Gain by the Copy, but from the Expectation I had of being fully satisfied in what I had so long desired to know. So I told him I would make him easy in that Respect. This quite transported him. He caressed me, and called me his Deliverer; and was then going open-mouthed to the Captain to tell him so; but I put a Stop to that; for, says I, (though I insist upon hearing your Story) the Captain may yet relent of his Purpose, and not leave you on shore; and if that should prove the Case, I shall neither part with my Money for you, nor you with your Interest in your Adventures to me: Whereupon he agreed I was right, and desisted.

When we had taken in best Part of our Water, and the Boat was going its last Turn, the Captain ordered up the strange Man, as they called him, and told him he must go on board the Boat, which was to leave him on shore, with some few Provisions. I happening to hear nothing of these Orders, they were so sudden, the poor Man was afraid, after all, he should have been hurried to Land without my Knowledge; but begging very hard of the Captain only for Leave to speak with me before he went, I was called, (though with some Reluctance; for the Captain disliked me, for the Liberties I frequently took with him, on account of his brutal Behaviour.) I expostulated with the cruel Wretch on the Inhumanity of the Action he was about; telling him, if he had resolved the poor Man should perish, it would have been better to have suffered him to do so, when he was at the last Extremity, than to expose him afresh, by this Means, to a Death as certain, in a more lingering and miserable Way. But the Savage being resolved, and nothing moved by what I said, I paid him Part of the Passage down, and agreed to pay the rest at our Arrival in *England*.

Thus having reprieved the poor Man, the next Thing was to enter upon my new Employ of Amanuensis. And having a long Space of Time before us, we allotted two Hours every Morning for the Purpose of writing down his Life from his own Mouth; and frequently, when Wind and Weather kept us below, we spent some Time of an Afternoon in the same Exercise, till we had quite compleated it. But then there were some Things in it so indescribable by Words, that if I had not had some Knowledge also in Drawing, our History had been very incompleat. Thus it must have been, especially, in the Description of the *Glumms* and *Gawrys* therein mentioned. In order to gain (that so I might communicate) a clear Idea of these, I made several Drawings of them, in all the Forms and Attitudes I could conceive from his Discourses and Accounts; and at length, after divers Trials, I made such exact Delineations, that he declared they could not have been more perfect Resemblances, if I had drawn them from the Life. Upon a Survey, he confessed the very Persons themselves could not have been more exact. I also drew with my Pencil the Figure of an aireal Engagement, which, having likewise had his Approbation, I have given a Draught of, Plate the *sixth*.

Then, having finished the Work to our mutual Satisfaction, I locked it up, in order to peruse it at Leisure, intending to have presented it to him at our Arrival in *England*, to dispose of as he pleased, in such a Way as might have conduced most to his Profit; for I resolved, notwithstanding our Agreement, and the Obligations he was under to me, that the Whole of that should be his own. But he, having been in a declining State sometime before we reached shore, died the very Night we landed; and his Funeral falling upon me, I thought I had the greatest Right to the Manuscript: Which however, I had no Design to have parted with; but shewing it to some judicious Friends, I have by them been prevailed with, not to conceal from the World, what may prove so very entertaining, and perhaps useful.

R. P.

C

Tab. III.

Boitard Fecit.

A Ganrey Extended for Flight.

Tab.V.
Boitard Fecit

A Glumm Swimming.

A

GENUINE ACCOUNT

OF THE

LIFE

OF

PETER WILKINS

VOLUME I

CHAPTER I

*Giving an Account of the Author's Birth and Family;
the Fondness of his Mother; his being put to an Academy at
sixteen by the Advice of his Friend; his Thoughts of his
own Illiterature*

I WAS born at *Penhale*, in the County of *Cornwall*, on the
21st Day of *December*, 1685, about four Months after my
Father *Peter Wilkins*, who was a zealous Protestant, of the
Church of *England*, had been executed by *Jefferys*,[1] in
Somersetshire, for joining in the Design of raising the Duke
of *Monmouth* to the *British* Throne. I was named, after my
Father and Grand-father, *Peter*, and was my Father's only
Child by *Alice* his Wife, the Daughter of *John Capert*, a
Clergyman in a neighbouring Village. My Grandfather was
a Shopkeeper at *Newport*, who, by great Frugality, and extra-
ordinary Application, had raised a Fortune of about one
hundred and sixty Pounds a Year in Lands, and a considerable
Sum of ready Money; all which at his Death devolved upon
my Father, as his only Child; who being no less parsimonious

than my Grandfather, and living upon his own Estate, had much improved it in Value, before his Marriage with my Mother; but, he coming to that unhappy End, my Mother, after my Birth, placed all her Affection upon me, (her growing Hopes as she call'd me) and used every Method, in my Minority, of encreasing the Store for my Benefit.

In this Manner she went on, till I grew too big, as I thought, for Confinement at the Apron-string, being then about fourteen Years of Age; and having met with so much Indulgence from her, for that Reason, found very little or no Contradiction from any body else; so I looked on myself as a Person of some Consequence, and began to take all Opportunities of enjoying the Company of my Neighbours, who hinted, frequently, that the Restraint I was under, was too great a Curb upon an Inclination like mine of seeing the World; but my Mother, still impatient of any little Absence, by excessive Fondness, and encouraging of every Inclination I seemed to have, when she could be a Partaker with me, kept me within Bounds of Restraint, till I arrived at my sixteenth Year.

About this time I got acquainted with a Country-Gentleman, of a small paternal Estate, which had been never the better for being in his Hands, and had some uneasy Demands upon it. He soon grew very fond of me, hoping, as I had Reason afterwards to believe, by a Union with my Mother, to set himself free from his Intanglements. She was then about Thirty-five Years old, and still continued my Father's Widow, out of particular regard to me, as I have all the Reason in the World to believe. She was really a beautiful Woman, and of a sanguine Complexion; but had always carried herself with so much Reserve, and given so little Encouragement to any of the other Sex, that she had passed her Widowhood with very few Solicitations to alter her Way of Life. This Gentleman, observing my Mother's Conduct, in order to ingratiate himself with her, had shewn numberless Instances of Regard for me, and, as he told my Mother, had observed many Things in my Discourse, Actions, and Turn of Mind, that presaged wonderful Expectations from me, if my Genius was but properly cultivated.

This Discourse, from a Man of very good Parts, and esteemed by every body an accomplished Gentleman, by Degrees wrought upon my Mother, and more and more inflamed her with a Desire of adding what Lustre she could to my applauded abilities, and influenced her so far as to ask his Advice in what Manner most properly to proceed with me. My Gentleman then had his Desire; for, he feared not the Widow, could he but properly dispose of her Charge; so, having desired a little Time to consider of a Matter of such Importance, he soon after told her, he thought the most useful Method of establishing me, would be at an Academy, kept by a very worthy and judicious Gentleman, about thirty or more Miles from us, in *Somersetshire*; where, if I could but be admitted, the Master taking in but a stated Number of Students at a Time, he did not in the least doubt, but I should fully answer the Character he had given her of me, and outshine most of my Cotemporaries.

My Mother, over-anxious for my good, seeming to listen to this Proposal, my Friend, as I call him, proposed taking a Journey himself to the Academy, to see if any Place was vacant for my Reception, and learn the Terms of my Admission; and in three Days Time returned with an engaging Account of the Place, the Master, the Regularity of the Scholars, of an Apartment secured for my Reception, and, in short, whatever else might captivate my Mother's Opinion in Favour of his Scheme; and indeed, tho' he acted principally from another Motive, as was plain afterwards, I can't help thinking, he believed it to be the best way of disposing of a Lad, sixteen Years old, born to a pretty Fortune, and who, at that Age, could but just read a Chapter in the Testament: For he had before beat my Mother quite out of her Inclination to a Grammar School in the Neighbourhood, from a Contempt, he said, it would bring upon me, from Lads much my Juniors in Years, by being placed in the first Rudiments of Learning with them.

Well, the whole Concern of my Mother's little Family was now employed in fitting me out for my Expedition; and as my

Friend had been so instrumental in bringing it about, he never missed a Day enquiring how Preparations went on, and, during the Process, by humouring me, ingratiated himself more and more with my Mother; but without seeming in the least to aim at it.

In short, the Hour of my Departure arrived; and tho' I had never been Master of above Sixpence at one Time, unless at a Fair, or so, for immediate spending, my Mother, thinking to make my Heart easy at our Separation, which had it appeared otherwise, would have broke hers, and spoiled all, gave me a double Pistole[1] in Gold, and a little Silver in my Pocket to prevent my changing it.

Thus I, the Coach waiting for us at the Door, having been preached into a good liking of the Scheme by my Friend, who now insisted upon making one of our Company to introduce us, mounted the Carriage with more Alacrity than could be expected for one who had never before been beyond the Smoak of his Mother's Chimney;[2] but the Thoughts I had conceived, from my Friend's Discourse, of Liberty in the Academick Way, and the Weight of so much Money in my Pocket, as I then imagined would scarce ever be exhausted, were prevailing Cordials to keep my Spirits on the Wing. We lay at an Inn that Night, near the Master's House, and the next Day I was initiated; and, at parting with me, my Friend presented me with a Guinea. When I found myself thus rich, I must say, I heartily wished they were all fairly at home again; that I might have Time to count my Cash, and dispose of such Part of it as I had already appropriated to several Uses then in Embryo.

The next Morning left me Master of my Wishes: For my Mother came and took her last (tho' she little thought it) Leave of me, and smothering me with her Caresses and Prayers for my well-doing, in the Heighth of her Ardour, put into my Hand another Guinea, promising to see me again quickly; and desiring me, in the mean time, to be a very good Husband, which I have since taken to be a Sort of prophetick Speech, She bid me farewel.

I shall not trouble you with the Reception I met from my Master, or his Scholars; or tell you, how soon I made Friends of all my Companions, by some trifling Largesses, which my Stock enabled me to bestow, as occasion required; but I must inform you, that after sixteen Years of Idleness at Home, I had but little Heart to my Nouns and Pronouns, which now began to be crammed upon me; and being the eldest Lad in the House, I sometimes regretted the Loss of the Time past, and at other times despaired of ever making a Scholar, at my Years; and was ashamed to stand like a great Lubber,[1] declining of *Hæc Mulier*, a Woman,[2] whilst my School-fellows, and Juniors by five Years, were engaged in the Love Stories of *Ovid*, or the luscious Songs of *Horace*: I own these Thoughts almost overcame me, and threw me into a deep melancholly, of which I soon after by Letter informed my Mother; who, (by the Advice as I suppose of my Friend, by this Time her Suitor) sent me Word to mind my Studies, and I should want for nothing.

CHAPTER II

How he spent his Time at the Academy; an Intrigue with a Servant-Maid there; she declares herself with Child by him; her Expostulations to him; he is put to it for Money; refused it from Home, by his Friend, who had married his Mother; is drawn in to marry the Maid; she lies-in at her Aunt's; returns to her Service; he has another Child by her

I HAD now been passing my Time for about three Months, in this melancholy Way; and you may imagine, under that Disadvantage, had made but little Progress in my Learning; when one of our Maids, taking Notice one Day of my Un-easiness, as I sat musing in my Chamber, according to my Custom, began to rally me, that I was certainly in Love,

I was so sad. Indeed, I never had a Thought of Love before; but the good-natur'd Girl, seeming to pity me, and seriously asking me the Cause, I fairly open'd my Heart to her; and for fear my Master should know it, gave her half a Crown to be silent. This last Engagement fixed her my Devotee, and from that Time, we had frequent Conferences, in Confidence together; till at length, Inclination, framed by Opportunity, produced the Date of a World of Concern to me; for, about six Months after my Arrival at the Academy, instead of proving my Parts by my Scholarship, I had proved my Manhood, by being the destined Father of an Infant, which my female Correspondent then assured me would soon be my own.

We nevertheless held on our frequent Intercourse; nor was I so alarmed at the News, as I ought to have been, till about two Months after, when *Patty* (for that was the only Name I then knew her by) explained herself to me, in the following Terms.—You know, Mr. *Peter*, how Matters are with me; I should be very sorry, for your Sake, and my own too, to reveal my Shame; but in spite of us both, Nature will shew itself; and truly, I think, some care should be taken, and some Method proposed, to preserve the Infant, and avoid, as far as may be, the Inconveniencies that may attend us; for, here is now no room for Delay.—This Speech, I own, gave me the first Reflection I ever had in my Life, and lock'd up all my Faculties for a long Time; nor was I able, for the Variety of Ideas that crowded my Brain, to make a Word of Answer, but stood like an Image of Stone; till *Patty*, seeing my Confusion, desired me to recollect my Reason, for as it was too late to undo what had been done, it remained now only to act with that Prudence, and Caution, which the Nature of the Case required; and that, for her Part, she would concur in every reasonable Measure I should approve of; but, I must remember, she was only a Servant, and had very little due to her for Wages, and not a Penny besides that; and, that there must necessarily be a Preparation made for the Reception of the Infant, when Time should produce it.—I now began to see the absolute Necessity of all she said; but, how to accomplish it, was not in me to comprehend.—My own small Matter of Money was gone, and had been so a long Time; we therefore agreed, I should write to my Mother for a fresh Supply; I did so, and, to my great Confusion, was answered by my former Friend, in the following Words.

Son PETER,

Your Mother and I are much surprised you should write for Money, having so amply provided for you; but as it is not many Months to *Christmas*, when possibly we may send for you home, you must make yourself easy till then; as a School-boy, with all Necessaries found him, can't have much occasion for Money. Your loving Father, *J. G.*

Imagine, if it is possible, my Consternation at the Receipt of this Letter. I began to think, I should be tricked out of what my Father and Grandfather had, with so much Pains and Industry, for many Years been heaping up for me; and had a thousand Thoughts altogether, justling out each other; so could resolve on nothing. I then shewed *Patty* the Letter, and we both condoled my hard Fortune, but saw no Remedy. Time wore away, and nothing done, or like to be, as I could see.—For my Part, I was like one distracted, and no more able to assist, or counsel what should be done, than a Child in Arms. At length poor *Patty*, who had sat thinking some Time, began, with telling me, she had formed a Scheme, which in some Measure might help us; but, fearing it might be disagreeable to me, she durst not mention it, till I should assure her, whatever I thought of That, I would think no worse of her, for proposing it.—This preparatory Introduction, startled me a great deal; for it darted into my Head, she waited for my Concurrence to destroy the Child; to which, I could never have consented. But, upon my assuring her, that I would not think the worse of her, for whatever she should propose, but freely give her my Opinion upon it; she told me, as she could see no other Way before us, but what tended to our Disgrace and Ruin, if I would marry her, she would immediately quit her Place, and retire to her Aunt, who had brought her up from a Child, and had enough, prettily to live upon; who, she did not doubt, would entertain her as my Wife, but she was assured, upon any other Score, or under any other Name, would prove her most inveterate Enemy.—When *Patty* had made an end, I was glad to find it no worse, and revolving Matters a little in my Mind, both as to Affairs at home, and the requested Marriage, I concluded upon this latter, and had a great Inclination to acquaint my Mother of it; but was diverted from that, by suspecting it might prove a good Handle for my new Father, to work with my Mother some Mischief against me; so determined to marry forthwith, send *Patty* to her Aunt's, and remain still at the Academy myself, till I should see what turn Things would take at home. Accordingly, the next Day, good Part of *Patty*'s Wages went to tie the Connubial Knot, and to the honest Parson for a Bribe to ante-date the Certificate; and she very soon after took up the rest, to defray her Journey to her Aunt's.

Though *Patty* was within two Months of her Time, she had so managed, that no one perceived it; and, getting safe to her Aunt's, was delivered of a Daughter, of which she wrote me Word, and said, she hoped to see me at the End of her Month. How, think I, can she expect to see me, Money I have none; and then, I despaired of Leave for a Journey, if I had it; and to go without Leave, would only arm *J. G.* against me, as I perceived plainly his Interest and mine were very remote Things; so I resolved to quit all Thoughts of a Journey, and wait till Opportunity better served, for seeing my Wife and Child, and our good Aunt, to whom we were so much obliged. —While these and such like Cogitations engrossed my whole Attention, I was most pleasingly surprised one Day, upon my return from a musing Walk, by the River Side, at the End of our Garden, where I frequently got my Tasks, to find *Patty* sitting in the Kitchen, with my old Mistress, my Master's Mother, who managed his House, he having been a Widower many Years. The Sight of her almost overcame me, as I had bolted into the Kitchen, and was seen by my old Mistress, before I had seen *Patty* was with her. The old Lady perceiving me discomposed, inquired into the Cause, which I directly imputed to the Symptoms of an Ague, that, I told her, I had felt upon me best Part of the Morning. She, a good motherly Woman, feeling my Pulse, and satisfying herself of its Disorder, immediately ran to her Closet to bring me a Cordial, which she assured me had done Wonders in the like Cases; so that I had but just Time to embrace *Patty*, and enquire after our Aunt and Daughter, before Madam returned with the Cordial. Having drank it, and given Thanks, I was going to withdraw, but she would not part with me so; for nothing less than my Knowledge, that this Cordial was of her own making, from whence she had the Receipt, and an exact Catalogue of the several Cures it had done, would serve her Turn; which, taking up full three Quarters of an Hour, gave room to *Patty* and me, to enjoy each others Glances for that Time, to our mutual Satisfaction. At last, the old Prattlebox having made a short Pause, to recover Breath, from the Narrative of the Cordial; Mr. *Peter*, says she, you look as if you did not know poor *Patty*; she has not left me so long that you should forget her; she is a good tight[1] Wench, and I was sorry to part with her; but she is out of Place, she says, and as that dirty Creature *Nan* is gone, I think to take her again. I told her, I well knew she was judge of a good Servant, and I did not doubt *Patty* was such, if she thought so; and then I made my Exit, lighter in Heart by a Pound than I came.

I shall not tire you any farther with the Amours between self and *Patty*; but to let you know, she quitted her Place again, seven Months after, upon the same Score.

CHAPTER III

Minds his Studies; informs his Master of his Mother's
Marriage, and Usage of him; hears of her Death;
makes his Master his Guardian; goes with him to
take Possession of his Estate; is informed all is given
to his Father-in-Law; Moral Reflections on his
Condition, and on his Father's Crimes

I WAS now near nineteen Years of Age; and though I had
so much more in my Head, than my School-Learning, I know
not how it happened, but ever since the Commencement of
my Amour with *Patty*, having somebody to disburthen my
Mind to, and participate in my Concerns, I had been much
easier, and had kept true tally with my Book, with more than
usual Delight; and being arrived to an Age, to comprehend
what I heard and read, I could, from the general Idea I had
of Things, form a pretty regular Piece of *Latin*, without being
able to repeat the very Rules it was done by; so that I had the
Acknowledgment of my Master, for the best Capacity he ever
had under his Tuition: This, he not sparing frequently to
mention it before me, was the acutest Spur he could have
applied to my Industry; and now, having his good Will,
I began to disuse set Hours of Exercise, but at my Conveniency applied myself to my Studies, as I best pleased,
being always sure to perform as much, or more, than he ever
enjoined me; till I grew exceedingly in his Confidence, and
by Reason of my Age (though I was but small, yet manly)
I became rather his Companion upon Parties, than his direct
Pupil.

It was upon one of these Parties, I took the Opportunity
to declare the Dissatisfaction I had at my Mother's second
Marriage. Sir, says I, surely I was of Age to have known it
first, especially, considering the Affection my Mother had
always shewn to me, and my never once having done the least
Thing to disoblige her; but, Sir, said I, something else I fear

is intended, by my Mother's Silence to me; for I have never received above three Letters from her, since I came here, which is now you know, three Years; and those were within the first three Months. I then shewed him the forementioned Letter I received from my new Father-in-Law, and assured him, that gave me the first Hint of this second Marriage.

I found, by the Attention my Master gave to my relation, he seemed to suspect this Marriage would prove detrimental to me; but not, on the sudden, knowing what to say to it, he told me, he would consider of it; and, by all Means, advised me to write a very obliging Letter to my new Father, with my humble Request, that he would please to order me home the next Recess of our Learning. I did so, under my Master's Dictation; and not long after received an Answer to the following Effect.

Son PETER,

Your Mother has been dead a good while; and as to your Request, it will be only expensive, and of little Use; for a Person who must live by his Studies, can't apply to them too closely.

This Letter, if I had a little hope left, quite subdued my Fortitude, and well nigh reduced me to Clay. However, with Tears in my Eyes, I shewed it to my Master; who, good Man, wishing me well; *Peter*, says he, what can this mean, here is some Mistery concealed in it; here is some ill Design on Foot; then, taking the Letter into his Hand, a Person who must live by his Studies, says he, here is more meant than we can think for. Why? Have not you a pretty Estate to live upon, when it comes to your Hands? *Peter*, says he, I would advise you to go to your Father, and inquire how your Affairs are left; but I am afraid to let you go alone, and will, when my Students depart at *Christmas*, accompany you myself, with all my Heart; for, you must know, I have advised on your Affair already, and find, you are of Age to chuse yourself a Guardian, who may be any Relation, or Friend you can confide in; and may see you have Justice done you. I immediately thanked him for the

D

Hint, and begged him to accept of the Trust, as my only Friend, having very few, if any near Relations; this, he with great Readiness complied with, and was admitted accordingly.

So soon as our Scholars were gone home, my Master lending me a Horse, we set out together, to possess ourselves of all my Father's real Estate, and such Part of the Personal as he had been advised would belong to me. Well, we arrived at the old House, but were not received with such extraordinary Tokens of Friendship, as would give the least room to suppose we were welcome. For my Part, all I said, or could say, was, that I was very sorry for my Mother's Death. My Father replied, so was he. Here we paused, and might have sat silent till this Time for me, if my Master, a grave Man, who had seen the World, and was unwilling any Part of our Time there, which he guessed would be short, should be lost, had not broke Silence. Mr. *G.* says he, I see the Loss of Master *Wilkins*'s Mother puts him under some Confusion; so that you will excuse me, as his Preceptor, and Friend, in making some Inquiry, how his Affairs stand, and how his Effects are disposed; as I don't doubt, you have taken care to schedule every Thing that will be coming to him; and though he is not yet of the necessary Age, for taking upon himself the Management of his Estate, he is nevertheless of Capacity to understand the Nature, and *Quantum* of it, and, to shew his Approbation of the Disposition of it, as if he was a Year or two older.—During this Discourse, Mr. *G.* turned pale, then reddened, was going to interrupt, then checked himself; but however, kept Silence, till my Master had done; when, with a Sneer, he replied, Sir, I must own myself a great Stranger to your Discourse; nor can I, for my Life, imagine, what your Harangue tends to; but sure I am, I know of no Estate, real, or personal, or any thing else belonging to young Mr. *Wilkins*, to make a Schedule of, as you call it: But this I know, his Mother had an Estate in Land, near two hundred a Year, and also a good Sum of Money, when I married her; but the Estate, she settled on me before her Marriage, to dispose of after her Decease, as I saw fit; and her Money and Goods are all come to my sole Use, as her Husband.—I was just ready to drop, while Mr. *G.* gave this Relation, and was not able to reply a Word; but my Master, though sufficiently shocked at what he had heard, replied; Sir, I am informed the Estate, and also the Money you mention, was Mr. *Wilkins*'s Father's at his Death; and I am surprized to think any one should have a better Title to them; than my Pupil, his only Child. Sir, says Mr. *G,* you are deceived, and tho' what you say seems plausible enough, and is in some Part true, as that the late Mr. *Wilkins* had such Estate, and some hundreds, I may say thousands, at his Death, yet you seem ignorant that he made a Deed just before entring into the fatal Rebellion, by which he gave my late Wife both the Estate, Money, and every thing else he had, absolutely, without any Conditions whatsoever; all which, on his unhappy Execution, she enjoyed, and now of Right, as I told you before, belongs to me; however, as I have no Child, if *Peter* behaves well under your Direction, I have Thoughts of paying another Year's Board for him, and then he must shift for himself.

Oh! cried I, for the Mercy of some savage Beast to devour me! Is this what I have been cocker'd up[1] for! Why was I not placed out to some laborious Craft, where I might have drudged for Bread in my proper Station! But, I fear, it is too late to inquire into what is past, and must submit.

My Master (good Man) was thunderstruck at what he had heard; and finding our Business done there, we took our Leaves, after Mr. *G.* had again repeated, that if I behaved well, my Preceptor should keep me another Year; which was all I must expect from him; and at my Departure he gave me a Crown Piece, which I then durst not refuse, for fear of offending my Master.

We made the best of our Way Home again to my Tutor's, where I stayed but a Week, to consider what I should do with myself. In this Time he did all he could to comfort me, telling me, if I would stay with him and become his Usher, he would compleat my Learning for nothing, and allow me a Salary for my Trouble. But my Heart was too lofty to think

of becoming an Usher, within so little a Way from mine own
Estate in other Hands. However, since I had not a Penny of
Money to endeavour at recovering my Right with, I told my
Master I would consider of his Proposal.

During my Stay with him, he used all Methods to make me
as easy as possible; and frequently moralliz'd with so much
Effect, that I was almost convinced I ought to submit, and be
content. Amongst the rest of his Discourse, he endeavoured
to shew me one Day, after I had been loudly condemning my
cruel Fortune, and saying I was born to be unhappy, that
I was mistaken, if I thought, or imagined, it was Chance or
Accident that had been against me, when I complained of
Fortune; for, says he, *Peter*, there is nothing done below, but
is at least fore-known if not decreed above; and our Business
in Life is to believe so: Not that I would have such Belief
make us careless, and think it to no Purpose to strive, as some
do; who being persuaded that our Actions are not in our own
Choice, but that, being pressed by an irresistable Decree, we
are forced to act this or that, fancy we must be necessarily
happy or miserable hereafter; Or, as others, who, for fear of
falling upon that shocking Principle, would even deprive the
Almighty of Fore-knowledge, lest it should consequentially
amount to a Decree; for (say they) what is foreknown, will,
and must be: But I would have you act so, as that, let either of
these Tenets be true, you may still be sure of making yourself
easy and happy: And for that Purpose let me recommend to
you a uniform Life of Justice and Piety; always choosing the
good rather than the bad Side of every Action; for this, say
they what they will to the contrary, is not above the Power
of a reasonable Being to practise; and doing so, you may without Scruple say, If there is Fore-knowledge of my Actions,
or they are decreed, I then am one who is fore-known or
decreed to be happy: And this, without further Speculation,
you will find the only Means always to keep you so; for all
Men, of all Denominations, fully allow this happy Effect to
follow good Actions. Again, *Peter*, a Person acting in a vicious
Course, with such an Opinion in his Head as above, must

surely be very miserable, as his very Actions themselves must pronounce the Decree against him: Whilst therefore we have not heard the Decree read, you see, we may easily give Sentence whether it be for Good or Evil to us, by the Tenour and Course of our own Actions.

You are not now to learn, *Peter*, that the Crimes of the Father are often punished in the Children, often in the Father himself, sometimes in both, and not seldom in neither, in this Life; and tho', at first, one should think the future Punishment, annexed to bad Actions, was sufficient, still it is necessary some should suffer here also for an Example to others; we being much more affected with what the Eye sees, than what the Heart only meditates upon.

Now, to bring it to our own Case; your Father, *Peter*, rose against the lawful Magistrate, to deprive him (it matters not that he was a bad one) of his lawful Power. Your Father's Policy was such, and his Design so well laid, as he thought, that upon any ill Success to himself, he had secured his Estate to go in the Way of all others he could wish to have it, and sits down very well contented, that, happen what would, he should bite[1] the Government, in preventing the Forfeiture. But lo his Policy is as a Wall of Sand blown down with a Puff, for it is to you it ought, even himself being Umpire, to have come, as no one would think, he could prize any before you his own Child. Now, could he look from the Grave, and know what passes here, and see Mr. *G.* in Possession of all he fancied he had secured for you, what a weak and short-sighted Creature would he find himself. If it be said, he did not know he should have a Child, then herein appears God's Policy beyond Man's; for he knew it, and has so ordered, that that Child should be disinherited; for, by the way, *Peter*, take this for a Maxim, wherever the first Principle of an Action is ill, no good Consequence can possibly ever be an Attendant on it. Could he, as I said before, but look up and see you, his only Child, undone, by the very Instrument he designed for your Security, how pungent would be his Anxiety. I say, *Peter*, tho' there is something so unaccountable, to human Wisdom, in such

Events of Things, yet there is something therein so reasonable and just withal, that by a prying Eye, the Supreme Hand may very visibly be seen in them. Now this being plainly the Case before us, and herein the Glory of the Almighty exalted, rest content under it, and let not this Disappointment, befallen you for your Father's Faults, be attended with others sent down for your own; but remember this, the Hand that depresses a Man, is no less able to exalt and establish him.

CHAPTER IV

Departs secretly from his Master; travels to Bristol; *religious Thoughts by the Way; enters on Shipboard, and is made Captain's Steward*

I SEEMED to be very well satisfied whilst my Master was speaking; but tho' I thought he talked like an Angel, my former Uneasiness seized me at parting with him. In short, without more Consideration, I rose in the Morning early and marched off; having first wrote to my Wife, at her Aunt's, relating the State of the Case to her, with my Resolution to leave *England*, the first Opportunity; giving her what Comfort I could, assuring her, if I ever was a Gainer in Life, she should not fail to be a Partaker, and promising also to let her know where I settled. I walked at a great Rate, for fear my Master's Kindness should prompt him to send after me; and taking the By-ways, I reached by dark Night a little Village, where I resolved to halt. Upon Inquiry, I found myself Thirty-five Miles from my Master's.—I had eaten nothing all Day, and was very hungry and weary, but my Crown Piece was as yet whole; however, I fed very sparingly, being over-pressed with the Distress of my Affairs and the Confusion of my Thoughts. —I slept that Night tolerably; but the Morning brought its Face of Horror with it. I had inquired over Night where I was, and been informed that I was not above sixteen Miles from

Bristol, for which Place I then resolved.—At my setting out
in the Morning, after I had walked about three Miles, and
had recollected a little my Master's last Discourse, I found
by Degrees my Spirit grew calmer, than it had been since
I left Mr. *G.* at my House, (as I shall ever call it;) and looking into myself for the Cause, found another Set of Thoughts
were preparing a Passage into my Mind, which did not carry
half the Dread and Terror with them that their Predecessors
had; for I began to cast aside the Difficulties and Apprehensions I before felt in my Way, and, encouraging the present
Motions, soon became sensible of the Benefit of a virtuous
Education; and though what I had hitherto done in the
immediate Service of God, I must own, had been performed
from Force, Custom, and Habit, and without the least Attention to the Object of the Duty; yet, as under my Mother at
Home, and my Master at the Academy, I had been always
used to say my Prayers, as they called it, Morning and Night;
I began with a Sort of superstitious Reflection, to accuse myself of having omitted that Duty the Night before, and also,
at my setting out in the Morning, and very much to blame
myself for it; and at the same Instant, even wondred at myself
for that Blame.—What, says I, is the real Use of this praying?
and to whom or to what do we pray? I see no one to pray to,
neither have I ever thought that my Prayers would be answered.
'Tis true, they are worded as if we prayed to God; but he is
in Heaven, does he concern himself with us, who can do him
no Service? Can I think all my Prayers that I have said, from
Day to Day, so many Years, have been heard by him? No
sure; if they had, I should scarce have sustained this hard
Fate in my Fortune. But hold, how have I prayed to him?
Have I as earnestly prayed to him, as I used to petition my
Mother for any thing when I wanted it against her Inclina-
tion? No, I can't say I have. And would my Mother have
granted me such Things, if she had not thought, I from my
Heart desired them, when I used to be so earnest with her?
No surely, I can't say she had any Reason for it. But I had
her indeed before me; now I have not God in my View, he is

in Heaven: Yet, let me see, my Master, and I can't help thinking he must know, used to say, that God is a Spirit, and not
confined by the Incumbrance of a Body, as we are; now, if it
is so, why may not he virtually be present with me, though
I don't perceive him? Why may he not be at once in Heaven,
and elsewhere? For, if he consists not of Parts, nothing can
circumscribe him. And truly, I believe it must be so; for if
he is of that supreme Power as he is represented, he could
never act in so unconfined a Capacity, under the Restraint of
Place; but if he is an operative[1] and purely spiritual Being,
then I can see no Reason, why his virtual[2] Essence should not
be diffused through all Nature; and then, which I begin to
think most likely, why should not I suppose him ever present
with me, and able to hear me? And why should not I, when
I pray, have a full Idea of the Being, tho' not of any corporeal
Parts or Form, of God; and so have actually somewhat to be
intent upon in my Prayers? and not do as I have hitherto done,
say so many Words only upon my Knees; which I can't help
thinking, may be as well without either Sense or Meaning in
themselves, as without a proper Object in my Mind to direct
them unto.

These Thoughts agitated me at least two Miles, working
stronger and stronger in me; till at length, bursting into Tears,
Have I been doing nothing, says I, in the Sight of God, under
the Name of Prayers, for so many Years? Yes, it is certainly
so. Well, by the Grace of God, it shall be so no longer, I'll
try somewhat more. So looking round about me, to see if
I was quite alone, I stept into an adjoining Copse, and could
scarce refrain falling on my Knees, till I came to a proper
Place for kneeling in. I then poured forth my whole Soul and
Spirit to God; and all my Strength, and every Member, every
Faculty, was to the utmost employed, for a considerable Time,
in that most agreeable as well as useful Duty. I would indeed
have began with my accustomed Prayers, and had repeated
some Words of them; when, as though against and contrary
to my Design, I was carried away by such rapturous Effusions,
that, to this Hour, when I reflect thereon, I can't believe, but

I was moved to them by a much more than human Impulse. However, this Extasy did not last above a Quarter of an Hour; but it was considerably longer before my Spirits subsided to their usual Frame.—When I had a little composed myself, how was I altered, how did I condemn myself for all my past Disquiet; what calm Thanks did I return for the Ease and Satisfaction of Mind I then enjoyed; and coming to a small Rivulet, I drank an hearty Draught of Water, and contentedly proceeding on my Journey, I reached *Bristol* about four a Clock in the Afternoon. Having refreshed myself, I went the same Evening to the *Kay*, to inquire what Ships were in the River, whither bound, and when they would depart. My Business was with the Sailors, of whom there were at that Time great Numbers there; but I could meet with no Employ, though I gave out, I would gladly enter myself before the Mast. —After I had done the best I could, but without Success, I returned to the little House I had dined at, and went to Bed very pensive. I did not forget my Prayers; but I could by no Means be roused to such Devotion as I felt in the Morning. Next Day I walked again to the *Kay*, asking all I met, who looked like Seafaring Men, for Employment; but could hear of none, there being many waiting for Births; and I feared, my Appearance (which was not so mean, as most of that Sort of Gentry's is) would prove no small Disappointment to my Preferment that Way. At last, being out of Heart with my frequent Repulses, I went to a landing Place just by, and as I asked some Sailors who were putting two Gentlemen on Shore, if they wanted a Hand on board their Ship, one of the Gentlemen, whom I afterwards found to be the Master of a Vessel bound to the Coast of *Africa*, turned back, and looking earnestly on me, young Man, says he, do you want Employment on board? I immediately made him a Bow, and answered, yes, Sir. Said he, there is no talking in this Weather, for it then blew almost a Storm, but step into that Tavern, pointing to the Place, and I'll be with you presently.—I went thither, and not long after came my future Master. He asked me many Questions, but the first was, Whether I had been at Sea? I told him no; but I did not doubt soon to learn the Duty of a Sailor. He then looked on my Hand, and, shaking his Head, told me it would not do, for I had too soft a Hand. I told him I was determined for the Sea, and that my Hand and Heart should go together; and I hoped my Hand would soon harden, though not my Heart. He then told me, it was pity to take such a pretty young Fellow before the Mast; but if I understood Accounts tolerably, and could write a good Hand, he would make me his Steward, and make it worth my while. I answered in the affirmative, joyfully accepting his Offer; but on his asking me where my Chest was, (for, says he, if the Wind had not been so strong against me, I had fallen down the River this Morning) I looked very blank, and plainly told him I had no other Stores than I carried on my Back. The Captain smiled. Says he, young Man, I see you are a Novice; why, the meanest Sailor in my Ship has a Chest, at least, and perhaps something in it; come, says he, my Lad, I like your Looks, be diligent and honest, I'll let you have a little Money to set you out, and deduct it in your Pay. He was then pulling out his Purse, when I begged him, as he seemed to shew me so great a Kindness, that he would order somebody to buy what Necessaries he knew I should want, for me, or I should be under as great a Difficulty to know what to get, and where to buy them, as I should have been at for want of them. He commended my Prudence, and said he would buy them and send them on board himself; so bid me trouble myself no more about them, but go to the Ship, in the return of his Boat, and stay there till he came; giving me a Ticket to the Boat's Crew to take me in. When I came to the Shore, the Boat was gone off, and at a good Distance; but I hailed them, and shewing my Ticket, they put back, and took me safe to the Ship; heartily glad that I was entred upon my new Service.

CHAPTER V

His first Entertainment on board; sets sail; his
Sickness; Engagement with a French *Privateer; is*
taken and laid in Irons. Twenty-one Prisoners turned
adrift in a small Boat with only two Days Provision

BEING once on board, and in Pay, I thought I was a Man
for myself; and set about considering how to behave; and no
body knowing, as yet, upon what footing I came on board,
they took me for a Passenger, as my Dress did not at all bespeak
me a Sailor; so every one, as I sauntered about, had something
to say to me. By and by comes a pert young Fellow up, Sir,
says he, your Servant; what, I see, our Captain has picked up
a Passenger at last. Passenger, says I, you are pleased to be
merry Sir, I am no Passenger. Why, pray, says he, what may
you be then? Sir, says I, the Captain's Steward. You impertinent Puppy, says he, what an Answer you give me; you the
Captain's Steward; No, Sir, that Place, I can assure you, is
in better Hands, and away he turned.—I knew not what to
think of it, but was terribly afraid I should draw myself into
some Scrape. By and by, others asked me, some one thing,
some another, and I was very cautious what Answers I made
them, for fear of Offence; till a gravish Sailor came and sat
down by me, and, after talking of the Weather, and other
indifferent Matters, pray, says I, Sir, who is that Gentleman
that was so affronted at me soon after I came on board? Oh,
says he, a proud insignificant Fellow, the Captain's Steward;
but don't mind him, says he, he uses the Captain himself as
bad; they have had high Words just before the Captain went
on Shore; and had he used me, as he did him, I should
have made no Ceremony of tipping him over-board, a Rascal.
Says I, you surprize me, for the Captain sent me on board
to be his Steward, and agreed with me about it this Afternoon. Hush, says he, I see how it will go; the Captain, if
that's the Case, will discharge him when he comes on board;

and indeed, I believe, he would not have kept him so long, but we have waited for a Wind, and he could not provide himself.

The Captain came on board at Night; and the first thing he did, was to demand the Keys of Mr. Steward, which he gave to me, and ordered him on Shore.

The next Morning the Captain went on Shore himself; but the Wind chopping about, and standing fair about Noon, he returned then with my Chest, and before Night we were got into sailing Order, and before the Wind, with a brisk Gale.

What happened the first fourteen Days of our Passage I know not, having been all that Time so sick and weak, I could scarcely keep Life and Soul together; but after grew better and better. We prosecuted our Voyage, touching, for about a Week, at the *Madeiras* in our Way. The Captain grew very fond of me, and never put me to hard Duty, and I passed my Time (under his Favour) very pleasantly. One Evening, being within sixty Leagues of the Cape of *Palmes*, calm Weather, but the little Wind we had against us, one of our Men spied a Sail, and gave the Captain notice of it. He not suspecting Danger, minded it little; and we made what Way the Wind would permit; but, Night coming on, and the calm continuing, about peep of Day, we perceived we were infallibly fallen in with a *French* Privateer; who, hoisting *French* Colours, called out to us to strike. Our Captain had scarce Time to consider what to do, they were so near us; but as he had twenty-two Men on board, and eight Guns, he could bring to;[1] so he called all Hands on Deck, and telling them the Consequence of a Surrender, asked them if they would stand by him. One and all swore, they would fight the Ship to the Bottom, rather than fall into the Privateer's Hands.—The Captain immediately gave the Word for a clear Deck, prepared his Firearms, and begged them to be active and obey Orders; and perceiving the Privateer out numbered our Hands by abundance, he commanded all the small Arms to be brought upon Deck loaded, and to run out as many of the Ship's Guns as she could bring to on one Side; and to charge them all with small

Shot; then stand to till he gave Directions.—The Privateer being a light Ship, and a small Breeze arising, run up close to us; first firing one Gun, then another, still calling out to us to strike; but we neither returned Fire or Answer, till he came almost within Pistol shot of us, and seeing us a small Vessel, thought to board us directly; but then our Captain ordered a broad Side, and immediately all Hands to come on Deck; himself standing there at the Time of our first Fire with his Fusee[1] in his Hand, and near him I stood with another. We killed eight Men and wounded several others. The Privateer then fired a broad Side through and through us. By this Time our Hands were all on Deck, and the Privateer pushing in hopes to grapple and board us, we gave them a Volley from thence, that did good Execution; and then all Hands to the Ship's Guns again, except four, who were left along with me to charge the small Arms. It is incredible how soon they had fired the great Guns, and were on Deck again. This last Fire, being with Ball, raked the Privateer miserably. Then we fired the small Arms, and away to the Ship's Guns. This we did three Times successively without Loss of a Man; and I believe if we could have held it once more, and no Assistance had come to the Privateer, she had sheered quite off: But our Captain spying a Sail at some Distance behind the Privateer, who lay to Windward of us, and seeing by his Glass it was a *Frenchman*, was almost dismayed; the same Sight put Courage into our Enemies, who thereupon redoubled the Attack; and, the first Volley of their small Arms, shot our Captain in the Breast, upon which he dropped dead without stirring. I need not say, that Sight shocked me exceedingly. Indeed, it disconcerted the whole Action; and though our Mate, a Man of good Courage and Experience, did all that a brave Man could do to animate the Men, they apparently[2] drooped, and the Loss of the Ship became inevitable; so we struck, and the *Frenchman* boarded us.

During the latter Part of the Engagement, we had two Men killed, and five wounded, who died afterwards of their Wounds. We, who were alive, were all ordered on board the

Frenchman, who, after rifling us, chained us two and two, and turned us into the Hold. Our Vessel was then ransacked; and the other Privateer, who had suffered much the Day before, in an Engagement with an *English* twenty-gun Ship of War, coming up, the Prize was sent by her into Port, where she herself was to refit.

In this Condition did I, and fourteen of our Crew, lie for six Weeks; till the Fetters on our Legs had almost eaten to the Bone, and the Stench of the Place had well nigh suffocated us.

The *Glorieux*, for that was the Name of the Privateer who took us, saw nothing further in five Weeks worth her Notice, which very much discouraged the Men; and consulting together, it was agreed, to cruise more Northward, between *Sierra Leon* and *Cape de Verd*; but, about Noon, next Day, they spied a Sail, coming West North West, with a fresh Gale. The Captain thereupon ordered all to be ready, and lie by for her. But, though she discerned us, she kept her Way, bearing only more Southward; when the Wind shifting to North-East, she ran for it, full before the Wind, and we after her with all the sail we could crowd; and though she was a very good Sailer, we gained upon her, being laden, and before Night, came pretty well up with her; but, being a large Ship, and the Evening haizy, we did not chuse to engage her till Morning. The next Morning we found she was slunk away; but we fetched her up, and, hoisting *French* Colours, fired a Shot; which she not answering, our Captain run along Side of her, and fired a broad Side; then slackening upon her, a hard Engagement ensued; the Shot thumping so against our Ship, that we Prisoners, who had nothing to do in the Action, expected Death, one or other of us, every Moment. The Merchant Man was so heavy loaded, and drew so much Water, that she was very unweildy in Action; so after a Fight of two Hours, when most of her Rigging and Masts were cut, and wounded, she struck. Twelve Men were sent on Board her, and her Captain and several Officers were ordered on Board us.

There were thirty-eight Persons in her, including Passengers: all of whom, except five, and the like Number which had been killed in the Action, were sent chained into the Hold to us, who had lain there almost six Weeks. This Prize put Monsieur into good Heart, and determined him to return Home with her. But in two Days Time, his new Acquisition was found to have leaked so fast near the Bottom, that before they were aware of it, the Water was risen some Feet. Several Hands were employed to find out the Leak; but all asserted it was too low to be come at; and as the Pumps, with all the Labour the Prisoners, who were the Persons put to it, could use, would not reduce it, but it still increased, they removed what Goods they could into the Privateer; and before they could unload it, the Prize sunk.

The next Thing they consulted upon, was, what to do with the Prisoners, who, by the Loss of the Prize, were now grown too numerous to be trusted in the Privateer; fearing too, as they were now so far out at Sea, by the great Addition of Mouths, they might soon be brought to short Allowance; it was (on both Accounts) resolved, to give us the Prize's Boat, which they had saved, and turn us adrift to shift for ourselves. There were in all forty-three of us; but the Privateer having lost several of their own Men in the two Engagements, they looked us over, and picking out two and twenty of us, who were the most likely Fellows for their Purpose, the remaining one and twenty were committed to the Boat, with about two Days Provision and a small Matter of Ammunition, and turned out.

CHAPTER VI

*The Boat, two hundred Leagues from Land, makes no
Way, but drives more to Sea by the Wind; the People
live nine Days at quarter Allowance; four die with
Hunger the twelfth Day; five more the fourteenth
Day; on the fifteenth they eat one just dead; want of
Water excessive; spy a Sail; are taken up; work their
Passage to the* African *Shore; are sent on a secret
Expedition; are Way-laid, taken Slaves, and sent up
the Country*

WHEN we, who were in the Boat, came to reflect on our
Condition, the Prospect before us appeared very melancholy;
tho' we had at first readily enough embraced the Offer, rather
than perish in so much Misery, as we suffered in our loath-
some Confinement. We now judged we were above two
hundred Leagues from Land, in about eight Degrees North
Latitude; and blowing North-East, a pretty stiff Gale, we
could make no Way, but rather lost, for we aimed at some
Port in *Africa*, having neither Sail, Compass, or any other
Instrument to direct us; so that all the Observation we could
make was by the Sun for running Southward, or as the Wind
carried us, for we had lost the North Pole.—As we had little
above two Days Provisions, we perceived a Necessity of
almost starving, voluntarily, to avoid doing it quite; seeing it
must be many Days before we could reach shore, if ever we
did, having visibly driven a great deal more Southward than
we were; nay, unless a sudden Change happened, we were
sure of perishing, unless delivered by some Ship that Providence might send in our Way.—In short, the ninth Day came,
but no Relief with it; and though we had lived at quarter
Allowance, and but just saved Life, our Food, except a little
Water, was all gone, and this caused us quite to despair.—
On the twelfth Day four of our Company died with hunger,
in a very miserable Way; and yet the Survivors had not

Strength left to move them to pity their Fellows. In truth we had sat still, attempting nothing in several Days; as we found that unless the Wind shifted, we only consumed the little Strength we had left, to no Manner of Purpose.—On the fourteenth day, and in the Night, five more died, and a sixth was near expiring; and yet, we, the Survivors, were so indolent, we would scarce lend a Hand to throw them overboard.—On the fifteenth day in the morning, our Carpenter, weak as he was, started up, and as the sixth Man was just dead, cut his Throat, and, whilst warm, would let out what Blood would flow; then, pulling off his old Jacket, invited us to Dinner, and cutting a large Slice off the Corpse, devoured it with as much seeming Relish, as if it had been Ox Beef. His Example prevailed with the rest of us, one after another, to taste and eat; and as there had been a heavy Dew or Rain in the Night, and we had spread out every Thing we had of Linnen and Woolen to receive it, we were a little refreshed by wringing our Cloaths, and sipping what came from them; after which we covered them up from the Sun, stowing them all close together to keep in the Moisture, which served us to suck at for two Days after, a little and a little at a Time; for now we were in greater Distress for Water, than for Meat.— It has surprised me many Times since, to think how we could make so light a Thing of eating our Fellow Creature just dead before our Eyes; but, I'll assure you, when we had once tasted, we looked on the Blessing to be so great, that we cut and eat, with as little Remorse, as we should have had for feeding on the best Meat in an *English* Market: And most certainly, when this Corpse had failed, if another had not dropped by fair Means, we should have used foul, by murdering one of our Number as a Supply for the rest.

Water, as I said before, to moisten our Mouths, was now our greatest Hardship, for every Man had so often drank his own, that we voided scarce any Thing but Blood, and that but a few Drops at a Time; our Mouths and Tongues were quite flead[1] with Drought, and our Teeth just falling from our Jaws; for, tho' we had tryed, by placing all the dead Men's

E

Jackets and Shirts one over another, to strain some of the Sea-Water through 'em by small Quantities, yet that would not deprive it of its pernicious Qualities; and tho' it refreshed a little in going down, we were so sick, and strained ourselves so much after it, that it came up again, and made us more miserable than before.—Our Corpse now stunk so, what was left of it, that we could no longer bear it on Board, and every Man began to look with an evil Eye on his Fellow, to think whose Turn it would be next; for the Carpenter had started the Question, and preached us into the Necessity of it; and we had agreed, the next Morning, to put it to the Lot who should be the Sacrifice.—In this Distress of Thought, it was so ordered, by good Providence, that, on the 21st Day, we thought we spied a Sail coming from the North-west, which caused us to delay our Lots, till we should see whether it would discover us or not; we hung up some Jackets upon our Oars to be seen as far off as we could, but had so little Strength left, we could make no Way towards it; however, it happened to direct its Course so much to our Relief, that, an Hour before Sunset, it was within a League of us, but seemed to bear away more Eastward, and our Fear was, that they should not know our Distress, for we were not able to make any Noise from our Throats, that might be heard fifty Yards; but the Carpenter, who was still the best Man amongst us, with much ado, getting one of the Guns to go off, in less than half an Hour she came up with us, and, seeing our deplorable Condition, took us all on Board, to the Number of eleven. Tho' no Methods were unessayed for our Recovery, four more of us died in as many Days. When the remaining seven of us came a little to ourselves, we found our Deliverers were *Portuguese*,[1] bound for Saint *Salvadore*.[2] We told the Captain, we begged he would let us work our Passage with him, be it where it would, to Shore; and then, if we could be of no further Service to him, we did not doubt getting into *Europe* again: But, in the Voyage, as we did him all the Service in our Power, we pleased him so well, that he engaged us to stay with him, to work the Ship home again, he having lost some Hands by Fevers soon after his setting Sail.

We arrived safe in Port; and, in a few Days, the Captain, who had a secret Enterprize to take in hand, hired a Country coasting Vessel, and sent her seventeen Leagues further on the Coast for Orders from some Factory or Settlement there. I was one of the nine Men who were destined to conduct her; but, not understanding *Portuguese*, I knew little of the Business we went upon. We were to coast it all the Way, but, on the tenth Day, just at Sun-rise, we fell in with a Fleet of Boats, which had way-laid us, and were taken Prisoners. Being carried ashore, we were conducted a long Way up the Country, where we were imprisoned, and almost starved: Tho' I never knew the Meaning of it; nor did any of us, unless the Mate, who, we heard, was carried up the Country, much further, to *Angola*;[1] but we never heard more of him, tho' we were told he would be sent back to us.

Here we remained under Confinement almost three Months, at the End of which Time our Keeper told us we were to be removed; and coupling us two and two together, sent a Guard with us to *Angola*; when, crossing a large River, we were set to Work in removing the Rubbish and Stones of a Castle, or Fortress, which had been lately demolished by an Earthquake and Lightning. Here we continued about five Months, being very sparingly dieted, and locked up everyNight.[2]

This Place however I thought a Paradise to our former Dungeon; and as we were not over-worked, we made our Lives comfortable enough, having the Air all Day to refresh us from the Heat, and not wanting for Company: For there were, at least, three hundred of us about the whole Work; and I often fancied myself at the Tower of *Babel*, each Labourer, almost, speaking in a Language of his own.

Towards the latter End of our Work, our Keepers grew more and more remiss in their Care of us. At my first coming thither, I had contracted a Familiarity with one of the Natives, but of a different Kingdom, who was then a Slave with me; and he and I being able tolerably to understand each other, he hinted to me, one Day, the Desire he had of seeing his own Country and Family; who, neither knew whether he was dead or alive, or where he was, since he had left them, seven Years before, to make War in this Kingdom; and insinuated, that as he had taken a great Liking to me, if I would endeavour to escape with him, and we succeeded, he would provide for me; for, says he, you see, now our Work is almost over, we are but slightly guarded, and if we stay till this Job is once finished, we may be commanded to some new Works, at the other End of the Kingdom, for ought we know; so that our Labours will only cease with our Lives; and, for my part, immediate Death, in the Attempt of Liberty, is to me, preferable to a lingring Life of Slavery.[1]

These and such like Arguments prevailed on me to ac-company him, as he had told me he had travelled most of the Country before, in the Wars of the different Nations; so, having taken our Resolution, the following Evening, soon after our Day's Work, and before the Time came for locking up, we withdrew from the rest, but within hearing; thinking, if we should then be missed, and called, we would appear, and make some Excuse for our Absence, but if not, we should have the whole Night before us.

When we were first put upon this Work, we were called over singly, by Name, Morning and Evening, to be let out and in, and were very narrowly observed in our Motions; but not one of us having been ever absent, our Actions were at length much less minded than before, and the Ceremony of calling us over was frequently omitted; so that we concluded, if we got away unobserved the first Night, we should be out of the Reach of Pursuers by the next; which was the soonest it was possible for them to overtake us, as we proposed to travel, the first Part of our Journey, with the utmost Dispatch.

CHAPTER VII

The Author escapes with Glanlepze, *a Native; their
Hardships in Travel; plunder of a Cotage; his Fears;
Adventure with a Crocodile; Passage of a River;
Adventure with a Lioness and Whelp; arrive at*
Glanlepze's *House; the Trial of* Glanlepze's *Wife's
Constancy; the tender meeting of her and her Husband;
the Author's Reflections thereupon*

HAVING now set out with all possible Speed, we seemed to
each other as joyful as we could; though it can't be supposed
we had no Fears in our Minds, the first Part of our Journey,
for we had many; but, as our Way advanced, our Fears subsided; and having, with scarce any Delay, pushed forwards
for the first twenty-four Hours, Nature then began to have
two very pressing Demands upon us, Food and Rest: But as
one of them was absolutely out of our Power to comply with,
she contented herself with the other, till we should be better
able to supply her, and gave a further Time till the next Day.

The next Morning found us very empty, and sharp set,
tho' a very sound Night's Rest had contributed its utmost to
refresh us. But what added much to our Discomfort was, that
tho' our whole Subsistance must come from Fruits, there was
not a Tree to be found at a less Distance than twelve Leagues,
in the open rocky Country we were then in; but a good
Draught of excellent Water, we met with, did us extraordinary
Service, and sent us with much better Courage to the Woods,
tho' they were quite out of the Way of our Rout; there, by
divers Kinds of Fruits, which, tho' my Companion knew very
well, I was quite a Stranger to, we satisfied our Hunger for the
present, and took a moderate Supply for another Opportunity. This retarded our Journey very much, for in so hard
Travel every Pound weighed six before Night.

I can't say this Journey, though bad enough, would have
been so discouraging, but for the Trouble of fetching our

Provisions so far; and then, if we meant not to loose half the next Day in the same Manner, we must double load ourselves, and delay our Progress by that Means; but we still went on, and in about eight Days got quite clear of *Angola*.

On the eighth Day, my Companion, whose Name was *Glanlepze*, told me, we were very near the Confines of *Congo*,[1] but there was one little Village still in *Angola*, by which we must pass, within half a League; and, if I would agree to it, he would go see what might be got here to supply ourselves with. I told him, I was in an unknown World, and would follow wherever he should lead me; but asked him if he was not afraid of the People, as he was not of that Country; he told me, as there had been Wars between them and his Country, for assisting their Neighbours of *Congo*, he was not concerned for any Mischief he should do them, or they him; but, says he, you have a Knife in your Pocket, and with that we will cut two stout Clubs, and then follow me, fear nothing.

We soon cut our Clubs, and marching on, in the Midst of some small Shrubs, and a few scattering Trees, we saw a little Hovel, larger, indeed, but worse contrived than an *English* Hogstie,[2] to which we boldly advanced; and *Glanlepze*, entring first, saluted an old Man who was lying on a Parcel of Rushes. The Man attempted to run away, but *Glanlepze* stopped him, and we tyed his Hands and Feet.[3] He then set up such a hideous Howl, that had not *Glanlepze* threatened to murder him, and prepared to do it, he would have raised the whole Village upon us; but we quieted him; and rumaging to find Provision, which was all we wanted, we, by good Luck, spied best Part of a Goat, hanging up behind a large Matt at the further End of the Room. By this Time in comes a Woman, with two Children very small. This was the old Man's Daughter, of about five and twenty. *Glanlepze* bound her also, and laid her by the old Man, but the two Children we suffered to lye untied. We then examined her, who told us, the old Man was her Father, and that her Husband having killed a Goat that Morning, was gone to carry Part of it to his Sister; that they had little or no Corn; and finding we wanted

Victuals, she told us, there was an earthen Pot we might boil
some of the Goat in if we pleased.

Having now seen all that was to be had, we were going to
make up our Bundle, when a Muletto,[1] very gently, put his
Head into the Doorway; him, *Glanlepze* immediately seized;
and bidding me fetch the great Mat, and the Goat's Flesh, he,
in the mean Time, put a long Rope, he found there, about the
Beast's Neck, and laying the Mat upon him, we packed up
the Goat's Flesh, and a little Corn in a *Calabash* Shell; and
then, turning up the Mat round about, skewered it together,
and over all we tyed the earthen Pot; *Glanlepze* crying out,
at every Thing we loaded, *it is no Hurt to plunder an Enemy*;
and so we marched off.

I own, I had greater Apprehensions from this Adventure,
than from any Thing before; for, says I, if the Woman's
Husband returns soon, or if she, or her Father, can release
themselves, they will raise the whole Village upon us, and we
are undone: But *Glanlepze* laughed at me, saying, we had not
an Hour's Walk out of the *Angola* Dominions; and that the
King of *Congo* was at War with them, in helping the King of
Loango,[2] whose Subject himself was; and that the *Angolans*
durst not be seen out of their Bounds on that Side the
Kingdom; for there was a much larger Village of *Congovians*
in our Way, who would certainly rise and destroy them, if
they came in any Numbers amongst them; and though, the
War being carried on near the Sea, the Borders were quiet,
yet, upon the least Stir, the whole Country would be in Arms,
whilst we might retire thro' the Woods very safely.

Well, we marched on, as fast as we could, all the Remainder
of that Day, till Moon-light, close by the Skirt of a long Wood,
that we might take Shelter therein, if there should be Occasion; and my Eyes were the best Part of the Way behind me;
but, neither hearing or seeing any Thing to annoy us, and
finding, by the Declivity of the Ground, we should soon be
in some Plain, or Bottom, and have a Chance of Water for us
all, and Pasture for our Muletto, who was now become one
of us, we would not halt, till we found a Bottom to the Hill;

which in half an Hour more we came to, and in some Minutes
after to a Rivulet of fine clear Water, where we resolved to
spend the Night. Here we fastned our Muletto by his Cord to
a Stake in the Ground; but perceiving him not to have sufficient Range to fill his Belly in before Morning, we, under
Glanlepze's Direction, cut several long Slips from the Mat,
and soaking them well in Water, twisted them into a very
strong Cord, of sufficient Length for the Purpose. And now,
having each of us brought a Bundle of dry fallen Sticks from
the Wood with us, and gathered two or three Flints as we
came along, we struck Fire on my Knife upon some rotten
Wood, and boiled a good Piece of our Goat's Flesh; and
having made such a Meal as we had neither of us made for
many Months before, we laid us down and slept heartily till
Morning.

As soon as Day broke we packed up our Goods, and, filling our *Calabash* with Water, we loaded our *Muletto*, and got
forward very pleasantly that Day, and several others following, and had tolerable Lodgings.

About Noon, one Day, travelling with great Glee, we met
an Adventure which very much daunted me, and had almost
put a Stop to my Hopes of ever getting where I intended. We
came to a great River, whose Name I have now forgot, near
a League over, but full, and especially about the Shores, of
large Trees which had fallen from the Mountains, and been
rolled down with the Floods, and lodged there in a shocking
Manner. This River *Glanlepze* told me we must pass. For
my part, I shrunk at the Sight of it, and told him, if he could
get over, I would not desire to prevent his meeting with his
Family, but as for my Share, I had rather take my Chance
in the Woods, on this Side, than plunge myself into such
a Stream, only for the Sake of Drowning. Oh! says *Glanlepze*,
then you can't swim. No, says I, there's my Misfortune. Well,
well, says the kind *Glanlepze*, be of good Heart, I'll have you
over. He then bad me go cut an arm full of the tallest of the
Reeds that grew there near the Shore, whilst he pulled up
another, where he then was, and bring them to him. The Side

of the River sloped for a good Way with an easy Descent, so
that it was very shallow where the Reeds grew, and they stood
very close together, upon a large Compass of Ground. I had
no sooner entred the Reeds a few Yards, to cut some of the
longest, but (being about Knee deep in the Water and Mud,
and every Step raising my Feet very high, to keep them clear
of the Roots, which were matted together) I thought, I had
trod upon a Trunck of one of the Trees, of which, as I said,
there was such Plenty thereabouts; and raising my other Foot,
to get that also upon the Tree, as I fancied it, I found it move
along with me; upon which, I roared out; when *Glanlepze*,
who was not far from me, imagining what was the Matter,
cried out, leap off, and run to shore to the Right. I knew not
yet what was the Case, but did as I was bid, and gained the
Shore. Looking back, I perceived the Reeds shake and rustle
all the Way to the Shore, by Degrees, after me. I was terribly
frightened, and ran to *Glanlepze*, who then told me the
Danger I had escaped, and that what I took for a Tree, was
certainly a large Alligator, or Crocodile.[1]

My Blood ran chill within me, at hearing the Name of such
a dangerous Creature; but he had no sooner told me what it
was, than out came the most hideous Monster I had ever seen.
Glanlepze ran to secure the Muletto; and then, taking the
Cord which had fastened him, and tying it to each End of
a broken Arm of a Tree that lay on the Shore, he marched up
to the Crocodile without the least Dismay, and beginning near
the Tail, with one Leg on one Side, and the other on the other
Side, he straddled over him, still mending his Pace as the
Beast crept forward, till he came to his Fore-Feet; then throwing the great Log before his Mouth, he by the Cord in his
Hand, bobbed it against the Creature's Nose, till he gaped
wide enough to have taken in the Muletto; then, of a sudden,
jerking the Wood between his Jaws with all his Force, by the
Cord, he gagged the Beast, with his Jaws wide open up to his
Throat, so that he could neither make use of his Teeth, or
shut his Mouth; he then threw one End of the Cord upon the
Ground, just before the Creatures's under Jaw, which, as he

by Degrees crept along over it, came out behind his Fore-Legs, on the contrary Side; and serving the other End of it in the same Manner, he took up those Ends and tied them over the Creature's Back, just within his Fore-Legs, which kept the Gag firm in his Mouth; and then calling out to me, for I stood at a good Distance, *Peter*, says he, bring me your Knife; I trembled at going so near, for the Crocodile was turning his Head this Way and that very uneasy, and wanting to get to the River again, but yet I carried it, keeping as much behind him as I could, still eyeing him which Way he moved, and at length tossed my Knife so near, that *Glanlepze* could reach it; and he, just keeping behind the Beasts Fore-feet, and leaning forward, first darted the Knife into one Eye, and then into the other, and immediately leaping from his Back, came running to me. So *Peter*, says he, I have done the Business. Ay! Business enough, I think, says I, and more than I would have done, to have been King of *Congo*. Why *Peter*, says he, there is nothing but a Man may compass by Resolution, if he takes both Ends of a Thing in his View at once, and fairly deliberates on both Sides, what may be given and taken from End to End. What you have seen me perform, is only from a thorough Notion I have of this Beast, and of myself, how far each of us hath Power to act and counter-act upon the other, and duly applying the Means. But, says he, this talk will not carry us cross the River; come, here are the Reeds I have pulled up, which I believe will be sufficient without any more, for I would not overload the Muletto. Why, says I, is the Muletto to carry them? No, they are to carry you, says he. I can never ride upon these says I. Hush, says he, I'll not loose you never fear. Come, cut me a good tough Stick, the Length of these Reeds. Well, says I, this is all Conjuration; but, I don't see a Step towards my getting over the River yet, unless I am to ride the Muletto upon these Reeds, and guide myself with the Stick. I must own, *Peter*, says he, you have a bright Guess. So, taking an Armful of the Reeds, and laying them on the Ground, now *Peter*, says he, lay that Stick upon those Reeds, and tie them tight at both Ends. I did so.

Now *Peter*, says he, lay yourself down upon them. I then laying myself on my Back, lengthwise, upon the Reeds, *Glanlepze* laugh'd heartily at me, and turning me about, brought my Breast upon the Reeds at the Heighth of my Armpits; and then taking a Handful of the Reeds he had reserved by themselves, he laid them on my Back, tying them to the Bundle, close at my Shoulders, and again at the Ends. Now *Peter*, says he, stand up; which I did; but, it was full as much as I could do. I then seeing *Glanlepze* laughing at the Figure I cut, desired him to be serious, and not put me upon loosing my Life for a Joke; for, I could not think what he would do next with me. He bid me never fear, and looking more soberly, ordered me to walk to the River, and so stand just within the Bank till he came; then leading the Muletto to me, he tied me to her, about a Yard from the Tail, and taking the Cord in his Hand, led the Muletto and me into the Water. We had not gone far before my Guide began to swim; then the Muletto and I were presently Chin deep, and I expected nothing but drowning every Moment; however, having gone so far, I was ashamed to cry out; when getting out of my Depth, and my Reeds coming to their bearing, up I mounted, and was carried on with all the Ease imaginable: My Conductor guiding us between the Trees so dexterously, that not one Accident happened to either of us all the Way, and we arrived safe on the opposite Shore.

We had now got into a very low, close, swampy Country, and our Goat's Flesh began to be very stale, through the heat not only of the Sun but the Muletto's Back; however, we pleased ourselves we should have one more Meal of it before it was too bad to eat; so having travelled about three Miles from the River, we took up our Lodging on a little Rising, and tyed our Muletto in a Valley about half a Furlong below us, where he made as good a Meal in his Way, as we did in ours.

We had but just supped, and were sauntring about to find the easiest Spot to sleep on, when we heard a rustling and a grumbling Noise, in a small Thicket just on our Right; which seeming to approach nearer and nearer, *Glanlepze* roused himself, and was on his Legs, just Time enough to see a Lioness, and a small Whelp which accompanied her, within thirty Yards of us, making towards us, as we afterwards guessed, for the Sake of our Goat's Flesh, which now smelt very strong.[1] *Glanlepze* whipped on the contrary Side of the Fire to that where the Goat's Flesh lay, and fell to kicking the Fire about at a great rate, which being made of dry Wood, caused innumerable Sparks to fly about us; but the Beasts still approaching in a couchant Manner, and seizing the Ribs of the Goat, and other Bones, for we had only cut the Flesh off, and grumbling and cracking them like rotten Twigs, *Glanlepze* snatched up a Fire-brand, flaming, in each Hand, and made towards them; which Sight so terrified the Creatures, that they fled with great Precipitation to the Thicket again.

Glanlepze was a little uneasy at the Thoughts of quitting so good a Lodging as we had found, but yet held it best to move farther; for as the Lions had left the Bones behind them, we must expect another Visit if we stayed there, and could hope for no Rest; and above all, we might possibly lose our Muletto; so we removed our Quarters two Miles further, where we slept with great Tranquility.

Reflections on the Nature of Mankind, have often astonished me. I told you at first, my Thoughts concerning Prayer, in my Journey to *Bristol*, and of the Benefit I received from it, and how fully I was convinced of the Necessity of it; which one would think was a sufficient Motive to a reasonable Creature to be constant in it; and yet it is too true, that not-withstanding the Difficulties I had laboured under, and Hard-ships I had undergone, and the Danger of starving at Sea, or being murdered for Food by my Fellows, when there was as urgent a Necessity of begging divine Assistance as can be conceived, I never once thought of it, or of the Object of it, or returned Thanks for my being delivered, till the Lioness had just left me: And then I felt near the same Force, urging me to return Thanks for my Escape, as I had impelling me to Prayer before; and I think I did so with great Sincerity.

I shall not trouble you with a Relation of the common

Accidents of our Journey, which lasted two Months and
better, or with the different Methods we used to get Subsistance; but shall at once conduct you to *Quamis*:[1] Only
mention that we were sometimes obliged to go about; and
were once stopped by a Cut that my Guide and Companion
receiv'd by a ragged Stone in his Foot, which growing very
bad almost deprived me of the Hopes of his Life; but, by
Rest, and constant sucking and licking it, which was the only
Remedy we had to apply, except green Leaves chewed, that
I laid to it by his Direction, to supple and cool it, he soon
began to be able to ride upon the Muletto, and sometimes to
walk a little.

I say, we arrived at *Quamis*, a small Place on a River of that
Name, where *Glanlepze* had a neat Dwelling, and left a Wife
and five Children when he went out to the Wars. We were
very near the Town when the Day closed, and, as it is soon
dark there after Sun-set, you could but just see your Hand at
our Entrance into it. We met nobody in the Way, but I went
directly to *Glanlepze*'s Door, by his Direction, and struck
two or three Strokes hard against it with my Stick. On this
there came a Woman to it stark-naked.[2] I asked her, in her own
Language, if she knew one *Glanlepze*? She told me, with a
deep Sigh, that once she did. I asked then, where he was?
She said with their Ancestors, she hoped, for he was the
greatest Warrior in the World; but, if he was not dead, he
was in Slavery. Now, you must know, *Glanlepze* had a mind
to hear how his Wife took his Death, or Slavery, and had put
me upon asking these Questions before he discovered himself.
I proceeded then to tell her, I brought some News of *Glanlepze*,
and was lately come from him, and by his Order. And does
my dear *Glanlepze* live, says she, flying upon my Neck, and
almost smothering me with Caresses, till I begged her to forbear, or she would strangle me, and I had a great deal more to
tell her; then ringing for a Light,[3] when she saw I was a white
Man, she seem'd in the utmost Confusion at her own Naked-
ness, and immediately retiring, she threw a Cloth round her
Waist, and came to me again. I then repeated to her, that her

Husband was alive and well, but wanted a Ransom to redeem himself, and had sent me to see what she could any Ways raise for that Purpose. She told me, she and her Children had lived very hardly ever since he went from her, and she had nothing to sell, or make Money of, but her five Children; that, as this was the Time for the Slaving Trade, she would see what she could raise by them, and if that would not do, she would sell herself and send him the Money, if he would let her know how to do it.

Glanlepze, who heard every Word that passed, finding so strong a Proof of his Wife's Affection, could hold out no longer, but, bursting into the Room, clasped her in his Arms, crying, no, *Zulika*, for that was her Name, I am free; there will be no Occasion for your or my dear Children's Slavery; and rather than have purchased my Freedom at that Rate, I would willingly have died a Slave myself. But my own Ears have heard the tender Sentiments my *Zulika* has for me. Then, drowned in Tears of Joy, they embraced each other so close, and so long, that I thought it impertinent to be seen with them, till their first Transports were over. So I retir'd without the House, till *Glanlepze* called me in, which was not in less than full half an Hour. I admired at the Love and Constancy of the Persons I had just left behind me; and, good Heaven, thinks I to myself, with a Sigh, how happy has this our Escape rendered *Glanlepze* and his Wife! what a mutual Felicity do they feel! And what is the Cause of all this? Is it that he has brought Home great Treasures from the Wars? Nothing like it, he is come naked. Is it that having escaped Slavery and Poverty he is returned to an opulent Wife, abounding with the good Things of Life? No such Thing. What then can be the Cause of this Excess of Satisfaction, this alternate[1] Joy, that *Patty* and I could not have been as happy with each other? Why, it was my Pride that interposed and prevented it. But what am I like to get by it, and by all this Travel, and these Hazards? Is this the Way to make a Fortune, to get an Estate? No surely, the very contrary. I could not forsooth labour for *Patty*, and her Children, where

I was known; but am I any better for labouring here, where
I am not known, where I have no body to assist me, than I
could have been where I am known, and where there would
have been my Friends about me, at least, if they could have
afforded no great Assistance. I have been deceived then, and
have travelled so many thousand Miles, and undergone so
many Dangers, only, to know at last, I had been happier at
home; and have doubled my Misery, for want of Consideration, that very Consideration, which, impartially taken, would
have convinced me, I ought to have made the best of my bad
Circumstances, and to have laid hold of every commendable
Method of improving them. Did I come hither to avoid daily
Labour or voluntary Servitude at home? I have had it in
Abundance. Did I come hither to avoid Poverty and Contempt? Here I have met with 'em ten fold. And now, after all,
was I to return Home empty and naked, as *Glanlepze* has
done; should I meet a Wife, as bare as myself, so ready to die
in my Embraces, and to be a Slave herself, with her Children,
for my Sake only? I fear not.

These and the like Reflections had taken Possession of me,
when *Glanlepze* called me in; where I found his Wife, in her
Manner, preparing our Supper, with all that Chearfulness
which gives a true Lustre to Innocence.

The Bustle we made, had by this Time awakened the Children; who, stark naked, as they were born, both Boys and Girls,
came crawling out, and black as Jett, from behind a Curtain, at
the further End of the Room, which was very long. The Father,
as yet, had only enquired after them, but, upon Sight of them,
he fell into an Extacy, kissing one, stroaking another, dandling
a third, for the eldest was scarce fourteen; but not one of them
knew him, for seven Years makes a great Chasm in young
Memories. The more I saw of this Sport, the stronger Impress-
ions *Patty* and my own Children made upon me. My Mind
had been so much employed on my own Distresses, that those
dear Ideas were almost effaced; but this moving Scene introduced them afresh, and imprinted 'em deeply on my Imagination, which cherished the sweet Remembrance.

CHAPTER VIII

How the Author passed his Time with Glanlepze *; his
Acquaintance with some* English *Prisoners ; they
project an Escape ; he joins them ; they seize a*
Portugueze *Ship, and get off ; make a long run from
Land ; want Water ; they anchor at a desert Island ;
the Boat goes on Shore for Water ; they lose their
Anchor in a Storm ; the Author and one* Adams *drove
to Sea ; a miraculous Passage to a Rock ;* Adams
drowned there ; the Author's miserable Condition

I PASSED my Time with *Glanlepze* and his Wife, who both
really loved me, with sufficient bodily Quiet, for about two
Years; my Business was chiefly, in company with my Patron,
to cultivate a Spot of Ground wherein we had planted Grain
and Necessaries for the Family; and once or twice a Week we
went a fishing; and sometimes hunted, and shot Venison.
These were our chief Employments; for as to Excursions for
Slaves, which is a Practice in many of those Countries, and
what the Natives get Money by, since our own Slavery,
Glanlepze and I could not endure it.

Though I was tolerably easy in my external Circumstances,
yet my Mind hankering after *England* made my Life still
unhappy; and that Infelicity daily increased, as I saw the less
Probability of attaining my Desire. At length, hearing of some
European Sailors, who were under Confinement for contra-
band Trade at a *Portuguese* Fort, about two Leagues from
Quamis, I resolved to go to see them; and if any of them
should be *English*, at least to enquire after my native Country.
I went, and found two *Dutchmen*, who had been Sailors in
British Pay several Years, three *Scotchmen*, an *Irishman*, and
five *Englishmen*; but all had been long in *English* Merchants
Service. They were taken, as they told me, by a *Portugueze*
Vessel, together with their Ship, as a *Dutch* Prize, under
Pretence of contraband Trade. The Captain was known to be

a *Dutchman*, though he spoke good *English*, and was then in *English* Pay, and his Vessel *English*: Therefore they would have it that he was a *Dutch* Trader, and so seized his Ship in the Harbour, with the Prisoners in it. The Captain, who was on Shore with several of his Men, was threatened to be laid in Irons, if he was taken; which obliged him and his Men to abscond, and fly over Land, to an *English* Factory,[1] for Assistance to recover his Ship and Cargoe; being afraid to appear, and claim it, amongst so many Enemies, without an additional Force. They had been in Confinement two Months, and their Ship confiscated and sold. In this miserable Condition I left them, but returned once or twice a Week, for a Fortnight or three Weeks, to visit them. These Instances of Regard, as they thought them, created some Confidence in me, so that they conversed with me very freely. Amongst other Discourse, they told me one Day, that one of their Crew, who went with the Captain, had been taken ill on the Way, and being unable to proceed, was returned; but as he talked good *Portuguese*, he was not suspected to belong to them; and that he had been to visit them, and would be there again that Day. I had a Mind to see him, so stayed longer than I intended, and in about an Hour's Time he came. After he was seated, he asked, who I was? and, privately, if I might be trusted? Being satisfied I might, for that I was a *Cornish* Man, he began as follows, looking narrowly about to see he was not overheard: My Lads, says he, be of good Courage, I have hopes for you, be but Men, and we shall see better Days yet. I wondered to what this Preface tended, when he told us, That since his return from the Captain, as he spoke good *Portugueze*, and had sailed on board *Portugueze* Traders several Years, he mixed among that People, and particularly among the Crew of the *Del Cruz*, the Ship which had taken them; that that Ship had partly unloaded, and was taking in other Goods for a future Voyage; that he had informed himself of their Strength, and that very seldom more than three Men and two Boys lay on Board; that he had hired himself to the Captain, and was to go on board the very next Day. Now,

F

says he, my Lads, if you can break Prison any Night after To-morrow, and come directly to the Ship, (telling them how she lay, for, says he, you can't mistake, you will find two or three Boats moored in the Gut¹ against the Church) I will be ready to receive you, and wee'll get off with her, in lieu of our Ship they have taken from us; for there is nothing ready to follow us.

The Prisoners listned to this Discourse very attentively; but scratched their heads, fearing the difficulty of it, and severer usage if they miscarried, and made several Objections; but, at last, they all swore to attempt it, the Night but one following. Upon which the Sailor went away, to prepare for their Reception on board. After he was gone, I surveyed his Scheme attentively in my own Mind, and found it not so difficult as I first imagined, if the Prisoners could but escape cleverly. So, before I went away, I told them, I approved of their Purpose; and as I was their Countryman, I was resolved, with their Leaves, to risk my Fortune with them. At this they seemed much pleased, and all embraced me. We then fixed the peremptory² Night, and I was to wait at the Water-Side, and get the Boats in Readiness.

The Prison they were in was a *Portugueze* Fort, which had been deserted ever since the building a much better on the other Side of the River, a Gun-shot lower. It was built with Walls too thick for naked Men to storm; the Captives were securely locked up every Night; and two Soldiers, or Centinels, kept watch in an outer Room, who were relieved from the Main Guard in the Body of the Building.

The expected Night arrived; and a little before Midnight, as had been concerted, one of the Prisoners cried out, he was so parched up, he was on Fire, he was on Fire. The Centinels were both asleep; but the first that waked, called at the Door, to know what was the Matter; the Prisoner still crying out, I am on Fire, the rest begged the Centinel to bring a Bowl of Water for him, for they knew not what ailed him.

The good natured Fellow, without waking his Companion, brought the Water, and having a Lamp in the Guard-Room, opened the Door; when the Prisoners seizing his Arms, and commanding him to silence, bound his Hands behind him, and his Feet together; then serving the other in the same Manner, who was now just awake, and taking from 'em their Swords and Musquets, they made the best of their Way over the Fort Wall; which, being built with Buttresses on the Inside, was easily surmounted. Being got out, they were not long a finding me, who had before this Time made the Boats ready, and was impatiently waiting for them; so in we all got, and made good Speed to the Ship, where we were welcomed by our Companion, ready to receive us.

Under Pretence of being a new entered Sailor, he had carried some *Madeira* Wine on board, and treated the Men and Boys so freely, that he had thrown 'em into a dead Sleep; which was a wise Precaution. There being now therefore no Fear of Disturbance, nor Interruption, we drew up the two Boats, and set all Hands at work to put the Ship under Way; and plyed it so closely, the Wind favouring us, that by eleven o'Clock the next Morning, we were out of Sight of Land; but we set the Men and Boys adrift, in one of the Boats, nigh the Mouth of the River.

The first Thing we did, after we had made a long run from Shore, was to consult what Course to steer. Now, as there was a valuable Loading on board, of Goods from *Portugal*, and others taken in since, some gave their Opinion for sailing directly to *India*, selling the Ship and Cargo there, and returning by some *English* Vessel. But that was rejected; for we did not doubt but Notice would be given of our Escape along the Coast; and if we should fall into the *Portuguese* Hands, we could expect no Mercy; besides we had not People sufficient for such an Enterprize. Others again, were for sailing the directest Course for *England*. But, I told them, as our Opinions were different, and no Time was to be lost, my Advice was, to stretch[1] Southward, till we might be quite out of Fear of Pursuit, and then, whatever Course we took, by keeping clear of all Coasts we might hope to come safe off.

My Proposal seem'd to please the whole Crew; so, crowding

all the Sail we could, we pushed Southward very briskly, before the Wind, for several Days. We now went upon examining our Stores, and found we had Flour enough, Plenty of Fish, and Salt Provisions, but were scant of Water and Wood: Of the first whereof there was not half a Ton, and but very little of the latter. This made us very uneasy; and being none of us expert in Navigation, farther than the common working of the Ship, and having no Chart on board, that might direct us to the nearest Land, we were almost at our Wit's End, and came to a short Allowance of Liquor. That we must get Water if we could, was indisputable; but where to do it puzzled us: As we had determined not to get in with the *African* Shore, on any Account whatever.

In this Perplexity, and under the Guidance of different Opinions, for we were all Captains now, we sometimes steered Eastward, and sometimes Westward for about nine Days; when we espied a little bluish Cloud-like Appearance, to the South-West. This continuing, we hoped it might be Land, and therefore made to it. Upon our nearer Approach, we found it to be, as we judged, an Island; but, not knowing its Name, or whether it was inhabited, we coasted round it two Days, to satisfy ourselves as to this last Particular. Seeing no living Creature on it during that time, and the Shore being very broken, we came to an Anchor about two Miles from it, and sent ten of our Crew in our best Boat, with some Casks, to get Water and cut Wood. The Boat returned at Night, with six Men, and the Casks fill'd, having left four behind, to go on with the cutting of Wood against next Day. Accordingly next Morning the Boat went off again, and made two Turns with Water and Wood ere Night; which was repeated for two or three Days after. On the sixth she went off for Wood only, leaving none but me and one *John Adams* a Board.

The Boat had scarce reach'd the Island, this last Turn, before the Day overcast, and there arose such a Storm of Wind, Thunder, Lightning, and Hail, as I had never before seen. At last our Cable broke close to the Anchor, and away we went with the Wind, full Southward by West; and not having Strength to keep the Ship upon a side wind, we were forced to set her Head right before it, and let her drive. Our Hope was, every Hour, the Storm would abate; but it continued with equal Violence for many Days; during all which Time, neither *Adams* or I had any rest; for one, or other of us was forced, and sometimes both, to keep her right before the Wind, or she would certainly have overset. When the Storm abated, as it did by Degrees, neither *Adams* or I could tell where we were, or even in what Part of the World.

I was sorry I had no better a Sailor with me, for neither *Adams* or myself had ever made more than one Voyage till now; so that we were both unacquainted with the Latitude, and scarce knew the Use of the Compass to any Purpose; and, being out of all Hope of ever reaching the Island, to our Companions, we neither knew which Way to steer, or what to do. And indeed, had we known where we were, we two only could not have been able to navigate the Ship to any Part we desired; or ever get to the Island, unless such a Wind as we had before, would of itself have driven us thither.

Whilst we were considering Day after Day what to do, though the Sea was now very calm and smooth, the Ship seemed to sail at as great a Rate as before; which we attributed to the Velocity she had acquired by the Storm, or to Currents that had set that Way by the Violence of the Winds. Contenting ourselves with this, we expected all soon to be right again; and as we had no Prospect of ever seeing our Companions, we kept the best look out we could, to see for any Vessel coming that Course, which might take us in; and resolved to rest all our Hopes upon that.

When we had sailed a good while after this manner, we knew not whither, *Adams* called out, I see land. My Heart leaped within me for Joy, and we hoped, the current that seem'd to carry us so fast, set in for some Islands or Rivers that lay before us. But still we were exceedingly puzzled at the Ship's making such Way; and the nearer and nearer we approached the Land, which was now very visible, the more speed the Ship made; though there was no Wind stirring. We had but just Time to think on this unexpected Phænomenon, when we found, that what we had taken for Land, was a Rock of an extraordinary Height, to which, as we advanced nearer, the Ship increased its Motion; and all our Strength could not make her answer her Rudder any other Way. This put us under the Apprehension of being dashed to Pieces immediately; and in less than half an Hour, I verily thought my Fears had not been groundless. Poor *Adams* told me he would try, when the Ship struck, if he could leap upon the Rock, and ran to the Head for that Purpose; but I was so fearful of seeing my Danger, that I ran under Hatches, resolving to sink in the Ship. We had no sooner parted, but I felt so violent a Shock, that I verily thought the Ship had brought down the whole Rock upon her, and been thereby dashed to Pieces; so that I never more expected to see the Light.

I lay under this Terror for at least half an Hour; waiting the Ship's either filling with Water or bulging[1] every Moment. But finding neither Motion in her, or any Water rise, or the least Noise whatsoever, I ventured with an aching Heart from my Retreat, and stole up the Hatchway, as if an Enemy had been on Deck, peeping first one Way, then another. Here nothing presented but Confusion; the Rock hung over the Hatchway, at about twenty Feet above my Head, our Foremast lay by the Board,[2] the Mainmast Yardarm was down, and great Part of the Mainmast snapped off with it, and almost every thing upon Deck was displaced. This Sight shocked me extremely; and calling for *Adams*, in whom I hoped to find some comfort, I was too soon convinced I had lost him.

CHAPTER IX

Wilkins *thinks of destroying himself; his Soliloquy;*
strange Accident in the Hold; his Surprize; can't
climb the Rock; his Method to sweeten his Water;
lives many Months on board; ventures to Sea in his
Boat several Times, and takes many Fish; almost
overcome by an Eel

AFTER I had stood a while in the utmost Confusion of
Thought, and my Spirits began to be a little composed, I was
resolved to see what Damage the Hull of the Ship had
received. Accordingly I looked narrowly, but could find
none, only she was immovably fixed in a Cleft of the Rock,
like a large Arch-way; and there stuck so fast, that tho', upon
fathoming, I could find no Bottom, she never moved in the
least, by the Working of the Water.

I now began to look upon *Adams* as a happy Man, being
delivered by immediate Death from such an inextricable
Scene of Distress, and wish'd myself with him a thousand
Times. I had a great Mind to have followed him into the other
World; yet, I know not how it is, there is something so
abhorrent to human Nature, in Self-Murder, be one's Condition what it will, that I was soon determined on the contrary
Side. Now again I perceived that the Almighty had given me
a large Field to expatiate in upon the Trial of his Creatures;
by bringing them into imminent Dangers, ready to overwhelm them, and at the same Time, as it were, hanging out the
Flag of Truce and Mercy to them. These Thoughts brought
me to my Knees, and I pour'd out my Soul to God, in a Strain
of Humiliation, Resignation to his Will, and earnest Petitions
for Deliverance, or Support in this Distress. Having finished,
I found myself in a more composed Frame; so having eaten
a Biscuit, and drank a Can of Water, and not seeing any
Thing to be done whereby I could better my Condition, I sat
me down upon the Deck, and fell into the following Soliloquy.

Peter, says I, what have you to do here? Alas, reply'd I to myself, I am fixed against my Will, in this dismal Mansion, destin'd, as Rats might be, to devour the Provisions only, and, having eat all up, to perish with Hunger for Want of a Supply. Then, says I, of what Use are you in the World, *Peter*? Truly, answer'd I, of no other Use, that I can see, but to be an Object of Misery for divine Vengeance to work upon, and to shew, what a deplorable State human Nature can be reduced to: For I can't think any one else can be so wretched. And again, *Peter*, says I, what have you been doing ever since you came into the World? I am afraid, says I, I can answer no better to this Question than to either of the former; for, if only reasonable Actions are to be reckoned among my Doings, I am sure I have done little worth recording. For, let me see, what it all amounts to: I spent my first sixteen Years, in making a Fool of my Mother; my three next in letting her make a Fool of me; and in being Fool enough myself to get me a Wife and two Children before I was twenty. The next Year was spent in finding out the Misery of Slavery from Experience. Two Years more I repin'd at the Happiness of my Benefactor, and at finding it was not my Lot to enjoy the same. This Year is not yet spent, and how many more are to come, and where they may be pass'd, and what they may produce, requires a better Head than mine even to guess at; but certainly my present Situation seems to promise nothing beside Woe and Misery. But hold a little, says I, and let me clearly state my own Wretchedness. I am here, 'tis true, but for any Good I have ever done, or any Advantage I have reaped in other Places, I am as well here as any where. I have no present Want of Food, or unjust or cruel Enemy to annoy me; so, as long as the Ship continues entire, and Provisions last, I shall do tolerably. Then, why should I grieve or terrify myself about what may come. What my frighted Imagination suggests may perhaps never happen. Deliverance, though not to be looked for, is yet possible. And my future Fate may be as different from my present Condition, as this is from the Hopes with which I lately flattered myself. And why, after all, may

I not die a natural Death here, as well as any where? All Mankind do die, and then there is an End of all.—An End of all, did I say,—no, there is something within that gives me the Lie, when I say so. Let me see, Death (my Master used to say) is not an End, but a Beginning of real Life. And may it not be so?—May I not as well undergo a Change, from this to a different State of Life, when I leave this World, as be born into it, I know not from whence? Who sent me into this World? Who framed me of two Natures so unlike, that Death cannot destroy but one of them? It must be the Almighty God: But all God's Works tend to some End. And if he has given me an immortal Nature, it must be his Intention that I should live somewhere and somehow for ever. May not this Stage of Being then be only an Introduction to, a Preparative for, another? There is nothing in this Supposition repugnant to Reason. Upon the whole; if God is the Author of my Being, he only has a Right to dispose of it; and I may not put an End thereto without his Leave. It is no less true, that my continuing therein during his Pleasure, and because it is so, may turn vastly to my Advantage in his good Time; it may be the Means of my becoming happy for ever, when it is his Will that I go hence. It is no less probable, that, dismal as my present Circumstances appear, I may be even now the Object of a kind Providence. God may be leading me by Affliction to Repentance of former Crimes; destroying those sensual Affections that have all my Days kept me from loving and serving him. I will therefore submit myself to his Will, and hope for his Mercy.

These Thoughts and many others I then had composed me very much, and by Degrees reconciled me to my destined Solitude. I walked my Ship, of which I was now both Master and Owner, and employed myself in searching how it was fastened to the Rock, and where it rested; but all to no Purpose, as to that particular. I then struck a Light, and went into the Hold, to see what I could find useful; for we had never searched the Ship since we took her.

In the Hold, I found Abundance of long Iron Bars, which

I suppose were brought out to be trafficked with the Blacks. I observed they lay all with one End close to the Head of the Ship, which I presumed was occasioned by the violent Shock they received when she struck against the Rock; but seeing one short Bar lying out beyond the Rest, though touching at the End one of the long Bars, I thought to take it up, and lay it on the Heap with the others; but the Moment I had raised the End next the other Bars, it flew out of my Hand, with such Violence, against the Head of the Ship, and with such a Noise, as greatly surprised me, and put me in fear it had broke through the Plank.

I just stay'd to see no harm was done, and run upon Deck, with my Hair stiff on my Head; nor could I conceive less, than that some subtil Spirit had done this Prank, meerly to terrify me.

It ran in my Pate several Days, and I durst upon no Account have gone into the Hold again, though my whole Support had lain there; nay, it even spoiled my Rest, for fear something tragical should befall me, of which this amazing Incident was an Omen.

About a Week after, as I was shifting myself, (for I had not taken my Cloaths off since I came there) and putting on a new Pair of Shoes which I found on Board, my own being very bad, taking out my Iron Buckles, I laid one of them upon a broken Piece of the Mast that I sat upon; when, to my Astonishment, it was no sooner out of my Hand, but up it flew to the Rock, and stuck there. I could not tell what to make of it; but was sorry the Devil had got above Deck. I then held several other Things, one after another, in my Hand, and laid them down where I laid the Buckle, but nothing stirred, till I took out the Fellow of that from the Shoes; when letting it go, away it jumped also to the Rock.

I mused on these Phenomena for some Time, and could not forbear calling upon God to protect me from the Devil, who must as I imagined have a Hand in such unaccountable Things, as they then seemed to me. But at Length Reason got the better of these foolish Apprehensions, and I began to think there might be some natural Cause of them, and next to be very desirous of finding it out. In order to this I set about making Experiments, to try what would run to the Rock, and what would not. I went into the Captain's Cabin, and opening a Cupboard, of which the Key was in the Door, I took out a Pipe, a Bottle, a Pocket-Book, a Silver Spoon, a Tea-cup, &c. and laid 'em successively near the Rock; when none of them answered; but the Key which I had brought out of the Cupboard, on my Finger, dropping off, while I was thus employed, no sooner it was disengaged, but away it went to it. After that I tryed several other Pieces of Iron-ware, with the like Success. Upon this, and the Needle of my Compass standing stiff to the Rock, I concluded that this same Rock contained great Quantity of Loadstone, or was itself one vast Magnet, and that our Lading of Iron was the Cause of the Ship's violent Course thereto, which I mentioned before.

This quite satisfied me, as to my Notion of Spirits, and gave me a more undisturbed Night's Rest than I had had before; so that now, having nothing to affright me, I passed the Time tolerably well in my Solitude, as it grew by Degrees familiar to me.

I had often wished it had been possible for me to climb the Rock; but it was so smooth in many Places, and craggy in others, and over hanging, continuing just the same to the Right and Left of me as far as ever I could see, that from the Impossibility of it, I discharged all Thoughts of such an Attempt.

I had now lived on board three Months, and perceived the Days grow shorter and shorter, 'till, having lost the Sun for a little Time, they were quite dark: That is, there was no absolute Day-light, or indeed visible Distinction between Day and Night; though it was never so dark, but I could see well enough upon Deck to go about.

What now concerned me the most was, my Water, which began to grow very bad (though I had plenty of it) and unsavory, so that I could scarce drink it; but had no Prospect

of better. Now and then indeed it snowed a little, which I
made some use of; but this was far from contenting me. Hereupon I began to contrive, and having nothing else to do,
I set two open Vessels upon Deck, and drawing Water from
the Hold, I filled one of my Vessels, and letting it stand a Day
and a Night, I poured it into the other, and so shifted it every
twenty-four Hours; this, I found, though it did not bring it
to the primitive[1] Taste, and render it altogether palatable,
was nevertheless a great Help to it, by incorporating the fresh
Air with it; so that it became very potable: And this Method
I constantly used with my drinking Water, so long as I stayed
on board the Ship.

It had now been sharp Weather for some Time; and the
Cold still increasing, this put me upon rumaging the Ship
further than ever I thought to do before; when opening a little
Cabin under Deck, I found a large Cargo of fine *French*
Brandy, a great many Bottles and some small Casks of *Madeira*
Wine, with divers Cordial Waters. Having tasted these, and
taken out a Bottle or two of Brandy, and some *Madeira*,
I locked up my Door, and looked no farther that Time.

The next Day I inquired into my Provisions; and some of
my Flesh having soaked out the Pickle, I made fresh Pickle,
and closed it up again. I that Day also found several Cheeses,
cased up in Lead, one of which I then opened and dined upon:
But what Time of Day or Night it was when I eat this Meal
I could not tell. I found a great many Chests well filled, and
one or two of Tools, which some Years after stood me in a very
good stead; though I did not expect they would ever be of that
Service when I first met with them.

In this Manner I spent my Time till I began to see broad
Day-light again, which cheared me greatly. I had been often
put in hopes, during the dark Season, that Ships were coming
towards me, and that I should once more have the Conversation of Mankind; for I had, by the small glimmering, seen
many large Bodies (to my thinking) move at a little Distance
from me, and particularly toward the re-appearing of the
Light; but though I hallowed as loud as I could, and often
fired my Gun, I never received an Answer.

When the Light returned, my Days increased in Proportion as they had before decreased; and gathering Comfort from that, I determined to launch my small Boat, and to coast along the Island, as I judged it, to see if it was inhabited, and by whom; I determin'd also to make me some Lines for Fishing, and carry my Gun, to try for other Game, if I found a Place for Landing: For though I had never, since my Arrival, seen a single living Creature but my Cat, except Insects, of which there were many in the Water, and in the Air, before the dark Weather, and then began to appear again; yet I could not but think there were both Birds and Beasts to be met with.

Upon launching my Boat, I perceived she was very leaky; so I let her fill, and continue thus a Week or more, to stop her Cracks; then getting down the Side of my Ship, I scooped her quite dry, and found her very fit for use; so, putting on board my Gun, Lines, Brandy Bottle, and a Cloaths-chest for a Seat, with some little Water, and Provisions for a Week, I once more committed myself to the Sea: Having taken all the Observation I could, to gain my Ship again, if any Accident should happen; tho' I resolved, upon no Account, to quit sight of the Rock willingly.

I had not row'd very long, before I thought I saw an Island to my right, about a League distant, to which I inclined to steer my Course, the Sea being very calm; but, upon surveying it nearer, I found it only a great Cake of Ice, about forty Yards high above the Water, and a Mile or two in length. I then concluded, that what I had before taken for Ships, were only these Lumps of Ice. Being thus disappointed as to my Island, I made what haste I could back to the Rock again, and coasted part of its Circumference; but tho' I had gone two or three Leagues of its Circuit, the Prospect it afforded was just the same.

I then try'd my Lines, by fastning several very long ones, made of the Log-line, to the Side of the Boat, baiting them with several different Baits, but took only one Fish of about four Pounds weight, very much resembling a Haddock; part of which I dress'd for my Supper, after my Return to the Ship, and it proved very good. Towards Evening I return'd to my Home, as I may call it.

The next Day I made a Voyage on the other Side of the Rock, tho' but to a small Distance from the Ship, with Intent only to fish, but took nothing. I had then a Mind to victual my Boat, or little Cruizer, and prepare myself for a Voyage of two or three Days; which I thought I might safely undertake, as I had never seen a troubled Sea since I came to the Island; for, tho' I heard the Wind often roaring over my Head, yet it coming always from the Land-side, it never disturbed the Water near Shore. I set out the same Way I went at first, designing to sail two or three Days out, and as many Home again; and resolved, if possible, to fathom the Depth as I went. With this View I prepared a very long Line, with a large Shot tyed in a Rag at the End of it, by way of Plummet; but I felt no Ground 'till the second Night. The next Morning I came into thirty fathom Water, then twenty, then sixteen. In both Tours I could perceive no Abatement in the Height or Steepness of the Rock.

In about fourteen Fathom Water I drop'd my Lines, and lay by for an Hour or two. Feeling several Jars, as I sat on my Chest in the Boat, I was sure I had caught somewhat; so pulling up my Lines, successively, I brought first a large Eel, near six Feet long, and almost as thick as my Thigh, whose Mouth, Throat, and Fins, were of a fine Scarlet, and the Belly as white as Snow: He was so strong, while in the Water, and weighty, I had much ado to get him into the Boat, and then had a harder Job to kill him; for though, having a Hatchet with me, to cut Wood in case I met with any landing Place, I chopped off his Head, the Moment I had him on board, yet he had several Times after that liked to have broken my Legs, and beat me overboard, before I had quite taken his Life from him; and, had I not whip'd off his Tail, and also divided his Body into two or three Pieces, I could not have master'd him. The next I pull'd up was a thick Fish like a Tench, but of another Colour and much bigger. I drew up several others, flat and long Fish, till I was tired with the Sport; and then I set out for the Ship again, which I reach'd the third Day.

During this whole time I had but one Shot, and that was as I came homewards, at a Creature I saw upon a high Crag of the Rock, which I fired at with Ball, fearing that my small Shot would not reach it. The Animal, being mortally wounded, bounded up, and came tumbling down the Rock, very near me. I pick'd it up, and found it to be a Creature not much unlike our Rabbits, but with shorter Ears, a longer Tail, and hoofed like a Kid, tho' it had the perfect Fluck[1] of a Rabbit. I put it into my Boat, to contemplate on when I arrived at the Ship; and plying my Oars, got safe, as I said, on the third Day.

I made me a Fire, to cook with, as soon as I had got my Cargo out of the Boat into my Ship, but was under Debate which of my Dainties to begin upon I had sometimes a Mind to have broil'd my Rabbit, as I called it, and boiled some of my Fish; but, being tired, I hung up my Flesh till the next Day, and boiled two or three Sorts of my Fish, to try which was best. I knew not the Nature of most of them, so I boiled a Piece of my Eel, to be sure, judging that, however I might like the others, I should certainly be able to make a good Meal of that. This Variety being ready, I took a little of my Oil out of the Hold for Sauce, and sat down to my Meal, as satisfied as an Emperor. But upon tasting my several Messes, though the Eel was rather richer than the smaller Fishes, yet the others were all so good, I gave them the Preference for that Time, and laid by the rest of the Eel, and of the other Fish, till the next Day, when I salted them for future spending.

I kept now a whole Week or more at home, to look further into the Contents of the Ship, bottle off a Cask of Madeira, which I found leaking, and to consume my new Stores of Fish, and Flesh; which being somewhat stale, when first salted, I thought would not keep so well as the old ones that were on board. I added also some fresh Bread to my Provision, and sweetened more Water, by the aforementioned Method; and when my necessary domestick Affairs were brought under, I then projected a new Voyage.

CHAPTER X

*Lays in great Store of Provision; resolves to traverse
the Rock; sails for three Weeks, still seeing it only;
is sucked under the Rock, and hurried down a
Cataract; continues there five Weeks; his Description
of the Cavern; his Thoughts, and Difficulties; his
Arrival at a great Lake; and his landing in the
beautiful Country of* Graundevolet

I HAD for a long Time wanted to see the other Side of the
Rock, and at last resolved to try if I could not coast it quite
round; for, as I reasoned with myself, I might possibly find
some landing Places, and perhaps a convenient Habitation
on Shore. But as I was very uncertain what Time that might
take up, I determined on having Provisions, Instruments of
divers Kinds, and necessary Utensils in plenty, to guard
against Accidents as well as I could. I therefore took another
Sea Chest out of the Hold of the Ship, and letting it into my
Boat, replenish'd it with a Stock of Wine, Brandy, Oil, Bread,
and the like, sufficient for a considerable Voyage. I also filled
a large Cask with Water, and took a good Quantity of Salt, to
cure what Fish I should take by the Way. I carried two Guns,
two Brace of Pistols, and other Arms, with Ammunition proportionable; also an Ax or two, a Saw to cut Wood, if I should
see any, and a few other Tools, which might be highly serviceable if I could land. To all these I added an old Sail, to make
a Covering for my Goods and Artillery against the Weather.
Thus furnished and equipped, having secur'd my Hatches
on board, and every Thing that might spoil by wet, I set out
(with a God's Speed) on my Expedition; committing myself
once more to Providence and the main Ocean,[1] and proceeding the same Way I went the first Time.

I did not sail extraordinary fast, but frequently fished in
proper Places, and caught a great deal; salting and drying
the best of what I took. For three Weeks Time and more,

Tab. I.

Boitard Fecit.

The Front of a Glumm Dreſst.

Tab. II.

Boitard Fecit.

The Back of a Glumm Dreſt.

I saw no Entrance into the Island, as I call it, nor any thing but the same unscalable Rock. This uniform Prospect gave me so little Hopes of landing, that I was almost of a mind to have return'd again. But, on mature Deliberation, resolving to go forward a Day or two more, I had not proceeded twenty-four Hours, when, just as it was becoming dark, I heard a great Noise, as of a Fall of Water; whereupon I purposed to lye by and wait for Day, to see what it was; but, the Stream insensibly drawing me on, I soon found myself in an Eddy; and the Boat drawing forward, beyond all my Power to resist it, I was quickly sucked under a low Arch, where, if I had not fallen flat in my Boat, having barely Light enough to see my Danger, I had undoubtedly been crushed to Pieces, or driven over-board. I could perceive the Boat to fall with incredible Violence, as I thought, down a Precipice, and suddenly whirled round and round with me; the Water roaring on all Sides, and dashing against the Rock with a most amazing Noise.

I expected every Moment my poor little Vessel would be staved against the Rock, and I overwhelm'd with Waters; and for that Reason never once attempted to rise up, or look upon my Peril, till after the Commotion had in some Measure ceased. At length, finding the Perturbation of the Water abate, and as if by Degrees I came into a smoother Stream, I took courage just to lift up my affrighted Head; but, guess if you can, the Horror which seiz'd me, on finding myself in the blackest of Darkness, unable to perceive the smallest Glimmer of Light.

However, as my Boat seemed to glide easily, I roused myself, and struck a Light; but if I had my Terrors before, what must I have now; I was quite stupified, at the tremendous View of an immense Arch over my Head, to which I could see no Bounds; the Stream itself, as I judged, was about thirty Yards broad, but in some Places wider in some narrower. It was well for me I happened to have a Tinder-box, or, though I had escaped hitherto, I must have at last perished; for in the narrower Parts of the Stream, where it ran swiftest, there

G

were frequently such Craggs stood out from the Rock, by Reason of the Turnings and Windings, and such Setts[1] of the Current against them, as, could I not have seen to manage my Boat, which I took great care to keep in the middle of the Stream, must have thrown me on them to my inevitable Destruction.

Happy it was for me also, I was so well victualled, and that I had taken with me two Bottles of Oyl, (as I supposed, for I did not imagine I had any more) or I had certainly been lost; not only through Hunger, for I was, to my Guess, five Weeks in the Vault or Cavern, but for want of Light, which the Oyl furnished, and without which all other Conveniences could have been of no Avail to me. I was forced to keep my Lamp always burning; so, not knowing how long my Residence was to be in that Place, or when I should get my Discharge from it, if ever, I was obliged to husband my Oyl with the utmost Frugality; and notwithstanding all my Caution, it grew low, and was just spent, in little above half the Time I stayed there.

I had now cut a Piece of my Shirt, for a Wick to my last Drop of Oyl, which I twisted and light. I burnt the Oyl in my Brass Tobacco-Box, which I had fitted pretty well to answer the Purpose. Sitting down, I had many black Thoughts, of what must follow the Loss of my Light, which I considered as near expiring, and that, I feared, for ever. I am here, thought I, like a poor condemned Criminal, who knows his Execution is fixed for such a Day, nay such an Hour, and dies over and over in Imagination, and by the Torture of his Mind, till that Hour comes: That Hour, which he so much dreads! and yet that very Hour which releases him from all further dread. Thus do I, my last Wick is kindled; my last Drop of Fuel is consuming; and I am every Moment apprehending the Shocks of the Rock, the Suffocation of the Water; and, in short, thinking over my dying Thoughts, till the Snuff of my Lamp throws up its last curling expiring Flame, and then my Quietus will be presently signed, and I released from my tormenting Anxiety. Happy Minute, come then, I only wait for thee.

My Spirits grew so low and feeble upon this, that I had recourse to my Brandy Bottle, to raise them. But as I was just going to take a Sip, I reflected that would only encrease Thirst, and therefore it were better to take a little of my white *Madeira*. So, putting my Dram-bottle again into the Chest, I held up one of *Madeira*, as I fancied, to the Lamp, and seeing it was white, for I had red too, I clapped it eagerly to my Mouth; when, the first Gulp gave me a greater Refreshment, and more cheered my Heart, than all the other Liquors I had put together could have done, insomuch as I had almost leaped over the Boat's Side for Joy: It is Oil, cry'd I aloud, it is Oil. I set it down carefully, with inexpressible Pleasure, and examining the rest of the Bottles I had taken for white *Madeira*, I found two more of those to be filled with Oil. Now, says I, here is the counterpart of my condemned Prisoner. For let but a Pardon come, though at the Gallows, how soon does he forget he has been an unhappy Villain. And I too have scarce a Notion now, how a Man in my Case could feel such Sorrow as I have, for want of a little Oil.

After my first Transport, I found myself grow serious; reflecting upon the Vigilance of Providence over us poor Creatures, and the various Instances wherein it interposes to save or relieve us, in Cases of the deepest Distress, where our own Foresight, Wisdom, and Power have utterly failed, and when, looking all around, we could discover no Means of Deliverance. And I saw a Train of Circumstances leading to the Incident I have just mentioned, which obliged me to acknowledge the Superintendence of Heaven over even my Affairs. And as the Goodness of God had cared for me thus far, and manifested itself to me now, in rescuing me, as it were, from being swallowed up in Darkness; I had ground to hope he intended a compleat Deliverance of me, out of that dismal Abyss, and would cause me yet to praise him in the full Brightness of Day.

A Series of these Meditations brought me, at the End of five Weeks, as nearly as I could compute it by my Lamp, to a prodigious Lake of Water, bordered with a grassy Down, about half a Mile wide, of the finest Verdure I had ever seen; this again was flanked with a Wood or Grove, rising like an Amphitheatre, of about the same Breadth; and behind, and above all, appeared the naked Rock, to an immense Height.

CHAPTER XI

His Joy on his Arrival at Land; a Description of the Place; no Inhabitants; wants fresh Water; resides in a Grotto; finds Water; views the Country; carries his Things to the Grotto

I T is impossible to express my Joy at the Sight of Day once more. I got on the Land as soon as possible, after my Dismission[1] from the Cavern, and kneeling on the Ground, returned hearty Thanks to God for my Deliverance, begging, at the same time, Grace to improve his Mercies, and that I might continue under his Protection, whatever should hereafter befal me, and at last die on my native Soil.

I unloaded my Vessel, as well as I could, and hauled her up on the Shore; and turning her upside down, made her a covering for my Arms and Baggage; I then sat down to contemplate the Place, and eat a most delightful Meal on the Grass, being quite a new Thing to me.

I walked over the green Swarth to the Wood, with my Gun in my Hand, a Brace of Pistols in my Girdle, and my Cutlass hanging before me. But when I was just entring the Wood, looking behind me, and all around the Plain, is it possible, says I, that so much Art, for I did not then believe it was natural, could have been bestowed upon this Place, and no Inhabitant in it? Here are neither Buildings, Huts, Castle, or any living Creature to be seen; it cannot be, says I, that this Place was made for nothing.

I then went a considerable Way into the Wood, and inclined to have gone much further, it being very beautiful, but, on second Thoughts, judged it best to content myself at present with only looking out a safe Retreat, for that Night; for however agreeable the Place then seemed, Darkness was at hand, when every thing about me would have more or less of Horror in it.

The Wood, at its first Entrance, was composed of the most charming flowering Shrubs that can be imagined; each growing upon its own Stem, at so convenient a Distance from the other, that you might fairly pass between them any Way, without the least Incommodity. Behind them grew numberless Trees, somewhat taller, of the greatest Variety of Shapes, Forms, and Verdures, the Eye ever beheld; each also, so far asunder, as was necessary for the spreading of their several Branches, and the Growth of their delicious Fruits, without a Bush, Briar, or Shrub amongst them. Behind these, and still on the higher Ground, grew an infinite Number of very large tall Trees, much loftier than the former; but intermixed with some Underwood, which grew thicker and closer, the nearer you approached the Rock. I made a shift to force my Way through these, as far as the Rock, which rose as perpendicular as a regular Building, having only here and there some Crags and Unevennesses. There was, I observed, a Space all the Way between the Underwood and the Rock, wide enough to drive a Cart in; and indeed I thought it had been left for that Purpose.

I walked along this Passage a good Way; having tied a Rag of the Lining of my Jacket at the Place of my Entrance, to know it again at my coming back, which I intended to be e're it grew dark; but I found so much Pleasure in the Walk, and surveying a small natural Grotto which was in the Rock, that the Day-light forsook me unawares; whereupon I resolved to put off my return unto the Boat till next Morning, and to take up my Lodging for that Night in the Cave.

I cut down a large Bundle of Underwood, with my Cutlass, sufficient to stop up the Mouth of the Grotto, and laying me down to rest, slept as sound, as if I had been on board my Ship; for I never had one Hour's Rest together, since I shot the Gulph, till this. Nature indeed could not have supported itself thus long under much Labour; but as I had nothing to do, but only keep the middle Stream, I began to be as used to guide myself in it, with my Eyes almost closed, and my Senses retired, as a Higler[1] is to drive the Cart to Market in his Sleep.

The next Morning I awaked sweetly refresh'd, and, by the Sign of my Rag, found the Way again thro' the Underwood to my Boat, I raised that up a little, took out some Bread and Cheese, and having eat pretty heartily, laid me down to drink at the Lake, which looked as clear as Chrystal, expecting a most delicious Draught: But, I had forgot it brought me from the Sea, and my first Gulp almost poisoned me. This was a sore Disappointment, for I knew my Water Cask was nigh emptied; and indeed, turning up my Boat again, I drew out all what remained, and drank it, for I was much athirst.

However, I did not despair; I was now so used to God's Providence, and had a Sense of its Operations so rivetted in my Mind, that though the vast Lake of salt Water was surrounded by an impenetrable Rock, or Barrier of Stone, I rested satisfied, that I should rather find even that yield me a fresh and living Stream, than I should perish for want of it.

With this easy Mind did I travel five or six Miles on the Side of the Lake, and sometimes stepped into the Wood, and walked a little there, till I had gone almost half the Diameter of the Lake, which lay in a circular, or rather an oval Figure. I had then Thoughts of walking back, to be near my Boat and Lodging, for fear I should be again benighted, if I went much further: But, considering I had come past no Water, and that possibly I might yet find some, if I went quite round the Lake, I rather chose to take up with a new Lodging, that Night, than to return: And I did not want for a Supper; having brought out with me more Bread and Cheese than had serv'd for Dinner, the Remainder of which was in the Lining of my Jacket. When it grew darkish, I had some Thoughts of eating; but I considered, as I was then neither very hungry nor dry, if I should eat, it would but occasion Drought, and

I had nothing to allay that with; so I contented myself for that Night, to lay me down Supperless.

In the Morning, I set forward again, upon my Water search; and hoped to compass the whole Lake that Day. I had gone about seven Miles more, when, at a little Distance before me, I perceived a small Hollow or Cut in the Grass, from the Wood to the Lake; thither I hasted with all speed, and blessed God for the Supply of a fine fresh Rill, which, distilling from several small Clefts in the Rock, had collected itself into one Stream, and cut its Way through the green Sod to the Lake.

I lay down with infinite Pleasure, and swallowed a most chearing Draught of the precious Liquid; and sitting on the Brink, made a good Meal of what I had with me, and then drank again. I had now got five sixths of the Lake's Circumference to go back again to my Boat; for I did not suspect any Passage over the Cavern's Mouth, where I came into the Lake; and I could not without much Trouble consider that if I would have this Water for a constant Supply, I must either come a long Way for it, or fix my Habitation near it. I was just going back again, revolving these uneasy Thoughts in my Breast, when this rose suddenly in my Mind, that if I could possibly get over the Mouth of the Cavern, I should not have above three Miles from my Grotto to the Water: Now as I could not get home that Night, otherwise than by crossing it, and as, if I lost my Labour, I should be but where I was; whereas if I should get over, it would very much shorten my Journey; I resolved to try whether the Thing was practicable: First, however, looking out for a resting Place, somewhere near my Water, if I should meet with a Disappointment.

I then walked into the Wood, where meeting with no Place of Retreat to my liking, I went to my Rill, and taking another Sup, determined not to leave that Side of the Lake, till Morning; but having some Time to spare, I walked about two Miles to view the Inlet of the Lake, and was agreeably surprized, just over the Mouth of the Cavern to see a large stone Arch, like a Bridge, as if it had been cut out of the Rock, quite across the Opening; this cheer'd me vastly, and pushing over it, I found a Path that brought me to my Boat before Night.

I then went up to my Grotto, for the third Night, in this most delightful Place; and the next Morning early I launched my Boat, and taking my Water Cask, and a small dipping Bucket with me, I rowed away for the Rill, and returned highly pleased with a Sufficiency of Water, whereof I carried a Bucket and a Copper Kettle full up with me to the Grotto. Indeed it was not the least Part of my Satisfaction, that I had this Kettle with me; for though I was in hopes, in my last Voyage, I should have come to some Shore, where I could have landed, and enjoy'd myself over some of my Fish, and for that Reason had taken it, notwithstanding Things did not turn out just as I had schemed, yet my Kettle proved the most useful Piece of Furniture I had.

Having now acquainted myself with the Circumference of the Lake, and settled a Communication with my Rill, I began to think of commencing Housekeeper. In order thereunto I set about removing my Goods up to the Grotto. By constant Application, in a few Days, I had gotten all thither but my two great Chests and my Water Cask; and how to drag or drive any of those to it, I was entirely at a Loss. My Water Cask was of the utmost Importance to me, and I had Thoughts sometimes of stopping it close, and roling it to the Place; but the Ascent through the Wood to the Grotto was so steep, that, besides the Fear of staving it, which would have been an irreparable Loss, I judged it impossible to accomplish it by my Strength; so, with a good deal of Discontent, I determined to remit both that and the Chests to future Consideration.

CHAPTER XII

*An Account of the Grotto; a Room added to it; a View
of that building; the Author makes a little Cart; also
a wet Dock for his Boat; goes in quest of Provision;
a Description of divers Fruits and Plants; he brings
home a Cart-load of different Sorts; makes Experiments
on them; loads his Cart with others; a great
Disappointment; makes good Bread; never sees the
Sun; the Nature of the Light*

HAVING come to a full Resolution of fixing my Residence
at the Grotto, and making that my capital Seat, it is proper to
give you some Description of it.

This Grotto then was a full Mile from the Lake, in the
Rock which encompassed the Wood. The Entrance was
scarcely two Feet wide, and about nine Feet high, rising, from
the Height of seven Feet upward, to a Point in the Middle.
The Cavity was about fifteen Feet long within, and about five
wide. Being obliged to lye lengthwise in it, full six Feet of it
were taken up at the further End for my Lodging only; as
nothing could stand on the Side of my Bed that would leave
me Room to come at it. The remaining nine Feet of the
Cave's Length were taken up, first, by my Fire Place, which
was on the deepest Side of the Door-way, ranging with my
Bed, (which I had set close to the Rock on one Side) and took
up near three Feet in length; and my Furniture and Provisions, of one Sort or other, so filled up the rest, that I had
much ado to creep between them into my Bed.

In the Chest which I had taken for a Seat in the Boat, as
aforesaid, upon breaking it open by the Water Side, I found
a Mattrass, some Shirts, Shoes, Stockings, and several other
useful Things, a small Case of Bottles with Cordials in them,
some Instruments of Surgery, Plaisters, and Salves: all which,
together with a large Quantity of Fish that I had salted,
I carried to the Grotto.

My Habitation being thus already over charged, and as I could not however bear the Thoughts of quitting it, or of having any of my Goods exposed to the Weather on the Outside, I was naturally bent on contriving how I should encrease my Accommodations. As I had no Prospect of enlarging the Grotto itself, I could conceive no other Way of effecting my Desire but by the Addition of an outer Room. This Thought pleased me very much, so that the next Day I set myself to plan out the Building, and trace the Foundation of it.

I told you before, there was about the Space of a Cart-way between the Wood and the Rock clear; but this Breadth, as I was building for Life, (so I imagined) not appearing to me spacious enough for my new Apartment, I considered how I should extend its Bounds into the Wood. Hereupon I set myself to observe what Trees stood at a proper Distance from my Grotto, that might serve as they stood, with a little Management of hewing and the like, to compose a noble Doorway, Posts, and Supporters; and I found, that upon cutting down three of the nearest Trees, I should answer my Purpose in this Respect; and that there were several others, about twenty Feet from the Grotto, and running parallel with the Rock, the Situation of which was so happily adapted to my Intention, that I could make them become, as I fancied, an Out-fence or Wall; so I took my Ax, to cut down my nearest Trees; but as I was going to strike, a somewhat different Scheme presented to my Imagination, that altered my Resolution.

In Conformity with this new Plan, I fixed the Height of my intended Ceiling, and sawed off my nearest Trees to that, sloping from the Sides to the Middle, to support cross Beams for the Roof to rest on, and left the Trunks standing, by Way of Pillars, both for the Use and Ornament of the Structure. In short, I worked hard every Day upon my Building for a Month; in which Time I had cut all my Timber into proper Lengths for my Out-works and Covering; but was at a great stand, how to fix my side Posts, having no Spade or Mattock, and the Ground almost as hard as flint; for to be sure it had

never been stirred since the Creation. I then thought I had
the worst Part of my Job to get over; however, I went on; and
having contrived, in most of my upright side Quarters, to
take the Tops of Trees, and leave on the lower Parts of the
Cleft, where they began to branch out and divide from the
main Stem, I set one of them upright against the Rock, then
laid one End of my long Ceiling-pieces upon the Cleft of it,
and laid the other End upon a Tree on the same Side, whose
Top I had also sawed off with a proper Cleft; I then went
and did the same on the other Side; after this, I laid on a
proper Number of cross Beams, and tyed all very firmly
together with the Bark of young Trees, stripped off in long
Thongs, which answered that purpose very well. Thus I proceeded, crossing, joining, and fastening all together, till the
whole Roof was so strong and firm, that there was no stirring
any Part of it. I then spread it over with small Lop-wood,[1]
on which I raised a Ridge of dried Grass and Weeds, very
thick, and thatched over the whole with the Leaves of a Tree
very much resembling those of a Palm, but much thicker, and
not quite so broad. The entire Surface, I might say, was as
smooth as a Dye; and so ordered, by a gentle Declivity every
Way, as to carry off the wet.

Having covered in my Building, I was next to finish and
close the Walls of it; the Skeleton of these was compos'd of
Sticks, crossing one another checker-wise and tyed together:
To fill up the Voids, I wove upon them the longest and most
pliable Twigs of the Underwood I could find; leaving only
a Door-way on one Side, between two Stems of a Tree, which,
dividing in the Trunk, at about two Feet from the Ground,
grew from thence, for the rest of its Height, as if the Branches
were a Couple of Trees a little distant from one another,
which made a Sort of Stile-way to my Room. When this was
all done, I temper'd up some Earth by the Lake Side, and
mixing it to a due Consistence with Mud, which I took from
the Lake, applyed it as a plaistering in this Manner: I divided
it into Pieces, which I rolled up of the Size of a Foot-Ball;
these Lumps I stuck close by one another on the Lattice,

pressing them very hard with my Hands, which forced part of them quite through the small Twigs, and then I smoothed both Sides with the back of my Saw, to about the Thickness of five or six Inches, so that by this Means I had a Wall round my new Apartment a Foot thick. This Plaister-work cost me some Time, and a great deal of Labour, as I had a full Mile to go to the Lake for every Load of Stuff, and could carry but little at once, it was so heavy; but there was neither Water for tempering, or proper Earth to make it with, any nearer. At last, however, I compleated my Building in every Respect but a Door, and for this I was forced to use the Lid of my Sea-Chest, which indeed I would have chosen not to apply that Way, but I had nothing else that would do; and there was however this Conveniency, that it had Hinges ready fixed thereon.

I now began to enjoy myself in my new Habitation, like the absolute and sole Lord of the Country; for I had neither seen Man nor Beast since my Arrival, save a few Animals in the Trees like our Squirrels, and some Water Rats about the Lake; but there were several strange kinds of Birds, I had never before seen, both on the Lake and in the Woods.

That which now troubled me most, was, how to get my Water nearer to me than the Lake, for I had no lesser Vessel than the Cask which held above twenty Gallons; and to bring that up was a Fatigue intolerable. My next Contrivance therefore was this: I told you I had taken my Chest-lid to make a Door for my Anti-chamber, as I now began to call it; so I resolved to apply the Body of the Chest also to a Purpose different from that it originally answered. In order to this I went to the Lake where the Body of the Chest lay, and sawed it thorough, within about three Inches of the Bottom; of the two Ends, having rounded them as well as I could, I made two Wheels, and with one of the Sides I made two more; I burnt a Hole through the Middle of each; then preparing two Axle-trees, I fastned them, after setting on the Wheels, to the Bottom of the Chest, with the Nails I had drawn out of it. Having finished this Machine, on which I bestowed no

small Labour, I was hugely pleased with it, and only wish'd
I had a Beast, if it were but an Ass, to draw it; however, that
Task I was satisfied to perform myself, since there was no
help for it; so I made a good strong Cord out of my Fishing
Lines, and fixed that to drag it by. When all was thus in readiness, filling my Water-Cask, I bound it thereon, and so
brought it to the Grotto, with such Ease, comparatively, as
quite charmed me. Having succeeded so well in the first Essay,
I no sooner unloaded, but down went I again with my Cart,
or Truckle[1] rather, to the Lake, and brought from thence on
it my other Chest, which I had left entire.

I had now nothing remaining near the Lake but my Boat,
and had half a Mind to try to bring that up too; but having so
frequent occasion for her, to get my Water in, which I used in
greater abundance now than I had done at first, a great Part
going to supply my domestick Uses, as well as for drinking,
I resolved against that, and sought out for a convenient Dock
to stow it in, as a Preservative against Wind and Weather,
which I soon after effected; for having pitched upon a swampy
Place, overgrown with a Sort of long Flags or Reeds, I soon
cut a Trench from the Lake, with a Sort of Spade or Board
that I had chopp'd and sharpen'd for that Use.

Thus having stowed my Boat, and looked over all my
Goods, and sorted them, and taken a Survey of my Provisions,
I found I must soon be in want of the last, if I did not forthwith procure a Supply; for though I had victualled so well
at setting out, and had been very sparing ever since, yet, had
it not been for a great Quantity of Fish I took and salted in
my Passage to the Gulph, I had been to seek[2] for Food much
sooner. Hereupon, I thought it highly prudent to look out
before I really wanted.

With this Resolution, I accoutred myself, as in my first
Walk, with my Instruments and Arms. But instead of travelling the Lake Side, I went along the Wood, and therein found
great Plenty of divers kinds of Fruits; though I could scarce
persuade myself to taste, or try the Effects of them, being so
much unlike our own, or any I had seen elsewhere. I observed

amongst the Shrubs abundance of a Fruit, or whatever else you may call it, which grew like a Ram's Horn; sharp at the Point next the Twig it was fastened to, and circling round and round, one Fold upon another, which gradually increased to the Size of my Wrist in the Middle, and then as gradually decreased, till it terminated in a Point again at the contrary Extream; all which Spiral, if it were fairly extended in Length, might be a Yard or an Ell[I] long. I surveyed this strange Vegetable very attentively; it had a Rind, or Crust, which I could not break with my Hand; but taking my Knife, and making an opening therewith in the Shell, there issued out a Sort of milky Liquor in great Quantity, to at least a Pint and half, which, having tasted, I found as sweet as Honey, and very pleasant. However, I could not perswade myself any more than just to taste it. I then found on the large Trees several Kinds of Fruits, like Pears or Quinces, but most of them exceeding hard and rough, and quite disagreeable: so I quitted my Hopes of them.

About three Miles from my Grotto, I met with a large Space of Ground full of a low Plant, growing only with a single woody Stalk half a Foot high, and from thence issued a round Head, about a Foot or ten Inches Diameter, but quite flat, about three Quarters of an Inch thick, and just like a Cream Cheese, standing upon its Edge. These grew so close together, that, upon the least Wind stirring, their Heads rattled against each other very musically; for tho' the Stalks were so very strong, that they would not easily either bend or break, yet the fanning of the Wind upon the broad Heads twisting the Stalks, so as to let the Heads strike each other, they made a most agreeable Sound.

I stood some time admiring this Shrub, and then cutting up one of them, I found it weighed about two Pounds; they had a tough green Rind or Covering, very smooth, and the Inside full of a stringy Pulp, quite white. In short, I made divers other Trials of Berries, Roots, Herbs, and what else I could find, but received little Satisfaction from any of them, for fear of bad Qualities. I returned back ruminating on what

Things I had seen, resolving to take my Cart the next Walk, and bring it home loaded with different kinds of them, in order to make my Trials thereof at Leisure. But my Cart being too flat, and wanting Sides, I considered it would carry very little, and that what it would otherwise bear, on that account, must tumble and roll off; so I made a Fire, and turned Smith; for with great to do, breaking off the Wards of a large Key I had, and making it red hot, I by Degrees fashioned it into a kind of Spindle, and therewith making Holes quite round the Bottom of my Cart, in them I stuck up Sticks, about two Feet high, that I had taper'd at the End to fit them.

Having thus qualified my Cart for a Load, I proceeded with it to the Wood, and cutting a small Quantity of each Species of Green, Berry, Fruit, and Flower, that I could find, and packing them severally in Parcels, I returned at Night heavy laden, and held a Council with myself, what Use they could most properly be applied to.

I had amongst my Goods, as I said, a Copper Kettle, which held about a Gallon; this I set over my Fire, and boiled something by Turns of every Sort in it, watching all the while, and with a Stick stiring and raising up one Thing and then another, to feel when they were boiled tender; but of upwards of twenty Greens which I thus dressed, only one proved eatable, all the rest becoming more stringy, tough, and insipid, for the cooking. The one I have excepted, was a round, thick, woolly leafed Plant, which boiled tender, and tasted as well as Spinage; I therefore preserved some Leaves of this, to know it again by, and, for Distinction, called it by the Name of that Herb.

I then began upon my Fruits, of the Pear and Quince kind, at least eight different Sorts, but I found I could make nothing of them, for they were most of them as rough and crabbed after stewing as before; so I laid them all aside. Lastly, I boiled my Ram's-horn and Cream-cheese, as I called them, together. Upon tasting the latter of these, it was become so watery and insipid, I laid it aside as useless. I then cut the other, and tasted the Juice, which proved so exceedingly pleasant, that I took a large Gulp or two of it, and tossed it into the Kettle again.

Having now gone through the several kinds of my Exoticks,[1] I had a Mind to re-examine them after cooling; but could make nothing of any of my Greens but the Spinage. I tried several Berries and Nuts too; but, save a few Sorts of Nuts, they were all very tasteless. Then I began to review the Fruits, and could find but two Sorts, that I had any the least hopes from. I then laid the best by, and threw the others away. After this Process, which took me up near a whole Day, and clearing my House of Good-for-nothings, I returned to re-examine my Cheese, that was grown cold, and was now so dry and hard I could not get my Teeth into it; upon which I was going to skim it away out of my Grotto, saying, go thou worthless, (for I always spoke aloud my Thoughts to myself): I say, I was just dispatching it, when I check'd my Hand, and, as I could make no Impression with my Teeth, had a mind to try what my Knife could do. Accordingly I began at the Edge of the Quarter, for I had boiled but a Quarter of it; but the Rind was grown so hard and brittle, that my Knife slipping, and raking along the cut Edge of it, scratched off some Powder as white as possible; I then scraped it backward and forward some time, till I found it would all scrape away in this Powder, except the Rind; upon which I laid it aside again for further Experiment.

During this Review my Kettle and Ram's-horn had been boiling, till hearing it blubber[2] very loud, and seeing there was but little Liquor in it, I whipped it off the Fire, for Fear of burning its Bottom, but took no further notice of it, till about two Hours after; when returning to the Grotto, I went to wash out my Kettle, but could scarce get my Ram's-horn from the Bottom; and when I did, it brought up with it a Sort of pitchy Substance, though not so black, and several gummy Threads hanging to it, drawn out to a great Length. I wondered at this, and thought the Shell of the Ram's-horn had melted, or some such Thing; 'till venturing to put a little of the Stuff on my Tongue, it proved, to my thinking, as good Treacle as I had ever tasted.

This new Discovery pleased me very much. I scraped all the sweet Thing up, and laid it near my Grotto, in a large Leaf of one of the Trees, (about two Feet long, and broad in Proportion) to prevent its running about. In getting this Curiosity out of my Kettle, I found in it a small Piece of my Cheese, which I suppose had been broke off in stirring; and biting it, for it was soft enough, I think it was the most luscious and delicate Morsel I ever put into my Lips. This unexpected good Fortune put me on trying the best of my Pears again; so setting on my Kettle, with very little Water, and putting some of my Treacle into it, and two of the best Pears quarter'd, I found, upon a little boiling, they also became an excellent Dainty.

Having succeeded so well, I was quite ripe for another Journey with my Cart: which I accordingly undertook, taking my Rout over the Stone Bridge, to see what the other Side of the Lake produced. In travelling thro' the Trees, I met, amongst other Things, with abundance of large Gourds, which, climbing the Trees, displayed their Fruit to the Height of twenty or thirty Feet above the Ground. I cut a great many of these, and some very large ones, of different Hues and Forms; which, of themselves, making a great Load, with some few new Sorts of Berries and Greens, was the gathering of that Day. But I must tell you, I was almost foiled in getting them home; for coming to my Stone-bridge, it rose so steep, and was so much ruggeder than the Grass or Wood-ground, that I was at a Set upon the first Entrance, and terribly afraid I should either break my Wheels, or pull of my Axle-trees. Hereupon, I was forced to unload, and carry my Cargoe over in my Arms to the other Side of the Bridge; whither having then, with less Fear but much Caution, drawn my Cart, I loaded again, and got safe home.

I was mightily pleased with the Acquisitions of this Journey, for now, thinks I, I shall have several convenient Family Utensils; so spent the next Day or two in scooping my Gourds and cleaning away the Pulp. When I had done this, finding the Rinds to be very weak and yielding, I made a good Fire,

H

and setting them round it at a moderate Distance, to dry, I went about something else without Doors. But alass my Hopes were ill founded; for coming home to turn my Gourds, and see how dry they were, I found them all warp'd, and turn'd into a Variety of uncouth Shapes. This put me to a stand; but however, I recovered some Pieces of them for use, as the bottom Parts of most of them, after paring away the Sides, would hold something, though they by no Means answered my first Purpose.

Well, thinks I, what if I have lost my Gourds, I have gained Experience; I will dry them next Time with the Guts in, and having stiffened their Rinds, in their proper Dimensions, then try to cleanse them. So next Morning, for I was very eager at it, I set out with my Cart for another Load; and having handed them over the Bridge, got safe with them to the Grotto. These by proper Management proved exceedingly valuable to me, answering, in one Way or other, the several Uses of Plates, Bottles, Pans, and divers other Vessels.

I now got a large Quantity of the vegetable Ram's-horn, and filled a great many of my Gourds with the Treacle it yielded; I also boiled and dried a large Parcel of my Cheeses, and hung them up for Use: For I had now for some Time made all my Bread of the latter, scraping and bruising the Flower,[1] and mixing it with my Treacle and Water; and this, indeed, made such a sweet and nourishing Bread, that I could even have lived wholly upon it: But I afterwards very much improved it, by putting the milky Juice of the Ram's-horn, unboiled, to my Flower, in a small Quantity, and then baking it on the Hearth, covered over with Embers: This detracted nothing from the Sweetness and Mellowness of my Bread, but made it much lighter than the Treacle alone would have done.

Finding there was no Fear of starving, but so far from it, that from Day to Day I found out something new to add to my Repasts, either in Substantials, or by Way of Desert, I set me down very well contented with my Condition. I had nothing to do, but to lay up Store against Sickness, and the dark Weather; which last I expected would soon be upon me, as the Days were now exceeding short. Indeed, tho' I had now been here six Months, I had never seen the Sun since I first entered the Gulph; and tho' there was very little Rain, and but few Clouds, yet the brightest Day-light never exceeded that of half an Hour after Sunset, in the Summer-time in *England*, and little more than just redned the Sky. For the first part of my Time here, there was but little if any Difference between Day and Night; but afterwards, what I might call the Night, or lesser Degree of Light, took up more Hours than the greater, and went on gradually encreasing as to Time, so that I perceived total Darkness approached, such as I had on board my Ship the Year before.

CHAPTER XIII

The Author lays in a Store against the dark Weather;
hears Voices; his Thoughts thereon; persuades himself
it was a Dream; hears them again; determines to see
if any one lodged in the Rock; is satisfied there is
nobody; Observations on what he saw; finds a strong
Weed like Whipcord; makes a drag Net, lengthens it;
catches a Monster; its Description; makes Oil of it

I HAD now well stored my Grotto with all Sorts of Winter Provisions; and feeling the Weather grow very cold, I expected, and waited patiently for, the total Darkness. I went little abroad, and employed myself within Doors, endeavouring to fence against the approaching Extremity of the Cold. For this Purpose, I prepared a Quantity of Rushes; which being very dry, I spread them smoothly on the Floor of my Bed-chamber a good Thickness, and over them I laid my Matrass. Then, I made a double Sheet of the Boat's Awning, or Sail, that I had brought to cover my Goods; and having scewered together several of the Jackets and Cloaths I found in the Chest, of them I made a Coverlid; so that I lay very commodiously, and made very long Nights of it, now the dark Season was set in.

As I lay awake one Night, or Day, I know not whether, I very plainly heard the Sound of several human Voices, and sometimes very loud; but tho' I could easily distinguish the Articulations, I could not understand the least Word that was said; nor did the Voices seem at all to me like such as I had any where heard before, but much softer and more musical. This startled me, and I rose immediately, slipping on my Cloaths, and taking my Gun in my Hand, (which I always kept charged, being my constant travelling Companion) and my Cutlass. Thus equipp'd, I walked into my Anti-chamber, where I heard the Voices much plainer, till, after some little Time, they by Degrees died quite away. After watching here and hearkening a good while, hearing nothing, I walked back into the Grotto, and laid me down again on my Bed. I was inclin'd to open the Door of my Anti-chamber, but I own I was afraid; beside, I considered, that if I did, I could discover nothing at any Distance, by reason of the thick and gloomy Wood that inclosed me.

I had a thousand different Surmises about the Meaning of this odd Incident; and could not conceive how any humane Creature should be in my Kingdom (as I called it) but myself, and I never yet see them, or any Trace of their Habitation. But then again I reflected, that though I had surrounded the whole Lake, yet I had not traced the out Bounds of the Wood, next the Rock, where there might be innumerable Grotto's like mine; nay perhaps some as spacious as that I had sailed through to the Lake; and that though I had not perceived it yet, this beautiful Spot might be very well peopled. But, says I again, if there be any such Beings as I am fancying here, surely they don't skulk in their Dens, like savage Beasts, by Day-light, and only patrole for Prey by Night; if so, I shall probably become a delicious Morsel for them e're long, if they meet with me. This kept me still more within Doors than before, and I hardly ever stirred out but for Water, or Firing. At length, hearing no more Voices, or seeing any one, I began to be more composed in my Mind, and at last grew persuaded, it was all a meer Delusion, and only a Fancy of mine, without any real Foundation; and sometimes, though I was sure I was fully awake when I heard them, I persuaded myself I had rose in my Sleep, upon a Dream of Voices; and recollected with myself the various Stories I had heard, when a Boy, of walking in one's Sleep, and the surprising Effects of it; so the whole Notion was now blown over.

I had not enjoy'd my Tranquillity above a Week, before my Fears were roused afresh, hearing the same Sound of Voices, twice the same Night; but not many Minutes at a Time. What gave me most Pain, was, that they were at such a Distance, as I judged by the Languor[1] of the Sound, that if I had opened my Door, I could not have seen the Utterers through the Trees, and I was resolved not to venture out; but then I determined, if they should come again, any thing near my Grotto, to open the Door, see who they were, and stand upon my Defence, whatever came of it: For, says I, my Entrance is so narrow and high, that more than one can't come at a time; and I can with Ease dispatch twenty of them before they can secure me, if they should be Savages; but if they prove sensible humane Creatures, it will be a great Benefit to me, to join myself to their Society. Thus had I formed my Scheme, but I heard no more of them, for a great while; so that at length beginning to grow ashamed of my Fears, I became tranquil again.

The Day now returning, and with it my Labours, I applied to my usual Callings; but my Mind run strangely upon viewing the Rock quite round, that is, the whole Circuit of my Dominions: for, thinks I, there may possibly be an Outlet through the Rock into some other Country, from whence the Persons I heard may come. As soon therefore as the Days grew towards the longest, I prepared for my Progress. Having lived so well at home since my Settlement, I did not care to trust only to what I could pick up in the Woods, for my Subsistance during this Journey, which would not only take up

Time in procuring, but perhaps not agree with me; so I resolved to carry a Supply with me, proportionate to the Length of my Perambulation. Hereupon considering, that though my Walk round the Lake was finished in two Days, yet as I now intended to go round by the Rock, the Way would be much longer, and perhaps more troublesome than that was; remembring also my Journey with *Glanlipze* in *Africa*, and how much I complained of the Fruits we carried for our Subsistance; these Circumstances, I say, laying together, I resolved to load the Cart with a Variety of Food, Bread and Fruits especially, and draw that with me.

Thus provided I sallied forth with great Chearfulness, and proceded in the main easily; though in some Places I was forced to make Way with my Hatchet, the Ground was so overrun with Underwood. I very narrowly view'd the Rock as I went, Bottom and Sides, all the Way, but could see nothing like a Passage through it; or indeed any more than one Opening, or Inlet, which I enter'd for about thirty Yards; but it was not above three Feet wide, and terminated in the solid Rock.

After some Days travel, (making all the Observations I could on the several Plants, Shrubs, and Trees, which I met with, particularly, where any of these occurr'd to me entirely new) finding myself a little faintish, I had a mind for a Sup of Ram's-horn Juice; so I cut me one; but, upon opening it, found therein only a pithy Pulp, and no Ways fit to taste. I supposed by this, I was too early for the Milk; it being three Months later, the last Year, when I cut them. Hereon, seeing one upon another Shrub, which, by its rusty Colour, I judged might have hung all the Winter, I opened that, and found it full of Milk; but, putting some of it into my Mouth, it was as sour as any Vinegar I ever tasted in my Life. So, thinks I, and said so too, for, as I told you before, I always spoke out; here's Sauce for something when I want it: and this gave me a Hint to store myself with these Gourds, to hang by for Vinegar the next Winter.

By this Time I had come almost to my Rill; when I enter'd

upon a large Plat[1] of Ground, miserably over-run with Weeds, matted together very thick. These choaked up my Wheels in such a Manner, that I could neither free them with my Hands, or get either backwards or forwards, they binding my Cart down like so many Cords; so that I was oblig'd to cut my Way back again, with my Hatchet, and take a sweep round in the Wood, on the Outside of these Weeds.

In all my Life I never saw any Thing of its Size, for it was not thicker than a Whipcord, so strong as this Weed; and what raised my Wonder, was the Length of it, for I drew out Pieces of it near fifty Foot long; and even they were broken at the End, so that it might be as long again for ought I know; for it was so matted, and twisted together, that it was a great Trial of Patience to untangle it; but that which was driest, and to me looked the rottenest and weakest, I found to be much the strongest. Upon Examination of its Parts, I discover'd it to be composed of an infinite Number of small Threads, spirally overlaying and infolding one another.

As I saw but few Things that I could not find a use for, so this I perceived would serve all the common Purposes of Packthread; a Thing I was often in want of. This inclined me to take a Load of it home with me. Indeed the Difficulty of getting a Quantity in the Condition I desired it puzzled me a little; for, says I, if I cut up a good deal of it with my Hatchet, as I first design'd, I shall only have small Lengths, good for little, and to get it in Pieces of any considerable Length, so as to be of Service, will require much Time and Labour; but reflecting how much I needed it, and of what Benefit it would be, I resolved to make a Trial of what I could do. So, without more Hesitation, I went to Work, and cutting a Fibre close to its Root, I extricated that Thread from all its Windings, just as one does an entangled Whipcord. When I had thus disengaged a sufficient Length, I cut that off; and repeating the like Operation, in about three Hour's Time, but with no little Toil, I made up my Load of different Lengths, just to my liking. Having finished this Task, I filled the Gourd, brought for that Purpose, with Water; and having first viewed the whole remaining Part of the Rock, I returned over the Stone Bridge home again.

This Journey, though it took me up several Days, and was attended with some Fatigue, had yet given me great Satisfaction; for now I was persuaded I could not have one Rival, or Enemy, to fear in my whole Dominions. And from the Impossibility, as I suppos'd, of there being any, or of the Ingress of any, unless by the same Passage I enter'd at, and by which I was well assured they could never return, I grew contented; and blamed myself for the Folly of my imaginary Voices, as I called them then, and took it for a Distemper of the Fancy only.

The next Day I looked over my Load of Matweed, having given it that Name, and separated the different Lengths from each other. I then found I had several Peices between forty and fifty Feet long, of which I resolved to get a good Number more, to make me a Drag-net, that I might try for some Fish in the Lake. A Day or two after, therefore, I brought home another Load of it. Then I picked out a smooth level Spot upon the green Swarth, and having prepared a great Number of short wooden Pegs, I strained a Line of the Matweed, about ten Feet long, tying it at each End to a Peg, and struck a Row of Pegs along by that Line, about two Inches asunder; I next strained another Line, of the same Length, parallel to that, at the Distance of forty Feet from it, and struck Pegs thereby, corresponding to the former Row; and from each Peg on one Side, to the opposite Peg on the other, I tied a like Length of my Matline, quite through the whole Number of Pegs; when the Work looked like the Inside of an Harpsichord; I afterwards drove Pegs, in like Manner, along the whole Length of the two outermost longer Lines, and tied shorter Lines to them; so that the whole Affair then represented the Squares of a Racket; the Corners of each of which Squares, I tied very tight with smaller Pieces of the Line, till I had formed a compleat Net of forty Feet long and ten wide.

When I had finished my Net, as I thought, I wrapped several Stones in Rags, and fastned them to the Bottom to sink it, and some of the smallest, unscooped, dry Gourds to the Top, to keep that Part boyant. I now longed to begin my new Trade, and carried the Net to my Boat, with that Intention; but, after two or three Hauls, I found it would not answer for want of Length; (though, by Chance, I caught a blackish Fish without Scales, a little bigger than a Whiting, but much longer, which stuck by the Gills in it;) so I left the Net in the Boat, resolving to make an Addition to it with all Speed, and returning to my Grotto, I supped on the Fish I had taken, and considered how to pursue my Enterprize with better Effect.

I provided me with another large Parcel of Line; and having brought two more Lengths to Perfection, I joined all together, and fixing one End on Shore, by a Pole I had cut for that Purpose, I launched my Boat, with the other End in it, taking a Sweep the Length of my Net, round to my Stick again; and getting on Shore, hauled up my Net, by both Ends together. I found now I had mended my Instrument, and taken a proper Way of applying it; for by this Means, in five Hauls, I caught about sixteen Fish, of three or four different Sorts, and one Shell-fish, almost like a Lobster, but without great Claws, and with a very small short Tail: which made me think, as the Body was thrice as long as a Lobster's in Proportion, that it did not swim backwards, like that Creature, but only crawled forwards, (it having Lobster-like Legs, but much shorter and stronger) and that the Legs all standing so forward, its Tail was, by its Motion, to keep the hinder Part of the Body from dragging upon the Ground, as I observed it did when the Creature walked on Land; it then frequently flacking[I] its short Tail.

These Fish made me rich in Provisions. Some of them I eat fresh, and the remainder I salted down. But of all the kinds, my Lobster was the most delicious Food, and made me almost three Meals.

Thus finding there were Fish to be had, tho' my present Tackle seemed suitable enough to my Family, yet could I not rest, till I had improved my Fishery, by inlarging my Net:

For, as it was, even with my late Addition, I must either sweep little or no Compass of Ground, or it would have no Bag behind me. Upon this I set to work, and shortly doubled the Dimensions of it. I had then a Mind to try it at the Mouth of my Rill; so taking it with me the next Time I crossed the Lake for Water, and fastening it to my Pole, close by the right Side of the Rill, I swept a long Compass round to the left, and closing the Ends, attempted to draw up in the hollow Cut of the Rill. But by the Time I had gathered up two thirds of the Net, I felt a Resistance that quite amazed me. In short, I was not able to stand against the Force I felt. Whereupon, sitting down in the Rill, and clapping my Feet to the two Sides of it, I exerted all my Strength, till finally I became Conqueror, and brought up so shocking a Monster, that I was just rising to run for my Life on the Sight of it. But recollecting that the Creature was hampered, and could not make so much Resistance on the Land as in the Water, I ventured to drag the Net up as far from the Rill as my Strength and Breath would permit me; and then running to the Boat for my Gun, I returned to the Net, to examine my Prize. Indeed I had not instantly Resolution enough to survey it; and when at length I assumed Courage enough to do so, I could not perfectly distinguish the Parts, they were so discomposed; but taking hold of one End of the Net I endeavoured to disentangle the Thing, and then drawing the Net away, a most surprising Sight presented itself: The Creature reared upright, about three Feet high, covered all over with long black shaggy Hair, like a Bear, which hung down from his Head and Neck quite along his Back and Sides. He had two Fins, very broad and large, which, as he stood erect, looked like Arms, and those he waved and whirled about with incredible Velocity; and though I wondered at first at it, I found afterwards, it was the Motion of these Fins that kept him upright; for I perceived when they ceased their Motion, he fell flat on his Belly. He had two very large Feet, which he stood upon, but could not run, and but barely walk on them; which made me in the less haste to dispatch him; and after he had stood upon his Feet

about four Minutes, clapping his Fins to his Sides, he fell
upon his Belly.

When I found he could not attack me, I was moving closer
to him; but, upon sight of my stirring, up he rose again, and
whirled his Fins about as before, so long as he stood. And
now I view'd him round, and found he had no Tail at all;
and that his hinder Fins, or Feet, very much resembled a large
Frog's, but were at least ten Inches broad, and eighteen long,
from Heel to Toe; and his Legs were so short, that when he
stood upright, his Breech bore upon the Ground. His Belly,
which he kept towards me, was of an Ash-colour, and very
broad, as was also his Breast. His Eyes were small and blue,
with a large black Sight[1] in the Middle, and rather of an oval
than round make. He had a long Snout like a Boar, and vast
Teeth. Thus having survey'd him near half an Hour living,
I made him rise up once more, and shot him in the Breast.
He fell, and giving a loud Howl, or Groan, expired.

I had then Time to see what else I had caught; and turning
over the Net, found a few of the same Fish I had taken before,
and some others of a flattish make, and one little Lump of
Flesh unform'd: which last, by all I could make of it, seemed
to be either a Spawn or young one of that I had shot.

The great Creature was so heavy, I was afraid I must have
cut him in Pieces to get him to the Boat: but with much ado,
having stowed the rest, I tumbled him on board. I then filled
my Water-cask, and rowed homewards. Being got to Land,
I was obliged to bring down my Cart, to carry my great Beast
Fish, as I termed him, up to the Grotto. When I had got him
thither, I had a Notion of first tasting, and then, if I liked his
Flesh, of salting him down, and drying him; so, having flead
him, and taken out the Guts and Intrails, I broiled a Piece
of him; but it made such a Blaze, that most of the Fat run into
the Fire, and the Flesh prov'd so dry and rank, that I could
no Ways endure it.

I then began to be sorry I had taken so much Pains for no
Profit, and had endangered my Net into the Bargain, (for that
had got a Crack or two in the Scuffle) and was thinking to

throw away my large, but worthless, Acquisition. However, as I was now prone to weighing all Things, before I threw it away, I resolved to consider a little; whereupon I changed my Mind. Says I, here is a good warm Skin, which, when dry, will make me a rare Cushion. Again, I have for a long while had no Light beside that of the Day; but now, as this Beast's Fat makes such a Blaze in the Fire, and issues in so great a Quantity from such a small Piece as I broiled, why may not I boil a good Tallow or Oil out of it? and if I can, I have not made so bad a Hand of my Time as I thought for.

In short, I went immediately to work upon this Subject, (for I never let a Project cool after I had once started it) and boiled as much of the Flesh as my Kettle would hold; and letting it stand to cool, I found it turned out a very good Oil for burning; though, I confess, I thought it would rather have made Tallow. This Success quickened my Industry; and I repeated the Operation, till I got about ten Quarts of this Stuff, which very well rewarded my Labour. After I had extracted as much Oil as I could from the Beast Fish, the Creature having strongly impress'd my Imagination, I conceived a new Fancy in relation to it; and that was, having heard him make a deep howling Groan at his Death, I endeavoured to perswade myself, and at last verily believed, that the Voices I had so often heard, in the dark Weather, proceeded from Numbers of these Creatures, diverting themselves in the Lake, or sporting together on the Shore: And this Thought, in its Turn, contributed to ease my Apprehensions in that Respect.

CHAPTER XIV

*The Author passes the Summer pleasantly; hears the
Voices in the Winter; ventures out; sees a strange
Sight on the Lake; his Uneasiness at it; his Dream;
Soliloquy; hears the Voices again, and perceives a
great Shock on his Building; takes up a beautiful
Woman; he thinks her dead, but recovers her; a
Description of her; she stays with him*

I PASSED the Summer, (tho' I had never yet seen the Sun's
Body) very much to my Satisfaction: partly, in the Work
I have been describing, (for I had taken two more of the Beast
Fish, and had a great quantity of Oil from 'em;) partly, in
building me a Chimney in my Antichamber, of Mud and
Earth burnt on my own Hearth into a sort of Brick; in making
a Window at one End of the abovesaid Chamber, to let in
what little Light would come through the Trees, when I did
not choose to open my Door; in moulding an earthen Lamp
for my Oil; and, finally, in providing and laying in Stores,
fresh and salt, (for I had now cured and dryed many more
Fish) against Winter. These, I say, were my Summer Employments, at Home, intermix'd with many agreeable Excursions.
But now, the Winter coming on, and the Days growing very
short, or indeed there being no Day, properly speaking, but
a kind of Twilight, I kept mostly in my Habitation: tho' not
so much as I had done the Winter before, when I had no light
within Doors, and slept, or at least lay still, great part of my
Time; for now my Lamp was never out. I also turned two of
my Beast-fish Skins into a Rugg to cover my Bed, and the
third into a Cushion, which I always sat upon, and a very soft
and warm Cushion it made. All this together rendered my life
very easy, yea even comfortable.

An indifferent Person would now be apt to ask, what would
this Man desire more than he had? To this I answer, that
I was contented, while my Condition was such as I have

been describing; but a little while after the Darkness, or Twilight, came on, I frequently heard the Voices again; sometimes a few only at a time, as it seem'd, and then again in great Numbers. This threw me into new Fears, and I became as uneasy as ever, even to the degree of growing quite Melancholly; tho', otherwise, I never received the least Injury from any thing. I foolishly attempted several Times, by looking out at my Window, to discover what these odd Sounds proceeded from; tho' I knew it was too dark to see any thing there.

I was now fully convinc'd, by a more deliberate Attention to 'em, that they could not be uttered by the Beast-fish, as I had afore conjectured, but only by Beings capable of articulate Speech: But then, what, or where they were, it galled me to be ignorant of.

At length one Night or Day, I can't say which, hearing the Voices very distinctly, and praying very earnestly, to be either delivered from the uncertainty they had put me under, or to have them removed from me, I took Courage, and arming myself with Gun, Pistols, and Cutlass, I went out of my Grotto, and crept down the Wood. I then heard them plainer than before, and was able to judge from what Point of the Compass they proceeded. Hereupon I went forward towards the Sound, till I came to the Verge of the Wood, where I could see the Lake very well by the dazzle of the Water. Thereon, as I thought, I beheld a Fleet of Boats, covering a large Compass, and not far from the Bridge. I was shock'd hereat beyond Expression. I could not conceive where they came from, or whither they would go; but supposed there must be some other Passage to the Lake, than I had found in my Voyage thro' the Cavern, and that for certain they came that Way, and from some Place, of which, as yet, I had no manner of Knowledge.

Whilst I was entertaining myself with this Speculation, I heard the People in the Boats laughing and talking very merrily; tho' I was too distant to distinguish the Words. I discern'd soon after all the Boats (as I still supposed 'em)

draw up, and push for the Bridge; presently after, tho' I was
sure no Boat entered the Arch, I saw a Multitude of People,
on the opposite Shore, all marching towards the Bridge; and
what was the strangest of all, there was not the least Sign of
a Boat now left upon the whole Lake. I then was in a greater
Consternation than before; but was still much more so, when
I saw the whole Posse of People, that as I have just said were
marching towards the Bridge, coming over it to my side of the
Lake. At this my Heart failed, and I was just going to run to
my Grotto for Shelter; but taking one look more, I plainly
discovered, that the People, leaping one after another from
the Top of the Bridge, as if into the Water, and then rising
again, flew in a long Train over the Lake, the length ways of
it, quite out of my Sight, laughing, hollowing and sporting
together: so that looking back again to the Bridge, and on the
Lake, I could neither see Person, Boat, or any thing else, nor
hear the least Noise or Stir afterwards for that Time.

I returned to my Grotto brim full of this amazing Adventure; bemoaning my Misfortune, in being at a Place, where
I was like to remain ignorant of what was doing about me.
For says I, if I am in a Land of Spirits, as now I have little
room to doubt, there is no guarding against them. I am never
safe, even in my Grotto; for that can be no Security against
such Beings as can sail on the Water in no Boats, and fly in
the Air on no Wings, as the Case now appears to me, who can
be here and there, and wherever they please. What a miserable
State, I say, am I fallen to? I should have been glad to have had
human Converse, and to have found Inhabitants in this Place;
but there being none, as I supposed hitherto, I contented
myself with thinking, I was at least safe from all those Evils,
Mankind, in Society, are obnoxious[1] to: But now, what may
be the Consequence of the next Hour I know not; nay, I am
not able to say, but whilst I speak, and show my Discontent,
they may at a distance conceive my Thoughts, and be hatching Revenge against me for my dislike of them.

The Pressure of my Spirits inclining me to repose, I laid
me down, but could get no rest; nor could all my most serious

Thoughts, even of the Almighty Providence, give me relief under my present Anxiety: And all this was only from my State of Uncertainty, concerning the reality of what I had heard and seen; and from the Earnestness with which I coveted a satisfactory Knowledge of those Beings who had just taken their Flight from me.

I really believe, the fiercest wild Beast, or the most savage of Mankind that had met me, and put me upon my Defence, would not have given me half the trouble that then lay upon me; and the more, for that I had no seeming Possibility of ever being rid of my Apprehensions: So, finding I could not sleep, I got up again; but as I could not fly from myself, all the Art I could use with myself, was but in vain to obtain me any Quiet.

In the Height of my Distress I had recourse to Prayer, with no small Benefit; begging, that if it pleased not the Almighty Power to remove the Object of my Fears, at least to resolve my Doubts about them, and to render them rather helpful than hurtful to me. I hereupon, as I always did on such Occasions, found myself much more placid and easy, and began to hope the best, 'till I had almost perswaded myself that I was out of Danger; and then laying myself down, I rested very sweetly, 'till I was wakened by the Impulse of the following Dream.

Methought I was in *Cornwall*, at my Wife's Aunt's; and enquiring after her and my Children, the old Gentlewoman inform'd me, both my Wife and Children had been dead some time, and that my Wife, before her Departure, desired her (that is her Aunt) immediately upon my Arrival to tell me, she was only gone to the Lake, where I should be sure to see her, and be happy with her ever after. I then, as I fancied, ran to the Lake, to find her. In my Passage she stopped me, crying, whither so fast *Peter*? I am your Wife, your *Patty*. Methought I did not know her, she was so altered; but observing her Voice, and looking more wistfully at her, she appeared to me, as the most beautiful Creature I ever beheld. I then went to seize her in my Arms; but the hurry of my Spirits awakened me.

When I got up, I kept at home, not caring even to look out at my Door. My Dream ran strangely in my Head, and I had now nothing but *Patty* in my Mind. Oh! cries I, how happy could I be with her, though I had only her in this Solitude. Oh! that this was but a Reality, and not a Dream. And indeed, though it was but a Dream, I could scarce refrain from running to the Lake to meet my *Patty*. But then I checked my Folly, and reasoned myself into some Degree of Temper again. However, I could not forbear crying out, What! nobody to converse with, nobody to assist, comfort, or counsel me! this is a melancholly Situation indeed. Thus I run on lamenting, till I was almost weary; when, on a sudden, I again heard the Voices. Hark! says I, here they come again. Well, I am now resolved to face them; come Life, come Death. It is not to be alone I thus dread; but to have Company about me, and not know who or what; is Death to me, worse than I can suffer from them, be they who, or what they will.

During my Soliloquy the Voices increased, and then by Degrees diminished as usual; but I had scarce got my Gun in my Hand, to pursue my Resolution of shewing myself to those who uttered them, when I felt such a Thump upon the Roof of my Antichamber, as shook the whole Fabrick, and set me all over into a Tremor; I then heard a sort of Shriek, and a Rustle near the Door of my Apartment: all which together seemed very terrible. But I, having before determined to see what, and who it was, resolutely opened my Door and leaped out. I saw nobody; all was quite silent, and nothing that I could perceive but my own Fears a moving. I went then softly to the Corner of the Building, and there looking down by the Glimmer of my Lamp, which stood in the Window, I saw something in human Shape lying at my Feet. I gave the Word, who's there? Still no one answered. My Heart was ready to force a Way through my Side. I was for a while fix'd to the Earth like a Statue. At length, recovering, I stepped in, fetched my Lamp, and returning, saw the very beautiful Face my *Patty* appeared under in my Dream; and not considering that it was only a Dream, I verily thought

I

I had my *Patty* before me, but she seemed to be stone dead. Upon viewing her other Parts, for I had never yet removed my Eyes from her Face, I found she had a sort of brown Chaplet, like Lace, round her Head, under and about which her Hair was tucked up and twined; and she seemed to me to be cloathed in a thin hair-coloured silk Garment; which, upon trying to raise her, I found to be quite warm, and therefore hoped there was Life in the Body it contained. I then took her into my Arms, and treading a Step backwards with her, I put out my Lamp; however, having her in my Arms, I conveyed her through the Door-way in the dark, into my Grotto; here I laid her upon my Bed, and then run out for my Lamp.

This, thinks I, is an amazing Adventure. How could *Patty* come here, and drest in Silk and Whalebone too? sure that is not the reigning Fashion in *England* now? But my Dream said she was dead. Why truly, says I, so she seems to be. But be it so, she is warm. Whether this is the Place for Persons to inhabit after Death or not, I can't tell, (for I see there are People here, though I don't know them;) but be it as it will, she feels as Flesh and Blood; and if I can but bring her to stir and act again as my Wife, what matters it to me, what she is; it will be a great Blessing and Comfort to me; for she never would have come to this very Spot, but for my good.

Top-full of these Thoughts, I re-entered my Grotto, shut my Door, and lighted my Lamp; when going to my *Patty*, (as I delighted to fancy her) I thought I saw her Eyes stir a little. I then set the Lamp farther off, for Fear of offending them if she should look up; and warming the last Glass I had reserved of my Madeira, I carried it to her, but she never stirred. I now supposed the Fall had absolutely killed her, and was prodigiously griev'd, when laying my Hand on her Breast, I perceived the Fountain of Life had some Motion. This gave me infinite Pleasure; so, not despairing, I dipped my Finger in the Wine, and moistened her Lips with it two or three Times; and I imagined they opened a little. Upon this I bethought me, and taking a Tea-spoon, I gently poured a few Drops of the Wine by that Means into her Mouth.

Finding she swallowed it, I poured in another Spoonful, and another, till I brought her to herself, so well as to be able to sit up. All this I did by a glimmering Light, which the Lamp afforded from a distant Part of the Room, where I had placed it, as I have said, out of her Sight.

I then spoke to her, and asked divers Questions, as if she had really been *Patty*, and understood me; in return of which, she uttered a Language I had no Idea of, though in the most musical Tone, and with the sweetest Accent I ever heard. It grieved me I could not understand her. However, thinking she might like to be upon her Feet, I went to lift her off the Bed; when she felt to my Touch in the oddest Manner imaginable: for while in one respect it was as though she had been cased in Whalebone, it was at the same Time as soft and warm, as if she had been naked.

I then took her in my Arms and carried her into my Anti-chamber again; where I would fain have entered into Conversation, but found she and I could make nothing of it together, unless we could understand one another's Speech. It is very strange, my Dream should have prepossessed me so of *Patty*, and of the Alteration of her Countenance, that I could by no Means persuade myself, the Person I had with me was not she; though, upon a deliberate Comparison, *Patty*, as pleasing as she always was to my Taste, would no more come up to this fair Creature, than a course Alewife would to *Venus* herself.

You may imagine, we stared heartily at each other, and I doubted not but she wondred as much as I, by what Means we came so near each other. I offered her every thing in my Grotto, which I thought might please her; some of which she gratefully received, as appeared by her Looks and Behaviour. But she avoided my Lamp, and always placed her Back toward it. I observing that, and ascribing it to her Modesty, in my Company, let her have her Will, and took care to set it in such a Position myself, as seem'd agreeable to her, tho' it deprived me of a Prospect I very much admired.

After we had sat a good while, now and then, I may say,

chattering to one another, she got up, and took a turn or two about the Room. When I saw her in that Attitude, her Grace and Motion perfectly charmed me, and her Shape was incomparable; but the Strangeness of her Dress put me to my Trumps, to conceive either what it was, or how it was put on.

Well, we supped together, and I set the best of every thing I had before her, nor could either of us forbear speaking in our own Tongue, tho' we were sensible neither of us understood the other. After Supper I gave her some of my Cordials, for which she shewed great Tokens of Thankfulness, and often, in her way, by Signs and Gestures, which were very far from being insignificant, expressed her Gratitude for my Kindness. When Supper had been some time over, I shewed her my Bed, and made Signs for her to go to it; but she seemed very shy of that, 'till I shewed her where I meant to lie myself, by pointing to myself, then to that, and again pointing to her and to my Bed. When at length I had made this matter intelligible to her, she lay down very composedly; and after I had taken Care of my Fire, and set the Things I had been using for Supper in their Places, I laid myself down too: For I could have no suspicious Thoughts, or fear of Danger, from a Form so excellent.

I treated her for some Time with all the Respect imaginable, and never suffered her to do the least part of my Work. It was very inconvenient to both of us, only to know each others Meaning by Signs; but I could not be otherwise than pleas'd to see, that she endeavoured all in her Power to learn to talk like me. Indeed I was not behind Hand with her in that Respect, striving all I could to imitate her. What I all the while wondered at was, she never shewed the least disquiet at her Confinement: For I kept my Door shut at first, thro' fear of loosing her, thinking she would have taken an Opportunity to run away from me; for little did I then think she could fly.

CHAPTER XV

Wilkins afraid of loosing his new Mistress; they live
together all Winter; a Remark on that; they begin
to know each others Language; a long Discourse
between them at cross purposes; she flies; they engage
to be Man and Wife

AFTER my new Love had been with me a Fortnight, finding
my Water run low, I was greatly troubled at the thought of
quitting her any time, to go for more; and having hinted it
to her, with seeming Uneasiness, she could not for a while
fathom my Meaning; but when she saw me much confused,
she came at length, by the many Signs I made, to imagine it
was my Concern for her which made me so; whereupon she
expressively enough signified I might be easy, for she did not
fear any thing happening to her, in my Absence. On this, as
well as I could declare my meaning, I intreated her not to go
away before my Return. As soon as she understood what
I signified to her, by Actions, she sat down, with her Arms
across, leaning her Head against the Wall, to assure me she
would not stir. However, as I had before nailed a Cord to the
outside of the Door, I tyed that for Caution's sake, to the Tree,
for fear of the worst: but I believe she had not the least
Design of removing.

I took my Boat, Net, and Water-Cask, as usual; desirous
of bringing her home a fresh Fish Dinner; and succeeded so
well as to catch enough for several good Meals, and to spare.
What remain'd I salted, and found she liked that better than
the fresh, after a few Days salting; tho' she did not so well
approve of that I had formerly pickled and dryed. As my Salt
grew very low, tho' I had been as sparing of it as possible, I
now resolved to try making some; and the next Summer
I effected it.

Thus we spent the Remainder of the Winter together, 'till
the Days began to be light enough for me to walk abroad

a little in the middle of them: for I was now under no Apprehensions of her leaving me; as she had before this time had so many Opportunities of doing so, but never once attempted it.

I must here make one Reflection upon our Conduct, which you will almost think incredible, *viz*. That we two, of different Sexes, not wanting our peculiar Desires, fully inflamed with Love to each other, and no outward Obstacle to prevent our Wishes, should have been together, under the same Roof, alone, for five Months, conversing together from Morning to Night, (for by this time she pretty well understood *English*, and I her Language) and yet, I should never have clasped her in my Arms, or have shewn any further amorous Desires to her, than what the Deference I all along paid her could give her room to surmise. Nay, I can affirm, that I did not even then know, that the Covering she wore, was not the work of Art, but the work of Nature; for I really took it for Silk: tho' it must be premised, that I had never seen it by any other Light, than of my Lamp. Indeed the Modesty of her Carriage, and Sweetness of her Behaviour to me, had struck into me such a Dread of offending her, that, tho' nothing upon Earth could be more capable of exciting Passion than her Charms, I could have died, rather than have attempted to salute[1] her only, without actual Invitation.

When the Weather cleared up a little, by the lengthening of Day light, I took Courage one Afternoon to invite her to walk with me to the Lake; but she sweetly excused herself from it, whilst there was such a frightful Glare of Light, as she said; but, looking out at the Door, told me, if I would not go out of the Wood, she would accompany me: so we agreed to take a Turn only there. I first went myself over the Style of the Door, and thinking it rather too high for her, I took her in my Arms and lifted her over. But even when I had her in this manner, I knew not what to make of her Cloathing, it sat so true and close; but seeing her by a steadier and truer Light in the Grove, tho' a heavy gloomy one, than my Lamp had afforded, I begged she would let me know of what Silk or other Composition her Garment was made. She smil'd, and ask'd me, if mine was not the same under my Jacket. No Lady, says I, I have nothing but my Skin under my Cloaths. Why what do you mean? replies she somewhat tartly; but indeed I was afraid something was the Matter, by that nasty Covering you wear, that you might not be seen. Are not you a *Glumm*?* Yes, says I, fair Creature. (Here, tho' you may conceive she spoke part *English*, part her own Tongue, and I the same, as we best understood each other, yet I shall give you our Discourse, Word for Word, in plain *English*). Then, says she, I am afraid you must have been a very bad Man, and have been *Crashee*,† which I should be very sorry to hear. I told her I believed we were none of us so good as we might be, but I hoped my Faults had not at most exceeded other Mens; but I had suffered Abundance of Hardships in my time; and that at last Providence having settled me in this Spot, from whence I had no Prospect of ever departing, it was none of the least of it's Mercies, to bring to my Knowledge and Company, the most exquisite Piece of all his Works, in her; which I should acknowledge as long as I lived. She was surpriz'd at this Discourse, and asked me, (if I did not mean to impose upon her, and was indeed an *Ingcrashee*‡ *Glumm*) why I should tell her I had no Prospect of departing from hence? Have not you, says she, the same Prospect, that I or any other Person has of departing? Sir, added she, you don't do well, and really I fear you are slit, or you would not wear this nasty cumbersome Coat, (taking hold of my Jacket Sleeve) if you were not afraid of shewing the Signs of a bad Life upon your natural Cloathing.

I could not for my Heart imagine what Way there was to get out of my Dominions; but certainly, thought I, there must be some or other, or she would not be so peremptory. And as to my Jacket, and shewing myself in my natural Cloathing, I profess she made me blush; and, but for shame, I would have stripped to my Skin, to have satisfied her. But, Madam, says I, pray Pardon me, for you are really mistaken; I have

* A man.   † Slit.   ‡ Unslit.

examined every Nook and Corner of this new World, in which
we now are, and can find no possible Outlet; nay, even by the
same way I came in, I am sure it is impossible to get out again.
Why, says she, what Outlets have you searched for, or what
way can you expect out, but the way you came in? And why
is that impossible to return by again? If you are not slit, is
not the Air open to you? Will not the Sky admit You to
patrole in it, as well as other People? I tell you, Sir, I fear
you have been slit for your Crimes; and tho' you have been
so good to me, that I can't help loving of you heartily for it;
yet, if I thought you had been slit, I would not, nay could
not, stay a Moment longer with you; no, tho' it should break
my Heart to leave you.

I found myself now in a strange Quandary, longing to
know what she meant by being slit; and had a hundred strange
Notions in my Head whether I was slit or not; for tho' I knew
what the Word naturally signified well enough, yet in what
manner, or by what Figure of Speech, she applied it to me,
I had no Idea of. But seeing her look a little angrily upon me,
pray Madam, says I, don't be offended, if I take the Liberty
to ask you what you mean by the word *Crashee*,* so often
repeated by you; for I am an utter Stranger to what you mean
by it. Sir, says she, pray answer me first, how you came here.
Madam, replied I, will you please to take a Walk to the Verge
of the Wood, and I will shew you the very Passage. Sir, says
she, I perfectly know the Range of the Rocks all round; and
by the least Description, without going to see them, can tell
from which you descended. In truth, said I, most charming
Lady, I descended from no Rock at all; nor would I for
a thousand Worlds attempt what could not be accomplished
but by my Destruction. Sir, says she, in some Anger, it is
false, and you impose upon me. I declare to you, says I,
Madam, what I tell you is strictly true, I never was near
the Summit of any of the surrounding Rocks, or any thing
like it; but as you are not far from the Verge of the Wood,
be so good as to step a little further, and I will shew you my

* Slit.

Entrance in hither. Well, says she, now this odious dazzle of Light is lessened, I don't care if I do go with you.

When we came far enough to see the Bridge; there, Madam, says I, there is my Entrance, where the Sea pours into this Lake from yonder Cavern. It is not possible, says she; this is another Untruth; and as I see you would deceive me, and are not to be believed, farewel; I must be gone. But hold, says she, let me ask you one thing more; that is, by what means did you come through that Cavern? you could not have used to have come over the Rock. Bless me, Madam, says I, do you think I and my Boat could fly? Come over the Rock did you say? No Madam, I sailed from the great Sea, the main Ocean, in my Boat, thro' that Cavern, into this very Lake here. What do you mean by your Boat, says she? You seem to make two Things of your Boat, you say you sailed with, and yourself. I do so, replied I, for, Madam, I take myself to be good Flesh and Blood, but my Boat is made of Wood and other Materials. Is it so, says she, and pray where is this Boat that is made of Wood and other Materials, under your Jacket? Lord! Madam, says I, you put me in fear, that you was angry; but now I hope you only Joke with me; what, put a Boat under my Jacket! No, Madam, my Boat is in the Lake. What! more Untruths, says she. No, Madam, I replied, if you would be satisfied of what I say, every Word of which is as true as that my Boat now is in the Lake, pray walk with me thither, and make your own Eyes judges, what Sincerity I speak with. To this she agreed, it growing Dusky; but assured me, if I did not give her good Satisfaction, I should see her no more.

We arrived at the Lake; and going to my wet Dock, now, Madam, says I, pray satisfy yourself, whether I spake true or no. She looked at my Boat, but could not yet frame a proper Notion of it. Says I, Madam, in this very Boat, I sailed from the main Ocean, thro' that Cavern, into this Lake; and shall at last think myself the happiest of all Men, if you continue with me, love me and credit me; and I promise you I'll never deceive you, but think my Life happily spent in your Service.

I found she was hardly content yet to believe what I told her of my Boat to be true; 'till I stepped into it, and pushing from the Shore, took my Oars in my Hand, and sailed along the Lake by her, as she walked on the Shore. At last, she seemed so well reconciled to me and my Boat, that she desired I would take her in. I immediately did so, and we sailed a good way; and as we return'd to my Dock, I described to her how I procured the Water we drank, and brought it to Shore in that Vessel.

Well, says she, I have sailed, as you call it, many a Mile in my Life time, but never in such a thing as this. I own it will serve very well, where one has a great many Things to carry from Place to Place; but, to be labouring thus at an Oar, when one intends Pleasure in sailing, is in my Mind a most ridiculous Piece of Slavery. Why, pray Madam, how would you have me sail? for, getting into the Boat only, will not carry us this way or that, without using some force. But, says she, pray where did you get this Boat, as you call it? O! Madam, says I, that is too long and fatal a Story to begin upon now; this Boat was made many thousand Miles from hence, among a People coal black, a quite different sort from us; and, when I first had it, I little thought of seeing this Country; but I will make a faithful Relation of all to you, when we come home. Indeed I began to wish heartily we were there, for it grew into the Night; and having strolled so far without my Gun, I was afraid of what I had before seen and heard, and hinted our Return; but I found my Motion was disagreeable to her, and so I dropped it.

I now perceiv'd, and wondered at it, that the later it grew, the more agreeable it seemed to her; and as I had now brought her into a good Humour again, by seeing and sailing in my Boat, I was not willing to prevent it's Increase: I told her if she pleas'd we would land, and when I had docked my Boat I would accompany her where and as long as she liked. As we talked, and walked by the Lake, she made a little run before me, and sprung into it. Perceiving this, I cryed out; whereupon she merrily called on me to follow her. The Light was then so dim, as prevented my having more than a confused Sight of her, when she jumped in; and looking earnestly after her, I could discern nothing more than a small Boat, on the Water, which skimm'd along at so great a Rate that I almost lost sight of it presently; but running along the Shore, for fear of losing her, I met her gravely walking to meet me; and then had entirely lost sight of the Boat upon the Lake. This, says she, accosting me with a Smile, is my way of Sailing, which, I perceive by the Fright you were in, you are altogether unacquainted with; and as you tell me you came from so many thousand Miles off, it is possible you may be made differently from me; but surely we are the part of the Creation which has had most Care bestow'd upon it: And I suspect from all your Discourse, to which I have been very attentive, it is possible you may no more be able to fly, than to sail, as I do. No, charming Creature, says I, that I can't, I'll assure you. She then stepping to the Edge of the Lake, for the Advantage of a Descent before her, sprung up into the Air, and away she went, further than my Eyes could follow her.

I was quite astonished. So, says I, then all is over, all a Delusion which I have so long been in, a meer Phantom! better had it been for me never to have seen her, than thus to lose her again! But what could I expect, had she stay'd? for it is plain she is no human Composition. But, says I, she felt like Flesh too, when I lifted her out at the Door.—I had but very little time for Reflection; for in about ten Minutes after she had left me in this Mixture of Grief and Amazement, she alighted just by me, on her Feet.

Her Return, as she plainly saw, filled me with a Transport not to be concealed; and which, as she afterwards told me, was very agreeable to her. Indeed I was some Moments in such an Agitation of Mind, from these unparallelled Incidents, that I was like one Thunder struck; but coming presently to myself, and clasping her in my Arms, with as much Love and Passion as I was capable of expressing, and for the first Time with any Desire, are you returned again, kind Angel, said I, to bless a Wretch who can only be happy in adoring you? Can it be, that you who have so many Advantages over me, should quit all the Pleasures that Nature has formed you for, and all your Friends and Relations, to take an Asylum in my Arms? But I here make you a tender of all I am able to bestow, my Love and Constancy.—Come, come, says she, no more Raptures, I find you are a worthier Man than I thought I had Reason to take you for; and I beg your Pardon for my Distrust, whilst I was ignorant of your Imperfections; but now, I verily believe all you have said is true; and I promise you, as you have seemed so much to delight in me, I will never quit you 'till Death, or other as fatal Accident shall part us. But we will now, if you chuse, go home, for I know you have been some time uneasy in this Gloom, tho' agreeable to me: For, giving my Eyes the Pleasure of looking eagerly on you, it conceals my Blushes from your Sight.

In this Manner, exchanging mutual Endearments, and soft Speeches, Hand in Hand, we arrived at the Grotto; where we that Night consummated our Nuptials, without further Ceremony than mutual solemn Engagements to each other: which are, in truth, the Essence of Marriage, and all that was there and then in our Power.

CHAPTER XVI

The Author's Disappointment at first going to bed
with his new Wife; some strange Circumstances
relating thereto; she resolves several Questions he asks
her, and clears up his Fears as to the Voices;
A Description of Swangeans

EVERY Calm is succeeded by a Storm, as is every Storm by it's Calm; for, after Supper, in order to give my Bride the Opportunity of undressing alone, which I thought might be most agreeable the first Night, I withdrew into the Antichamber, 'till I thought she was laid; and then, having first disposed of my Lamp, I moved softly towards her, and stepped into Bed too; when, on my nearer approach to her, I imagined she had her Cloaths on. This struck a thorough Damp over me; and asking her the Reason of it, not being able to touch the least bit of her Flesh, but her Face and Hands, she burst out a laughing; and running her Hand along my naked Side, soon perceived the Difference, she before had made such doubt of, between herself and me. Upon which she fairly told me, that neither she, or any Person she had ever seen before, had any other Covering than what they were born with, and which they would not willingly part with but with their Lives. This shocked me terribly; not from the Horror of the thing itself, or any distaste I had to this Covering, for it was quite smooth, warm, and softer than Velvet, or the finest Skin imaginable; but from an Apprehension of her being so wholly incased in it, that tho' I had so fine a Companion, and now a Wife, yet, I should have no conjugal Benefit from her, either to my own Gratification, or the Increase of our Species.

In the Height of my Impatience, I made divers Essays for unfolding this Covering, but unsuccessfully. Surely, says I, there must be some Way of coming at my Wishes; or why should she seem so shy of me at first, and now we are under Engagements to each other, meet me half Way with such a yielding Compliance. I could, if I had had Time to spare, have gone on, starting Objections and answering them, in my own Breast, a great while longer, (for I now knew not what to make of it;) but being prompted to act as well as think, and feeling, as tenderly as possible, upon her Bosom, for the Folds or Plaits of her Garment, she lying perfectly still, and perceiving divers flat broad ledges, like Whalebone, seemingly under her Covering, which closely infolded her Body, I thought, it might be all laced on together, somewhat like Stays, and felt behind for the Lacing. At length, perceiving me so puzzled, and beyond Conception vexed at my Disappointment; of a sudden, lest I should grow outragious, which I was almost come to, she threw down all those seeming

Ribbs, flat to her Side, so imperceptably to me, that I knew nothing of the Matter, though I lay close to her; 'till putting forth my Hand again to her Bosom, the softest Skin and most delightful Body, free from all Impediment, presented itself to my Wishes, and gave up itself to my Embraces.

I slept very soundly 'till Morning, and so did she; but at waking I was very solicitous to find out what Sort of Being I had had in my Arms, and with what Qualities her Garment was endued, or how contrived, that notwithstanding all my fruitless Attempts to uncover her, she herself could so instantaneously dispose of it, undiscerned by me: Well, thought I, she is my Wife, I will be satisfied in every Thing, for surely she will not now refuse to gratify my Curiosity.

We rose with the Light; but surely no two were ever more amorous, or more delighted with each other. I being up first, lighted the Fire, and prepared Breakfast of some Fish Soup, thickened with my Cream-Cheese; and then calling her, I kept my Eye towards the Bed to see how she dress'd herself; but throwing aside the Cloaths, she stepped out ready dressed, and came to me. When I had kissed her, and wished her a good Day, we sat down to Breakfast; which being soon over, I told her, I hoped every Minute of our Lives would prove as happy as those we so lately passed together; which she seemed to wish with equal Ardour. I then told her, now she was my Wife, I thought proper to know her Name, which I had never before asked, for fear of giving Uneasiness; for, as I added, I did not doubt, she had observed in my Behaviour, ever since I first saw her, a peculiar Tenderness for her, and a sedulous Concern not to offend; which had obliged me, hitherto, to stifle several Questions I had to ask her, whenever they wou'd be agreeable to her. She then bid me begin, for as she was now my Wife, whilst I was speaking it became her to be all Attention, and to give me the utmost Satisfaction she could in all I should require, as she herself should have so great an Interest in every thing for the Future which would oblige me.

Compliments (if in compliance with old Custom I may call 'em so, for they were by us delivered from the Heart) being a little over on both sides, I first desired to know what Name she went by, before I found her: For, says I, having only hitherto called you Madam, and my Lady; besides the future Expression of my Love to you in the Word *Dear*, I would know your original Name, that so I might join it with that tender Epithet. That you shall, says she, and also my Family at another Opportunity; but as my Name will not take up long Time to repeat at present, it is YOUWARKEE. And pray, says she, now gratify me with the Knowledge of yours. My dear *Youwarkee*, says I, my Name was PETER WILKINS when I heard it last; but that is so long ago, I had almost forgot it. And now, says I, there is another Thing you can give me a Pleasure in. You need then only mention it, my dear *Peter*, says she. That is, says I, only to tell me, if you did not, by some Accident, fall from the Top of the Rock over my Habitation, upon the Roof of it, when I first took you in here; and whether you are of the Country upon the Rocks? She, softly smiling, answered, my dear *Peter* you run your Questions too thick; as to my Country, which is not on the Rocks, as you suppose, but at a vast Distance from hence, I shall leave that, 'till I may hereafter, at more Leisure, speak of my Family, as I promised you before; but as to how I came into this Grotto, I knew not at first, but soon perceived your Humanity had brought me in, to take Care of me, after a terrible Fall I had: not from the Rock, as you suppose; for then I must not now have been Living to enjoy you; but from a far less considerable Height in the Air. I'll tell you how it happened. A Parcel of us young People were upon a merry *Swangean*,* round this *Arkoe*,† which we usually divert our selves with at set Times of the Year, chasing and pursuing one another, sometimes soaring to an extravagant Height, and then shooting down again with surprising Precipitancy, 'till we even touch the Trees; when, of a sudden, we mount again and away. I say, being of this Party, and pursued by one of my Comrades, I descended down to the very Trees, and she after me; but,

* Flight.
† Water surrounded with a Wood.

as I mounted, she over-shooting me, brushed so stiffly against the upper part of my *Graundee*,* that I lost my bearing; and being so near the Branches, before I could recover it again, I sunk into the Tree, and rendered my *Graundee* useless to me, so that down I came, and that with so much Force, that I but just felt my Fall, and lost my Senses. Whether I cryed out or no upon my coming to the Ground I cannot say; but if I did, my Companion was too far gone by that time to hear or take Notice of me; as she probably, in so swift a Flight, saw not my Fall. As to the Condition I was in, or what happened immediately afterwards, I must be obliged to you for a Relation of that: But one thing I was quickly sensible of, and never can forget, *viz.* that I owe my Life to your Care, and Kindness to me.

I told her she should have that part of her Story from me another time; but, says I, there is something so amazing in these Flights, or *Swangeans*, as you call them, that I must, as the Questions for this Day, beg you would let me know, what is the Method of 'em? what's the Nature of your Covering? (which was at first such an Obstacle to my Wishes) how you put it on? and how you Use it in your *Swangean*?

Surely, my dearest *Peter*, says she, but that I can deny you nothing, since you are my *Barkatt*,† which you seem so passionately to desire, the latter of your Questions would not be answered, for it must put me to the Blush. As to our Method of Flight, you saw somewhat of that, last Night; tho' in a Light hardly sufficient for you; and, for the Nature of my Covering, you perceive that now: but to shew you how it is put on, as you call it, I am afraid it will be necessary, as far as I can, to put it off, before I can make you comprehend that; which having done, the whole will be no further a Mystery. But, not to be tedious, is it your Command that I uncover? Lay that upon me, it shall be done. Here I was at a Plunge, whether to proceed, or drop the Question. Thinks I, if my Curiosity should be fatal to me, as I may see some-

* The Covering and Wings of Skin they flew with.
† Husband.

thing I can never bear hereafter, I am undone. She waits the Command! why so? I know not the Consequence. What shall I do? At last, somewhat resolutely, I asked her, Whether her Answer, either way, to my Command, would cause her to leave me, or me to love her less. She seeing my Hesitation, and perceiving the Cause, was so pleased, that she cryed out, No, my dear *Peter*, nor that, nor all the force on Earth, shall ever part me from you. But I conceive you are afraid, you shall discover something in me, you may not like; I fear not that; but an immodest Appearance before you, I can't suffer myself to be guilty of, but under your own Command.

My lovely *Youwarkee*, says I, delay then my Desires no longer; and since you require a Warrant from me, I do command you to do it. Immediately her *Graundee* flew open, (discovering her naked Body, just to the Hip, and round the Rim of her Belly,) and expanding itself, was near six Feet wide. Here my Love and Curiosity had a hard Conflict; the one to gain my Attention to the *Graundee*, and the other to retain my Eyes and Thoughts on her lovely Body, which I had never beheld so much of before. Tho' I was very unwilling to keep her uncovered too long, I could not easily dismiss so charming a Sight. I attentively view'd her lovely Flesh, and examined the Case that enshrined it: but as I shall give you a full Description of this *Graundee* hereafter, in a more proper Place, I will mention it no further here, than to tell you, that when I had narrowly surveyed the upper part of it, she in a Moment contracted it round her so close, that the nicest Eye could not perceive the joining of the Parts.

Indeed my dear *Youwarkee*, says I, you had the best of Reasons for saying you was not fearful I should discover any thing in you displeasing; for, if my Bosom glow'd with Love before, you have now therein raised an ardent Flame, which neither Time or ought else will ever be able to extinguish. I now almost conceive how you fly: Tho' yet I am at a Loss to know, how you extend and make Use of the lower part of your *Graundee*, which rises up and meets the upper; but

K

I will rather guess at that, by what I have seen, than raise the Colour higher in those fair Cheeks, which are however adorn'd with Blushes. Then running to her, and taking her in my Arms, I called her the Gift of Heaven; and left off further Interrogatories 'till another Opportunity.

CHAPTER XVII

Youwarkee cannot bear a strong Light; Wilkins makes her Spectacles which help her; a Description of them

YOUWARKEE and I having no other Company than one another's, we talked together almost from Morning to Night, in order to learn each others Dialect. But how compliable soever she was in all other Respects, I could not perswade her to go out with me to fetch Water, or to the Lake, in the Day time. It being now the light Season, I wanted her to be more abroad; but she excused herself, telling me her People never came into those luminous Parts of the Country, during the false Glare, as they called it, but kept altogether at Home, where their Light was more moderate and steddier; and that the Place where I resided, was not frequented by them for half the Year; and at other Times only upon Parties of Pleasure; it not being worth while to settle Habitations, where they could not abide always. She said *Normbdsgrsutt*, was the finest Region in the World, where her King's Court was, and a vast Kingdom. I asked her twice or thrice more to name the Country to me; but not all the Art we could use, her's in dictating, and mine in endeavouring to pronounce it, would render me Conqueror of that poor Monosyllable, (for as such it sounded from her sweet Lips:) So I relinquished the Name to her; telling her, whenever she had any more Occasion to mention the Place, I desired it might be under the Stile of *Doorpt Swangeanti*;* which she promised; but

* The Land of Flight.

wondered, as she could speak the other so glibly, as she called it, I could not do so too.

I told her, that the Light of my Native Country was far stronger than any I had seen since my Arrival at *Graundevolet*, (for that, I found by her, was the Name my Dominions went by;) and that we had a Sun, or Ball of Fire, which roll'd over our Heads every Day, with such a Light and such a Heat, that it would sometimes almost scorch one, it was so hot; and was of such Brightness, that the Eye could not look at it without Danger of Blindness. She was heartily glad, she said, she was not born in so wretched a Land; and she did not believe there was any other so good as her own. I thought no Benefit could arise from my Combating these innocent Prejudices, so I let 'em alone.

She had often lamented to me, the Difference of our Eye-Sight, and the Trouble it was to her, that she could not at all Times go about with me; 'till it gave me a good deal of Uneasiness to see her Concern. At last I told her, that tho' I believ'd it would be impossible to reduce my Sight to the Standard of her's, yet I was perswaded, I could bring her's to bear the strongest Light I had ever seen in this Country. She was mightily pleased with the Thought of that, and said she wished I might; for she was sensible of no Grief, like being obliged to stay at Home, when I went abroad on my Business; and was resolved to try my Experiment, if I pleased; and in the mean Time should heartily pray for the Success.— I light on the following Invention.

I rumaged over all my old Things, and by good Luck found an old crape Hatband. This I tried myself, single, before my own Eyes, in the strongest Light we had; but, believing I had not yet obscured it enough, I doubled it, and then thought it might do; but for fear it should not, I trebled it; and then it seemed too dark for Eyes like mine to discover Objects thro' it, and so I judged it would suit her's: For I was determined to produce something, if possible, that would do, at first, without Repetition of Tryal; which I thought would only deject her more, by making her look on the Matter as impracticable.

I now only wanted a proper Method for fixing it on her; and this I thought would be easily effected; but had much more Difficulty in it than I imagined. At first I purposed to tye the Crape over her Eyes; but trying it myself, I found it very rough and fretting. I then designed fixing it to an old Crown of a Hat, that held my Fish Hooks and Lines, and so let it hang down before her Face: but that also had its Inconveniences, as it would flap her Eyes in windy Weather, and would be not only useless but very troublesome in Flight: so that I was scarce ever more puzzled before. At last I thought of a Method that answered exceedingly well; the Hint of which I took from somewhat I had seen with my Master, when I was at School, which he called Goggles, and which he used to tie round his Head, to skreen his Eyes in riding. The thing I made upon that Plan was compos'd of old Hat, pieces of Ram's-horn, and the above mentioned Crape.

When I had finished the whole Apparatus, I tried it first upon myself, and finding great Reason to believe it would perfectly answer the Intention, I ran directly to *Youwarkee*. Come, says I, my Dear, will you go with me to the Water Rill? for I must fetch some this Morning. She shook her Head, and with Tears in her Eyes wished she could; but, says she, let me see how light it is abroad? No, says I, my Love, you must not look out till you go. Indeed, says she, if it did not affect my Eyes and Head, you should not ask me twice. Well, says I, my *Youwarkee*, I am now come to take you with me; and that you may not suffer by it, turn about, and let me apply the Remedy I told you of for your Sight. She wanted much to see first what it was; but I begged her to forbear, till she tried whether it would be useful or not. She told me, she would absolutely submit to my Direction; so I adjusted the thing to her Head. Now, says I, you have it on, let us go out and try it; and let me know the Moment you find the Light offensive, and take particular Notice how you are affected. Hereupon away we marched, and I heard no Complaint in all our Walk to the Lake.

Now my dear *Youwarkee*, says I, when we got there, what

do you think of my Contrivance, can you see at all? Yes, very well, says she. But, my dear *Peter*, you have taken the Advantage of the twilight, I know, to deceive me; and I had rather have stay'd at Home, than have subjected you to return in the Night, for the Sake of my Company. I then assured her it was Mid-Day, and no later, which pleased her mightily; and to satisfy her, I untied the String behind, and just let her be convinced it was so. When I had fixed the Shade on her Head again, she put up her Hands, and felt the several Materials of which it consisted; and after expressing her Admiration of it, so my dear *Peter*, says she, you have now encumbered yourself with a Wife indeed, for since I can come abroad in a glaring Light, with so much Ease, you will never henceforward be without my Company.

Youwarkee being thus in Spirits, we launched the Boat, watered, took a Draft of Fish, and return'd; passing the Night at home, in talking of the Spectacles, (for that was the Name I told her they must go by) and of the Fishing: for that Exercise delighted her to a great Degree. But, above all, the Spectacles were her chief Theme; she handled 'em and look'd at 'em again and again, and ask'd several rational Questions about them; as how they could have that Effect on her Eyes, enabling her to see, and the like. She ventured out, with them on, next Day by herself; and as she threatned, she was as good as her Word, for she scarcely afterwards let me go abroad by myself, but accompanied me every where freely, and with Delight.

CHAPTER XVIII

Youwarkee *with Child ;* Wilkins's *Stock of Provisions ;*
no Beast or Fish in Youwarkee's *Country ; the*
Voices again ; her Reason for not seeing those who
uttered 'em ; she bears a Son ; a hard Speech in her
lying in ; divers Birds appear ; their Eggs gathered ;
how Wilkins *kept Account of Time*

ABOUT three Months after we were married, as we called it,
Youwarkee told me she believed she was Breeding; and I was
mightily pleased with it: for tho' I had had two Children
before, by *Patty*, yet I had never seen either of them; so that
I longed to be a Father. I sometimes amused myself with
whimsical Conjectures, as whether the Child would have
a *Graundee*, or not; which of us it would be most like; how we
should do without a Midwife; and what must become of the
Infant, as we had no Milk, in Case *Youwarkee* could not suckle
it. Indeed I had leisure enough for indulging such Reveries;
for having laid in our Winter Stores, my Wife and I had
nothing to do but enjoy our selves over a good Fire, pratling
and toying together, making as good Chear as we could: and
truly that was none of the worst; for we had as fine Bread as
need to be eaten; we had Pears preserved; all Sorts of dry'd
Fish; and once a Fortnight, for two or three Days together,
had fresh Fish; we had Vinegar; and a biting Herb, I had
found, for Pepper; and several Sorts of Nuts; so there was
no want.

It was at this Time, after my Return from watering one
Day, where *Youwarkee* had been with me; that, having taken
several Fish, and amongst them some I had not before seen,
I asked her, as we were preparing and salting some of them,
how they managed Fish in her Country, and what Variety
they had of them there? She told me, she neither ever saw,
or heard of a Fish in her Life, 'till she came to me. How!
says I, no Fish amongst you? why you want one of the greatest

Dainties that can be set upon a Table. Do you wholly eat
Flesh, says I, at *Doorpt Swangeanti*? Flesh, says she, laugh-
ingly, of what? Nay, says I, you know best what the Beasts
of your own Country are; we have in *England*, where I was
born and bred, Oxen, very large Hogs, Sheep, Lambs, and
Calves; these make our ordinary Dishes; then, we have Deer,
Hares, Rabbits, and these are reckoned Dainties; besides
numberless kinds of Poultry, and Fish without stint. I never
heard of any of these things in my Life, says *Youwarkee*; nor
did I ever eat any thing but Fruits, and Herbs, and what is
made from them at *Normbdsgrsutt*. You will speak that
crabbed Word, says I, again. I beg your Pardon, my Dear,
says she: at *Doorpt Swangeanti*, I say, nor I, or any one else,
to my Knowledge, ever eat any such thing. But seeing you
eat Fish, as you call them, I made no Scruple of doing so too;
and like them very well, especially the salted ones: for I never
tasted what you call Salt, neither, 'till I came here. I can't
think, says I, what sort of a Country yours is, or how you all
live there. O says she, there's no want; I wish you and I were
there.—I was afraid I had talked too much of her Country
already, so we called a new Cause.

Soon after Winter had set in, as we were in Bed one Night,
I heard the Voices again. And tho' my Wife had told me of her
Country Folks, *Swangeans*, in that Place, I being frighted
a little, waked her; and she hearing them too, cry'd out, there
they are, it is ten to one but my Sister or some of our family
are there; hark! I believe I hear her Voice. I myself hearkened
very attentively; and by this time understanding a great deal
of their Language, I not only could distinguish different
Speakers, but knew the Meaning of several of the Words they
pronounced.

I would have had *Youwarkee* have gotten up, and called
to them. Not for the World, says she, have you a Mind to
part with me? Tho' I have no Intent to leave you, as I am
with Child, if they should try to force me away, without
my Consent, I may receive some Injury, to the Danger of
my own Life, or at least of the Child's. This Reason perfectly

satisfying me, endeared the loving Creature to me ten times more, if possible, than ever.

The next Summer brought me a *Yawm,** as fair as Alabaster. My Wife was delivered without the usual Assistance, and had as favourable a Labour as could be. The first thing I did, after giving her some Fish Soup, made as skilfully as I was able, and a little Cordial, was, to see if my Yawm had the *Graundee,* or not. Finding it had, so, says I, to *Youwarkee,* you have brought me a legitimate Heir to my Dominions, whose Title sure can't be disputed, being one of you. Tho' I spoke this, with as much Pleasure, and in as endearing a way, as ever I spoke in my Life, and quite innocently; the poor *Youwarkee* burst into Tears, to such Excess, there was no pacifying her. I asked her the Reason of her Grief, begged and intreated her to let me know what disturbed her; but all in Vain; 'till seeing me in a violent Passion, such as I had never before appeared to be in, she told me, she was very sorry I should Question her Fidelity to me. She surprized me in saying this, as I never had any such Apprehension. No, my dearest Wife, says I, I never had any such Suspicion as you Charge me with, I can safely affirm; nor can I comprehend your Meaning by imputing such a thing to me. Oh! says she, I am sure you have no Cause for it, but, you said *the poor Child was one of us,* as much as to intimate, that had it been your own, it would have been born as you were, without the *Graundee:* Which Thought I can't bear; and if you continue to think so, it must end me; therefore take away my Life now, rather than let me live to see my further Misery.

I was heartily sorry for what I had said, when I saw the Effects of it, tho' I did not imagine it could have been perverted to such a contrary Meaning. But considering her to be the faithfullest and most loving Creature upon Earth, and that true Love can't bear any thing that touches upon, or can be applied (though with ever so forced a Construction) to an opprobrious or contemptuous Meaning, I attributed her groundless Resentment, to her Excess of Fondness only for

* Man Child.

me; and falling upon the Bed by her, and bathing her Face in my Tears, I assured her, the Interpretation she had put on my Words, was altogether foreign from the view they were spoken with; professing to her, that I never had, nor ever could have, the least Cause of Jealousy. On my confirming this absolute Confidence in her Virtue, by the strongest Asseverations, she grew fully convinced of her Error, and acknowledged she had been too rash in censuring me: and growing pleased at my fresh Professions of Love to her, we presently were reconciled, and became again very good Friends.

When *Youwarkee* had gathered Strength again, she prov'd an excellent Nurse to my *Pedro*, for that was the Name I gave him, so that he soon grew a charming Child, able to go in his twelfth Month, and spoke in his twentieth. This and two other lovely Boys I had by her within three Years; every one of which she brought up with the Breast, and they thriv'd delicately.[1]

I don't mention the little intervening Occurrences which happened during this Period; they consisting chiefly of the old Rota,[2] of fishing, watering, providing in the Summer for the Winter, and in managing my Saltwork: which, altogether, kept me at full Imployment, comfortably to maintain an encreasing Family.

In this time, I had found out several new Sorts of Eatables. I had observed, as I said before, abundance of Birds about the Wood and Lake, in the Summer Months. These, by firing at 'em two or three times, on my first coming, I had almost caused to desert my Dominions. But as I had, for the last two or three Years, given no Disturbance at all to them, they were now in as great Plenty as ever: And I made great Profit of them, by the Peace they enjoy'd; and yet my Table never wanted a Supply, fresh in the Summer, or salted and pickled in Winter.

I took Notice, it was about *October* these Birds used to come; and most of the Month of *November* they were busy in laying their Eggs, which I used at that time to find in great Plenty, along the Banks of the Lake, in the Reeds, and made great Collections of them; I used also to find a great many in the Woods, amongst the Shrubs and Underwood. These furnished our Table various Ways; for, with my Cream Cheese Flower, and a little Mixture of Ramshorn Juice, I had taught my Wife to make excellent Puddings of 'em; abundance of them also we eat boiled or fryed, alone, and often as Sauce to our Fish. As for the Birds themselves, having long omitted to Fire at them, I had an effectual Means of taking them otherwise, by Nets, which I set between the Trees, and also very large pitfal Nets, with which I used to catch all Sorts, even from the size of a Thrush to that of a Turkey. But as I shall say more of these when I come to speak of my Ward,[1] by and by, and of my Poultry, I shall omit any further mention of 'em here.

You may perhaps wonder how I could keep an Account of my Time so precisely, as to talk of the particular Months. I will tell you. At my coming from *America*,[2] I was then exact; for we set sail the fourteenth of *November*, and struck the first or second Day of *February*. So far I kept perfect Reckoning. But, after that, I was not so exact: Tho' I kept it as well as my Perplexity would admit even then, 'till the Days shortning upon me, prevented it.

Hereupon I set about making a Year for myself. I found the Duration of the comparative Darkness, or, what might with me be termed Night, in the Course of the twenty four Hours or Day, gradually encreased for six Months; after which it decreased reciprocally, for an equal Time, and the lighter part of the Day took it's turn, as in our Parts of the World, only inversely: so that, as the Light's Decrease became sensible about the middle of *March*, it was at the greatest Pitch the latter end of *August*, or beginning of *September*; and from thence, on the contrary, went on decreasing to the close of *February*, when I had the longest Portion of Light. Hereupon, dividing my Year, into two Seasons only, I began the Winter half in *March*, and the Summer half in *September*. Thus my Winter was the Spring and Summer Quarters of us in *Europe*, and my Summer those of our Autumn and Winter.

From my settling this Matter, I kept little Account of Days or Weeks, but only reckoned my Time by Summer and Winter: so that I am pretty right as to the Revolutions of these; tho' the Years, as to their Notation, I kept no Account of, nor do I know what Year of the Lord it now is.

CHAPTER XIX

Wilkins's Concern about Cloathing for Pedro, *his eldest Son; his Discourse with his Wife about the Ship; her Flight to it; his melancholy Reflections 'till her Return; an Account of what she had done, and of what she brought; she cloaths her Children, and takes a second Flight*

As my Boy *Pedro* grew up, tho', as I said before, he had the *Graundee*, yet it was of less Dimensions than it ought to have been, to be useful to him; so that it was visible, he could never fly; for it would scarce meet before, whereas it ought to have reached from Side to Side both ways. This pleased my Wife to the Heart; for now she was sure, whatever I had done before, I could not suspect her. Be that as it will, the Boy's *Graundee* not being a sufficient Vestment for him, it became necessary he should be cloathed.

I turned over my Hoard, but could find nothing that would do; or, at least, that we knew how to fit him with. I had described my own Country Vest[I] for Lads to *Youwarkee*, and she form'd a tolerable Idea of it, but we had no Tackle to alter any thing with. O my Dear, says I, had I but been born with the *Graundee*, I need not be now racking my Brains to get my Child Cloaths. What do you mean by that, says she? Why, says I, I would have flown to my Ship, (for I had long before related to her all my Sea Adventures, 'till the Vessel's coming to the magnetical Rock) and have brought some such Things from thence, as you, not wanting them in this Country, can have no Notion of. She seemed mighty inquisitive, to understand how a Ship was made, what it was most like to, how a Person who never saw one might know it only by the Description, and how one might get into it; with Abundance of the like Questions. She then inquired, what sort of things those Needles and several other Utensils were, which I had at times been speaking of; and in what part of a Ship they usually kept such Articles. And I, to gratify her Curiosity, as I perceived she took a Pleasure in hearing me, answered all her Questions to a Scruple: not then conceiving the secret Purpose of all this Inquisitiveness.

About two Days after this, having been out two or three Hours in the Morning, to cut Wood; at coming Home I found *Pedro* crying, ready to break his Heart, and his little Brother Tommy, hanging to him, and crawling about the Floor after him: the youngest (pretty Baby) was fast asleep upon one of the Beast Fish Skins, in a Corner of the Room. I asked *Pedro* for his Mother, but the poor Infant had nothing further to say to the Matter, than Mammy run away, I cry, Mammy run away, I cry. I admired[1] where she was gone, never before missing her from our Habitation. However, I waited patiently 'till Bed-time, but no Wife. I grew very uneasy then. Yet, as my Children were tired and sleepy, I thought I had best go to Bed with them, and make quiet. So, giving all three their Suppers, we lay down together. They slept; but my Mind was too full to permit the Closure of my Eyes. A thousand different Chimeras swam in my Imagination relating to my Wife. One while I fancied her carried away by her Kinsfolks; then, that she was gone of her own accord to make Peace with her Father. But that thought would not fix, being put aside by her constant Tenderness to her Children, and Regard to me; whom I was sure she would not have left without Notice. But alass! says I, she may even now be near me, but taken so ill she can't get Home; or, she may have dyed suddenly, in the Wood. I lay tumbling and tossing in great Anxiety, not able to find out any excusable Occasion she could have, of so long Absence. And then, thinks I, if she should either be

dead, or have quite left me, which will be of equally bad
Consequence to me, what can I do with three poor helpless
Infants. If they were a little more grown up, they might be
helpful to me, and to each other; but at their Age, how shall
I ever rear them, without the Tenderness of a Mother: And
to see them pine away before my Face, and not know how to
help them, will distract[1] me.

Finding I could neither Sleep, or lye still, I rose, intending
to search all the Woods about, and call to her, that if any
Accident had prevented Sight of her, she might at least hear
me. But upon opening the Door, and just stepping out, how
agreeably was I surprized, to meet her coming in, with something on her Arm. My dear *Youwarkee*, says I, where have
you been? What has befallen you to keep you out so long?
The poor Children have been at their Wit's end to find you;
and I, my Dear, have been unconsolable; and was now, almost
distracted, coming in search of you.

Youwarkee looked very blank, to think what Concern she
had given me and the Children. My dearest *Peter*, says she,
(kissing me) pray forgive the only thing I have ever done to
offend you, and the last Cause you shall ever have, by my
good Will, to complain of me; but walk within Doors, and
I will give you a farther Account of my Absence. Don't you
remember what delight I took the other Day to hear you talk
of your Ship? Yes, says I, you did so, but what of that? Nay,
pray, says she, forgive me for I have been to see it. That's
impossible, says I: And truly this was the first time I ever
thought she went about to deceive me. I do assure you, says
she, I have; and a wonderful Thing it is; but if you distrust
me, and what I say, I have brought Proof of it; step out with me
to the Verge of the Wood, and satisfy yourself. But pray, says
I, who presented you with this upon your Arm? I vow, says
she, I had forgot this; yes, this will, I believe, confirm to you
what I have said. I turn'd it over and over; and looking wish-
fully upon her, says I, this Waistcoat, indeed, is the very
fellow to one that lay in the Captain's Locker, in the Cabbin.
Say not the very fellow, says she, but rather say the very same;

for I'll assure you it is so; and had you been with me, we might have got so many things for ourselves and the Children, we should never have wanted more, tho' we lived these hundred Years; but as it is, I have left something without the Wood, for you to bring up. When we had had our Talk out, she hearing the Children stir, took them up, and was going, as she always did, to get their Breakfasts. Hold, says I, this Journey must have fatigued you too much already, lay yourself to Rest, and leave every thing else to me. My Dear, says she, you seem to think this Flight tiresome, but you are mistaken; I am more weary with Walking to the Lake, and back again, than with all the Rest. Oh, says she, if you had but the *Graundee*, flying would rest you, after the greatest Labour; for the Parts which are moved with Exercise on the Earth, are all at Rest in Flight; as, on the contrary, the Parts used in Flight are, when on earthly Travel. The whole Trouble of Flight is, in mounting from the plain Ground; but when once you are upon the *Graundee*, at a proper Height, all the rest is Play, a meer Trifle; you need only think of your Way, and incline to it, your *Graundee* directs you as readily as your Feet obey you on the Ground, without thinking of every Step you take: it does not require Labour, as your Boat does, to keep you a going.

After we had composed ourselves, we walked to the Verge of the Wood, to see what Cargo my Wife had brought from the Ship. I was astonished at the Bulk of it; and seeing, by the outside, it consisted of Cloaths, I took it, with much ado, upon my Shoulders, and carried it Home. But upon opening it, I found far more Treasure than I could have imagined: for there was a Hammer, a great many Spikes and Nails, three Spoons, about five Plates of Pewter, four Knives and a Fork, a small China Punch Bowl, two Chocolate Cups, a Paper of Needles, and several of Pins, a Parcel of coarse Thread, a pair of Shoes, and Abundance of such other things as she had heard me Wish for and Describe; besides as much Linnen and Woollen, of one Sort or another, as made a good Package for all the other things; with a great Tin Porridge Pot, of about two Gallons, tyed to the outside: and all these as nicely stowed, as if she had been bred a Packer.

When I had viewed the Bundle, and poized the Weight; how was it possible, my dear *Youwarkee*, said I, for you to bring all this? You could never carry them in your Hands. No, no, replied she, I carried them on my Back. Is it possible says I, for your *Graundee* to bear yourself and all this Weight too, in the Air, and to such an Height as the Top of these Rocks? You will always, replies she, make the Height a part of your Difficulty in flying; but you are deceived; for as the first Stroke, (I have heard you say often) in Fighting, is half the Battle, so it is in Flying; get but once fairly on the Wind, nothing can hurt you afterwards. My Method, let me tell you, was this: I clim'd to the highest part of the Ship, where I could stand clear, having first put up my Burthen, which you have there; and then, getting that on my Back, near my Shoulders, I took the two Cords you see hang loose to it, in my two Hands, and extending my *Graundee*, leaped off, flat-wise, with my Face towards the Water; when, instantly, playing two or three good Strokes with my *Graundee*, I was out of Danger: Now, if I had found the Bundle too heavy to make my first Strokes with, I should directly have turned on my Back, dropped my Bundle, and floated in my *Graundee* to the Ship again, as you once saw me float on the Lake. Says I, you must have flown a prodigious Distance to the Ship, for I was several Days sailing, I believe three Weeks, from my Ship, before I reached the Gulph; and after that, could be little less than five Weeks, (as I accounted for it) and at a great Rate of Sailing too, under the Rock, before I reached the Lake; so that the Ship must be a monstrous Way off. No, no, says she, your Ship lies but over yon Cliff, that rises as it were with two Points; and as to the Rock itself, it is not broader than our Lake is long: But what made you so tedious in your Passage was, many of the windings and turnings in the Cavern returning into themselves again; so that you might have gone round and round 'till this time, if the Tide had not luckily struck you into the direct Passage: This, says she,

I have heard from some of my Countrymen, who have flown up it, but could never get quite thro'.

I wish with all my Heart, says I, Fortune had brought me first to Light in this Country; or (but for your Sake I could almost say) had never brought me into it at all: For, to be a Creature of the least Significancy of the whole Race about one, is a melancholy Circumstance. Fear not, says she, my Love, for you have a Wife will hazard all for you, tho' you are restrained: And as my Inclinations and Affections are so much yours, that I need but know your Desires, to execute them, as far as my Power extends; surely you, who can act by another, may be content to forego the Trouble of your own Performance. I perceive, indeed, continued she, you want mightily to go to your Ship, and are more uneasy, now you know it is safe, than you was before; but that being past my Skill to assist you in, if you will command your Deputy, to go backwards and forwards in your stead, I am ready to obey you.

Thus ended our Conversation about the Ship for that time. But it left not my Mind so soon; for a stronger Hankering after it pursued me now than ever, since my Wife's Flight; but to no purpose.

We sat us down, and sorted out our Cargo, Piece by Piece; and having found several things proper for the Children, my Wife longed to enter upon some piece of Work towards Cloathing *Pedro*, in the Manner she had heard me talk of; and laid hard at me, to shew her the Use of the Needles, Thread, and other things she had brought. Indeed, I must say, she proved very tractable; and from the little Instruction I was able to give her, soon outwrought my Knowledge: For I could only shew her that the Thread went thro' the Needle, and both thro' the Cloth to hold it together; but for any thing else I was as ignorant as she. In much less Time than I could have imagined, she had cloathed my Son *Pedro*, and had made a sort of Mantle for the youngest. But now, seeing us so smart, (for I took upon me sometimes to wear the green Waistcoat she had brought, under my dirty Jacket) she began to be ashamed of herself, as she said, in our fine Company; and afterwards (as I shall soon acquaint you) got into our Fashion.

Seeing the Advantages of her Flight to the Ship, and that so many Conveniencies arose from it, she was frequently at me to let her go again. I should as much have wished for another Return of Goods, as she, but I could by no Means think of parting with my Factor; for I knew her Eagerness to please me, and that she would stick at nothing to perform it; and, thinks I, should any Accident happen to her, by over loading, or otherwise, and I should lose her, all the other Commodities of the whole World put together would not compensate her Loss. But as she so earnestly desired it, and assured me she would run no hazards, I was prevailed on at length, by her incessant Importunities, to let her go; tho' under certain Restrictions, which she promised me to comply with. As first, I insisted upon it, that she should take a Tour quite round the Rock; setting out the same way I had last gone with my Boat; and, if possible, find out the Gulph, which I told her she could not mistake, by Reason of the Noise the Fall of the Water made; and desired her to remark the Place, so as I might know, within Side, where it was without. And then, I told her, she might review and search every Hole in the Ship as she pleas'd; and if there were any small things she had a Mind to bring from it, she was welcome, provided the Bundle she should make up, was not above a fourth part either of the Bulk or Weight of the last. All which, she having engaged punctually to observe, she bid me not expect her 'till I saw her, and she would return as soon as possible. I then went with her to the Confines of the Wood, (for I told her I desired to see her mount) and she, after we had embraced, bidding me to stand behind her, took her Flight.

L

CHAPTER XX

*The Author observes her Flight; a Description of
a* Glumm *in the* Graundee; *she finds out the Gulph,
not far from the Ship; brings Home more Goods;
makes her a Gown by her Husband's Instruction*

I HAD ever since our Marriage been desirous of seeing
Youwarkee fly, but this was the first Opportunity I had of it;
and indeed the Sight was worthy of all the Attention I paid
it; for I desired her, slowly, to put herself in proper Order
for it, that I might make my Observation the more accurately;
and shall now give you an Account of the whole Apparatus:
Tho' several Parts of the Description were taken from subse-
quent Views; for it would have been impossible to have made
just Remarks of every thing at that once, especially as I only
view'd her back Parts then.

I told you before, I had seen her *Graundee* open, and quite
extended, as low as her Middle; but that being in the Grotto,
by Lamplight, I could not take so just a Survey as now, when
the Sort of Light we ever had was at the brightest.

She first threw up two long Branches or Ribbs of the Whalebone, as I called it before, (and indeed, for several of its
Properties, as Toughness, Elasticity, and Plyableness, nothing
I have ever seen can so justly be compared to it) which were
jointed behind to the upper Bone of the Spine, and which,
when not extended, lye bent over the Shoulders, on each side
of the Neck forwards, from whence, by nearer and nearer
Approaches, they just meet at the lower Rim of the Belly, in
a sort of Point;* but when Extended, they stand their whole
Length above the Shoulders, not perpendicularly, but spreading outwards, with a Webb of the softest and most plyable
and springy Membrane, that can be imagined, in the Interspace between them, reaching from their Root or Joint on
the Back, up above the hinder part of the Head, and near

* Plate I.

half way their own length;* but, when closed, the Membrane
falls down in the Middle, upon the Neck, like an Handkerchief.†
There are also two other Ribs, rising as it were from the same
Root, which, when open, run horizontally, but not so long as
the others.‡ These are filled up, in the Interspace between
them and the upper ones, with the same Membrane; and on
the lower Side of this is also a deep Flap of the Membrane, so
that the Arms can be either above or below it in Flight; and
are always above it when closed. This last Rib, when shut,
flaps under the upper one, and also falls down with it before,
to the Waist, but is not join'd to the Ribs below. Along the
whole Spine-bone runs a strong flat broad grisly[1] Cartilage,
to which are join'd several other of these Ribs; all which open
horizontally, and are filled in the Interspaces with the above
Membrane, and are jointed to the Ribs of the Person just
where the Plane of the Back begins to turn towards the Breast
and Belly; and, when shut, wrap the Body round to the Joints
on the contrary Side, folding neatly one Side over the other.
At the lower Spine are two more Ribs, extended horizontally
when open, jointed again to the Hips, and long enough to meet
the Joint on the contrary side cross the Belly; and from the
Hip Joint, which is on the outermost Edge of the Hip-Bone,
runs a plyable Cartilage quite down the outside of the Thigh
and Leg to the Ancle; from which there branch out divers
other Ribs, horizontally also, when open, but when closed
they encompass the whole Thigh and Leg, rolling inwards,
cross the back of the Leg and Thigh, till they reach and just
cover the Cartilage. The Interspaces of these are also filled
up with the same Membrane. From the two Ribs which join
to the lower Spine-bone there hangs down a sort of short
Apron, very full of Plaits, from Hip Joint to Hip Joint, and
reaches below the Buttocks, half way or more to the Hams.§
This has also several small limber Ribs in it. Just upon the
lower Spine-Joint, and above the Apron, as I call it, there are
two other long Branches, which, when close, extend upon the
Back, from the point they join at below to the Shoulders,

* Plate III.   † Plate II.   ‡ Plate III.   § Plate II.

where each Rib has a Clasper, which, reaching over the Shoulders, just under the Fold of the uppermost Branch or Ribs, hold up the two Ribs flat to the Back, like a V;* the Interspaces of which are also filled up with the aforesaid Membrane. This last piece, in flight, falls down almost to the Ancles;† where the two Claspers, lapping under each Leg, within side, hold it very fast; and then also the short Apron is drawn up, by the strength of the Ribs in it, between the Thighs forward, and covers the Pudenda and Groin, as far as the Rim of the Belly.‡ The whole Arms are covered also from the Shoulders to the Wrist with the same delicate Membrane, fastened to Ribs, of proportionable Dimensions, and jointed to a Cartilage on the outside, in the same Manner as on the Legs.

It is very surprizing to feel the Difference of these Ribs when open, and when closed; for, closed, they are as plyable as the finest Whalebone, or more so, but, when extended, are as strong and stiff as a Bone. They are tapering, from the Roots; and are broader or narrower, as best suits the Places they occupy and the Stress they are put to, up to their Points: which are almost as small as a Hair. The Membrane between them is the most elastic thing I ever met with; occupying no more Space, when the Ribs are closed, than just from Rib to Rib, as flat and smooth as possible; but, when extended, in some Postures, will dilate itself surprizingly. This will be better comprehended by the Plates, as to the Machinery, where you will see several Figures of *Glumms* and *Gawrys* in different Attitudes, than can be exprest by Words.

As soon as my Wife had expanded the whole *Graundee*, being upon plain Ground, she stooped forward, moving with a heavy rigling[1] motion at first, which put me into some Pain for her: but after a few Strokes, beginning to rise a little, she cut thro' the Air like Lightning; and was soon over the Edge of the Rock, and out of my Sight.

It is the most amazing thing in the World to observe the large Expansion of this *Graundee*, when open; and when

* Plate II. † Plate IV. ‡ Plate III.

closed, (as it all is in a Moment, upon the Party's descent) to see it sit so close and compact to the Body, as no Taylor can come up to it; and then the several Ribs lye so justly disposed in the several Parts, that instead of being, as one would imagine, a Disadvantage to the Shape, they make the Body and Limbs look extreamly elegant; and by the different Adjustment of their Lines, on the Body and Limbs, the whole, to my Fancy, somewhat resembles the Dress of the old Roman Warriors, in their Buskins; and to Appearance seems much more noble than any factitious[1] Garb I ever saw, or can frame a Notion of to myself.

Tho' these People, in height, shape, and limb, very much resemble the *Europeans*, there is yet this Difference; that their Bodies are rather broader and flatter, and their Limbs, tho' as long, and well shaped, are seldom so thick as ours: And this I observed generally in all I saw of them, during a long time among them afterwards: But their Skin, for Beauty and Fairness, exceeds ours very much.

My Wife having now taken her second Flight, I went home, and never left my Children 'till her Return. This was three Days after our parting. I was in Bed, with my little ones, when she knocked at the Door. I soon let her in, and we received each other with a glowing welcome. The News she brought me was very agreeable. She told me, she first went and pryed into every Nook in the Ship; where she had seen such things, could we get at them, as would make us very happy. Then she set out the way I told her to go, in order to find the Gulph. She was much afraid she should not have discovered it, tho' she flew very slow, that she might be sure to hear the Water-fall, and not over shoot it. It was long 'ere she came at it; but, when she did, she perceiv'd she might have spared most of her Trouble, had she set out the other way; for after she had flown almost round the Island, and not before, she began to hear the Fall, and upon coming up to it, found it to be not above six Minutes flight from the Ship. She said, the Entrance was very narrow, and, she thought, lower than I represented it; for she could scarce discern any Space between the Surface of the Water and the Arch-way of the Rock. I told her, that might happen from the rise or fall of the Sea itself. But I was glad to hear the Ship was no farther from the Gulph; for my Head was never free from the thoughts of my Ship and Cargoe. She then told me, she had left a small Bundle for me without the Wood, and went to look after her Children. I brought up the Bundle: And tho' it was not near so large as the other, I found several useful things in it, wrapped up in four or five Yards of dark blue Woollen Cloth, which I knew no Name for, but which was thin and light, and about a Yard wide. I asked her where she met with this Stuff? She answered, where there was more of it, under a thing like our Bed, in a Cloth like our Sheet, which she cut open, and took it out of. Well, says I, and what will you do with this? Why, I will make me a Coat, like yours, says she, for I don't like to look different from my dear Husband and Children. No *Youwarkee*, replied I, you must not do so; if you make such a Jacket as mine, there will be no Distinction between *Glumm* and *Gawry*;* the *Gawren Praave*,† in my Country, would not on any Account go dressed like a *Glumm*; for they wear a fine flowing Garment, called a Gown, that sits tight about the Waist, and hangs down from thence in folds, like your *Barras*,‡ almost to the Ground, so that you can hardly discern their Feet, and no other part of their Body but their Hands and Face, and about as much of their Necks and Breasts as you shew in your *Graundee*.

Youwarkee seemed highly delighted with this new fancied Dress, and worked Day and Night at it, against the cold Weather. Whilst she employed herself thus, I was busied in providing my Winter Stores; which I was forced to do alone now, herself and Children taking up all my Wife's time. About a Fortnight after she had began Mantuamaking,[1] she presented herself to me one Day, as I came from Work, in her new Gown. And truly, considering the scanty Description

---

* Man and Woman.
† Modest Women.
‡ The back Flap of the *Graundee*.

I had given her of such a Garment, it appeared a good comely Dress. Tho' it had not one Plait about the Body, it sat very tight thereto, and yet hung down full enough for a Countess: for she would have put it all in, all the Stuff she had, had there been as much more of it. I could see no Opening before, so asked her how she got it on. She told me, she laid along on the Ground, and crept thro' the Plaits at the Bottom, and sewed the Body round her, after she had got her Hands and Arms thro' the Sleeves. I wondered at her Contrivance, and smiling, shew'd her how she should put it on, and also how to Pin it before; and after she had done that, and I had turned up about half a Yard of Sleeve, which then hung down to her Fingers Ends, I kissed her, and called her my Country Woman, of which and her new Gown she was very proud for a long time.

CHAPTER XXI

The Author gets a Breed of Poultry, and by what means; builds them an House; how he managed to keep them in Winter

ONE Day as I was traversing the Woods, to view my Bird-traps, looking into the Underwood, among the great Trees on my right Hand, I saw a Wood Hen (a Bird I used to call so, from its Resemblance in Make to our *English* Poultry) come out of a little Thicket. I know not whether my Rustling, or what, had disturbed it, but I let her pass, and she ran away before me. When she was fairly out of sight, I stepped up, and found she had a Nest and sixteen Eggs there. I exactly marked the Place; and taking away one of the Eggs, I broke it, at some distance from the Nest, to see how forward they were; and I had no sooner broke the Shell, but out came a young Chicken. I then looked into the Nest again, and taking up more of the Eggs, I found them all just splintered in the Shell, and ready for Hatching. I had immediately a Desire to save them, and bring them up tame; but I was afraid if I took them away before they were hatched, and a little strengthened under the Hen, they would all dye, so I let them remain 'till next Day. In the mean while I prepared some small Netting, of such a proper Size, as I conceived would do; and with this I contrived, by fastning it to Stakes which I fixed in the Ground, to surround the Nest, and me on the outside of it. All the while I was doing this the Hen did not stir, so that I thought she had either been absent when I came, or had hatched and gone off with the young ones. As to her being gone, I was under no Concern, for I had no Design to catch her, but only to confine the Chickens within my Net, if they were hatched. But however I went nearer, and peeping in, found she sat still, squeezing herself as flat to the Ground as she could. I was in twenty Minds whether to take her first, and then catch the Chickens, or to let her go off, and then clap upon them; but as I proposed to let her go, I thought, if she would sit still 'till I had got the Chickens, that would be the best Way. So I softly kneeled down before her, and sliding my Hand under her, I gently drew out two, and put 'em in a Bag I had in my left Hand. I then dipped again and again, taking two every turn. But going a fourth time, as I was bringing out my Prize, the Hen jumped up, flew out, and made such a Noise, that tho' I the Minute before saw six or seven more Chicks in a Lump, where she had sat, and kept my Eye upon them, yet, before I could put the last two I had got into my Bag, these were all gone, and in three Hours search I could not find one of them; tho' I was sure they could not pass my Net, and must be within the compass of a small Room, my Toils inclosing no more: After tiring myself with looking for them, I marched home with those eight I had got.

I told *Youwarkee* what I had done, and how I intended to manage the little Brood, and, if I could, to bring them up tame. We kept them some Days very warm, by the Fire, and fed them often, as I had seen my Mother do with her early Chickens; and in a Fortnight's time they were as stout and familiar[1] as common Poultry. We kept them a long while in the House; and when I fed them I always used[1] them to a particular Whistle, which I also taught my Wife, that they might know both us and their feeding time; and in a very short while they would come running upon the usual Sound, like Barn-door Fowls to the Name of Biddy.[2]

There happened in this Brood to be five Hens and three Cocks; and they were now so tame, that, having cut their Wings, I let them out, when the Weather favoured, at my Door; where they would pick about in the Wood, and get best part of their Subsistance; and having used them to roost in a Corner of my Antichamber, they all came in very regularly at Night, and took their places. My Hens, at the usual Season, laid me abundance of Eggs, and hatched me a Brood or two, each, of Chickens; so that now I was at a Loss to know what to do with them, they were become so numerous. The Antichamber was no longer a proper Receptacle of such a Flock, and therefore I built a little House, at a small Distance from my own, on purpose for their Reception and Entertainment. I had by this time cleared a Spot of Ground, on one side of my Grotto, by burning up the Timber and Underwood which had covered it; this I inclos'd, and within that Inclosure I raised my Aviary; and my Poultry thrived well there, seem'd to like their Habitation, and grew very fat.

My Wife and I took much Delight in visiting and feeding 'em, and it was a fine Diversion also to my Boys; but at the end of Summer, when all the other Birds took their annual Flight, away went every one of my new raised Brood with them, and one of my old Cocks, the rest of the old set remaining very quiet with me all the Winter. The next Summer, when my Chicks of that Year grew up a little, I cut their Wings, and by that Means preserved all but one; which I suppose was either not cut so close as the rest, or his Wings had grown again. From this Time I found by long Experience, that not two, out of an hundred that had once wintered with me, would ever go away, tho' I did not cut their Wings; but all of the same Season would certainly go off with the Wild ones, if they could any ways make a Shift to fly. I afterwards got

a Breed of black Necks; which was a Name I gave them from
the peculiar Blackness of their Necks, let the rest of their
Bodies be of what Colour they would, as they were indeed of
all Colours. These Birds were as big or bigger than a Turkey,
of a delicious Flavour, and were bred from Turkey Eggs,
hatched under my own Wood Hens, in great plenty. I was
forced to clip these, as I did the other young Fowl, to keep
'em; and at length they grew very tame, and would return
every Night during the dark Season. The greatest Difficulty
now was, to get Meat for all these Animals, in the Winter,
when they would sit on the Roost two Days together, if I did
not call and feed them; which I was sometimes forced to do
by Lamp-light, or they would have starved in cloudy Weather.
But I overcame that want of Food by an accidental Discovery;
for I observ'd my Blacknecks, in the Woods, jump many times
together at a sort of little round Heads or Pods, very dry,
which hung plentifully upon a Shrub that grew in great
Abundance there. I cut several of these Heads, and carrying
them home with me broke them, and took out a Spoonful or
more from each Head of small yellow Seeds; which giving
to my Poultry, and finding they greedily devoured them,
I soon laid in a Stock for twice my Number of Mouths;
so that they never after wanted. I tried several times to
raise a breed of Water Fowl, by hatching their Eggs under
my Hens; but not one in ten of the Sorts,[1] when hatched,
were fit to eat; and those that were, would never live and
thrive with me, but got away to the Lake, I having
no sort of Water nearer me: so I dropped my Design of
Water Fowl as impracticable. But by breeding and feeding my Land Fowl so constantly in my Farm-Yard, I
never wanted of that sort at my Table; where we eat
abundance of them: for my whole side of the Lake, in a
few Years, was like a Farm-Yard, so full of Poultry, that
I never knew my Stock; and upon the usual Whistle they
would flock round me from all Quarters. I had every
thing now but Cattle, not only for the Support, but Convenience and Pleasure of Life; and so happily should I

I have fared here, if I had had but a Cow and Bull, a Ram and Sheep, that I would not have changed my Dominions for the Crown of *England*.

CHAPTER XXII

Reflections on Mankind; the Author wants to be
with his Ship; projects going, but perceives it
impracticable; Youwarkee offers her Service, and
goes; an Account of her Transactions on Board;
Remarks on her Sagacity; she dispatches several
Chests of Goods through the Gulph to the Lake; an
Account of a Danger she escaped; the Author has
a Fit of Sickness

STRANGE is the Temper of Mankind, who, the more they enjoy, the more they covet. Before I received any Return from my Ship, I rested tolerably easy, and but seldom thought upon what I had left behind me in her; thinking myself happy in what I had, and compleatly so, since my Union with my dear Wife. But after I had got what I could never have expected, I grew more and more perplexed for want of the rest; and thought I should never enjoy true Happiness while even a Plank of the Ship remained. My Head, be I where I would, or at what I would, was ever on board. I wished for her in the Lake, and could I but have got her thither, I thought I should be an Emperor. And tho' I wanted for nothing to maintain Life, and had so good a Wife and five Children I was very fond of, yet the one thing I had not, reduced the Comfort of all the rest to a scanty Pattern, even so low as to destroy my whole Peace. I was even mad enough to think of venturing up the Cavern again, but was restrained from the Attempt by the certain impracticableness of it. Then I thought *Youwarkee* should make another trip to the Ship: But what can she bring from it, says I to myself, in respect of what must be left

behind? Her whole Life won't suffice to clear it in, at the Rate
she can fetch the Loading hither, in Parcels. At last a Project
started; that as there were so many Chests on Board,
Youwarkee should fill some of them, and send them thro'
the Gulph, to take their Chance for the Lake. This, at first
Sight, seemed feasable; but then I considered, how they could
be got from the Ship to the Gulph; and, again, that they
would never keep out the Water, and if they fill'd, with
a lading in them, they would sink; or, if this did not happen,
they might be dashed to pieces against the Craggs in the
Cavern. These Apprehensions stopped me again; 'till, unwilling to quit the thought, true, says I, this may happen to
some, but if I get but one in five, it is better than nothing. Thus
I turned and wound the Affair in my Mind; but Objections
still started, too obstinate to be conquered.

In the height of my Soliloquy, in comes *Youwarkee*; and
seeing my dejected Look, would needs know the meaning of
it. I told her plainly, that I could get no rest from Day to Day,
ever since she first went to the Ship, to think such a number
of good Things lay there, to be a Prey to the Sea, as the Ship
wasted, when they might be of such infinite Service here;
and that since her last Flight I had suffered the more, when
I thought how near the Gulph was to the Ship: So that could
I but get thither myself, with my Boat, I would contrive to
pack up the Goods in the Chests that were on Board, and,
carrying them in the Boat, drop them near the Draft of the
Water, which of itself would suck them under the Rock, down
the Gulph; and when they were passed thro' the Cavern,
I might take them up in the Lake. Well, says she, *Peter*, and
why can't I do this for you? No, says I, even this has its
Objections. Then I told her what I feared of their taking
Water, or dashing against the Rock, and twenty other ways
of frustrating my Views; but above all, says I, how can you
get such large and weighty things to the Gulph without a Boat?
There is another Impossibility! it won't do.

Youwarkee eyed me attentively. Prithee, my dear *Peter*,
says she, set your Heart at rest about that. I can only try; if

no good is to be done, you shall soon know it, and must rest contented under the Disappointment. I told her, if I was there, I could take all the Things out of a Chest, and then melt some Pitch, and pour into every Crack, to keep out the Water, when they were set a Float. Pitch, says she, what's that? Why, says I, that is a nasty, hard, black, sticking thing, that stands in Tubs in the Ship; and which, being put over the Fire, in any thing to melt, will grow liquid; and, when it is cold, be hard again; and will resist the Water and keep it out. Says she, how can I put this Pitch within side of the Chest lid, when I have tyed it up? It is to no manner of purpose, says I, to talk of it, so there's an end of it. But, says she, suppose yourself there, what Things would you bring first? I then entered into a long detail of Particulars, saying, I would have this and that, and so on, 'till I had scarce left out a Thing I either knew of or could suppose to be in the Ship; and for fear I had not mentioned all, says I, at last, if I was there, I believe I should leave but little portable behind me.

So, so, my dear, says *Youwarkee*, you would roll in Riches, I find, but you have mentioned never a new Gown for me. Why ay, says I, I would have that too. But how would you melt the Pitch? says she. O, says I, there is a Tinder-Box and Matches, in a Room below, upon the side of the Fire Hearth; and then I let her see one I had brought with me, and shew'd her the Use of the Flint and Steel. Well, my Dear, says she, will you once more trust me? I told her, her going would be of little more Use than to get a second Gown, or some such thing; but if she was desirous, I would let her make another Flight, on her Promise to be back as soon as possible.

In the Evening she set out, and stayed two Days, and 'till the Night of the third. I would here observe, that tho' it was much lighter and brighter on the outside of the Rock, where the Ship lay, than with us at *Graundevolet*, yet, having always her Spectacles with her, I heard no more complaint of the Glare of Light she used to be so much afraid of: Indeed she always avoided the Fire and Lamp at home, as much as she could; because she generally took off her Spectacles within

Doors; but when at any time she had them on, she could bear both well enough.

Upon her Return again, she told me she had shipped some Goods to Sea for me, which she hoped would arrive safe, (for by this time, she had had my seafaring Terms so often over, she could apply them very properly) and that they were in six Chests, which she had pitched after my Directions. Ay, says I, you have pitched them into the Sea, perhaps, but after my Directions, I am satisfied, was beyond your Ability. You *Glumms*, says she, think us *Gawrys* very ignorant, but I'll satisfy you we are not so dull of Apprehension as you would make us; did not you show me, one Day, how your Boat was tarred and caulked, as you call it? I did, says I, what then? I'll tell you, says she. When I had emptied the first Chest, and set it properly, I looked about for your Pitch, which, at last, I found by it's sticking to my Fingers; I then put a good Piece into a sort of a little Kettle, with a long Handle, that lay upon the Pitch.—O, the Pitch Ladle, says I.—I know not what you call it, says she, but then I made a Fire, as you told me, and melted that Stuff; afterwards turning up the Chest sideways, and then endways, I poured it into it, and let it settle in the Cracks, and with an old Stocking, such as yours, dipped into the Pitch, I rubbed every place where the Boards joined. I then set the Chest on the side of the Ship, and when the Pitch was cold and hardned in it, filled it top full of things. But when I had done thus, and shut the Lid, I found that would not come so close, but I could get the Blade of a Knife thro', any where between it and the Chest; whereupon, I cut some long Slips of the Cloth I was packing up, and fitting them all round the Edge of the Chest, I dipped them into the Pitch, and laid them on hot; and where one Slip would not do, I put two; and shutting the Lid down close upon them, I nailed it, as I had seen you do some things, quite round; then tying a Rope to the Handle, I tipped the Chest into the Sea, holding the Rope; I watched it some time, and seeing it swim well, I took flight, with the Rope in my Hand, and drew the Chest after me to the Gulph, when, letting go the Rope, away it went.

I served five more in the same Manner. And now, my dearest, I am here to tell you, I hope you will be able to see at least some of them, one time or other, in the Lake.

I admired in all this at the Sagacity of the Gawrys. Alas! thinks I, what narrow hearted Creatures are Mankind? Did not I heretofore look upon the poor Blacks in *Africa* as little better than Beasts, 'till my friend *Glandlipze* convinced me, by disabling the Crocodile, the Passage of the River, and several other Atchievements, that my own Excellencies might have perished in a Desert, without his Genius; and now what could I, or almost any of us Master-pieces of the Creation (as we think ourselves) and Heavens peculiar Favourites have done, in this present Case, that has been omitted by this Woman, (for I may justly stile her so in an eminent Degree) and that in a way to which she was bred an utter Stranger.

After what I had heard from *Youwarkee*, I grew much more cheerful; which she (poor Creature) was remarkably pleased with. She went with me constantly once, and sometimes twice, a Day, for several Days together, to see what Success at the Lake; 'till at length she grew very impatient, for fear, as she afterwards told me, I should either think she had not done what she said, or had done it in an ineffectual Manner. But one Day, walking by the Lake, I thought I saw something floating in the Water, at a very great Distance. *Youwarkee*, says I, I spy a Sail; then running to my Boat, and taking her in, away we went, plying my Oars with all my might, for I longed to see what it was. At nearer View I perceived it to be one of my Wife's Fleet. But what added to my Satisfaction, was, to see *Youwarkee* so pleased, for she could scarcely contain herself.

When we came close to it, up she started; now, my dear *Peter*, says she, torment yourself no more about your Goods on Board, for if this will do, all shall be your own. She then lent me a Hand to take it in; but we had both Work enough to compass it, the Wood had soaked in so much Water. We then made the best of our way homewards to my wet Dock; when, just as we had landed our Treasure, we saw two more

Boxes coming down the Stream, both together; whereupon we launched again, and brought them in, one by one: For I did not care to trust them both on one Bottom, my Boat being in Years, and grown somewhat crazy.[1]

We had now made a good Day's Work of it; so, mooring the Boat, we went home, intending to be out next Morning early with the Cart, to convey our Imports to the Grotto.

After Supper, *Youwarkee*, looking very earnestly at me, with Tears just glittering in her Eyes, broke out in these Words, What should you have thought, *Peter*, to have seen me come sailing, drowned, thro' the Cavern, tied to one of your Chests? Heaven forbid such a Thought! my Charmer, says I. But, as you know I must have been rendered the most miserable of all living Creatures by such a Sight, or any thing else that would deprive me of you; pray tell me how you could possibly have such a Thought in your Head? She saw she had raised my Concern, and was very sorry for what she had said. Nothing, nothing, says she, my Dear; it was only a Fancy just come into my Head. My dear *Youwee*, says I, you must let me know what you mean; I am in great Pain till you explain yourself: for I am sure there is something more in what you say than Fancy; therefore, pray, if you love me, keep me on the Rack no longer. Ah! *Peter*, says she, there was but a Span between me and Death, not many Days ago; and when I saw the Line of the last Chest we took up just now, it gave me so much Horror, I could scarce keep upon my Feet. My Dear *Youwee*, proceed, says I, for I can't bear my Torment 'till I have heard the worst. Why, *Peter*, says she, now the Danger is over, I shall tell you my Escape, with as much Pleasure as I guess you will take in hearing of it. You must know, my Life, says she, that having cast that Chest into the Sea, as I was tugging it along, by that very Line, it being one of the heaviest, and moving but slowly, I twisted the String several times round my Hand, one Fold upon another, the easier to tow it; when, drawing it rather too quick into the Eddy, it pulled so hard against me, towards the Gulph, and so quick, that I could no way loosen or disengage the Cord from my

Fingers, but was drag'd thereby to the very Rock; against which the Chest struck violently: My last Thought, as I supposed it, was of you, my Dear, (on which she clasped me round the Neck, in sense of her past Agony;) when, taking myself for lost, I forbore further Resistance; at which Instant the Line, slackning by the Rebound of the Chest, fell from my Hand of itself; and the Chest, returning to the Rock, went down the Current. I took a Turn or two round on my Graundee, to recollect my past Danger, and went back to the Ship, fully resolved to avoid the like Snare for the future. Indeed I did not easily recover my Spirits, and was so terrify'd with the Thought, that I had half a Mind to have left the two remaining Chests behind me: But, as Danger overcome gives fresh Resolution, I again set to work, and discharged them also down the Gulph, as I hope you will see in good Time.

My Heart bled within me all the while she spoke; and I even felt ten Times more than she could have suffered by the Gulph. My dearest *Youwee*, says I, why did not you tell me this Adventure sooner? It is too soon I fear now, says she; for she then saw the Colour forsake my Lips, my Eyes grow languid, and myself dropping into her Arms. She screamed out, and ran to the Chest, where all was empty; but turning every Bottle up, and, from the remaining Drops in each, collecting a small Quantity of Liquor, and putting it by little and little to my Lips, and rubbing my Wrists and Temples, she brought me to myself again: But I continued so extreamly sick for some Days after, that it was above a Week before I could get down with my Cart to fetch up my Chests.

When I was able to go down, *Youwarkee* would not venture me alone, but went herself with me. We then found two more of the Chests, which we landed; and I had Work sufficient for two or three Days, in getting them all up to the Grotto, they were so heavy, and all the way thro' the Wood being up Hill.

We had five in Hand, and watched several Days for the sixth, when seeing nothing of it, we gave it over for lost. But one Day, as I was going for Water, *Youwarkee* would go with me, and urged our carrying the Net, that we might drag for

M

some Fish. Accordingly we did so. And now having taken
what we wanted, we went to the Rill, and pushing in the Head
of the Boat (as I usually did, for by that means I could fill the
Vessel as I stood on board) the first thing that appeared was
my sixth Chest. *Youwarkee* spyed it first, and cry'd, pointing
thereto, O *Peter*, what we have long wished for, and almost
despaired of, is come at last; let us meet and welcome it.
I was pleas'd with the Gaiety of her Fancy; I did as she
desired; we got it into the Boat, after merrily saluting it, and
so returned home. It took us up several Days time in searching,
sorting, and disposing our Cargoe, and drying the Chests:
For the Goods themselves were so far from being wetted or
spoiled, that even those in the last Chest, which had lain so
long in the Water, had not taken the least Moisture.

Youwarkee was quite alert at the Success of her packing,
but left me to ring her Praises: which I did not fail of doing,
more than once, at unpacking each Chest, and could see her
Eyes glow with Delight, to see she had so pleased me.

She had been so curious as to examine almost every thing
in the Ship; and as well of Things I had described, and she
did know, as of what she did not, brought me something for
a Sample: But, above all, had not forgot the blue Stuff; for
the moment she had seen that, she destin'd it to the Use of
herself and Children.

CHAPTER XXIII

The Religion of the Author's Family

YOUWARKEE and I having fixed ourselves by degrees into
a settled Rota of Action, began to live like Christians; having
so great a Quantity of most sorts of Necessaries about us.
But I say we lived like Christians, on another Account; for
you must not think, after what I have said before, that I and
my Family lived like Heathens: No, I'll assure you, they, by

degrees, knew all I knew; and that, with a little artificial Improvement, and a well regulated Disposition, I hoped, and did not doubt, would carry them all to Heaven. I would many a Time have given all my Interest in the Ship's Cargoe for a Bible; and a hundred Times griev'd that I was not Master of a Pocket one, which I might have carried every where about me. I never imagin'd there was one aboard; and if there were, and *Youwarkee* should find it, I suppos'd it would be in *Portugueze*, which I knew little of; so it would be of small Service to me, if I had it.

Since I am upon the Topic of Religion, it may not be amiss, once for all, to give you a small Sketch of my religious Proceedings, after coming into my new Dominions. I have already told you, that, from my first Stop at the Rock, I had prayed constantly Morning and Evening; but I can't say I did it always with the same Efficacy. However, my imperfect Devotions were not without good Effect: And I am confident, wherever this Course is pursued with a right View, sooner or later the Issue will prove the same to others as I found it to myself:—I mean, that Mercies will be remembered with more Gratitude, and Evils be more disregarded, and become less burthensome: And surely the Person whose Case this is, must necessarily enjoy the truest Relish of Life. As daily Prayer was my Practice, in answer to it I obtained the greatest Blessing and Comfort my solitude was capable of receiving: I mean my Wife; whose Character I need not farther attempt to blazon, in any faint Colours of my own, after what has been already said; her Acts having spoken her Virtues beyond all verbal Description.

After we were married, as I call it, that is, after we had agreed to become Man and Wife, I frequently prayed before her, and with her, (for by this Time she understood a good deal of my Language;) at which, tho' contrary to my Expectation, she did not seem surprised, but readily kneeled by, and joyned with me. This I liked very well. And upon my asking her one Day, after Prayer, if she understood what I had been doing, (for I had a Notion she did not) Yes, verily, says she, you have been making Petitions to the Image of the great *Collwar*.* Pray, says I, (willing gently to lead her into a just Sense of a supreme Being) who is this *Collwar*? And where does he dwell? He it is, says she, that does all Good and Evil to us. Right, says I, it is in some Measure so; but he can't of himself do Evil, absolutely and properly, as his own Act. Yes, says she, he can; for he can do all that can be done; and as Evil can be done, he can do it. So quick a Reply startled me. Thinks I, she will run me a Ground presently; and from being a Doctor,[1] as I fancy'd myself, I shall become but a Pupil to my own Scholar. I then asked her where the great *Collwar* dwelt? She told me in Heaven, in a charming Place. And can he know what we do, says I? Yes, reply'd she, his Image tells him every thing; and I have prayed to his Image, which I have often seen; and it is filled with so much Virtue, that it is his second Self: For there is only one of them in the World; who is so good, he gives several Virtues to other Images of himself, which are brought to him, and put into his Arms to breath upon; and the only thing I have ever regretted since I knew you, is, that I have not one of them here to comfort and bless us and our Children.

Tho' I was sorry for the Oddity of her Conceptions, I was almost glad to find her so ignorant; and pleased myself with thinking, that as she had already a confused Notion of a supreme Power, I should soon have the Satisfaction of bringing her to a more rational Knowledge of him.

Pray, *Youwee*, says I, what is your God made of? Why of Clay, says she, finely painted; and looks so terrible, he would make you tremble to behold him. Do you think, says I, that is the true *Collwar*'s real Shape, if you could see himself? She told me yes; for that some of his best Servants had seen him, and took the Representation from himself. And, pray, do you think he loves his best Servants, as you call them, and is kind to them? You need not doubt it, says she. Why then, reply'd I, how came he to look so terrible upon them, when they saw him, as you say they did? For I can see no Reason,

* God.

how terrible soever he looks to others, why he should shew himself so to those he loves. I should rather think, as you say he is kind to them, that he should have two Images, a placid one for his good, and a terrible one for his bad, Servants. Or else, who by seeing him, can tell whether he is pleased or angry? For even you yourself, *Youwee*, when any thing pleases you, have a different Look from that you have when you are angry; and little *Pedro* can tell whether he does well or ill, by your Countenance: Whereas, if you made no Distinction, but looked with the same Face on all his Actions, he would as readily think he did well as ill in committing a bad Action. *Youwarkee* could not tell what to say to this, the Fact seeming against her.

I then asked her, if she thought the Image itself could hear her Petitions? She reply'd, yes. And can he, says I, return you an Answer? She told me, he only did that to his best Servants. Did you ever hear him do it? says I: For unless he can speak too, I should much suspect his hearing; and you being one of his best Servants, seeing you love him, and pray heartily to him, why should you not hear him as soon as others? No, says she, there are a great Number of Glumms on purpose to serve him, pray for us to him, and receive his Answers. But to what Purpose then, says I, is your praying to him, if their Prayer will serve your Turn? O, says she, the Image hears them sooner than us, and sends the Petitions up to the great *Collwar*, and lets him know who makes them, and desires him to let them have what they want. But suppose, says I, for Arguments sake, that you could see the great *Collwar*, or know where he was, and should pray to himself, without going about to his Image first; do you think he could not hear you? I can't tell that, says she. But how then, says I, can he tell what (if it could speak) his Image says, which is as far from him as you are? And, pray, do you think he can hear an Image which he did not make, which could not make itself, and which can neither hear, nor see, nor speak; better than he can hear a *Glumm* whom he did make, and who made that Image, and who himself can hear, and see, and speak to him? She paused here a good while. At last, says she, Why, truly, I cannot think but he might as well, or better, hear me than the Image. Why then, said I, don't you make your Petitions to himself, and not to the Image? It is for the Reason I have given you, my Dear *Youwarkee*, that I pray to him, and not to his Image, or any Representation of him upon Earth; and, consequently, am more sure of being heard and answered. Indeed, says she, I never thought of that before; for our *Ragans** always charged me to pray to the Image; or to let them know what I wanted, and they would pray to him for me; and they have had many a *Rappin†* of me for so doing, and sometimes two or three, when they told me I should have what I wanted: But you have convinced me it is better to pray to himself, and I shall always do it hereafter.

Having conducted my Scholar thus far, I left off, thinking I had now laid a solid Basis, that I need be in no fear for my Superstructure: And as the slower you build, the firmer it settles; I thought fit to let this first Work settle into a firm Principle, before I raised any further Doctrine upon it, which, as Occasion offered, I determined to pursue. I propagated no theological Notions in my Children, 'till they were capable of conceiving the Truth of them from Principles of Reason; but only inculcated on them Justice, Truth, and Love to myself, their Mother, and each other. Having brought my Wife firmly to believe in a supreme Being (let her call him what she would) who could hear our Prayers, see our Actions, and answer our Petitions as he sees fit; and to an Assurance that his Love to us is so great, that he will do what is most beneficial for us, tho' it should not always prove what we think so; the great Truths, concerning his Dispensations in our Creation and Redemption, and our Duty towards him, follow'd of course, as direct Consequences of such his Love and Knowledge of us; and she easily came into 'em. Accordingly, I opened the Doctrine of the Creation to her as well as I could. I am sorry to say, my Explication of this great Point

---

* Priests, or holy Men.
† Cake of Marmalade.

was not so just, so particular, and clear as it might have been, if I had had a Bible; any more than was the succeeding History of our Redemption: However, in general, I explained both so effectually, that tho' it required Time to ground her in the full practical Faith of it, yet the Opinion she had of me, and my Fidelity to her, with the Reasons I was able to urge for what I taught her, persuaded her I was in the Right, and disposed her to hearken to what I delivered; and then her own zealous Application, with God's Grace, soon brought her to a firm Belief in it, and a suitable Temper and Conduct with respect to God and Man.

After I had began with my Children, I frequently referred their further Instruction to their Mother; for I have always experienced, that a superficial Knowledge, with a Desire of becoming a Teacher, is, in some Measure, equivalent to better Knowledge: For it not only excites every Principle one has to the utmost, but makes Matters more clear and conspicuous even to oneself.

By these Means, and the divine Blessing thereon, in a few Years, I may fairly say, I had a little Christian Church in my own House, and in a flourishing way too, without a *Schismatick* or *Heretick* amongst us.

CHAPTER XXIV

The Author's Account of his Children; their Names;
they are exercised in Flying; his Boat crazy;
Youwarkee *intends a Visit to her Father, but first*
takes another Flight to the Ship; sends a Boat and
Chests thro' the Gulph; cloaths her Children; is with
Child again, so her Visit is put off; an Inventory of
the last Freight of Goods; the Author's Method
of treating his Children; Youwarkee, *her Son*
Tommy, *with her Daughters* Patty *and* Hallicarnie,
set out to her Father's

I HAD now lived here almost fourteen Years; and besides the
three Sons before-mentioned, had three Girls and one Boy.
Pedro, my eldest, had the *Graundee*, but too small to be useful;
my second Son, *Tommy*, had it compleat; so had my three
Daughters; but *Jemmy* and *David*, the youngest Sons, none
at all. My eldest Daughter I named *Patty*, because I always
call'd my first Wife so: I say, my first Wife, tho' I had no other
Knowledge of her Death than my Dream; but am from that as
verily perswaded, if ever I reach *England* I shall find it so, as
if I had heard it from her Aunt's own Mouth. My second
Daughter my Wife desired might be call'd by her Sister's
Name, *Hallicarnie*; and my Youngest I named *Sarah*, after
my Mother. I put you to the Trouble of writing down the
Names, for as I shall hereafter have frequent Occasion to
mention the Children severally, it will be pleasanter for myself and you to call them by their several Names of Distinction, than to call them my second Son, or my eldest
Daughter, and so forth.

My Wife now took great Delight in exercising *Tommy* and
Patty (who were big enough to be trusted) in flight, and would
often skim round the whole Island with them before I could
walk half thro' the Wood. And she would teach them also to
swim or sail; I know not which to call it, for sometimes you

should see them dart out of the Air, as if they would fall on their Faces into the Lake, when, coming near the Surface, they would stretch their Legs in an horizontal Posture, and in an Instant turn on their Backs, and then you could see nothing from the Bank, to all Appearance, but a Boat sailing along, the *Graundee* rising at their Head, Feet, and Sides, so like the Sides and Ends of a Boat, that you could not discern the Face, or any Part of the Body.* I own, I often envied them this Exercise, which they seemed to perform with more Ease than I could only shake my Leg, or stir an Arm.

Tho' we had perpetually *Swangeans* about us, and the Voices, as I used to call them, I could never once prevail on my Wife to shew herself, or to claim any Acquaintance with her Country-folks. And what is very remarkable in my Children, is, that my three Daughters and *Tommy*, who had the full *Graundee*, had exactly their Mother's Sight, *Jemmy* and *David* had just my Sight, and *Pedro*'s Sight was between both, tho' he was never much affected with any Light: But I was obliged to make Spectacles for *Tommy* and all my Daughters when they came to go abroad.

I had in this Time twice enlarged my Dwelling, which the Encrease of my Family had rendred necessary. The last Alteration I was enabled to do in a much better Manner, and with more Ease, than the first; for, by the Return of my Flota,[1] I had gotten a large Collection of useful Tools: Several of Iron, where the Handles or Wood-work preponderated the Iron; but such as were all, or greatest Part, of that Metal had got either to the Rock, or were so fast fixed to the Head of the Ship, that it was difficult to remove them; so that my Wife could get comparatively few of this latter Sort; tho' some she did. It was well, truly, I had these Instruments, which greatly facilitated my Labours; for I was forced to work harder now than ever, in making Provision for us all; and my Sons *Pedro* and *Tommy* commonly assisted. I had also had another Importation of Goods thro' the Gulph, which still added to my Convenience. But my Boat made me shudder every Time

* Plate V.

I went into her. She had leaked again and again, and I had patch'd her till I could scarce see a Bit of the old Wood. She was of unspeakable Use to me, and yet I could not venture myself in her, but with the utmost Apprehension and trembling. I had been intending a good while, now I had such Helps, to build a new one, but had been diverted by one Avocation or other.

About this Time, *Youwarkee*, who was now upwards of thirty-two Years of Age, the fondest Mother living, and very proud of her Children, had formed a Project of taking a Flight to *Arndrumnstake*, a Town in the Kingdom of *Doorpt Swangeanti*, as I called it, where her Father, if living, was a *Colamb*,* under *Georigetti* the Prince of that Country. She imparted her Desire to me, asking my Leave; and she told me, if I pleased, she would take *Patty* and *Tommy* along with her. I did not much dislike the Proposal, because of the great Inclination I had, for a long time, to a Knowledge of, and Familiarity with, her Countrymen and Relations; and now I had so many of her Children with me, I could not think she would ever be prevailed on, but by Force, to quit me and her Offspring, and be contented to loose six for the sake of having two with her; especially as she had shewed no more Love for them than the rest: So I made no Hesitation, but told her she should go.

I expected continually I should hear of her Departure; but she saying no more of it, I thought she had dropt her Design, and I did not chuse to mention it. But one Day, as we were at Dinner, looking mighty seriously, she said, My Dear, I have considered of the Journey you have consented I should take, but in order thereto it is necessary that I prepare several Things for the Children, especially those who have no *Graundee*, and I am resolved to finish them before I go, that we may appear with Decency, both here and at *Arndrumnstake*: For I am sure my Father, whose Temper I am perfectly acquainted with, will, upon Sight of me and my little ones, be so overjoyed, that he will forgive my Absence, and Marriage,

* Governor.

provided he sees Reason to believe I have not match'd un-
worthily, unbecoming my Birth; and after keeping me and
the Children with him, it may be two or three Months, will
accompany me home again himself, with a great Retinue of
Servants and Relations; or, at least, if he is either dead or
unable for Flight, my other Relations will come, or send
a Convoy to take Care of me and the Children: And, my Dear,
as I shall give them all the Encomiums I can of you, and of my
Situation with you, while I am among them; I would have
them a little taken with the Elegance of our domestick Condition when they come hither, that they may think me happy in
you and my Children: For I would not only put my Family
into a Condition to appear before them, but to surprize the
old Gentleman and his Company, who never in their Lives
saw any Part of Mankind with another Covering than the
Graundee. When she had done, I expressed my Approbation
of her whole System, as altogether prudent; and she proceeded immediately to put it in Execution. To work she went,
opened every Chest, and examined their Contents. But while
she was upon the hunt, and selecting such Things as she
thought fit for her Purpose, she recollected several Articles
she had observed in the Ship, which she judged far more for
her Turn, than any she had at home. Hereupon she prayed
me to let her take another Trip to the Vessel, and to carry
Tommy with her.

   After so many Trials, and such happy Experience of her
wise and fortunate Conduct, I consented to her Flight, and
away went she and her Son. Upon their Return, which was in
a few Days, she told me what they had been doing, and said,
as she so often heard me complain of the Age of my Boat, and
fear to sail in her, she had fitted me out a little Ship, and hoped
it would in due Time arrive safely. As she passed quickly on
to other Things, I never once thought of asking her what she
meant by the little Ship she spoke of; but must own, that like
a foolishly fond Parent, I was more intent on her telling me
how *Tommy* had found a Hoard of Playthings, which he had
packed up for his own Use.

As to this last Particular, I learn'd, by the Sequel of the Story, when the Spark, proud of his Acquisition, came to me, That he had been peeping about in the Cabin, whilst his Mother was packing the Chests, and seeing a small brass Knob in the Wainscot, took it for a Plaything, and pulling to get it out, opened a little Door of a Cupboard, where he had found some very pretty Toys, that he positively claim'd for himself: Among which were, a small plain gold Ring, and a very fine one set with Diamonds, which he shewed me upon two of his Fingers. I wondered how the Child, who had never before seen such Things, or the Use of them, should happen to apply these so properly; but he told me, in playing with this, meaning the Diamond Ring, about his Fingers, it slipped over his middle Finger Joint, and he could not get it off again, so he put the other upon another Finger to keep it Company.

We watched daily, as usual on such Occasions, for the Arrival of our Fleet. It was surprizing, that none of the Chests which *Youwarkee* shot down the Gulph were ever half so long in their Passage as I was myself, but some came in a Week, some in a few Days more, and even some in less: Which I attributed to their following directly the Course of the Water, shooting from Shelf to Shelf as the Tide set; and I believe my keeping the Boat I sailed in so strictly and constantly in the Middle of the Stream, was the Reason of my being detained there so long. In less than a Fortnight, every thing came safe but one Chest, which, as we never heard of it, I suppose was either sunk or bulged.[1]

Being one Day upon Shore, watching to see if any thing more was come thro' the Cavern, I spied at a Distance somewhat looking very black and very long, and by the Colour and Shape thereof I took it for a young Whale. Having observed it some Time making very little Way, I took my old Boat and followed it; but was afraid to go near it, lest a Stroke with its Tail (which I then fancied I saw move) might endanger my Boat and myself too; but creeping nearer and nearer, and seeing it did not stir, I believed it to be dead; whereupon taking Courage, I drew so close, that at length I plainly perceived it

was the Ship's second Boat turned upside down. It is not easy
to express the Joy I felt on this Discovery. It was the very
Thing I was now, as I have said, in the greatest Want of.
I presently laid hold of it, and brought it ashore; and it was
no small Pleasure to find, on examining, that tho' it had lain
so long dry, it was yet quite sound, and all its Chinks filled
up in its Passage: And it prov'd to me, afterwards, the most
beneficial Thing I could have had from the Ship.

I got all my Goods home from the Lake to my Grotto, by
means of the Cart, as usual. My Wife and Daughters waited
with Impatience for me to unpack, that they might take
Possession of such Things as would be needful for rigging
out the Family, against the supposed Reception of the old
Glumm, and had set all the Chests in the Order they desired
they might be opened in. But *Tommy* running to me, with
a pray Daddy open my Chest first, pray give me my Playthings first, it was (to satisfy him) concluded in Favour of his
Demand. So, he pointing to the Chest which he regarded as
his Property, I opened it, whilst his Eyes were ready to pierce
thro' it, 'till I came to his Treasure. There, there they are,
Daddy, says he, as soon as I had uncovered 'em. And indeed,
when I saw them, I could not but much commend the Child
for his Fancy; for the first Things that appeared were a silver
Punch or Wine Can and a Ladle, then a gold Watch, a Pair of
Scissars, a small silver Chaffing-dish and Lamp, a large Case
of mathematical Instruments, a Flagellet,[1] a Terrella,[2] or
globular Loadstone, a small Globe, a Dozen of large silver
Spoons, and a small Case of Knives and Forks and Spoons:
In short, there was, I believe, the greatest Part of the *Portuguese* Captain's valuable Effects.

These *Tommy* claiming as his own proper Chattels, I could
not help interposing somewhat of my Authority in the Affair.
Hold, hold Son, says I, these Things are all mine: But as
I have several of you, who will all be equally pleased with
them; though, as the first Finder, you may be entitled to the
best Share, you are not to grasp the Whole; you must all have
something like an Equality: And as to some Things which may

be equally useful to us all, they must be set up to be used upon Occasion, and are to be considered as mine and your Mother's Property. I thereupon gave each of them a large silver Spoon, and with a Fork I scratched the Initials of their Names respectively on 'em, and divided several of the Trifles amongst them equally. And now *Tommy*, says I, you, for your Pains, shall have this more than the rest, offering him the Flagellet. *Tommy* looked very gloomy; and though he durst not find Fault, his Dissatisfaction was very visible, by cooly taking it, tossing it down, and walking gravely off. I thought, says I, *Tommy*, I had made a good Choice for you; but, as I find you despise it, here *Pedro*, do you take that pretty Thing, since your Brother slights it. *Tommy* replied (speaking but half out, and a little surly, more than I ever observed before) let him take it, if he will, I can get Bits of Sticks enough in the Wood.

My Method had always been to avoid either beating or scolding at my Children, for preferring their own Opinion to mine; but I ever let Things turn about so, that from their own Reason they should perceive they had erred in opposing my Sentiments; by which means they grew so habituated to submit to my Advice and Direction, that, for the most part, my Will was no sooner known to them, than it became their own Choice: But then I never willed according to Fancy only, but with Judgment, to the best of my Skill.

Tommy therefore (as I said before) having shewn a Disapprobation of my Doings; to convince him of his Mistake, I took the Flagellet from *Pedro*, and now *Pedro*, says I, let me teach you how to manage this Piece of Wood, as *Tommy* calls it, and then let me see if in all the Grove he can cut such another. On this I clapt it to my Mouth, and immediately played several Country Dances and Hornpipes on it: For tho' my Mother had scarce taught me to read, I had learnt Musick and Dancing, being, as she called them, Gentleman-like Accomplishments. My Wife and Children, especially *Tommy*, all stared as if they were wild, first on me, then on one another, whilst I played a Country Dance; but I had no sooner struck up an Hornpipe, than their Feet, Arms, and Heads, had so many Twitchings and convulsive Motions, that not one quiet Limb was to be seen amongst them; till having exercised their Members as long as I saw fit, I almost laid them all to Sleep with *Chevy Chase*, and so gave over.

They no sooner found themselves free from this Enchantment, than the Children all husled round me in a Cluster, all speaking together, and reaching out their little Hands to the Instrument. I gave it *Pedro*. There, says I to him, take this slighted Favour as no such contemptible Present.

Poor *Tommy*, who had all this while looked very simple, burst into a Flood of Tears, at my last Words, as if his Heart would have broke; and running to me, fell on his Knees, and begged my Pardon, hoping I would forgive him. I took him up, and kissing him, told him he had very little offended me; for, as he knew, I had more Children to give any thing to which either of the rest despised, it was equal to me who had it, so it was thankfully received. I found that did not satisfy: Still in Tears, he said, might he not have the Stick again, as I gave it to him first? *Tommy*, says I, you know I gave it to you first; but you disapproving my Kindness, I have now given it *Pedro*, who, should I against his Will take it from him, would have that Reason to complain which you have not, who parted with it by your own Consent; and therefore, *Tommy*, as I am determined to acquaint you, as near as I can, with the strict Rules of Justice, there must no more be said to me of this Matter. Such as this was my constant Practice amongst them; and they having always found me inflexible from this Rule, we seldom had any long Debates.

Tho' I say the Affair ended so, with regard to what I had to do in it, yet it ended not so with *Tommy*; for tho' he knew he had no Hopes of moving me, he set all his Engines at work to recover his Stick (as he called it) by his Mother's and Sister's Interest. These solicited *Pedro* very strongly to gratify him. At length *Pedro* (he being a Boy of a most humane Disposition) granted their Desire, if I would give leave; and I having signified, that, the Cause being now out of my Hands, he might do as he pleased, he generously yielded it. And indeed he could not have bestowed it more properly; for *Tommy* had the best Ear for Musick I ever knew; and in less than a Twelve-month could far outdo me, his Instructor, in Softness and Easiness of Finger; and was also Master of every Tune I knew, which were neither inconsiderable in Number, or of the lowest Rate.

Youwarkee, with her Daughters, sat close to Work, and had but just compleated her whole Design for the Family Cloathing when she told me she found herself with Child again. As that Circumstance ill-suited a Journey, she deferred her Flight for about fifteen Months; in which Time she was brought to Bed, and weaned the Infant, which was a Boy, whom I named *Richard*, after my good Master at the Academy. The little Knave thrived amain, and was left to my further Nursing during its Mammy's Absence: Who, still firm to her Resolution, after she had equipped herself and Companions with whatever was necessary to their travelling, and locked up all the Apparel she had made, till her Return, because she would have it appear new when her Father came, set out with her Son *Tommy* and my two Daughters *Patty* and *Hallicarnie*; the last of which, by this Time, being big enough also to be trusted with her Mother.

CHAPTER XXV

*Youwarkee's Account of the Stages to Arndrumnstake;
the Author uneasy at her Flight; his Imployment in
her Absence, and Preparations for receiving her Father;
how he spent the Evenings with the Children*

MY Wife was now upon her Journey to her Father's; but where that was, or how far off, it was impossible for me to conceive by her Description of the Way: For she distinguished it not by Miles or Leagues, but by *Swangeans*, and Names of

Rocks, Seas, and Mountains, which I could neither comprehend the Distance of from each other, or from *Graundevolet*
where I was. I understood by her indeed there was a great Sea
to be passed, which would take her up almost a Day and Night,
having the Children with her, before she reached the next
Arkoe; though she could do it herself, she said, and strain
hard, in a Summer's Night: But if the Children should flag
by the Way, as there was no Resting-place between us and
Battringdrigg, the next *Arkoe*, it might be dangerous to them;
so she would take the above Time for their Sakes. After this,
I found by what she said, there was a narrow Sea to pass, and
a prodigious Mountain, before she reached her own Country;
and that her Father's was but a little beyond that Mountain.
This was all I could know in general about it. At their Departure, she and the Children had taken each a small Provision
for their Flight, which hung about their Necks in a sort of
Purse.

I can't say, notwithstanding this Journey was taken with my
Concurrence and Consent, that I was perfectly easy when they
were gone; for my Affection for them all would work up
imaginary Fears, too potent for my Reason to dispel, and
which at first sat with no easy Pressure upon my Mind. This,
my pretty Babies at home perceiving, used all the little winning
Arts they could to divert and keep up my Spirits; and from
Day to Day, by taking them abroad with me, and playing
with, and amusing them at home, I grew more and more
perswaded that all would go right with the Absent, and that
in due Time I should see them return again.

But as the Winter set in, I went little abroad, and then we
employed ourselves within Doors, in preparing several
Things, which might not only be useful and ornamental, if
the old *Glumm* should come to see us, but might also divert
us, and make the Time pass less tediously. The first Thing
I went upon was a Table; which, as my Family consisted of
so many, I intended to make big enough for us all. With that
View I broke up a Couple of Chests, and taking the two Sides
of one of them, I nailed them Edge to Edge, by strong thick

N

Pieces underneath, at each End, and in the Middle; then I took two Chest-lids with their Hinges, nailing one to each Side of my middle Piece, which made two good Flaps; after this, with my Tools, of which I had now a Chest full, I chopped out of new Stuff and planed four strong Legs quite square, and nailed them strongly to each Corner of my middle Board; I then nailed Pieces from one Leg to the other, and nailed the Bed likewise to them; then I fastened a Border quite round, within six Inches from the Bottom, from Foot to Foot, which held all fast together. When all this was done, still my Table was imperfect, I could not put up the Flaps, having no proper Support. To remedy this, I sawed out a broad Slip from a Chest Side, and boring a large Hole through the Centre, I spiked it up to the under-side of the Table's Bed, with a Spindle I contrived, just loose enough to play round the Head of the Spike, filing down that Part of the Spindle which passed through the Bed of the Table, and rivetting it close; so that when my Flaps were set up, I pulled the Slip cross-ways of the Table, and when the Flaps were down, the Slip turned under the Top of the Table, lengthways; next under each Flap, I nailed a small Slip, the lengthways of the Flaps, to raise them on a Level (when up) with the Top of the Table. When I had thus compleated the several Parts of this needful Utensil, I spent some Time and Pains, by scraping and rubbing, to render it all as elegant as could be; and the Success so well answered my Wish, that I was not a little proud of the Performance: And what rendered my Work thereon a still more agreeable Task, was, my pretty Infants Company, who stood by, expressing their Wonder and Approbation at every Stroke.

Now I had gotten a Table, I wanted Chairs to it; for as yet we had only sat round the Room upon Chests, which formed a Bench of the whole Circumference, they stood so thick. There was no moving of them without a monstrous Trouble, every Time I might have Occasion to set out my Table; besides, if I could have dragged them backwards and forwards, they were too low to be commodious for Seats; so I resolved to make some Chairs, and Stools also, that might be manageable. I will not trouble you with the Steps I took in the Formation of these; only, in general, you must know, that some more Chests I broke up to that Purpose served me for Timber, out of which I framed six sizeable handsome Chairs, and a competent Number of Stools.

But now that I was turned Joiner I had another Convenience to provide for. I had nothing wherein to inclose Things, and preserve 'em from Dust, except the Chests; and they were quite unfit for holding Liquors, Victuals, and such like Matters, in open Shells, as most of my Vessels were. Wherefore, having several Boards now remaining, of the Boxes I had broken up for Chairs and Stools, I bethought me of supplying this great Deficiency; so, of these spare Boards, in a Workman-like Way, (for by this Time I was become a tolerable Mechanic) I composed a very tight Closet, holding half a Dozen broad Shelves, shut up by a good Pair of Doors, with a Lock and Key to fasten 'em.

These Jobs took me up almost three Months, and I thought I had not employed them idly, but for the Credit and Service of my Family. I was now again at Leisure for farther Projects. I was uncertain as to my Wife's Return, how soon she might be with me, or how much longer she might stay; but I was sure I could do nothing in the mean while more grateful, than encreasing, by all means in my Power, the Accommodations of my House, for the more polite as well as convenient Reception of her Father, or any else who might accompany her home, in the Way of a Retinue, as she talked of. I saw plainly I had not Room for lodging of them, and that was a Circumstance of main Importance to be provided for. Hereupon I thought of adding a long Apartment to one of my outer Rooms, to range against the Side of the Rock; but reflecting, that such a Thing would be quite useless, unless I could finish it in Time, so as to be compleat when my Guests came and not knowing how soon that might be, I resolved to quit this Design; and I fell upon another, which might do as well, and required much less Labour, and fewer Days, to perfect.

I remembered that amongst those Things my Wife had packed up on board the Ship, and which came home through the Gulph, there were two of the largest Sails, and a Couple of smaller Size. These I carried to the Wood, and tried them in several Places, to see where they might be disposed to most Advantage, in the Nature of a Tent; and having found a convenient Spot to my Purpose, I cut divers Poles for Supporters, and making Straining-lines of my Mat-weed, I pitched a noble one, sufficient to cover or entertain a numerous company, and so tight every where as to keep out the Weather. The front of this new appartment I hung with blue cloth; which had a very genteel Effect: I had almost forgotten to tell you, that I contrived so, (by hanging one of the smaller sails across, just in the Middle, which I could let down, or raise up at Pleasure) as to divide the Tent, occasionally, into two distinct Rooms.

When I had proceeded thus far, there were still wanting Seats for this additional Building, as I may call it; and though I could spare some Chests to sit on, I found they would not half do. For a Supplement then I took my Ax, and felled a Couple of great Trees, one from each Side of the Tent, sawed off the Tops, and cut each of the Trunks in two, about the Middle; these huge Cylinders I rolled into the Tent with a good deal of Toil and Difficulty; two of them I thrust into the inner Division, and left two in the outer; I placed them as Benches on both Sides; then with infinite Pains I shaved the upper Face of each smooth and flat, and pared off all the little Knots and Roughnesses of the Front, so that they were fitted to sit on; and their own Weight fixed them in the Place where I intended them to be. At the upper End of the further Chamber I set three Chests lengthwise, for Seats, or any other Use I might see fit to put them to.

During these Operations we were all hard at it, and no Hand idle, but *Dicky* in Arms, and *Sally*, whom he kept in full Employ; but *Pedro*, being a sturdy Lad, could drive a Nail, and lift or carry the Things I wanted; and *Jemmy* and *David*, tho' so young, could pick up the Chips, hold a Nail, or the Lamp, or be some way or other useful: For I always preached to them the Necessity of earning their Bread before they eat it, and not think to live on mine and their Brother's Labour.

The Nights being pretty long, after Work was over, and *Sarah* had fed her Brother, and laid him in his Hammock, we used to sit all down to enjoy ourselves at a good Meal; for we were never regular at that till Night; and then after Meal, my Wife being absent, one or other of the young ones would begin with something they had before heard me speak of, by saying, *Daddy*, how did you use to do this or that in *England*; then all Ears were immediately open to catch my Answer, which certainly brought on something else, done either there or elsewhere; and by their little Questions and my Answers they would sometimes draw me into a Story of three Hours long, till perhaps two out of three of my Audience were falling asleep, and then we all went to Bed.

I verily believe my Children would, almost any of them, from the frequent Repetition of these Stories, have given a sufficient Account of *England*, to have gained a Belief from almost any *Englishman* of their being Natives there.

I frequently observed, that when we had begun upon *Cornwall*, and traversed the Mines, the Sea-Coast, or talked of the fine Gentlemen's Seats, and such Things, one would start up, and, if the Discourse flagged ever so little, would cry, ay but *Daddy*, what did you do when the Crocodile came after you out of the Water; and another, before that Subject was half ended, (and I was forced to enter on every one they started) would be impatient for the Story of the Lion; and I always took notice, that the Part each had made the most Reflections on was always most acceptable to the same Person: But poor *Sally* would never let the Conversation drop without some Account of the *Muletto*, it was such a pretty gentle Creature she said.

CHAPTER XXVI

The Author's Concern at Youwarkee's *Stay;*
Reflections on his Condition; hears a Voice call him;
Youwarkee's *Brother* Quangrollart *visits him with*
a Companion; he treats them at the Grotto; the
Brother discovers himself by Accident; Wilkins
produces his Children to him

MY Head, as well as my Hands, had now been employed for
five Months, in adjusting all Things in the most suitable
Manner for the Reception of *Youwarkee* and her Friends; but
nobody coming, and light Days getting forward apace, I began
to grow very uneasy, and had formed divers Imaginations of
what might occasion her Stay. Thought I, I am afraid all the
Pains I have been taking will be to no Purpose; for either her
Father will not let her return, or she has of herself come to
such a Resolution: For she knows I cannot follow her, and
had rather perhaps live, and enjoy the three Children she has
with her, amidst a Number of her Friends and Acquaintance,
than spend the Remainder of her Days with me and all our
Offspring in this Solitude.—But then I reflected, she chose it
herself, or at least declared herself perfectly satisfied, yea
delighted, therewith; and here are her Children with me, the
major Part of them.—Yet, what can I think; since her Return
is put off till the *Swangeans* are over at this *Arkoe*, she will
never bring her Relations now, in this unseasonable Time for
Flight: Therefore I must think, if she intended to return at all,
it would have been before now; and as the Case is not so, my
Fear of losing her intirely prevails greatly. O! says I, that we
had but a Post here, as we have in *England*; there we can communicate our Thoughts at a Distance to each other, without
any Trouble, and for little Charge! What a Country is this to
live in, and what an improper Creature am I to live in it!
Had I but the *Graundee*, I would have found her out by this
Time, be she where she would; but, whilst every one about

me can pass, repass, and act as they please, I am fixed here like one of my Trees, bound to the Spot, or upon Removal to die in the Attempt. Alas! why did I beget Children here, but to make them as wretched and inconsolable as myself. Some of them are so formed, indeed, as to shift for themselves; but they owe it to their Mother, not to me. What! am I a Father, of Children who will be bound one Day to curse me! Severe Reflection! yet I never thought of this till now. But, am I the only Father in such a Case? No surely: For am not I as much bound to curse my Father, as my Children are to curse me? He might have left me happy if he would, I would them if I could. Again, are there not others, who, by improper Junction with Persons diseased in Body, or vicious in Mind, have intailed greater Misery upon their Posterity, than I have on mine? My Children are all healthy, strong, and sound, both in Body and Mind; and is not that the greatest Blessing that can be bestowed on our Beings? But they are imprisoned in this *Arkoe*. What then? with Industry here is no Want; and as they increase, they may settle in Communities, and be helpful to each other. I have lived well here, nigh sixteen Years, and it was God's Pleasure I should be here; and can I think I was placed here, with an Injunction contrary to the great Command, *Increase and multiply*? If that were so, can it be possible I should have received the only Means of propagating, as it were from Heaven itself? No, it was certainly as much my Maker's Will, that I should have Posterity here, as that I myself should at first be brought hither. This is a large and plentiful Spot, and capable of great Improvement, when there shall be Hands sufficient. How many petty States are less than these my Dominions? I have here a Compass of near twenty Miles round, and how many Thousands grow voluntarily grey in a far less Circuit.

I had hardly finished my Reflections (for I was sitting by myself in my Tent upon one of the Trees I had turned into Benches) when I heard a musical Voice call *Peter*, *Peter*. I started; what's this, says I; it is not *Youwarkee*'s Voice; what can this mean? Listening, I heard it again; but at so great a Distance, I could but just perceive the Sound. Be it where it will, says I, I'll face it. Thus speaking, I went out of the Tent, and hearkned very attentively, but could hear nothing. I then run for my Gun, and walked through the Wood as fast as I could to the Plain; but still I neither saw or heard any thing. I was then in hopes of seeing somebody on the Lake, but no one appeared: for I was fully determined to make myself known to whomsoever I should meet, and, if possible, to gain some Intelligence of my Wife. But after so much fruitless Pains, my Hopes being at an End, I was returning, when I heard *Peter, Peter*, again, at a great Distance; the Sound coming from a different Quarter than at first. Upon this I stopped, and heard it repeated, and it was as if the Speaker approached nearer and nearer. Hereupon I stepped out of the Wood, (for I had just re-entered it upon my Return home) when I saw two Persons upon the *Swangean*, just over my Head. I cried out, Who's that; and they immediately called again, *Peter, Peter. Ors clam gee*, says I, that is, here am I. On this they directly took a small Sweep round, (for they had overshot me before they heard me) and alighted just by me: When I perceived them to be my Wife's Countrymen, being dressed like her, with only broader Chaplets about their Heads, as she had told me the *Glumms* all wore. After a short Obeisance, they asked me if I was the *Glumm Peter, Barkett*** to *Youwarkee*? I answered, I was. They then told me they came with a Message from *Pendlehamby, Colambo*† of *Arndrumn-stake*, my *Goppo*,‡ and from *Youwarkee* his Daughter. I was vastly rejoiced to see them, and to hear only the Name of my Wife. But though I longed to know their Message, I trembled to think of their mentioning it, as one of them was just going to do, for fear of hearing some things very displeasing: So I begged them to go through the Wood with me to the Grotto, where we should have more Leisure and Convenience for Talk, and where, at the same time, they might take some Refreshment. But though I had thus put off their Message, I could not forbear enquiring by the way, after the Health of

---

* Husband.   † Governor.   ‡ Father-in-Law.

my *Goppo*, and my Wife and Children, how they got to
Arndrumnstake, and how they found their Relations and
Friends. They told me all were well; and that *Youwarkee*, as
she did on me, desired I would think on her with true Affection. I found this was the Phrase of the Country. As for the
rest, I hoped it would turn out well at last, tho' I dreaded
to hear it.

Being arrived at the Grotto, I desired my Guests to sit
down, and take such Refreshment as I could prepare them.
When they were seated, I went to work in order to provide
'em a Repast. Seeing my Fire piled up very high, and burning
fierce, and the Children about it, they wondered where they
were got, and who they had come to, and turned their Faces
from it; but I setting some Chairs, so that the Light might not
strike on their Eyes, they liked the Warmth well enough:
Tho', I remarked, the Light did not affect them so much as
it had done *Youwarkee*.

Whilst I was cooking, the poor Children got all up in
a Corner, and stared at the Strangers, not being able to conceive where they came from; and by Degrees crept all backwards into the Bedchamber, and hid themselves; for they had
never before seen any body but my own Family.

I observed that one of my Guests paid more than ordinary
Respect to the other; and tho' their *Graundees* made no Distinction between them, yet there was something, I thought,
much more noble in the Address and Behaviour of the latter;
and taking notice that he was also the chief Spokesman, I
judged it proper to pay my Respects to him in a somewhat
more distinguishing Manner; though, so as not to offend the
other if I should happen to be mistaken.

I first presented a Can of my *Madeira*, and took care, as if
by Accident, to give it to Mr. Uppermost, as I thought him;
who drank half of it, and would have given the Remainder to
his Companion; but I begged him to drink it all up, and his
Friend should be served with some presently: He did so, and
thanked me by lifting his Hand to his Chin. I then gave the
other a Can of the same Liquor, which he drank, and returned

Thanks as his Companion had before. I then took a Can my-self, and telling them I begged leave to use the Ceremony of my own Country to them, I drank, wishing their own Health, and that of all Relations at *Arndrumnstake*. He that I took for the Superior, fell a laughing heartily; ha, ha, ha, says he, this is the very Way my Sister does every Day at *Arndrumnstake*. Your Sister Sir, says I, pray has she ever been in *Europe* or in *England*. Well, says he, I have plainly discovered myself, which I did not intend to do yet; but truly Brother *Peter*, I mean none other than your own Wife, *Youwarkee*.

The Moment I knew who he was, I rose up, and taking him by the Right-hand, lifted it to my Lips, and kissed it. He likewise immediately stood up, and we embraced each other with great Tenderness. I then begged him, as I had so worthy and near a Relation of my Wife's with me, that he would not delay the Happiness I hoped for, in a Narrative from his Mouth, how it fared with my Father, Wife, and Children, and all their Kinsfolks and Friends, whom I had so often heard mentioned by my dearest *Youwarkee*, and so earnestly desired to see.

My Brother *Quangrollart* (for that he told me was his Name) was preparing to gratify my Impatience; but seeing I had set the Entertainment on the Table, which consisted chiefly of Bread, several Sorts of Pickles and Preserves, with some cold salted Fish; he said, that eating would but interrupt the Thread of his Discourse, and therefore, with my Leave, he would defer the relating of what I desired for a little while; which we all thinking most proper, I desired him and his Friend (who might be another Brother for ought I knew) to refresh themselves with the poor Modicum I was able to provide them.

Whilst my Brother *Quangrollart* was looking upon and handling his Plate, being what he had never before seen, his Friend had got the Handle of one of the Knives in his Mouth, biting it with all his Force; but finding he could make nothing of that End, he tried the other, and got to champing the Blade. Perceiving what he was at, though I could not help laughing,

I rose, and begging Pardon, took the Knife from him; telling him, I believed he was not acquainted with the Use of that Instrument, which was one of my Country Implements; and that the Design of it, which was called a Knife, and of that other, pointing to it, called a Fork, were, the one to reduce the Food into Pieces proper for chewing, and the other to convey it to the Mouth without daubing the Fingers, which must happen in handling the Food itself. And I then shewed him what Use I put them to, by helping each of them therewith to somewhat, and by cutting a Piece for myself, and putting it to my Mouth with the Fork.

They both smiled, and looked very well pleased; and then I told 'em that the Plate was the only Thing that need be daubed, and when that was taken away, the Table remained clean. So, after I had helped each of them for the first Time, I desired them to help themselves where they liked best: And, to say the Truth, they did so, more dextrously than I could have expected.

During our Repast, we had frequent Sketches of the Observations they made in their Flight, and of the Places where they had rested; and I could plainly see, that neither of them had ever been at this *Arkoe* before, by hinting, that if they had not taken such a Course, they had missed me.

I took particular notice which Part of my Entertainment they eat most of, that I might bring a fresh Supply of that when wanted; and I found, that tho' they eat heartily of my Bread and Preserves, and tasted almost of every thing else, they never once touched the Fish; which put me upon desiring I might help them to some. At this they looked upon each other, which I readily knew the Meaning of, and excused themselves, expressing great Satisfaction in what they had already gotten. I took however a Piece of Fish on my own Plate, and eating very heartily thereof, my Brother desired me to give him a Bit of it; I did so, taking care to cut it as free from Bones as I could, and for greater Security cautioning him, in case there should be any, to pick them out, and not swallow them. He had no sooner put a Piece in his Mouth, but, *Rosig*, says he to his Friend, this is *Padsi*. I thought indeed I had puzzled my Brother when I gave him the Fish, but by what he said of it he puzzled me; for I knew not what he meant by *Padsi*, my Wife having told me they had no Fish: or, else, I should have taken that Word for their Name of it. However, I cut *Rosig* a Slice; and he agreeing it was *Padsi*, they both eat heartily of it.

While we were at Dinner, my Brother told me he thought he saw some of my Children just now; for his Sister had informed him she had five more at home; and he asked me why they did not appear, and eat with us. I excused their Coming, as fearing they would only be troublesome; and said, when we had done they should have some Victuals. But he would not be put of, and entreated me to admit 'em. So I called them by their Names, and they came, all but *Dicky*, who was asleep in his Hammock. I told them, that *Reglumm*,* pointing to *Quangrollart*, was their Uncle, their Mamma's Brother, and ordered them to pay their Obeisance to him, which they severally did. I then made them salute *Rosig*. This last would have had them sit down at Table; but I positively forbid that; and giving each of them a little of what we had before us, they carried it to the Chests and eat it there.

When we had done, the Children helped me to clear the Table, and were retiring out of the Room; but then I recalled them, and desired their Uncle to excuse their Stay: For as he had promised me News of their Mammy and her Family, it would be the Height of Pleasure to them to hear him. He seemed very much pleased with this Motion, desiring by all Means they might be present while he told his Story. Whereupon I ordered them to the Chests again, while *Quangrollart* delivered his Narrative.

* Gentleman.

CHAPTER XXVII

Quangrollart's *Account of* Youwarkee's *Journey, and Reception at her Father's*

HAVING set on the Table some Brandy and *Madeira*, and each of us taken one Glass of both, I shewed by the Attentiveness of my Aspect and Posture how desirous I was he should proceed to what he had promised. Observing this, he went on in the following Manner. Brother *Peter*, says he, my Sister *Youwarkee*, as I don't doubt you will be glad to hear of her first, arrived very safe at *Arndrumnstake*, the third Day after she left you, and after a very severe Flight to the dear little *Hallycarnie*,* who was a full Day and a Night on her *Graundee*; and at last would not have been able to have reached *Battingdrigg* but for my Sister's Assistance, who, taking her sometimes on her Back for a short Flight, by those little Refreshments enabled her to perform it; but from *Battingdrigg*, after some Hours Rest, they came with Pleasure to the *White Mountains*, from whence, after a small Stay, they arrived at *Arndrumnstake*.

They alighted at our *Covett*,† but were opposed at their Entrance by the Guards, to whom they did not chuse to discover themselves, till Notice was given to my Father; who, upon hearing that some Strangers desired Admittance to him, sent me to introduce them, if they were proper for his Presence, or else give Orders for such other Reception as was suitable to them.

When I came to the Guard, I found three *Gawreys* and a *Glumm Boss*,‡ whose Appearance and Behaviour, I must own, prejudiced me very much in their Favour. I then asked from whence they came, and their Business with the *Colamb*? *Youwarkee* told me they came not about Business of publick Concern, relating to the *Colamb*'s Office, but out of a dutiful Regard, as Relations, to kiss his Knees. My Father, said I,

---

* One of *Wilkins*'s Daughters.   † Capital Seat.   ‡ A Youth.

shall know it immediately; but first, pray inform me of your Name? Your Father, replied *Youwarkee*, are you my Brother *Quangrollart*? My Name is so, says I, but I have only one Sister, now with my Father, and how I can be your Brother, I am not able to guess. Have you never had another Sister, says she? Yes, says I, but she is long since dead; her Name was *Youwarkee*. At my mentioning her Name, she fell upon my Neck in Tears, crying, my dear Brother, I am that dead Sister *Youwarkee*, and these with me are some of my Children, for I have five more; but pray how does my Father and Sister? I started back at this Declaration, to view her and the Children, fearing it was some gross Imposition; not in the least knowing or remembring any thing of her Face, after so long an Absence; but I desired them to walk in, 'till I told my Father.

The Guard, observing the several Passages between us, were amazed to think who it could be had so familiarly embraced me; especially as they plainly saw I only played a passive Part in it.

When I went in, I did not think proper directly to inform my Father what had happened; but calling my Sister *Hallycarnie*, I let her into the Circumstances of this odd Affair, and desired her Advice what to do: For, says I, surely this must be some Imposture; and as my Father has scarce yet subdued his Sorrow for my Sister's Loss, if this *Gawry* should prove a Deceiver, it will only revive his Affliction, and may prove, at this Time, extreamly dangerous to him: Therefore let's consider, what had best be done in the Matter.

Hallycarnie, who had attentively weighed all I said, seemed to think it was some Cheat, as well as I did; for we could neither of us conceive, that any thing but Death, or being *slit*, could have kept *Youwarkee* so long from the Knowledge of her Relations; and, that neither of them could be the Case, was plain, if the Person attending was *Youwarkee*. Besides, Brother, says *Hallycarnie*, she cannot surely be so much altered in fifteen Years, but you must have known her: And yet, now I think, it is possible, you being so much younger, may have forgot her; but whilst we have been talking of her,

I have so well recollected her, that I think I could hardly be imposed upon by any Deceiver.

I then desired her to go with me to the Strangers, and see if she could make any Discovery. She did so, and had no sooner enter'd the *Abb*,* but *Youwarkee* called out, my dear Sister *Hallycarnie*; and she as readily recollecting *Youwarkee*, they in Transport embraced each other; and then your Wife presenting to us her three Children, it proved the tenderest Scene, except the following, I ever saw.

My Father having kept his Chamber some Time with a Fever, and, though he was pretty well recovered, having not yet been out of it; we consulted how we might introduce our Sister and her Children to him, with as little Surprize as might be, for Fear of a Relapse, by too great a Hurry of his Spirits. At length we concluded, I should go tell him, that some Strangers had arrived, desiring to see him; but, on Inquiry, finding their Business was too trifling to trouble him upon, I had dispatched them: I was then to say, how like one of them was to my Sister *Youwarkee*; and, whilst I was speaking, *Hallycarnie* was to enter, and keep up the Discourse, till we should find a proper Opportunity of Discovery. I went in therefore, as had been agreed; and, upon mentioning the Name of *Youwarkee*, my Father fetched a deep Sigh, and turned away from me in Tears. At that Instant *Hallycarnie* came in as by Accident; Sir, says she, what makes you so sad, are you worse to-day! O! says he, I have heard a Name that will never be out of my Heart, till I am in *Hoximo*.† What, I suppose my Sister? 'Tis true, replied he, the same. Says she, I fancied so; for I have just seen a Stranger as like her as two *Dorrs*‡ could be, and would have sworn it was she, if that had been possible. I thought my Brother had been so imprudent as to mention her to you; and I think he did not do well to rip up an old Sore he knew was almost healed, and make it break out afresh. Ah! no, Child, says my Father, that Sore never has, or can be healed. O great Image! why can't

* Room.   † A Place where the Dead are buried.
‡ A Fruit like an Apple.

I by some Means or other be ascertained what End she came to.

Sir, says my Sister, I think you are much to blame for these Exclamations, after so long Absence: For, if she be dead, what Use are they of, and if she be not, all may be well, and you may still see her again. O never, never, says my Father; but could I be sure she was alive, I would take a *Swangean*, and never close my *Graundee*, till I found her, or dropt dead in the Search. And suppose you could meet with her, Sir, says I, the very Sight would overcome you, and be dangerous. No, believe me, Boy, says he, I should then be fully easy and composed; and were she to come in this Moment, I should suffer no Surprize, but Pleasure. No Surprize, Sir, says I? Not if she were alive and well, says he. Then Sir, says *Hallycarnie*, will you excuse me if I introduce her; and went out directly, without staying for an Answer.

When she was gone, *Quangrollart*, says my Father sternly, what is the Meaning of your's and your Sister's playing thus upon my Weakness? It is what I can upon no Account forgive. It looks as if you were weary of me, and wanted to break my Heart. To what Purpose is all this Prelude of yours, to introduce to me somebody, who, by her Likeness to my Daughter, may expose me to your Scoff and Raillery? This is a Disobedience I never expected from either of you.

The great Image attend me! says I, Sir, you have much mistaken me; but I will not leave you in Doubt, even till *Hallycarnie*'s Return; you shall see *Youwarkee* with her; for all our Discourse, I'll assure you, has but been concerted to prepare you for her Reception, with three of her Children. And am I then (says he in a Transport) still to be blessed? You are Sir, says I; assure yourself you are.

By this Time we heard them coming; but my poor Father had not Power to go to meet them: And upon *Youwarkee*'s nearer Approach, to fall at his Knees, his Limbs failing him, he sunk, and, without speaking a Word, fell backwards on a *Cught Drappec*,* which stood behind him; and being quite

* A Bed or Couch, covered with a sort of Cotton.

motionless, we concluded him to be stone dead. On this, the Women became intirely helpless, screaming only, and wringing their Hands in extravagant Postures. But I, having a little more Presence of Mind, called for the *Calentar*,* who, by holding his Nose, pinching his Feet, and other Applications, in a little Time brought him to his Senses again.

You may more easily conceive than I describe, both the Confusion we were all in, during my Father's Disorder, and the Gratulations upon his Recovery: So, as I can give you but a defective Account of these, I shall pass 'em by, and come to our more serious Discourse, after my Father and your Wife had, without speaking a Word, wept themselves quite dry on each other's Necks.

My Father then looking upon the three Children, (who were also crying to see their Mammy cry) and who are these, says he? These Sir, says *Youwarkee*, are three (of eight) of your Grand-children. And where is your *Barkatt*, says he? At home with the rest Sir, replied she, who are some of them too small to come so far yet: But Sir, says she, pray excuse my answering you any more Questions, till you are a little recovered from the Commotion I perceive my Presence has brought upon your Spirits; and as Rest, the *Calentar* says, will be exceedingly proper, I will retire with my Sister till you are better able to bear Company. My Father was with much Difficulty prevailed with to part with her out of his Sight; but the *Calentar* pressing it, we were all dismissed, and he lay down to Rest.

My Brother would have gone on, but I told him, as it grew near Time for Repose, and he and *Rosig* must needs be fatigued with so long a Flight, if they pleased (as I had already heard the most valuable Part of all he could say, in that my Father received my Wife and Children so kindly, and that he left them all well) we would defer his farther Relation till the next Day: Which they both agreeing to, I laid them in my own Bed, myself sleeping in a spare Hammock.

* A sort of Doctor in all great Families.

CHAPTER XXVIII

A Discourse on Light; Quangrollart *explains the
Word* Crashee; *believes a Fowl is a Fruit; gives
a further Account of* Youwarkee's *Reception by her
Father, and by the King;* Tommy *and* Hallycarnie
provided for at Court; Youwarkee *and her Father
visit the* Colambs, *and are visited; her Return put off
till next Winter, when her Father is to come with her*

THE next Day I prepared again of the best of every thing
for my new Guests. I killed three Fowls, and ordered *Pedro*,
(who was as good a Cook almost as myself) to get them ready
for boiling, whilst we took a Walk to the Lake. Tho' we went
out in the clearest Part of the Morning, I heard no Complaint
of the Light. I took the Liberty to ask my Brother, if the
Light did not offend him; for I told him my Wife could not
bear so much without Spectacles. What is that Spectacle, says
he? Something I made your Sister, says I, to prevent the
Inconvenience of too much Light upon her Eyes. He said the
Light was scarce at all troublesome to him, for he had been
in much greater, and was used to it; and that the *Glumms*,
who travelled much abroad, could bear more Light than the
Gawrys, who staid much at home: these stirring but little out,
unless in large Companies, and that of one another, and very
rarely admitting *Glumms* amongst them before Marriage. For
his own Part, he said, he had an Office at *Crash Doorpt*,*
which, though he executed chiefly by a Deputy, obliged him
to reside there sometimes for a long Season together; and that
being a more luminous Country than *Arndrumnstake*, Light
was become familiar to him; for it was very observable, that
some who had been used to it young, though they might in
Time overcome it, yet at first it was very uneasy.

I was upon the Tenter whilst he spoke, lest, before he had
done, a Question, I had a thousand Times thought to have

* The Country of the *Slitts.*

asked my Wife, should slip out of my Head, as it had so often done before: and was, what I had for Years desired to be resolved in, *viz.* What the Meaning of the Word *Slitt* was, when applied to a Man? So, on his pausing, I said, that his Mention of *Crash-doorpt* reminded me of inquiring what *Crashee* meant, when applied to a *Glumm*, or *Gawry*. It would be no hard Task, he said, to satisfy me in respect of that, as I already understood the Nature of the *Graundee*; whereupon he went on thus: '*Slitting* is the only Punishment we use to incorrigible Criminals: Our Method is, Where any one has committed a very heinous Offence, or, which is the same Thing, has multiplied the Acts of Offence, he has a long String tied round his Neck, in the Manner of a Cravat; and then two *Glumms*, one at each End, take it in their Hands, standing Side by Side with him; two more stand before him, and two behind him; all which in that Manner take Flight, so that the String keeps the Criminal in the Middle of them; thus they conduct him to *Crash-Doorpt*, which lies farther on the other Side of *Arndrumnstake*, than this *Arkoe* does on this Side of it, and is just such an *Arkoe* as ours, but much bigger within the Rocks. When they come to the *Covett* they alight, where my Deputy immediately orders the Malefactor to be *slit*, so that he can never more return to *Normnbdsgrsutt*, or indeed by any means get out of that *Arkoe*, but must end his Days there. The Method of *Slitting* is thus, The Criminal is laid on his Back with his *Graundee* open, and after a Recapitulation of his Crimes and his Condemnation, the Officer, with a sharp Stone, *slits* the *Gume** between each of the *Filas*† of the *Graundee*, so that he can never fly more. But what is still worse to new Comers, if they are not very young, is, the Light of the Place, which is so strong, that it is some Years before they can overcome it, if ever they do.'

This Discourse gave me a great Pleasure; thereupon I repeated the Dialogue that had pass'd between me and *Youwarkee* about my being *slit*, and how we had held an Argument a long Time, without being able to come at one

* The Membrane. † Ribs.

another's Meaning. But pray Brother, says I, how comes that light Country to agree so well with you? Why, says he, the *Colambat** of *Crash-Doorpt* is reckoned one of the most honourable Employments in the State, by reason of the Hazard of it, and the Person accepting it must be young; it was, by my Father's Interest at Court, given to me at nine Years of Age; my Friend *Rosig* has followed my Fortune in it ever since, being much about my Age, and has a Post under me there: In short, by being obliged to be so much there, and from so tender an Age too, I have pretty well enured myself to any Light.

By this Time we had got home again to Dinner, which *Pedro* had set out as elegantly as my Country could afford, consisting of Pickles and Preserves, as usual, a Dish of hard Eggs, and boiled Fowls with Spinage.

My Guests, as I expected, stared at the Fowls, but never offered to touch them, or seemed in the least inclinable to do so. I was afraid they would be cold, and begged them to let me help them. I put a Wing on each of their Plates, and a Leg on my own; but perceiving they waited to see how I managed it, I stuck in my Fork, cut off a Slice, dipped it in the Salt, and put it in my Mouth. Just as I did they did, and appeared very well pleased with the Taste. I never in my Life, says *Rosig*, saw a *Crullmott*† of this Shape before; and laid hold of a Leg, (taking it for a Stick I had thrust in, as he told me afterwards) intending to pull it out; but finding it grew there, Mr. *Peter*, says he, you have the oddest shaped *Crullmotts* that ever I saw, pray what Part of the Woods do they grow in? Grow in, says I? Ay, says he, I mean whether your *Crullmott*-Trees are like ours or not? Why, says I, these Fowls are about my Yard and the Wood too. What, says he, is it a running Plant like a *Bott*.‡ No, no, says I, a Bird that I keep tame about my House; and these, (shewing him the Eggs) are the Eggs of these Birds, and the Birds grow from them. Prithee, says *Quangrollart*, never let's inquire what they are till we have dined; for my Brother *Peter* will give us nothing we need be afraid of.

* Government.   † A Fruit like a Melon.   ‡ A Gourd.

It growing into the Night, by that Time we rose from Table, I set a Bowl of Punch before them, made with my Treacle and sour Rams-horn Juice, which they pulled off[1] plentifully. After some Bumpers had gone round, I desired my Brother to proceed where he left off, in the Account of my Wife's Reception with her Father.

When my Father, says he, had recovered himself by some Hours Repose, the first Thing he did was to order my Sister *Youwarkee* to be called; who coming into his Presence, he took her from her Knees, kissed her, and ordered all to depart but myself and *Hallycarnie*. Then bidding us sit down, says he to your Wife, Daughter, your Appearance, whom I have so long lamented as dead, has given me the truest Cordial I could have received, and I hope will add both to my Health and Years. I have heard, you suspect my Anger for some Part of your past Conduct (for she had hinted so to her Sister and me) which you justly enough imagine may be censured; but, my dear Life, I am this Day (what I did not expect any more to be) a Father of a new-born Child; and not of one only, but of many; and this Day, I say, Daughter, shall not be spent in Sorrow and Excuses, or any thing to interrupt our mutual Felicity; neither will I ever hereafter permit you to beg my Forgiveness, or attempt to palliate any of your Proceedings; for know, Child, that a Benevolence freely bestowed, is better than twice its Value obtained by Petition: I therefore, as in Presence of the great Image, your Brother and Sister, at this Instant, erase from my Mind for-ever what Thoughts I may have had prejudicial to the Love I ever bore you, as I will have you to do all such as may cloud the unreserved Complacency you used to appear with before me: And now *Quangrollart*, says he, let the Guard be drawn out before my *Covvett*, and let the whole Country be entertained, for seven Days; proclaim Liberty to all Persons confined; and let not the least Sorrow appear in any Face throughout my *Colambat*.

I retired immediately, and gave the necessary Orders for the speedy Dispatch of my Father's Commands; which indeed were performed to the utmost; and nothing for seven

Days was to be heard, through the whole District of *Arn-drumnstake*, but Joy and the Name of *Youwarkee*.

My Father, so soon as he had dispatched the above Orders, sent for the Children before him, whom he kissed and blessed, frequently lifting up his Eyes in Gratitude to the Great Image, for the unexpected Happiness he enjoyed on that Occasion; and then he ordered *Youwarkee* to let him know what had befallen her in her Absence, and where she lived, and with whom.

Youwarkee was setting out with some indirect Excuses; but my Father absolutely forbid her, and charged her only to mention plain Facts, without Flourishes. So she began with her *Swangean*, and the accidental Fall she had, your taking. her in after it, and saving her Life. She told him, your continued Kindness so wrought upon her, that she found herself uncapable of disesteeming you, but never shewed her Affection, till, having examined every Particular of your Life, and finding you a worthy Man, she could not avoid becoming your Wife; and she said, the Reason why she always declined being seen by her Friends, in their *Swangeans*, was, for Fear she should be forced from you, tho' she longed to see us; and that at last, she was come by your Consent; and, that had it rested there only, she might have come much sooner; for that you would often have had her shew herself to her Friends, when you heard them, having strong Desires yourself to be known to them.

My Father upon hearing this, was so charmed with your Tenderness and Affection to his Daughter, that you already rival his own Issue in his Esteem, and he is perswaded he can never do enough for you or your Children.

The Noise of *Youwarkee*'s Return, and my Father's Rejoicing, soon spread over all *Normnbdsgrsutt*; and King *Georigetti* sent Express to my Father, to command him to attend with your Wife and Children at *Brandleguarp*, his Capital. Thither accordingly we all went, with a grand Retinue, and staid twenty Days. The King took great Delight, as well as the Ladies of the Court, to hear *Youwarkee* and her Children talk

English, and in being informed of you and your Way of Life; and, so fond was *Yurcumbourse* (who, though not the King's Wife, is instead of one) of my Nephew *Tommy*, that, upon my Father's Return, she took him to herself, and assured my Sister, he should continue near her Person till he was qualified for better Preferment. The King's Sister *Jahamel*, would also have taken *Patty* into her Service; but she begged to be permitted to attend her Mother to *Arndrumnstake*; so *Hallycarnie* her Sister, who chose to continue with *Jahamel*, was received in her Room.

Upon my Father's Return to *Arndrumnstake*, he found no less than fifteen Expresses from several *Colambs*, desiring to rejoice with him on the Return of his Daughter, with particular Invitations to him and her to spend some Time with them. My Father, though he hates more Pomp than is necessary to support Dignity, could do no less than severally visit them, with *Youwarkee*, attended by a grand Retinue, spending more or less Days with each; hoping when that was over, he should have some little Time to spend in Retirement with his Daughter before her Departure, who now began to be uneasy for you, who, she said, would suffer the greatest Concern in her Absence; but, upon their Return from those Visits, at about the End of four Months Progress, they found themselves in as little Likelihood of Retirement as the first Day: For the inferior *Colambs* were continually posting away, one after another, to perform their Respects to my Father, and all the inferior Magistrates of smaller Districts sending to know when they might be permitted to do the same. Poor *Youwarkee*, who saw no End of it, expressed her Concern for you in so lively a Manner to my Father, that, finding he could by no Means put a Stop to the Good-will of the People, and not bearing the Thoughts of *Youwarkee*'s Departure, till she had now received all their Compliments, he resolved to keep her with him till the next Winter set in in these Parts, and then to accompany her himself to *Graundevolet*. In the mean while, that you might not remain in an uneasy Suspence what was become of my Sister, he ordered me to dispatch Messengers express to inform you of the Reasons of her Stay: But I told him, if he pleased, I would execute that Office myself, with my Friend *Rosig*; with which he was very well pleased, and enjoined me to assure you of his Affection, and that he himself was Debtor to you for the Love and Kindness you had shewn his Daughter.

Thus Brother, says *Quangrollart*, I hope I have acquitted myself of my Charge to your Satisfaction; and it only now remains that I return you my Acknowledgments for your hearty Welcome to myself and Friend: Which (with Concern I speak it) I am afraid I shall not have an Opportunity to return at *Arndrumnstake*, the Distance being so immensely great, and you not having the *Graundee*. To-morrow Morning my Friend and I will set out on our Return home.

Quangrollart having done, I told him I could not but blush at the Load of undeserved Praises he had laid on me; but, as he had received his Notion of my Merits from a Wife, too fond to let my Character sink for want of her Support, it would be sufficient if himself could conceive of, and also represent me at his Return, in no worse a Light than other Men; and though it gave me Pain to think of losing my Wife so long, yet his Account of her Health, and the Company he assured me she would return in, would doubly compensate my Loss; and I begged of him, if it might be, with any Convenience, he would let some Messenger come the Day before her, to give me notice of their Approach. As to their Departure on the morrow, I told them I could by no Means think of that; as I had proposed to catch them a Dinner of fresh Fish in the Lake, and to shew them my Boat, and how and where I came into this *Arkoe*; believing, by what I had observed, it would be no small Novelty to them. So having engaged them one Day more, we parted for that Night to Rest.

CHAPTER XXIX

The Author shews Quangrollart *and* Rosig *his
Poultry; they are surprized at them; he takes them
a fishing; they wonder at his Cart, and at his shooting
a Fowl; they are terribly frightened at the firing of
the Gun;* Wilkins *pacifies them*

I WAS heartily sorry to lose my Brother thus quickly, and
still more so, to find it would be a long Time yet 'ere I should
see my Wife; however, I was resolved to behave as chearfully
as possible, and to omit nothing I could do, the few remaining
Hours of *Quangrollart's* Stay with me, to rivet myself
thoroughly in his Esteem, and to dismiss him with a most
cordial Affection to me and the rest of my Children here with
him. I rose early in the Morning to provide a good Breakfast
for my Guests, and considering we should be in the Air most
Part of that Day, I treated them with a Dish of hot Fish Soup,
and set before them on the Table a jovial Bottle of Brandy,
and my silver Can: This last Piece I chose to shew them, as
a Specimen of the Richness of my Houshold Furniture, and
the Grandeur of my living, concealing most of my other
Curiosities, till *Pendlehamby* my Father-in-Law's Arrival;
for I thought it would be imprudent not to have somewhat
new of this Kind to display at his Entertainment.

After a plenteous Meal, we set out on our pleasurable
Expedition; having told *Pedro* what to get for Dinner, and
that I believed we should not return till late.

We first took a Turn in the Wood; but I did not lead them
near my Tent, because I did not chuse my Wife should hear
of that till she came. I then shewed them my Farm-yard and
Poultry; which they were strangely surprized at, and wondered
to see so many Creatures come at my Call, and run about my
Legs, only upon a Whistle, tho' before there were only two or
three to be seen. They asked me an hundred Questions about
the Fowl, which I answered, and told them, these were some

such as they had eaten, and called *Crullmotts*, the Day before.
I afterwards carried them to hear the Music of those Plants
that I call my Cream-cheese; which, as there happened to be
a small Breeze stirring, made their usual Melody.

When we had diverted ourselves some time in the Wood,
we went to the wet Dock, where I shewed them my Boat. At
first View they wondered what Use it was for; to satisfy them
in that I stepped in, desiring them to follow me; but seeing the
Boat's Agitation, they did not chuse to venture, till I assured
them they might come with the greatest Safety: At length,
with some Persuasion, and repeated Assurances, I prevailed
on them to trust themselves with me.

We first rowed to the Bridge, where I informed them by
what Accident I was drawn down the Stream, on the other
Side of the Rock, and after a tedious and dangerous Passage,
discharged safe in the Lake through that Opening.

I then told them how surprized I had been, just before I
knew *Youwarkee*, with the Sight of her Country Folks; first
on the Lake, and then taking Flight from that Bridge; and
what had been my Thoughts, and how great my Terrors on
that Occasion.

After we had viewed the Bridge, I took them to my *Rill*,
(for by this time they were reconciled to the Boat, and would
help me to row it) and shewed them how I got Water. I then
landed them to see the Method of Fishing; for which Purpose
I laid my Net in proper Order, and fixing it as usual, I brought
it round out at the *Rill*, and had a very good Hawl, with which
I desired them to help me up; for though I could easily have
done it myself, I had a Mind to let them have a Hand in the
Sport, with which they were pleased. I perceived however,
the Fish were not agreeable to them; for when any one came
near their Hands, they avoided touching it. Notwithstanding,
having got the Net on shore, I laid it open: But to see how they
stared at the Fish, creeping backwards, and then at me and the
Net, it made me very merry to myself, though I did not care
to shew it.

I drew up at that Draught twenty-two Fishes in all, of which a few were near an Ell long, several about two Feet, and some smaller. When they saw me take up the large ones in my Arms, and tumble them into the Boat, they both, unrequested, took up of the small ones, and put them in likewise; but dropping them every Time they struck their Tails, the Fish had commonly two or three Falls 'ere they came to the Boat.

I asked them how they liked that Sport, and they told me it was something very surprizing that I should know just where the Fish were, as they could see none before I pulled them up, and yet they did not hear me whistle. I perceived by this, they imagined I could whistle the Fish together as well as the Fowls, and I did not undeceive them; being well enough pleased they should think me excellent for something, as I really thought they were on account of the *Graundee*.

Upon our Return, when I had docked my Boat, as there were too many Fish to carry up by Hand to the Grotto, I desired them to take a Turn upon the Shore till I fetched my Cart for it. I made what haste I could, and brought one of my Guns with me, which I determined upon some Occasion or other to fire off; for I took it they would be more surprised at the Explosion of that, than at any thing they had yet seen. Having loaded my Fish, and marched backwards, they eyed my Cart very much, and wondered what made the Wheels move about so; taking them for Legs it walked upon, till I explained the Reason of it, and then they desired to draw it, which they did with great Eagerness, one at a Time, the other observing its Motions.

As we advanced homewards, there came a large Water-Fowl, about the Size of a Goose, flying cross us. I bid them look at it, which they did. Says my Brother, I wish I had it. If you have a mind for it, says I, I'll give it you. I wish you would, says he, for I never saw any thing like it in my Life. Stand still then, says I, and stepping two or three Yards before them, I fired, and down it dropt. I then turned about, to observe what Impression the Gun had made on them, and could not help laughing to see them so terrified. *Rosig*, before

I could well look about, had got fifty Paces from me, and my Brother was lying behind the Cart of Fish. I called and asked them what was the Matter, and desired them to come to me, telling them they should receive no Harm, and offered my Brother the Gun to handle; but he, thanking me as much as if he had, retired to *Rosig*.

Finding they made a serious Affair of it, for I saw them whispering together, I was under some Apprehension for the Consequences of my Frolick. Thinks I, if under this Disgust they take Flight, refusing to hear me, and report that I was about to murder them, or tell any other pernicious Story to my Father of me, I am absolutely undone, and shall never see *Youwarkee* more. So I laid down the Gun by the Fish, and moving slowly towards them, expostulated with them upon their Disorder; assuring them, that though the Object before them might surprize them, it was but a common Instrument in my Country, which every Boy used to take Birds with; and protested to them, that the Gun of itself could do nothing without my Skill directing it; and that they might be sure I should never employ that, but to their Service. This, and a great deal more, brought us together again; and when we came to reasoning cooly, they blamed me for not giving them Notice. Says I, there was no Room for me to explain the Operation of the Gun to you, whilst the Bird was on the Wing; for it would have been gone out of my Reach before I could have made you sensible of that, and so have escaped me; which, as you desired me to get it you, I was resolved it should not do. But for yourselves, surely you could have no Diffidence in me: That is highly unbecoming of Man to Man, especially Relations; and, above all, a Relation to whom you have brought the welcomest News upon Earth, in the Love of my dear Father, and his Reconciliation to my Wife.

At last, by Degrees, I brought them to confess, that it was only a groundless sudden Terror which suppressed their Reason for a while; but that what I said was all very true; and as their serious Reflection returned, they were satisfied of it. I then stepped for the Bird, and brought it to them: It was

a very fine feathered Creature, and they were very much
delighted with the Beauty of it, and desired it might be laid
upon the Cart, and carried home.

All the Way we went afterwards to the Grotto, nothing was
to be heard from them but my Praises, and what a great and
wise Man Brother *Peter* was; and no Wonder now, Sister
Youwarkee, (says *Quangrollart*) once knowing him, could
never leave him. It was not my Business to gainsay this, but
only to receive it with so much Modesty as might serve to
heighten their good Opinion of me; and I found, upon my
Wife's Return, that *Quangrollart* had painted me in no mean
Colours to his Father.

I once more had the Pleasure of entertaining them, with
the old Fare, and some of the fresh Fish, Part boiled and Part
fryed; which last they chose before the boiled. We made
a very chearful Supper, talking over that Day's Adventures,
and of their ensuing Journey home; after which we retired to
Rest, mutually pleased. We all arose early, the next Morning.
We took a short Breakfast; after which *Quangrollart* and
Rosig stuck their Chaplets with the longest and most beautiful
Feathers of the Bird I shot, thinking them a fine Ornament.
Being now ready for Departure, they embraced me and the
Children, and were just taking Flight, when it came into my
Head, that as the King's Mistress had taken *Tommy* into her
Protection, it might possibly be a Means of ingratiating him in
her Favour, if I sent him the Flagellet, (for I had, in my Wife's
Absence, made two others near as good, by copying exactly
after it.) I therefore desired to know, if one of them would
trouble himself with a small Piece of Wood, I very much
wanted to convey to my Son. *Rosig* answered, with all his
Heart; if it was not very long he would put it into his *Colapet*.*
So I stepped in, and fetching the Flagellet, presented it to
Rosig. My Brother seeing it look oddly, with Holes in it,
desired (after he had asked if it was not a little Gun) to have
the handling of it. It was given him, and he surveyed it
very attentively. Being inquisitive into the Use of it, I told

* A Bag they always carry round the Neck.

him it was a musical Instrument, and played several Tunes upon it; with which he and his Companion were in Raptures. I doubt not, they would have sat a Week to hear me, if I would have gone on; but I desiring the latter to take care of its Safety, he put it in his *Colapet*, and away they went.

The End of the FIRST VOLUME

A

GENUINE ACCOUNT

OF THE

LIFE

OF

PETER WILKINS

VOLUME II

CHAPTER I

Peter *prepares for his Father's Reception; Arguments*
about his Beard; expects his Wife; Reflections on
her not coming; sees a Messenger on the Rock; has
Notice of Pendlehamby's *Arrival, and prepares*
a Treat

THE News my late Visitors had brought me, set my Mind
quite at ease; and now, having leisure to look into my own
Affairs, with the Summer before me, I began to consider what
Preparations I must make against the Return of my Wife; for
according to the Report I had heard, I concluded there would
be a great Number of Attendants; and, as her Father would
no doubt pique himself upon the Grandeur of his Equipage,
if his Followers should see nothing in me, but a plain dirty
Fellow, I should be contemned, and perhaps my Wife, thro'
my means, be slighted; or, at least, lose that Respect the Report
of me had in a great measure procured her.

The first thing therefore that I did, was to look into
my Chests again, wherein I knew there were many of the

Portuguese Captain's Cloaths, and take out such as would be most suitable to the Occasion, and lay them all by themselves. I found a blue Cloth laced Coat double-breasted, with very large gold Buttons, and very broad gold Buttonholes, lined with white Silk; a Pair of black Velvet Breeches, a large gold-laced Hat, and a Point[1] Neckcloth, with two or three very good Shirts, two Pair of red-heeled Shoes, a Pair of white, and another of scarlet Silk Stockings, two silver-hilted Swords, and several other good things; but upon Examination of these Cloaths, and by a Letter or two found in the Pockets of some of them, directed to Captain *Jeremiah Vauclaile*, in *Threadneedle-Street*, *London*, I judged these belonged to the *English* Captain, taken by the *Portuguese* Ship in *Africa*. I immediately tried some of them on, and thought they became me very well, and laid all those in particular Chests, to be ready when the Time came, and set them into one of my inner Rooms.

Upon examining the Contents of another Chest, I found a long scarlet Cloak laced, a Case of Rasors, a Pair of Scissars, and Shaving-glass; a Long-wig, and two Bob-wigs,[2] and laid them by; for I was determined, as I might possibly have no other Opportunity, to make myself appear as considerable as I could.

When I had digested in my Mind upon what Occasions I would appear in either of them, and laid them in proper Order, *Pedro*, and I went several Days to work with the Net, and caught abundance of Fish, which I salted, and dried; and we cut a great Quantity of long Grass to dry, and spread in my Tent, for the lower Gentry, and made up a little Cock of it; we also cut, and piled up a large Parcel of Fire-wood; and as I had now about thirty of the best Fish-skins, each of which would cover four Chairs, I nailed them on for Cushions to my Chairs, and the rest I sewed together, and made Rugs of them.

I had observed, that my Brother *Quangrallort*, and *Rossig*, neither of them had Beards, and as they were quite smooth chinned, I conjectured that none of their Countrymen had any; so, says I, if that is the case, as I have now both Scissars, and Rasors; I will e'en cut off mine, to be like them: I then set up my Glass, taking my Scissars in hand; but had not quite closed them for a Snip, when I considered, that as I was not of their Country, and was so different from them in other respects, whether it would not add to my Dignity, to appear with my Beard before them: This I debated some time, and then determined in favour of my Beard; but as this Question still ran in my Mind, and I wavered sometimes this way, sometimes that; I some Days after prepared again for Execution, and took a large Snip off; when, says I, how can I tell whether I can shave after all, I have not tried yet, and if I can't, how much more ridiculous shall I look with stubbed Hair here and there, than with this comely Beard? I must say, I never in my Life had so long a Debate with myself; it holding upwards of two Months, varying, almost every time I thought of it: 'Till one Day, dressing myself in a Suit I had not before tried on, and looking in the Glass; it can never be, says I, that this grave Beard should suit with these fine Cloaths: No, I will have it off I am resolved. I had no sooner given another good Snip, than spying the Cloak, I had a mind to see how I looked in that: Ay, says I, now I see I must either wear this Beard, or not this Cloak. How majestick does it look? So sage, so grave, it denotes Wisdom, and Solidity; and if they already think well of me, don't let me be Fool enough to relinquish my Claim to that, for a gay Coat. I had no sooner fixed on this, than I took up all the Implements to put again into the Chest; and the last of them being the Glass, I would have one more Look, before I parted with it: But, my Beard made such a horrid, frightful Figure, with the three great Cuts in it, that, tho' it grieved me to think I must part with it just when I had come to a Resolution to preserve it, I fell to work with my Scissars, and off it came; and after two or three Trials, I became very expert with my Rasor.

Winter coming on, as I knew I must soon have more Occasion than ever for a Stock of Provision, from the Increase of Mouths I expected; I laid in a Stock for a little Army, and when the Hurry of that was over, I kept a sharp Look-out

P

upon the Level, in Expectation of my Company; and had once a mind to have brought my Tent thither, to entertain them in: But it was too much trouble for the Hands I had, so I dropp'd the Design. I took one or other of the Children with me every Day, and grew more and more uneasy, at hearing nothing of them; and, as uncertain Attendance naturally breeds Thoughtfulness, and the Hours in no Employ pass so leisurely, as in that; my Mind, presaged numberless intervening Accidents, that might, if not intirely prevent their coming, at least postpone it.

Thinks I, and that I fixed for my Standard, *Youwarkee*, I'm sure, would come if she could; but then, says I, here is a long Flight, and to be undertaken by an old Man too, for I thought my Father-in-Law much older than I afterwards found him, who is now safe, and quiet at home; and having his Daughter with him, is no doubt desirous of continuing so: Now what cares he for my Uneasiness, he can find one Pretence or other, no doubt, of drilling on¹ the Time till the dark Weather is over; and then, forsooth, it will be too light to come; and thus shall I be hung up in Suspence for another Year: Or what if my Brother, as he called himself, for he may be no more a Brother of mine, than the Pope's, for aught I know, came only on a Pretence, to see how I went on; and not finding, for all his sham Compliments to me, his Sister married to his Father's liking, should advise him not to send my Wife back again; and so all the Trouble I have had on their Account, should only prove a standing Monument of my foolish Credulity! Nay, it is not impossible, but as I have already had one Message, to inform me *Tommy* and *Hallycarnie* are provided for, as much as to say, in plain *English*, I shall see them no more, so I may soon have another, by some sneaking Puppy or other, whom I suppose I am to treat for the News, to tell me, my Wife, and *Patty* are provided for too, and I am to thank my kind Benefactors, for taking so great a Charge off my Hands. Am I? No; I'll first set my Tent, Cloaths, Chairs, and all other Mementos of my Stupidity on fire, and by perishing, what's left of us, in the Blaze, exterminate at once the wretched Remains of a deserted Family. I hate to be made a Fool of.

I had scarce finished my Soliloquy, when I heard a monstrous sort of Groan, or Growl in the Air, like Thunder at a Distance. What's that, *Pedro*, says I? I never heard the like before, Daddy, says he. Look about Boy, says I, do you see any thing? We heard it again; Hark! says *Pedro*, it comes from that End of the Lake. While we were listening to the third Sound, says *Pedro*, Daddy, yonder is something black upon the Rock, I did not see just now. Why? it moves, says I, *Pedro*, here is News, good or bad. Hope the best, Daddy, says *Pedro*, I wish it may be Mammy. No, says I, *Pedro*, I don't expect her before I hear from her. Why then, says *Pedro*, here they come; I can plainly descern three of them. If my Brother *Tommy* should be there, Daddy? No, says I, *Pedro*, no such good News; they tell me, *Tommy*'s provided for, and that's to suffice for the Loss of my Child: And yet, *Pedro*, if I could get you settled in *England*, in some good Employ, I should consent to that; but what *Tommy*'s to be, I know not.

By this time, the three Persons were so near, that seeing us, they called out, *Peter*; and I, making Signs for them to alight, they settled just before me, and told me, that *Pendlehamby*, and *Youwarkee* would be with me by Light next Day.

I had no sooner heard this, but so far was I from firing my Tent, that I invited them to my Grotto, set the best Cheer before them, and with Over-haste to do more than one thing at once, I even left undone, what I might have done.

I asked them, who came with my Father? and they told me, about two hundred Guards: That knocked me up[1] again, as I had but prepared for about sixty; thinks I, my Scheme is all untwisted. I then asked them, what loud Noise it was, and if they heard it, just before I saw them over the Rock. They told me, they heard only the Gripsack [Trumpet] they brought with them, to distinguish them from ordinary Messengers; and then one of them shewed it me, for I had before only taken it for a long Staff in his Hand: But, says he, you will hear them much louder Tomorrow, and longer, before they come to you.

Having entertained them to their Content, I sent them to rest, not chusing to ask any Questions; for I avoided anticipating the Pleasure of hearing all the News from *Youwarkee* herself. However, the Boys and I prepared what Provisions of Fowl and Fish we could in the Time, to be ready cold, against they came, and then lay down ourselves.

CHAPTER II

Peter *settles the Formality of his Father's Reception;*
Description of their March, and alighting, receives
his Father; conducts him to the Grotto; offers to
beg Pardon for his Marriage; is prevented by
Pendlehamby; Youwarkee *not known in* English
Habit; Quarters the Officers in the Tent

My Mind ran so all Night upon settling the Formality with which I should receive *Pendlehamby*, that I got little or no Rest. In the Morning I spread my Table in as neat a manner as I could, and having dressed myself, *Pedro*, *Jemmy*, and *David*, we marched to the Plain; myself carrying a Chair, and each of them a Stool. I was dressed in a Cinnamon-coloured Gold-button Coat, Scarlet Waistcoat, Velvet Breeches, white Silk Stockings, the Campain-wig[1] flowing, a Gold-laced Hat and Feather, Point Cravat, Silver Sword, and over all my Cloak: As for my Sons, they had the Cloaths my Wife made before she went.

When we heard them coming, I marshalled the Children in the Order they were to sit, and charged them to do as they saw me do; but to keep rather a half Pace backwarder than me; and then sitting down in my Chair, I ordered *Pedro* to his Stool on my Right-hand, and *Jemmy* to his on my Left, and *David* to the Left of *Jemmy*.

I then sent two of the Messengers to meet them, with Instructions to let *Youwarkee* know where I waited for them, that they might alight at a small Distance before they came to me. This she having communicated to her Father, the Order ran through the whole Corps immediately, when and where to alight.

It will be impossible for me, by Words, to raise your Ideas adequate to the Grandeur of the Appearance this Body of Men made, coming over the Rock; but, as I perceive your Curiosity is on the Stretch to comprehend it, I shall faintly aim at gratifying you.

After we had heard, for some time, a Sound as of distant rumbling Thunder, or of a thousand Bears in Consort, serenading in their hoarsest Voices, we could just perceive, by the Clearness of the Dawn gilding the Edge of the Rock, a black Stream arise above the Summit of it, seemingly about forty Paces broad; when the Noise increasing very much, the Stream arose broader and broader; and then you might perceive Rows of Poles, with here and there a Streamer; and as soon as ever the main Body appeared above the Rock, there was such an universal Shout, as rent the Air, and echoing from the opposite Rock, returned the Salute to them again. This was succeeded with a most ravishing Sound of Voices, in Song, which continued till they came pretty near me; and then the first Line, consisting of all the Trumpets, mounting a considerable Height, and still blowing, left Room for the next Ranks, about twenty a-breast, to come forward beneath them; each of which dividing in the Middle, alighted in Ranks, at about twenty Paces Distance from my Right and Left, making a Lane before me, at the farther End of which *Pendlehamby* and his two Daughters alighted, with about twenty of his Guards behind them; the Remainder, consisting of about twenty more, coming forward over my Head, and alighting behind me; and during this whole Ceremony, the Gripsacks sounded with such a Din, it was astonishing.

Poor *Youwarkee*, who knew nothing of my Dress, or of the Loss of my Beard, was Thunderstruck when she saw me, not being able to observe any Visage I had, for my great Wig, and Hat; but putting a good Face on the matter, and not doubting, but if the Person she saw was not me, she should soon find her Husband, for she knew the Children by their Cloaths, she came forward at her Father's Right-hand, I sitting as great as a Lord, till they came within about thirty Paces of my Seat; and then gravely rising, I pulled off my Hat, and made my Obeisance; and again, at ten Steps forwarder: So that I made my third low Bow, close at the Feet of *Pendlehamby*; the Children all doing the same. I then kneeling with one Leg, embraced his Right-knee; who raising me up, embraced me. Then retiring three Steps, and coming forward again, I embraced *Youwarkee*, some time; during which, the Children observed my Pattern with *Pendlehamby*, who took them up, and kissed them.

I whispered *Youwarkee*, to know if any more of her Relations were in the Train, to whom I ought to pay my Compliments; she told me, only her Sister *Hallycarnie*, just behind her Father: I then saluted her, and stepping forward to the old Gentleman's Left-hand, I ushered him thro' the Lines of Guards to my Chair; where I caused him to sit down, with *Youwarkee*, and *Hallycarnie* on each side, and myself on the left of *Hallycarnie*.

After expressing the great Honour done me by *Pendlehamby* in this Visit; I told him, I had a little Grotto, about half a Mile thro' the Wood, to which if he pleased to command, we would retire; for I had only placed that Seat, to relieve him, immediately upon his Descent.

Pendlehamby rose, and all the Gripsacks sounded; he leading *Youwarkee* in his Right-hand, and I *Hallycarnie* in mine.

At the Grotto, my Father being seated, taking *Youwarkee* in my Hand, we paid our Obedience to him. I would have asked his Pardon, for taking his Daughter to Wife without his Leave, and was going on in a set Speech, I had studied for the Purpose: But he refused to hear me, telling me I was mistaken, he had consented. I was replying, I knew he had been so good to pass it over, but that would not excuse—when he again interrupted me, by saying, if I approve it, and esteem you, what can you desire more; so, finding the Subject ungrateful,[1] I desisted.

I then gave each of them a silver Can of *Madiera*, and *Youwarkee* retired. I soon made an Excuse to follow her, to learn if she was pleased with what I had done. Says she, my dearest, what is come to you; I'll promise you, but for fear of surprizing my Father, I had disowned you for my Husband. Dear *Youwee*, says I, do you approve my Dress, for this is the *English* Fashion. This, *Peter*, says she, I perceived attracted all Eyes to you, and indeed is very showy, and I approve it in regard to those we are now to please; but, you are not to imagine I esteem you more in this, than your own old Jacket; for it is *Peter* I love, in this, and all things else; but step in again, I shall only dress, and come to you.

My Wife, being dressed in her *English* Gown, just crossed the Room where my Father sat, to see *Dicky*, who was in another side Room. I was then setting by, and talking with him. Son, says my Father, I understood you had no other Woman in this Arkoe, but my Daughter; for surely, you have no Child so tall as that, pointing to my Wife. No Sir, said I, that is a Friend. Is she come to you, says he, in my Daughter's Absence? O Sir, says I, she is very well known to my Wife.

Whilst we were talking, in comes *Youwarkee*, with the Child in her Arms, which she kept covered to her Wrists, with her Gown-sleeve, to hide her Graundee; and, playing with the Child, talked only *English* to it. Is this your youngest Son? says my Father. I told him yes. Pray Madam, says I, bring the Child to my Father. Madam, says he, you have a fine Baby in your Arms, has his Mother seen him since she came home? He speaking this in his own Tongue, and *Youwarkee* looking at me, as if she could not understand him, I interpreted it to her. My Sister then desired to see the Child, but I was forced again to interpret, there too. In short, they both talked with my Wife near half an Hour, but neither of them knew her; till at last, saying in her own Language, that is your Grand-daddy, my dear *Dicky*; the old Gentleman smoked her out; I'll be slit, says he, if that is not *Youwarkee*. Its impossible, says *Hallycarnie*. Indeed Sister, says *Youwarkee*, you are mistaken; and my Father, protesting he had not the least

Suspicion of her, till she spoke in his Tongue, rose, and kissing her, and the Child, desired her to appear in that Habit during his Stay.

I asked *Pedro* what Provision had been made for the Guards. Son, says my Father, I bring not this Number of People to eat you up; they have their Subsistance with them; and he would by no means suffer me to allow them any. I then desired to know if there were any Officers, or others, to whom he would have shewn any particular Marks of Distinction. Son, says the old Glumm, you seem to have studied Punctillios; and tho' I should be sorry to incommode you for their sakes, if you could procure some Shelter, and Sleep-room, for about twenty of them, who are Superiors, ten at a time, while the rest are on Duty, I should be glad. I told him, I had purposely erected a Tent, which would, with great ease, accomodate a greater number; and as they were of Distinction, with his Leave, I insisted upon providing for them; to which, with some Reluctance, I procured his Consent.

When *Pendlehamby* was refreshed, he would go with me, to see the Officers Quarters; and shewing him my Tent, he, having never seen such a thing before, was going to climb up the Out-side of it, taking it for Earth. Hold Sir, said I, you can't do so: Then taking him to the Front of it, I turned aside the blue Cloth, and desired him to walk in; at which he seemed wonderfully pleased, and asked me how it was made. I told him, in as few Words as I could; but he understood so little of it, that any thing else I had said, might have done as well. He mightily approved it, and calling the chief Officer, told him, that was their Quarters. Then, turning to the Officer, I desired he would command my House, and that Provision should be supplied to his Quarters daily; at which, he hesitating; I assured him, I had my Father's Leave for what I offered; whereupon, he stroked his Chin.

I then asked him, if he had any clever Fellows under him, to serve them, and dress their Provisions; but, he hoped, he said, they were ready dressed, as his Men knew little of that Matter; but for any other piece of Service, as many as I pleased, should be at my Command.

CHAPTER III

The Manner of their Dinner; believe the Fish and
Fowl to be Fruits; hears his Brother and the Colambs
are coming; Account of their lying; Peter's
Reflections on the want of the Graundee; they view
the Arkoe; Servants harder to please than their
Masters; Reason for different Dresses the same Day

PENDLEHAMBY, having a mind to view my Arkoe, took
a long Walk with *Hallycarnie* in the Wood, till Dinner-time;
and, he having before told me, that some of his Guards always
waited on him at Meals; I ordered their Dinner before his
Return, sending a large Dish of cold Fowls, cut into Joints,
into the Tent, to be spread on clean Leaves I had laid on the
Chests, and setting a sufficient Quantity of Bread, and Fish
there also, I desired the Officers present to refresh themselves now; and the rest, when relieved, should have a fresh
Supply. I saw there was an Oddity in their Countenances,
which at first, I did not comprehend; but presently turning
about to the Superior, Sir, says I, tho' this Food may look
unusual to you, it is what my Island affords, and you'll be
better reconciled to it, after tasting: So, taking a Piece of
Fowl, and dipping it in the Salt, I eat a bit myself, and recommended another to him; who, eating it, they all fell to without further Scruple: Above all things commending the Salt,
as what they had never tasted the like of before, tho' they
thought they had, both of the Fish, and Fowl.

I then told them where my Supply of Water came from,
and that they must furnish themselves with that, by their
own Men.

Upon the Return of my Father, and Sister, the Gripsack
sounded for Dinner; when four Officers on Duty, entring,
desired, as their Posts, to have the serving up of the Dishes;
one of them, I perceived, having set on the first Dish, never
stirred from behind *Pendlehamby*; but upon his least Word,

or Sign, ordered the others what to do, or bring, which he only presented to my Father; and he frequently gave him a Piece from his own Plate; but the other Officers served at the Table promiscuously.

After Dinner, I brought in a Bowl of Punch; when, begging leave to proceed in my Country Method, I drank to my Father's Health. So, Daughter, says he to my Wife, we are at the old Game again. Son, says he, this is no Novelty to me, *Youwarkee* constantly drinking to the Health of her dear *Peter*, and the Children at *Grandevolet*, and obliging us, to pledge her, as she called it; but I thank you, and will return your Civility: So, taking a Glass, Son and Daughter, says he, long Life, Love, and Unity attend you, and my Grand-children. *Youwarkee*, and I, both rising till he had done, returned him our Thanks.

When we had sat some time, Son, says my Father, you and your Wife having lived so retired, I fear my Company, and Attendants, must put you to an Inconvenience: Now, as my Son intends you a Visit also, in Company with several of my Brother *Colambs*; if we shall be too great a Load upon you, declare it, for they will be at *Battingdrig* Arkoe To-morrow, to know whether it will be agreeable for them to proceed.

You know Son, says my Father, the Mouth is a great Devourer, and that the Stock your Family can't consume in a Year, by multiplying their Numbers may be reduced in a Day; now freely let me know, for you say you provided for us, how your Stock stands; that you may not only pleasure us, but we not injure you.

I told him, as for dried Fish, I had a vast Quantity, and that my Fowls were so numerous, I knew not my Stock; as to Bread, I had a great deal, and might have almost what more I would; and then for fresh Fish, the whole Province of *Arndrumstake* could not soon devour them; but for my Pickles, and Preserves, I had neither such large Quantities, or Con-veniencies to bestow them, if I had.

If this be the Case Son, says my Father, I may send your Brother Word to proceed; and dispatched ten Messengers with a Gripsack, to hasten his Son's Arrival.

It now began to be time for Rest, and the old Gentleman growing pretty mellow, with the Punch; which, by the hearty Pulls he took at it, I perceived was no disagreeable Entertainment to him; I conducted him to his Repose, and disposing of the rest of the Family, *Youwarkee* and I, with great Impatience retired.

You may imagine, I was sincerely glad to find myself once more alone with my *Youwarkee*; when, after a Transport of mutual Endearments, I desired to know how *Pendlehamby* first received her; which she told me, with every Circumstance, in so affecting a Manner, that the Tears forced Passage from my Eyes, in perfect Streams, and I loved the dear Man ever after, as my own Father.

She told me, *Tommy* was in great Favour at Court, before her Brother returned from me; but, ever since I sent him the Flagellet, he had been caressed[1] above measure, and would soon be a great Man. That *Hallycarnie*, was a constant Attendant on *Jahamel*, both in her Diversions, and Retirement; and she did not doubt, would in time, marry very well. As for *Patty*, she said her Father intended, with my Leave, to adopt her his own Child.

My Wife slept very sound after her Journey; but, my Hurry of Spirits denying me that Refreshment, I never, so much as now, lamented the want of the Graundee; for thinks I, now I have once again tasted the Sweets of Society, how shall I ever relish a total Desertion of it, which in a few Days must be the Case, when all this Company are fled, and myself am reduced to my old Jacket, and Water-cart again. Now, if I was as others here are, I might make a better Figure than they, by my superior Knowledge of things, and have the World my own: Nay, I would fly to my own Country, or to some other part of the World; where, even the Strangeness of my Appearance would procure me a good Subsistance. But, says I, if with my Graundee I should loose my Sight, or only be able to live in the Dark in *England*? why I should be full as bad as I am here; for no Body would be able to keep me Company abroad, as my Hours for the Air would be theirs of Retirement;

and then, at home, it would be much the same; no one would prefer my Company in a dark Room, in the Day-time, when they could enjoy others in the Light of the Sun; then, how should I be the better for the Graundee? Unless I fixed a Resolution of living here, or here-abouts; and then, to get into Company, I must retire to still darker Regions, which my Eyes are no ways adapted to; in short, I must be quite new moulded, new made, and new born too, before I can attain my Desires. Therefore, *Peter*, says I, be content, you have been happy here, in your Wife and Children without these things; then never make yourself so wretched, as to hope for a Change which can never possibly happen, and which, perhaps, if obtained, might undo you; but, intend only what you can compass, by weighing all Circumstances, and your Felicity will lie in very narrow Bounds; free, from two of the greatest Evils a Man can be beset by, Hopes, and Fears; two inseperable Companions, and deadly Enemies to Peace: For a Man is destroyed by Hope, thro' Fear of Disappointment. This brought me a Shew of Peace again; surely, says I, I am one of the most unaccountable amongst Mankind: I never can reflect, till I am worn down with Vexation. O *Glaulepze*, *Glaulepze*! says I, I shall never forget thy Speech after engaging the Crocodile; that every thing was to be attained by Resolution, by him that takes both Ends of a thing in his View at once, and fairly deliberates what may be given, and taken, from End to End. Surely, says I, this ought to be engraven on Brass, as I wish it was on my Heart; it would prevent me many painful Hours, help me with more Ease to compass attainable Ends, and to rest contented, under Difficulties insuperable: And, if I live to rise again, I will place it, where it shall never more be out of my Sight, and will enforce it, not only more and more on myself, but on my Children.

With this Thought, I dropped on Sleep, and with this, I awaked again; and the first thing I did, was to find a proper Place to write it, which, having fixed for the Door of my Cupboard, I took a burnt Stick, for my Pencil, and wrote as follows. 'He that is resolved to overcome, must have both

Ends of an Object in View at once, and fairly deliberate what may be given, and taken, from End to End; and then pursue the Dictates of cool Reason.' This, I wrote first in *English*, and then in the *Doorpt Swangeantine* Tongue; and, having read it twice or thrice over, I went for Water, and Fish, and returned before the Family were up.

I took care To-day also, that the Officers should be as well served as possible, and where an Accomodation must be wanting, I rather chose to let it fall on my Father, than on them; for I had ever observed it to be an easier thing, to satisfy the Master than the Man; as the Master weighs Circumstances, and from a natural Complaisancy in himself, puts a humane Construction upon that Error, or Omission, which the Servant wholly attributes to Slight, and Neglect.

My Company being abroad, about the Time I expected their Return, I dressed myself as the Day before, only without my Cloak, and in a black Bob-wig; and took a Turn to meet them.

Pendlehamby, spying me first among the Trees, Daughter *Youwarkee*, says he, you have an Husband, I think, for every Day in the Week; who's this, my Son *Peter*? Why, he is not the same Man he was Yesterday. She told him, she had heard me say, we changed our Apparel almost every Day in *England*; nay, sometimes twice, or thrice the same Day. What? says *Pendlehamby*, are they so mischievous there, they are fearful of being known in the latter, by those who saw them in the former Part of the Day?

By this time I was come up, and after paying due Compliments, says *Youwarkee*, my Father did not know you, my Dear, you are so altered in your other Wig; and I told him, in your Country, they not only change Wigs, but their whole Cloathing, two or three times a Day, sometimes. Son, says my Father, if it be so, I can't guess at the Design, of a Man's making himself, unlike himself. O, Sir, says I, it is owing to the different Functions he is to perform, that Day: As suppose, in the Morning he is to pursue Business, with his Inferiors, or meet at our Coffee-Houses, to hear, and chat over the News of the Day: He appears in a light, easy Habit, proper for Dispatch, and comes home dirty. Then, perhaps, he is to dine with a Friend at Mid-day; before whom, for Respect's sake, not chusing to be seen in his dirty Dress, he puts on something handsomer; and, after spending some time there; he has, it may be, an Appointment at Court, a Play, or with his Mistress; in all which last Cases, if he has any thing better than ordinary, it is a part of good Breeding to appear in that: But, if the very best was to be used in common, it might soon become the worst, and not fit for a nice Man to stir abroad in. The different Custom of Countries, you have told me of, says my Father, is surprizing. Here are we born with our Cloaths on, which always fit, be we ever so small, or large; nay, are never the worse for constant wearing; and you must be eternally altering, and changing Colour, Shape, and Habit: But, says he, where do they get all these things? Does every Man make just what he likes? No, says I, there are a particular Set of Men, whose Business it is to make for all the rest. What? says he, I suppose their Lasks [Slaves] make them. No Sir, they are Filgays, [Freemen] says I. It is their Trade, they do it for a Livelihood, being paid by them they work for. A Suit of these Cloaths, says I, taking up the Flap of my Coat, will cost what we call twelve or fourteen Pounds in Money. I don't understand you, says he. Why Sir, says I, that is as much, as will provide one moderate Man with all the necessary things of Life for two Months. Then, says he, these nice Men must be very rich. No, Sir, said I, there you are under a Mistake; for if a Man, very rich, and who is known to be so, neglects his Habit, it is taken to be his Choice; but, one who is not known to be rich, and is really not so, is by appearing gay sometimes thought to be so; for he comes little abroad, and pinches miserably at home; first to get that gay Suit, and then acts on the same part to preserve it; till some lucky hit may help him to the Means of getting another; as it frequently happens, by a good Marriage: For tho' he is but seldom seen in public, yet always appearing so fine when he is, the Ladies, whose Fancies are frequently more tickled with Shew than Sense, admitting him only at first as a Companion, are at last, if worth any thing, taken in the Toils he is ever spreading for them; and, becoming his Wife, produce a standing Fund to make him a rich Man in reality, which he but personated before.

Pendlehamby could not well understand all I said; and I found by him, that all the Riches they possessed were only Food and Slaves; and, as I found afterwards when amongst them, they know the want of nothing else: But, I am afraid, I have put them upon another way of thinking, tho' I aimed at what we call civilizing of them.

CHAPTER IV

Quangrallort *arrives with the* Colambs; *streightned for Accommodation; remove to the Tent;* Youwarkee *not known;* Peter *relates Part of his Travels; Dispute about the Beast-Fish Skins*

SLEEPING longer than usual, I was awakened next Morning by a Gripsack from *Quangrallort*; upon hearing of which, I roused immediately, thinking they were at my Door; but the Messenger told me, they could not be there in what I understood by his Signs to be about two Hours; for they have no such Measure for Time, as Hours: So I dressed at leisure, and then went to *Youwarkee*, and waked her; *Youwee*, says I, your Brother will be here presently, and I having a mind you should appear as my Country-woman, would have you dress yourself.

We walked down to the Level, and but just saved our Distance; for the Van of them were within the Arkoe before we arrived, and with such a Train after them, as seemed to reach the whole Length of the Arkoe. The Regularity and Order of their Flight was admirable, and the Break of the Trumpets so great, sounding all the way they came, (for we had not only one Set of them, but at least thirty, there being so many *Colambs* and petty Princes in the Train, each with fifty Attendants) that I wondered how they could bear it. As the Principals alighted, which was at least an hundred Paces from me, the Gripsacks still kept Wing, sounding as long as we stayed.

This, was a very tedious Ceremony, for the Guards alighting with their *Colambs*, ranged just as *Pendlehamby*'s had done, but reached as far as the Eye could see. As they moved towards us, *Youwarkee*, and I, having stood still some time, moved slowly forward to meet them.

It would have surprized you, to have seen the Deference they paid us; and, I believe, the Guards took us for something above the mortal Race. *Youwarkee* shewed no part of her Graundee, having her Sleeves down to her Wrists, white Silk Stockings, and red-heeled Shoes; so that none of them knew her for one of them.

The first that we met was my Brother, to whom we had only an Opportunity of paying our Compliments *en passant*, before another Grandee came up, who was succeeded by another, and another, to the number of thirty; some out of Respect to my Father and Brother, and some out of mere Curiosity to see me; and as fast as each had paid his Salutes, he passed us, till we found we had no more to meet; when we turned about, and fell in with the Company.

When we came to the Grotto, I was very much put to it for Room, we scarce being able to stand upright by each other, much less to sit down; which my Father perceiving, my dear Friends, says he, had my Son known, in time, of so much good Company, he would have been better provided with Seats for us all; but considering all we see is the Labour only of his own Hands, we should rather admire at the many Conveniencies we see here, than be uneasy there are no more: And, Son, says he, as we are now so large a Body, I propose that we adjourn to the Officers Quarters, and let them take ours. I returned my Father Thanks for the Hint, and led the way, the rest following; where we found Room enough and to spare.

Tho' *Youwarkee* was with us all Dinner-time, helping the
Guests, we had no sooner done, but says *Quangrallort*, aloud,
Brother *Peter*, are we not to see my Sister? I not hearing
perfectly what he said, tho' I perceived he spoke to me; Sir,
says I. My Sister *Youwarkee*, says he, why won't she appear?
here are several of her good Friends, as well as myself, will be
glad to see her. My Father then laughed so heartily, that the
rest taking notice of it, my poor Brother was put to the Blush.
Son, says my Father, don't you know your own Sister? We
have not seen her yet, says one of the *Colambs*, or any Lady,
but your Daughter *Hallycarnie*, and that Attendant. My
Brother, then seeing how it was, came up to salute my Wife;
but even then had his Scruples, till he saw her smile; and then
begged Pardon for his Oversight, as did all the *Colambs*, upon
saluting her: My Brother declaring, that as she was somewhat
behind me on the Level, he had only paid her the Respect of
his Chin, taking her for some one attending me. The *Colamb*
following my Brother, assured her, the little Regard shewn
her by *Quangrallort*, who he thought should know best where
to bestow his Respects, was the Reason of his taking no more
Notice of her; and each, confessing his Mistake arose from
too nearly copying the Steps of his immediate Predecessor,
they all made excuse, and the Mistake made us very merry, till
they proposed taking a Turn in the Woods, it being a great
Novelty to them, they said; but I begged they would leave me
behind, to prepare for their Return.

Having refreshed themselves after they came home,
Quangrallort, being put upon it by some of the *Colambs*, told
me, I could not render a more acceptable Favour to the whole
Company, than to relate to them an Account of my Adventures; for tho', says he, I told them last Night what I remembered to have heard from you; yet the Variety was so great,
I could not deliver the Facts in Order, as I heard them, but
was obliged to take here a-piece, and there another, as they
occurred to me, making rather several Stories of it, than
a continued Series of Facts.

All the *Colambs* immediately seconded the Motion, and

Q

desired me to begin. I then ordering a clear Table, and a Bowl of Punch, and having drank all the Company's Healths, began my Narration, hoping to have finished it before Bedtime; but they pressing me to be very particular, and frequently one or other requiring Explanations upon particular Facts; and then one making a Remark upon something, which another answering, and a third replying to; they got the Talk out of my Hands, so long, that having lost themselves in the Argument, and forgot what I said last, they begged my Pardon, and desired me to go on: When one, who in Contemplation of one Fact had lost best part of another, prayed me to go on from such an Incident, and another from one before that; so that I was frequently obliged to begin, half way back again. This Method not only spun out my Story to a very great Length, but instead of its being finished that Evening, as I had purposed, it was scarce well begun before Bed-time drew on: So I just having brought them to *Angola*, told them, as it grew late, if they pleased, I would finish the Remainder next Night; which they agreed to.

Quangrallort then asked my Father, if he had been fishing since he came; but he told him, he knew not what he meant. Then all the Company desired I would shew them what that was. I told them they might command me as they pleased; so we appointed the next Morning for that Exercise; but, Gentlemen, says I, your Lodging to Night gives me the greatest Pain; for I know not what I shall do about that. I have a few Beast-Fish Skins, which are very soft and hairy, but not a Sufficiency for so many Friends as I would at present be proud to oblige: But I can lay them as far as they will go, upon as much dry Reeds and Grass as you please. I then sent a Servant to *Youwarkee* for the Skins; after which, they one and all crying out, if they had but good dry Reeds, they desired no better Lodging: I dispatched Hands, to bring away a large Parcel of it to the Tent; which they did in a trice. Then waiting on those few who lay at the Grotto to their Quarters, and having sent *Youwarkee* to her Sister, I returned to the Tent, to take up my own Lodging with those I had left there.

I had not yet entred the Tent, when I heard a perfect Tumult within, every one talking so loud, and all together, that I verily thought they had fallen out, and were going to Handycuffs;[1] however, I resolved to go in amongst them, and try to compose their Difference: When just entring, and they spying me, several ran to me, with each a Skin in his Hand, the rest following as fast as they could. Gentlemen, says I, I hoped to have found you all at Rest. So we should have been, says one of them, but for these, what you call 'ems. It is my unspeakable Misfortune, says I, that I have no more at your Service, and am sorry I should cause them to be brought, since each of you can't have one. Says one of them, I don't want one, I have seen enough of it. Then, Gentlemen, says I, it is possible there may be so many more of that *Colamb*'s Mind, that there may be sufficient for those who desire them. They neither knew what to make of me, or I of them, all this while; till an old *Colamb* perceiving our Mistake, Mr. *Peter*, says he, we have only had a Dispute—I am sorry at my Heart for it, says I; but I perceived you were very warm, before I entred, and am in great Hopes of compromising Matters, to all your Satisfactions. I was going, says the same *Colamb*, to tell you we had a Dispute about what these Things were, nothing else. I was then struck on a Heap, being quite ashamed they should think I suspected they had been quarrelling for the Skins; and how to come of,[2] I knew not. You'll excuse me Sir, says I, for expressing a Concern that you could not each have one, to examine into at the same time, that one of you need not have waited to make your Remarks, till the other had done. No Occasion, no Occasion for that, Mr. *Peter*, said they all together; we shall have Leisure enough to examine them to-morrow; but we want to know what they are, and where they grow. Gentlemen, says I, each of these is the Cloathing of a particular Fish. And where do they grow, said they? In the Lake, says I; they are a living Creature, who inhabit that great Water; I often catch them when I am fishing; the same Exercise we shall go upon to-morrow.

I had much ado to persuade them they did not grow on

Trees, which I was then much more surprized at, than some time after, that I returned their Visit: But having satisfied them, and given them some possible Hopes they might see one alive next Day, they were very well contented; and we all lay down to Rest.

CHAPTER V

Go a fishing; catch a Beast-Fish; afraid of the Gun; how Peter *altered his Net; a Fish-dinner for the Guards; Method of dressing and eating it*

I APPEARED before them in the Morning in my old Jacket, and an old Hat with Brims indented almost to the Crown, a Flannel Nightcap, and checker'd Shirt. How now Son? says my Father, what have we here? Sir, says I, this will shew you the Use of our *English* Fashion I mentioned the other Day, and the Necessity of it. You see me in this indifferent Habit, because my next Business requires it; but when I come back, and have no further Dirty-work to do, I shall then dress, as near as I can, to qualify me for your Company.

Are you for moving Gentlemen? says my Brother; I believe it is time: They then all arising, we went to the Lake; where getting into my Boat, and telling them, that any six of them might go with me, they, never having seen such a thing before, and not much liking the Looks of it, all made Excuses; till my Brother, assuring them it was very safe, and that he had sailed in it the last Trip, three or four of them, with my Father, and *Hallycarnie*, who was very desirous of seeing me fish, got in; and we sailed a great way up the Lake, taking my Gun as usual with me.

It gave me exceeding Delight, to see the whole Body of the People then in the Arkoe on the Graundee; some hovering over our Heads, and talking with us; others flying this way, others that, till I had pitched upon a Spot to begin my Operation; when rowing to Shoar, and quitting my Boat, the whole Body of People settled just by me, staring at me and my Net, and wondering what I was doing. I then taking a Sweep as usual, got some of the Soldiers to assist me to Shoar with it; but, when the Cod[1] of the Net landed, and the Fish began to dash with their Tails at the Water's Edge, away ran all my Soldiers, frighted out of their Wits to think what was coming: But it being a large Hale,[2] and a shelving Bank, I could not lift it to the Level myself; which, my Brother, who had seen the Sport before, perceiving, tho' not one of the rest stirred, lent me a Hand, and we got it up.

You can't imagine, what Surprize appeared in every Face upon opening the Net, and seeing all the Fish naked; they drew up by degrees closer and closer, for I let the Fish lie some time for their Observation; but seeing the large Fish, upon my handling them, flap their Tails, they very expeditiously retired again. I then, tossed several of them into the Boat; but two of them being very large, and rough-scaled ugly Fish, I did not think I could lift them myself, so desired Assistance; but no body stirred: I expected some of the *Colambs* would have ordered their Men to have helped me; but they were so terrified with seeing me handle them, that they could not have the Conscience to order their Men on so severe a Duty, till a common Man came to me, and taking the Tail, and I the Head, we tossed them both into the Boat.

I went higher up the Lake than usual, in hopes of a Beast-Fish, to shew them; but, tho' I could not meet with one, I had several very great Hales, and took three or four of my Lobsters, very large ones. This was the second Trial I had made of my Net, since I had altered it, and gave me great Satisfaction; for I could now take as many Fish at one Draught, as I could before have done at ten; I had found, that tho' my Net was very long, yet for want of a Bag, or Cod to inclose the Fish, many that were included within its Compass would, whilst I drew round, swim to the Extreams, and so get out, for want of some Inlet to enter at; for which reason, I sawed off the Top of a Tree, at about ten Feet from the Ground, and drawing a Circle of six Feet Diameter round the Tree, on the Ground,

I stuck it round with small Pegs, at two Inches Distance; then I drove the like Number of Nails round the Top of the Trunk of the Tree, and straining a Length of Matline from each Peg on the Ground to a correspondent Nail on the Tree, I tied my Matline in Circles round the strained Lines, from Top to Bottom, about two Inches Distance at the Bottom, but at a less Distance where the strained Lines grew nearer to each other towards the Top; and having secured all the Ends, by some Line twisted round them, I cut a Hole in the Middle of my Net, and tied the large Ground End over the Hole in the Net, and gathered the small End up in a Purse, tying it up tight; and by this means, I now scarce lost any Fish, which once were within the Sweep of my Net.

Having had so good Success, I had a Design of returning; but thought, as I could now so easily entertain a Multitude, I might as well take another Hale or two, and make an handsome Treat for the Soldiery: Then coming up to my Drill's Mouth,[1] I fixed my Implements for a Draft there, and beginning to draw up, I found great Resistance in the Net, and got two or three to help me; but, coming near Shoar, when the Company saw the Net tumble and roll, and rise and fall, they all ran as if they were mad; till I called them, and told the *Colambs*, it was only one of the Fish whose Skins I had shewn them; upon which, by that time I had discharged the Fish from the Net, they were all round me again. But, no sooner had he got loose, than up he rose, whirled his Wings, and at the same Instant uttered such a Groan, that my whole Company retreated again, thinking me somewhat more than a Man, who could face so dreadful an Enemy. I intreated them to come and view it; but finding no Arguments could bring them nearer, I edged round till I got him between me and the Water, and shot him dead.

Upon the Report of my Gun, the whole Field was in the Air, darting and screaming, as I have often seen a Flight of Rooks do on the same Occasion; and I am apt to believe some of them never returned again, but went directly home.

I was a little concerned to see the Confusion I had caused;

and laying down my Gun, my Brother, who tho' at a Distance when I shot, knowing what I was at, and coming up to me, it put the rest upon their Consideration; and they alighted one by one, at a Distance, till they were all on the Level again.

My Father, and the *Colambs*, who were the first that durst approach, wondered what I had done, and how the Fish came to be dead, and whence so much Fire and Smoak proceeded, for they were sure I brought none with me; and asked me abundance of Questions: But, as I knew I must have Occasion for answering to the same thing twenty times over, had I entred upon an Explanation there, I deferred giving them Satisfaction till we came home; when all at once might be capable of hearing what was said. So, I told them, the most necessary thing at present was, to stow the Fish in the Boat; for it was the largest I had ever taken, and I could not wholly do it myself. I made several Efforts for Help, but in vain; till the same Soldier who had helped me with one of the first Fish came to my Relief, and, desiring my Orders what to do, assisted me; and the rest seeing the Difficulty we both had to manage it, one or two more of them coming up, we shipped it on board.

I then called the *Colambs* to me, telling them, I was sorry I had given such a general Disturbance to them, by shooting the Fish; but, as they kept at too great a Distance from me to have Notice of my Design, and if I had followed them the Fish might have escaped before my Return, I was obliged to do as I did; which was without any possibility of hurting them: But, as I had given them such a Fright, I hoped they would this one Day give me an Opportunity of complimenting their Guards with a Fish-dinner, if we could any way contrive to dress it; for whoever did that must be able to bear the close Light of a large Fire. They all shook their Heads, but my Brother; who told me, he had in his Retinue six Men from Mount *Alkoe* [a burning Mountain] purposely retained for their strong Sight, to attend him always to *Crashdoorpt*; who, he believed, for the Benefit of the rest, would undertake the

Cookery, if I would shew them how. I desired he would give them Orders to attend me on the other Side the Lake, and I would instruct them at my landing; and then I crossed over with my Booty.

Finding the Mount *Alkoe* Men waiting for my landing, I asked if they could bear the Sight of Fire. They told me, they were used to much greater Light and Flames than I had ever seen, they believed. Very good, said I, then get into my Boat, three of you, and hand out that Fish to the Shore. I found they were more afraid of the Fish than of the Fire; for not one of them stirred till I got in and tossed out several small ones; and then taking up a large one, help me some body, says I, they looking a little at one another; till one of them venturing to take it, the rest fell heartily to work, and dispatched the whole Lading presently. I then laid a small Parcel upon my Cart, for our own eating, and the Officers, and sending them to the Grotto, I gave the Cooks their Charge.

Now, says I, my Lads, do you serve all the rest of the Fish as I do this; cutting it open at the same time, and throwing away the Guts, and I will send each of you such an Instrument as I use here, pointing to my Knife. I shall order six large Heaps of Wood to the Level, to be piled up there: When you have done the Fish, do you set fire to the Heaps, and let them burn till the Flame is over, and the Coals are clear; then lay on your Fish, and if any are too large to be managable, cut them in proper Pieces, and with Sticks, which I will send you, turn them over and over, walking round the Fire, and with the forked End of the Stick toss the least off first, and afterwards the greater; but be sure, throw the Fish as far as ever you can from the Fire, amongst the Men, that they may not be obliged to come too near it; and in this manner go on, till either they have enough, or your Fish are gone; and when you have done, come to the Grotto for your Reward.

I then set abundance of Hands to work to carry Wood, to be laid in six Heaps, two hundred Paces from each other, and told them how to pile it. I then prepared six long taper Sticks with forked Ends, and ordered more Hands to divide the Fish equally to the Piles. I sent others with Salt, and Bread; and I ordered them to let me know when all was ready.

While these Preparations were making, my Tent Visitors had all dined, and my Cart had returned with the Beast-Fish, which the Company desired might be brought in; when every one passed his Judgment upon it, and a long Dissertation we had, on the marvelous Works of *Collwarr*. I let them go on with their Show, tho' I could have disproved most of their Conclusions, from the little Knowlege I had of things; but I never was Knight-Errant enough to oppose my Sentiments to a Multitude already prepossessed on the other Side of the Question; for this reason, because I have ever observed, that where several have imbibed the same ridiculous Principle in Infancy, they never want Arguments, tho' ever so ridiculous, to support it: And, as no one of them can desert it without impeaching the Judgment of the rest, they encourage each other in their Obstinacy, and quite out-vote a single Person; and then, the Laugh beginning on the strongest Side, nothing is so difficult as to get it out of their Hands; but when a single Man in the wrong hears a just Argument from a single Antagonist, which he can't contradict, he imbibes its Force; and whilst that lasts, as nothing but a better Argument, with better Reasons, can remove it, he from thenceforth adopts his Adversary's Reasons for his own, to oppose against his own former Opinion.

In the Height of our Disputations on the Beast-Fish, came News that the Broil was going to begin; and, as I expected very good Diversion at it, I invited the Company to go see it, telling them, in my Opinion, it would exceed the Sport in taking them. We passed thro' the Wood till we came amongst the Shrubs, where I placed them to be out of Harm's-way; and the Fire, which was now nothing but Cinders, was of no Inconvenience to them. They were pleased with it to per-fection; for first, the six Men who walked round the Fires, by the glowing Light of the Embers and the shining of their Graundees, looked like Men on fire; then, to see each Fire surrounded with a Circle of Men, at the Diameter of near two hundred Paces, as close as they could well stand, by a more distant Shine of the Fire, had a very pleasant Effect: But, when the Broilers began to throw the Fish about, for each Man stood with some Salt and a Cut of Bread in his Hand, to see a Body of an hundred Men running for it, and whilst they were stooping and scrambling for that, to see a hot Fish fall on the Back of one, which was whipped off by another, who scalding his Mouth with it, threw it in the Face of a third, when a fourth, fifth, and sixth pulling it in Pieces ran away with it; and to see the different Postures, Courses, and Groups during this Exercise and Running-feast, was the most agreeable Farce my Guests had ever seen in their Lives; and, to the great Saving of my Liquors, kept us in the Wood for full three Hours, not a Soul stirring till the Feast was over.

We spent best Part of this Evening in Discourse on the Passages of the Day; the Reflections on which not being concluded till Bed-time, my Adventures were postponed till the next Night; but we had first concluded upon a Shooting for the next Morning; for they were all extreamly desirous of knowing how I did it, at a time they should have Opportunity of seeing me, and making Remarks; and I, being unwilling they should think me a Conjurer, agreed to make them Masters of Part of the Mystery of Powder and Ball.

CHAPTER VI

A Shooting proposed; all afraid of the Gun but one private Guard; his Behaviour; Pendlehamby at Peter's Request makes him a General; Peter's Discourse thereon; Remainder of his Story; the Colambs return

THIS being the fifth Morning, I cleaned up my best Gun, and prepared my Balls, and we all took a Walk towards the Bridge, every one admiring my Gun, as we went; but I could get none of them to carry it, and we had, at least, five hundred Questions proposed about it. I told them they need not be afraid of it, for it was only Wood, and Iron; but they knew nothing of Iron. I then shewed them how I made it give Fire, by snapping the Cock; they thought it was very strange. I then put a little Powder in the Pan, and made it Flash, and shewing them the empty Pan, they would not be persuaded but I had taken away the Powder, before the Flash, or else, they said, it was impossible that it should be all gone, upon flashing only; for they said it was a little Nut, using the same Word to express both Nut and Seed. I then desired one of them to put in some Powder, and snap it himself; but having prevailed with him to try the Experiment, if I had not thro' Caution held my Hand upon the Barrel, the Gun had been on the Ground; for the Moment it flashed, he let go, and ran for it.

I had a great Inclination to gain the better of their Prejudices, and used abundance of Arguments to prove the Gun as innocent a thing as a Twig I took up; and that it was the Powder, which when set on fire, the Flame thereof wanting more Room, than the Powder itself did, forced itself, and all that opposed it, out of the Mouth of the Gun, with such Fury as to make the Noise they heard; and being just come to the Rock, now, says I, you shall see that what I tell you is true. They told me, they desired nothing more than that I would make them understand it, for it was the strangest thing they had ever seen. Well then, says I, observe; I put in thus much Powder only, and with this Rag I stop it down close. Now, says I, you see by the Length of this Stick, that the Rag and Powder take up the Space only of a Finger's Depth on the Inside of the Gun. They saw that plainly, they said; but how could that kill any thing? Now look again, says I, I put in a little more Powder, as I did before when I made a Flash, and you see there is a little Hole from this Powder thro' the Side of the Gun to the Powder within. Do you observe that this communicates with that, thro' this Hole? Yes, they said, they did. Now, says I, when I put fire to this, it sets fire to that within; which Fire, turning to Flame, and wanting Room, bursts out at the Mouth of the Gun: And to shew you with what Force it comes out, here handle this round Ball, giving them a Bullet to handle; you feel how heavy it is; now can any of you throw this Ball as far as that Rock? for I stood a good hundred Paces from it. They told me, no. And don't you think, says I, that if the Force of the Fire made by this Powder can throw this Ball to that Rock, that Force must be very great? They said, they thought it must; but believed it to be impossible. But, says I, if it not only throws it to the Rock, but beats out a Piece of the Stone, must not that be much more violent? They agreed it must. Then putting in the Ball, now, says I, we will try. I then ordered one to daub a Part of the Rock, about Breast high, with some Mud, and first to observe about it, if the Rock was any where fresh broken, or not; who, returning, reported that the Rock was all of a Colour, and sound, but somewhat ragged all about the Mud. Did you lay the Mud on smooth, says I? He replied, yes. Then lifting up my Gun, I perceived they were creeping off; so, I took it down again, and calling, reasoned with them upon their Fears. What Mischief, says I, can you apprehend from this Gun in my Hand? Should I be able to hurt you with it, are you not all my Friends, or Relations; could I be willing to do it? If the Gun of itself could hurt, would I handle it as I do? For shame, be more courageous, rouse your Reason, and stand by me; I shall take care not to hurt you; it looks as if you mistrusted my Love to you; for this Gun can do nothing, but what I direct it to.

By such like Persuasions, rough and smooth, I prevailed upon the major Part of the *Colambs* and Officers to stand near me to see me fire; and then I shot; but tho' my Words had engaged them to stand it, I had no sooner snapped, but the Graundees flew all open, tho' they closed again immediately; and then, we fell to Question and Answer again. I desired them to walk to the Rock, and sent the Person who put up the Mark before, to see, and shew us exactly what Alteration there was; he told us, there was a round Hole in the Mud, pointing to it, which he did not leave there, and taking away the Mud, a thick Shiver[1] of the Rock followed it. They then all agreed, that the Ball must have made both the Hole in the Mud, and also splintered the Rock; and stood in amaze at it, not being able to comprehend it: But by all the Art I had I could not prevail with a Man of them to fire the Gun himself, till it had been buzzed about a good while, and at last came to my Ears, that a common Soldier behind said he should not be afraid of it, if the Gentleman would show him how.

I then ordered the Fellow to me, and he told me, with a composed Look, that it had always been his way of thinking, that what he saw another do, he could do himself, and could not rest till he had tried: And Sir, says he, if this Gun, as you call it, does not hurt you, why should it hurt me? And if you can make it hit that Rock, why should not I? when you have told me how you manage it. Are not you the Man that first helped me up with the large Fish Yesterday, says I? He told me he was.

I was prodigiously pleased with the Fellow's Spirit, and, says I, my Friend, if you will, and I live, you shall hit it before you have done. I then shewed him the Sight of the Gun, and how to hold it; and being perfect in that, now, says I, shut your left Eye, and observe with your Right, till this Knob, and that Notch, are exactly even with each other, and the Middle of that Mark; and when they are so, pull this Bit with your Fore-finger, holding the Gun tight to your Shoulder. He so exactly pursued my Directions, that he hit the very Middle of the Mud; and then, without any Emotion, walked up with the Gun in his Hand, as I had done before; and turning to me, very gravely, Sir, says he, it is hit. I told him, the best Marksman on Earth could not be sure of coming so near his Mark. He stroked his Chin,[2] and giving me the Gun again, was walking to his Place; but I stopped him, and seeing something so modest and sincere in his Countenance and Behaviour, and so generous in his Spirit, I asked him to which *Colamb* he belonged. He told me to *Colamb Pendlehamby*. To my Father? says I, then sure I shall not be denied.

I took him with me to my Father, who was not yet come up to the Rock. Sir, says I, there is a Favour I would beg of you. Son, says he, what is it you can ask, that I can refuse you? Says I, Sir, this Man belongs to your Guards; now there is something so noble and daring in his Spirit, and yet so meek and deserving in his Deportment, that if you will load me with Obligation, it is to make him an Officer: He is not deserving of so ill a Station as a private Man.

My Father looking at me, Son, says he, there is something to be done before he can be qualified for what you require. This, thinks I, is a put-off. Pray Sir, says I, what can a Man of Courage, Sense, and a cool Temper want, to qualify him for what I ask? Something, says he, which none but myself can give; and that, at your desire, I will supply him with. Then, my Father calling him, Lask *Nasgig* bonyoe, says he, that is, Slave *Nasgig* lie down. *Nasgig*, for that was his Name, immediately fell on his Face, with his Arms, and Hands, strait by his Sides; when my Father, setting his left Foot on *Nasgig*'s Neck, pronounced these Words: Lask, I give thee Life, thou art a Filgay. Then *Nasgig* raising himself on his Knees, made Obeisance to my Father, and standing up stroaked his Chin; and my Father taking him by the Hand, in token of Equality, the Ceremony ceased.

Now Son, says my Father, let me hear your Request? It is only, Sir, said I, Preferment for the deserving, equal to his Merit. My Father asked him if he understood the Duty of a Gorpel, [a sort of Ensign.] He did not reply yes, but beginning, gave a compendious sort of History of his whole Duty; at which, all the *Colambs* were very much surpris'd; for even his Comrades were not apprized, or ever imagined he knew more of Military Affairs than themselves. My Father then asked him, if he knew how to behave as a Cluff [Captain]; but he made as little Difficulty of that as the other, going thro' the several Parts of Duty in all the different Branches, in Peace and War, at Home and Abroad. Son, says my Father, it is a Mystery to me, you should have found out more in an Hour, than I myself could in half an Age; for this Man was born in my Palang [Town], of my own Lask, and has been mine, and my Father's, these forty Years. I shall be glad if you will look on the rest of my Lasks, and give me your Opinion; I may have more as deserving. I told him, such as *Nasgig* were not to be met with very often; and when they were found, ought to be cherished accordingly.

Sir, says I, Nature works upon the same sort of Materials divers ways; on some in sport, and some in earnest; and if the necessary Qualifications of a great Man are impressed on our Mass, 'tis odds but we improve regularly into one, tho' it may never be publickly known, or even to ourselves, till a proper Occasion: For as a curious Genius will be most inquisitive after, and is most an end retentive of Knowledge; so no Man is less ostentatious of it. He covets Knowledge, not from the Prospect of Gain, but meerly for its own sake; the very knowing, being his Recompence: And if I may presume to give you a Hint, how properly to bestow your Favours, let it be on Persons like this; for the vain knowing Man, who is always shewing it, as he for the most part labours for it, to shew out with, and procure his Rise by it, were it not for the Hopes of that, would not think Knowledge worth attaining; and as his Rise is his Aim, if he could invent any more expeditious Method than that, he would not pretermit any ill Act, that might advance him according to his Lust of rising. But the Man who aims at Perfection, from his natural Inclination, must, to attain his End, avoid all ill Courses, as Impediments to that Perfection he lusts after: And that, by *Nasgig*'s Worth being so little known, I'll answer for it, is his Character. And this being true, yourself will deduce the Consequence, which is the fitter Man to bear place; for with me it is a Maxim, He that labours after Truth for Truth's sake, and that he surely must who proposes no worldly View in it, can't arrive at his Ends by false Methods; but is always the truest Friend to himself and others, the trustiest Subject to his Lord, and the most faithful Servant to his God.

My Father then turning to me, Son, says he, you have enlightened me more than ever I was before, and have put me on a new way of thinking; for which I am to return you many Thanks. And the whole Company doing the same, says my Father, I lost a brave General-Officer lately, who was destined to the Western Wars, which are breaking out; and have been long debating in my Mind, to whom I should commit his Corps; and, but for the Hazard of the Enterprize, I would have now given it to *Nasgig*; but shall be loth to lose him so soon, after I am acquainted with his Worth; so will think of some other Post nearer my Person for him, less dangerous, tho' perhaps, not so honourable.

Great Sir, says *Nasgig*, I am too sensible of the Honour already done me, to think any Post wherein I may continue to serve you either too mean, or too hazardous for me: And as Valour is no where so conspicuous, as in the greatest Dangers, I shall esteem my Blood spent to great Advantage in any Enterprize where my Duty under your Command leads me: I therefore the rather humbly request this dangerous Post, that I may either lose my Life in your Service, or live to see you justified in your Advancement of me, by the whole Nation. For what can I do, or how can I demonstrate my Affection to your Person and Pleasure, in an inactive State?

Here the whole Level rang with Applause to *Nasgig*.

My Father then giving his Hand to *Nasgig*, in token of Friendship, and his Word for Investiture in the Command of that vacant Post, the whole Level again resounded with Long live *Pendlehamby*, and his Servant *Nasgig*.

This being the last Day of my Company's stay, for they had agreed to go homewards next Morning, some of them moved to return the sooner, that they might have time to hear out my Story. So that our stay was very little longer.

In our return home *Nasgig* singled me out, to return his Acknowledgements for my Favour, and viewing my Gun, told me, they had no such thing growing in his Country. I told him, if he had it would do no good, without my Powder. I then at his Request described what I had heard of our Method of Fighting in Battle in *Europe*; and mentioning our Cannon, he said, he supposed they killed every Man they hit.

No, says I, not so bad as that; sometimes they hit the Flesh only, and that is commonly cured; sometimes break a Leg, or Arm, and that may in time be cured, some so well, as to be useful again, and others are cut off, and healed up again; but if the Ball hits the Head, or Vitals, it is commonly mortal. O, says he, give me the Head or Vitals then, no broken Limbs for me.

After Dinner, at their Request, I went on with my Story, at repairing the Castle, and my Escape with *Glaulepze*, and so on to the Crocodile; when I repeated his Speech to me on that Account, and told them, it had made such an Impression upon me, that I had endeavoured to make it the leading Thought of my Mind, and had set it down upon one of my Doors at the Grotto, that it might the oftner be in my Sight, when any Difficulty arose.

One of the *Colambs* begged Pardon for interrupting, but told me, tho' he understood what *Glaulepze* meant, he could not tell how I could set what he said down at my Grotto, or have it in my Sight; and desired me to explain that. I would have told my Guest I took it down in Writing, if that would not have puzzled the Cause more; but, to go the nearest way I could, I told him, we had a Method in my Country, of conveying to a Man at a great Distance whatever we have a mind to say to him; and in such a manner, that no Body but himself would know, what we would have him know. And pausing here a little, to consider the easiest Method of demonstrating this to their Senses, they told me, they had gone as far as their Conjectures could carry them, but could conclude on nothing so probable as sending it by a Messenger. I told them, that in part was my way; but my Messenger should not know the Message he carried. That gravelled them quite, and they were unanimous, that was what could not be done. By this time I had sent for a Wood-coal, to write with upon my Deal-table; and kneeling down to the Table, I began to write, 'Honoured Sir, I send this to gain by your Answer to it an Account of your Arrival at *Arndruumstake*.' I then called them all to me: Now, says I, suppose I want to know how my Father

R

gets back to *Arndruumstake*, my way is this, I set down so
many Words as will express my Meaning to my Father, after
the manner you see on this Table, and make a little Distance
between each Word, which is the same thing as you do in
speaking; for there, if you run one Word into another, and
don't give each its proper Sound, who can understand you?
For tho' you speak what contains all the Words, yet, without
the proper Sound and Distinction, it is only Confusion. Do
you understand that? They told me they did. Then, says I,
these are the Words I would have my Father know, I being
at this Arkoe, and he at *Arndruumstake. Honoured Sir*, and so
I read on; here, says I, you must take us to be Countrymen,
and that he and I understand both the same Method. Now
look, this Word, which ends where you see the Gap, stands
for *honoured*, and this next for *Sir*, the next for *I*, and so on;
and we both using the same Method, and seeing each others
Words, are able to open our Minds at a Distance.—I was now
in Hopes I had done, and was going on with my Story; but,
says one of the *Colambs*, Mr. *Peter*, tho' this is a Matter that
requires Consideration, I plainly see how you do it, by agreeing that all these Strokes, put into this Form, shall stand for
the Word *honoured*, and so on, as you say, let who will make
them; but have not you set down there the Word *Arndruumstake*? Yes, says I; why then, says he, none of your Countrymen could understand what that means. No? says I, smiling,
but they could. Says he, you say, you agree what Strokes shall
stand for one Word, and what for another; but then, how could
your Countryman, who never knew what Strokes you would
set down for *Arndruumstake*, know that your Strokes meant
that very Country? For that you could not have agreed upon,
before either of you knew there was any such Place.

I was at a loss, without spending more Words than I was
willing about it, how to answer this close Reasoner; and talking of Syllables, and Letters, would only have perplexed the
Affair more; so I told him the readiest for dispatch, that as
every Word consisted of one or more distinct Sounds, and as
some of the same Sounds happened in different Words, we

did not agree so much upon making our Strokes stand for several Words, as for several Sounds; and those Sounds, more or less of them, added together, made the particular Words. As for Example, says I, *Arn* is one Sound, *druum* is another Sound, and *stake* is another; now, by our knowing how to set down these several Sounds by themselves, we can couple them, and apply them to the making up any Word, in the manner we please; and therefore he, by seeing those three Sounds together, knows I mean *Arndruumstake*, and can speak it as well, tho' he never heard the whole Word spoken together, as if he heard me speak to him. I have some little Notion of what you mean, says he, but not clear enough to express myself upon it; and so, go on, go on, and pray what did you do about the Reeds?

I then resuming my Discourse where I left off, compleated my Narration that Night; but I could perceive the Water in my Father's Eyes, when I came to the Account of *Youwarkee*'s Fall, and the Condition I took her up in.

When I had done, they adjusted the Order of their Flight, for avoiding Confusion, one to go so long before another, and the junior *Colambs* to go first.

In the Morning nothing was to be heard but the Gripsacks; the Men were all ranged in Order to go off with their respective *Colambs*; and after all Compliments passed, the junior *Colamb* arising, walked half-way the Wood, where his Gripsack standing to wait for him, preceded him to the Level, the next Gripsack standing ready to sound as soon as the first removed; and this was the Signal for the second *Colamb* to move; so that each *Colamb* was a Quarter of a Mile before the other.

My Father was the last but two; but I shall never forget his Tenderness, at parting with his Daughter and Grandchildren, and I may say with myself too; for by this time he had a high Opinion of me. *Patty* went with my Father, she so much resembling my Wife, that my Father said, he should still have his two Daughters in his Sight, having her with him.

At parting, I presented *Nasgig* with a broad Sword, and shewing him the Use of it, with many Expressions of Gratitude on his Part, and Respect on mine, he took flight after the rest.

CHAPTER VII

Peter finds his Stores low; sends Youwarkee *to the
Ship; receives an Invitation to* Georigetti's *Court*

FOR the first few Days after our Company had left us,
Youwarkee could not forbear a Tear now and then for the
Loss of her Father and Sister; but I endeavoured not to see
it, lest I should, by persuading her to the contrary, seem to
oppose what I really thought was a further Token of the
Sweetness of her Disposition; but it wore off by degrees, and
having a clear Stage again, it cost us several Days to settle ourselves, and put our confused Affairs in Order; and when we
had done, we blessed ourselves that we could come and go,
and converse with the pleasing Tenderness we had hitherto
always done.

She told me, nothing in the World but her Concern for so
tender a Father, and the Fear of displeasing me if she dis-
obliged him, should have kept her so long from me; for her
Life had never been so sweet and serene as with me and her
Children; and if she was to begin it again, and chuse her
Settlement and Company, it should be with me in that Arkoe.
I told her, tho' I was intirely of her Opinion for avoiding a Life
of Hurry, yet I loved a little Company, if for nothing else but
to advance Topicks for Discourse, to the Exercise of our
Faculties; but I then agreed, it was not from meer Judgment
I spoke, but from Fancy. But *Youwee*, says I, it will be proper
for us to see what our Friends have left us, that we don't want
before the time comes about again: Then she took her part,
and I mine; and having finished, we found they would hold
out pretty well, and that the first thing to be done, was to get
the Oil of the Beast-Fish.

When we came to examine the Brandy and Wine, I found
they had suffered greatly; so I told *Youwarkee*, when she could
spare time, she should make another Flight to the Ship; and,
says I, pray look at all the small Casks of Wine or Brandy, or

be they what they will, if they are not above half full, or thereabouts, they will swim, and you may send them down. I
desired her to send a Fire-shovel, and Tongs, describing them
to her; and there are abundance of good Ropes between Decks,
rolled up, send them, says I, and any thing else you think we
shall want, as Plates, Bowls, and all the Cutlasses and Pistols,
says I, that hang in the Room by the Cabin: For I would,
methinks, have another Cargoe, as it may possibly be the last;
for the Ship can't hold for ever.

Youwarkee, who loved a Jaunt to the Ship mightily, sat
very attentive to what I said, and told me, if I pleas'd, she
would go the next Day; to which I agreed.

She stayed on this Trip till I began to be uneasy for her,
being gone almost four Days, and I was in great Fear of some
Accident; but she arrived safe, telling me, she had sent all she
could any ways pack up; and any one who had seen the Arrival
of her Fleet would have taken it for a good Ship's Cargoe, for
it cost me full three Weeks to land and draw them up to the
Grotto; and then we had such a Redundancy of things, that
we were forced to pile them upon each other, to the Top of
the Room.

It began to draw towards long Days again, when one Morning in Bed I heard the Gripsack. I waked *Youwarkee*, and told
her of it; and we both got up, and were going to the Level,
when we met six Glumms in the Wood, with a Gripsack before
them, coming to the Grotto. The Trumpeter, it seems, had
been there before; but the others, who seemed to be of a better
Rank, had not. We saluted them, and they us; and *Youwarkee*
knowing one of them, we desired them to walk to the Grotto.

They told us, they came Express from *Georigetti*'s Palace,
with an Invitation to me and *Youwarkee* to spend some time
at his Court. I let them know, what a Misfortune I lay under
in not being born with the Graundee, since Providence had
pleased to dispose of me in a Part of the World where alone it
could have been of such infinite Service to me; or I should
have taken it for the highest Honour, to have laid myself at
their Master's Feet: And after some other Discourse, one of

them pressed me to return his Master my Answer; for they had but a very little time to stay. I told them, they saw plainly, by bareing my Breast to them, that I was under an absolute Incapacity for such a Journey, and gratifying the highest Ambition I could have in the World; for I was pinned down to my Arkoe, never more to pass the Barrier of that Rock. One of them then asking, if I should chuse to go, if it was possible to convey me thither; I told him, he could scarce have the least Doubt, was my Ability to perform such a Journey equal to my Inclination to take it, that I should in the least hesitate at obeying his Master. Sir, says he, you make me very happy, in the Regard you shew my Master; and I must beg Leave to stay another Day with you. I told him, they did me great Honour; but little thought what it all tended to.

We were very facetious; and they talked of the number of Visitors I had here; and they mentioned several Facts which had happened, and amongst the rest that of *Nasgig*, who they said, since his Return, had been introduced by *Pendlehamby* to the King, and was for his great Prudence and Penetration become *Georigetti*'s great Favourite. They told me, War was upon the Point of breaking out, and several other Pieces of News, which, as they did not concern me, I was very easy about.

The next Morning they desiring to walk, and view what was most remarkable in my Arkoe, and above all to see me fire my Gun, which they had heard so much of; I gratified them at a Mark, and hit the Edge of it, and found them quite staunch, without the least Start at the Report. I paid them a Compliment upon it, and told them how their Countrymen had behaved, even at a second firing: But, says he who was the chief Spokesman, and knew I found as much as I could tell him, that second Fright was from seeing Death the Consequence of the first; and tho' you had then to do mostly with Soldiers, you must not think they chuse Death more than others, tho' their Duty obliges them to shun it less.

The same Person then desired me to shew him how to fire the Gun; which I did, and believe he might hit the Rock some where or other; but he did not seem to admire the Sport, and I having but few Balls left, did not recommend the Gun to the rest.

A little before Bed-time, the Strangers told me, they believed I should see *Nasgig* next Morning. I presently thought there was somewhat more than ordinary in this Visit; but could no ways dive to the Bottom of it.

Just before they went to Rest, they ordered the Trumpeter to be early on the Rock next Morning; and, upon the first Sight of *Nasgig*'s Corps, to sound Notice of it, for us to be ready to receive him.

CHAPTER VIII

Nasgig *comes with a Guard to fetch* Peter; *long Debate about his going;* Nasgig's *Uneasiness at* Peter's *Refusal; relates a Prediction to him, and Proceedings thereon at* Georigetti's *Court;* Peter *consents to go; prepares a Machine for that Purpose*

WE were waked by the Trumpet, giving Notice of *Nasgig*'s coming; I did not care to enquire of the Stranger into the Particulars of his Embassy; for be it what it will, thinks I, *Nasgig* is so much my Friend, that I can know the Motives of it from him, and, or I am much deceived, he is too honest to impose upon me: But I had but little time for Thought, for upon our entring the Level, we found him and his Train, of at least an hundred Persons, just alighting before us.

We embraced, and professed the particular Pleasure Fortune had done us, in once more meeting together. When we arrived at the Grotto, he told me, he was assured I had been informed of the Occasion of his Visit; and that it would be the greatest Honour done to his Country, that could be imagined. He then laid his Hand on my Beard, which was now of about five Months Growth, having never shaved it since my Father went, and told me, he was glad to see that. And are you not so to see me, says I? Yes surely, says he, for I prize that for your sake. But, says I, pray be open with me and tell me, what you mean by my being informed of the Occasion of your coming? Why, says he, of *Georigetti*'s Message to you; as it will be of such infinite Service to our Country: And, says he, if you had not consented to it, the Messengers had returned and stopped me. True, says I, one of the Messengers told me the King would be glad to see me; which as I, so well as he, knew it was impossible he should; in return to his Compliment, I believe I might say, what a Happiness it would be to me if I could wait on him. But pray what is your immediate Message, for I hear you are in great Favour at Court, and would never have come hither with this Retinue in so much Ceremony, on a trifling Account.

My dear *Peter*, says *Nasgig*, know that your Fame has reached far and near since I saw you before; and our State tho' a large and populous one, and once of mighty Power and twice its present Extent, by the Revolt of the western Part of it who chose themselves a King, has been so miserably harrassed by Wars, that the Revolters, who are ever fomenting Discontent and Rebellion amongst us, will, by the Encroachments they daily make on us, certainly reduce us at last to a Province under their Government; which will render us all Slaves to an usurped Power, set up against our lawful Sovereign. Now, these things were foretold long enough before they actually began to be transacted; but all being then at Peace, and no Prospect of what has since happened, we looked not out for a Remedy, till the Disease became stubborn and incurable. Pray, says I, by whom were the things you mention foretold? By a very ancient and grave Ragam, says he. How long ago, says I? O, above four times the Age of the oldest Man living, says he. And when did he say it would happen, says I? That, says he, was not quite so clear then. But how do you know, says I, that he ever said any such thing? Why the thing itself was so peculiar, says he, and the Ragam delivered it so positively, that his Successors have ever since pronounced it twelve times a Year publickly Word for Word, to put the People in mind of it, and from whom they must hope for Relief; and now the long expected time being come, we have no hopes but in your Destruction of the Tyrant-Usurper. I destroy him, says I! if he is not destroyed till I do it, I fear your State is but in a bad Case. My good Friend *Peter*, says he, you or no body can do it. Pugh, says I, *Nasgig*, I took you for a Man of more Sense, notwithstanding the Prejudices of Education, than to think, because you have seen me kill a Beast-Fish, that could not come to hurt me, at the Distance of twenty Paces; that I can kill your Usurper, at the Distance he is from me. No, my good Friend, says *Nasgig*, I know you take me to have more Judgment than to think so. Why, what else can I do, says I? unless he will come hither to be killed by me. Dear *Peter*, says he, you will not hear me out. I will, says I, say on. You, as I said before, being the only Person that can, according to our Prediction, destroy this Usurper, and restore Peace among us; my Master *Georigetti*, and the whole State of *Norrunbdsgrsutt*, were going to send a splendid Embassy to you; but your Father advising to repose the Commission wholly in me, they all consented to it, and I am come to invite you over to *Brandleguarp* for that Purpose. I know you will tell me you have not the Graundee, and can't get thither: But I am assured you have what is far better; the Wisdom you have will help you to surmount that Difficulty, which our whole Moucherat can't get over. And I am sure did you apply half the Thought to accomplish it, you seem to do to invent Excuses against it, you would easily overcome that. And now, dear Friend, continues he, refuse me not; for as my first Rise was owing to your Favour, so my Downfal as absolutely attends your Refusal.

Dear *Nasgig*, says I, you know I love you, and could refuse you nothing in my Power; but for me to be mounted in the Air, I know not how, over these Rocks, and then drowned by a Fall into the Sea, which is a necessary Consequence of such a mad Attempt; and all this, in Prosecution of a Project founded upon an old Wife's Tale, is such a Chimera, as all

Men of Sense would laugh at; as if there was no way of destroying me, but with a Guard of an hundred Men, to souse me into the wide Ocean. A very pretty Conqueror of Rebels I should prove truly, kicking for Life, till the next Wave sent me to the Bottom.

Nasgig looked then so grave, I almost thought I should have heard no more of it; but after a short Pause, *Peter*, says he, I am sorry you make so light of sacred things; a thing foretold so long ago by a holy Ragam, kept up by undoubted Tradition ever since in the manner I have told you, in part performed, and now waiting your Concurrence for its Accomplishment; but if I can't prevail with you, tho' I perish at my Return, I dread to think you may be forced without Thanks to perform, what generously to undertake will be your greatest Glory.

Pray, says I, *Nasgig*, for now I perceive you are in earnest, what may this famous Prediction be?

Ah, *Peter*, says *Nasgig*, to what Purpose should I relate so sacred a Prediction to one who, tho' the most concerned in it, makes such a Jest of it?

His mentioning me as concerned in it, raised my Curiosity once more to desire a Relation of it. Why should I relate it, says he, if you are resolved not to fulfil it? I told him, I had no Resolution against any thing that related to my own good, or that of my Friends; but the greatest Question with me, says I, is, whether I am at all concerned in it. O, clearly, clearly, says he, there is no doubt of it, it must mean you or no body. I told him I must judge by the Words of it, that I was the Person intended by it; and till that was apparent to my Reason, it would be difficult to procure my Consent to so perilous an Undertaking. And, says he, will you upon hearing it judge impartially, and go with me if you can take the Application to yourself? I can't go quite so far as that, says I, but this I'll promise you, I'll judge impartially, and if I can so apply it to myself, that it must necessarily mean me and no other, and if you can convince me I may go safely, I will go.

Nasgig was so rejoiced at this, he was at a loss how to express himself. My dear *Peter*, says he, you have given me new Life; our State is free, our Persons free, we're free, we're free; and *Peter*, says he, now I have given Vent to my Joy, you shall hear the Prediction.

You must know, this holy Ragam lived four Ages ago; and from certain Dreams and Revelations he had had, set himself to overturn our Country-Worship of the great Image; and by his Sanctity of Life and sound Reasonings, had almost effected it under the Assistance of *Begsurbeck* then our King, who had fully embraced his Tenets; but the rest of the Ragams opposing him, and finding he could not advance his Scheme, he withdrew from the Ragams, to a close Retirement for several Years; and just before his Death, sending for the King and all the Ragams, he told them, he should certainly die that Day; and that he could not die at Peace, till he had informed them what had been revealed to him; desiring them to take Notice of it, not as a Conjecture of his own, but a certain Verity which should hereafter come to pass. Says he, 'You know you have rejected the Alteration in your Religion I proposed to you; and which *Begsurbeck*, here present, would have advanced; and now I must tell you, what you have brought upon yourselves. As for *Begsurbeck*, he shall reign the longest and most prosperously, of all your former and future Kings; but in twice his time out-run, the West shall be divided from the East, and bring Sorrow, Confusion, and Slaughter, till the Waters of the Earth shall produce a Glumm, with Hair round his Head, swimming and flying without the Graundee; who, with unknown Fire and Smoak, shall destroy the Traitor of the West, settle the ancient Limits of the Monarchy, by common Consent establish what I would have taught you, change the Name of this Country, introduce new Laws and Arts, add Kingdoms to this State, and force Tributes from the Bowels of the Earth, of such things as this Kingdom shall not know till then, and shall never afterwards want; and then shall return to the Waters again. Take care, says he, you miss not the Opportunity when it may be had; for once lost, it shall never, never more return; and then, wo, wo, wo, to my poor Country.' The Ragam having said this, expired.

This Prediction made so great an Impression on *Begsurbeck*, that he ordered all the Ragams singly before him, and heard them repeat it; which having done, and made himself perfect in it, he ordered it to be pronounced twelve times in the Year, on particular Days, in the Moucherat, that the People might learn it by heart; that they and their Children being perfect in it, might not fail of applying it, when the Man from the Waters should appear with proper Description.

Thus *Peter*, says he, has this Prediction been kept up in our Memories as perfectly, as if it had but just been pronounced to us.

Tis very true, says I, here may have been a Prediction, and it may have been as you say, handed down very exactly from *Begsurbeck*'s Days till now; but, how does that affect me? how am I concerned in it? Surely, if any Marks would have denoted me to be the Man; some of the *Colambs*, who have so lately left me, and were so long with me, would have found them out in my Person, or among the several Actions of my Life I recounted to them.

Upon the Return of the *Colambs* from you, says *Nasgig*, they told his Majesty what they had heard and seen at *Grande-volet*; and the Story was conveyed thro' the whole Realm; but every Man has not the Faculty of Distinction: Now, one of the Ragams when he had heard of you, applying you to the Prediction, and that to you, soon found our Deliverer in you; and, at a public Moucheratt, after first pronouncing the Prediction, declared himself thereon to the following Effect:

'May it please your Majesty, and you the honourable *Colambs*, the reverend Ragams, and People of this State, says he; you all know, that our famous King *Begsurbeck*, who reigned at the time of this Prediction, did live sixty Years after it in the greatest Splendor, and died at the Age of one hundred and twenty Years, having reigned full ninety of them; and herein you will all agree with me, that no King before, or since, has done the like. You all likewise know, that within two hundred Years after *Begsurbeck*'s Death, that is, about twice his Reign of ninety Years outrun, the Rebellion in the West began, which has been carried on ever since; and our Strength diminishing, as theirs increases, we are now no fair Match for them; but are fearful of being undone. So far, you will agree Matters have tallied with the Prediction; and now, to look forward to the time to come, it becomes us to lay hold of the present Opportunity for our Relief; for that, once slipp'd, will never return; and, if I have any Skill in Interpretations, now is the time of our Deliverance.

'Our Prediction foretells the past Evils, their Increase and Continuance, till the Waters of the Earth shall produce a Glumm: Here I must appeal to the honourable *Colambs* present, if the Waters have not done so, in the Person of Glumm *Peter* of *Grandevolet*; as they have received it from his own Report.'

All the *Colambs* then rising, and making Reverence to the King, declared it was most true.

'The next part says the Ragam, is, he is to be hairy round his Head; and how his Person in this respect agrees with the Prediction, I beg leave to be informed by the *Colambs*.'

The *Colambs* then rising, declared, that having seen and conversed with him, they could not observe any Hair on the Fore-Part of his Head; But I answered, that when I left you, I well remembered your having short Stubbs of Hair upon your Cheeks, and Chin; which I had no sooner mentioned, than your Father arose and told the Assembly, that tho' he did not mind it whilst he was with you; yet he remembered, that his Daughter a Year before had told him, that you had Hair on your Face before, as long as that behind.

This again putting new Life into the Ragam, he proceeded. 'Then let this, says he, be put to the Trial, by an Embassy to Glumm *Peter*; and if it answers, there will be no Room to doubt the rest. Then, says the Ragam, it is plain by the Report of the *Colambs*, that Glumm *Peter* has not the Graundee.

'As to the next Point, he is to swim and fly. Now I am informed he swims daily, in a thing he calls a Boat.' To which, the *Colambs* all agreed. 'And now, says he, that he flies too, that must be fulfilled; for every Word must have a Meaning, and that indeed he must do, if ever he comes hither. I therefore advise, that a Contrivance be some how found out, for conveying Glumm *Peter* thro' the Air to us; and then, we shall answer that Part of the Prediction; and I think, and don't doubt, but that may be done.

'Now, says he, let us see the Benefit predicted to us, upon the Arrival of Glumm *Peter*. Our Words are; who, with unknown Fire and Smoak, shall destroy the Traitor of the West. What can be plainer than this? For I again appeal to the *Colambs*, for his making unknown Fire and Smoak.

'Thus far, says the Ragam, we have succeeded happily towards a Discovery of the Person; but it ends not here, with the Death of the Traitor; but such other Benefits are to accrue, as are mentioned in the following Part of the Prediction; they are Blessings yet to come; and who knows the End of them?

'I hope, says the Ragam, I have given Satisfaction in what I have said, and shall now leave it to the Care of those, whose Business it is to provide, that none of those Woes pronounced against us may happen; by missing the time, which when gone, will never return.'

The Assembly were coming to a Resolution of sending you a pompous Embassy; but your Father prevailed, for sending me only: For, says he, my Son thinks better of him, than of the rest of our whole Race. So this important Affair was committed to me, with Orders to prepare a Conveyance for you; which I cannot attempt to do, but shall refer myself to your more solid Judgment, in the Contrivance of it.

I had sat very attentive to *Nasgig*, and from what he had declared, could not say, but there was a very great Resemblance between myself and the Person predicted of; but then, says I, they are Idolaters, Providence would not interpose in this Affair, when all the Glory of its Success must redound to an Idol. But, says I, has not the same thing often happened from oracular Presages, where the Glory must redound to the false Deity? But what if, as is predicted, their Religion is to be changed to the old Ragam's Plan, and that will be to the Abolishion of Idolatry? I know not what to say, but if

I thought my going would gain a single Soul to the eternal Truth, I should not scruple to hazard my Life in the Attempt.

I then called in *Youwarkee*, told her the whole Affair of the Prediction, which she had often heard, I found, and could have repeated. I told her, that the King and States had pitched on me, as the Person intended by their Prediction; and that *Nasgig* was sent to fetch me over; and indeed, says I, *Youwee*, if this be a true Prediction, it seems very applicable to me as far as I can see. Yes truly, says she, so it does, now I consider it in the Light you say the Ragam puts it. Why, says I, Prophecies and Predictions are never delivered so plain as to mention Names; but yet, upon the Solution, they become as intelligible as if they did; the Circumstances tallying so exactly. But what would you have me do? shall I, or shall I not go? Go! says she, how can you go? O, says I, never fear that. If this is from above, Means will soon be found; Providence never directs Effects without Means.

Youwarkee, whose Head ran only on the Dangers of the Undertaking, had a violent Conflict with herself; the Love of me, of her Children, and of her Country, divided her so, she was not capable of advising. I pressed her Opinion again, when she told me to follow the Dictates of my own Reason, and, but for the Dread of losing you, and for my Childrens sakes, says she, I should have no Choice to make when my Country is at Stake; but you know best.

I told *Youwarkee*, that I really found the Prediction the plainer the more I thought of it; and that above all, the Change of Religion was the uppermost: For, if I can reduce a State from the Misery and Bondage of Idolatry, to a true Sense of the Supreme Being, and seemingly by his own Direction; shall I fear to risque my own Life for it, or will he suffer me to perish, till somewhat, at least, is done towards it? And how do I know but the whole Tendency of my Life has been by Impulse hither, for this very Purpose? My dear *Youwee*, says I, fear nothing, I will go.

I called *Nasgig* and told him my Resolution, and that he had nothing now to do but prepare a Means of conveying me.

He said, he begged to refer that to me, for my own Thoughts would suggest to me both the safest and easiest Means.

I wanted to venture on the Back of some strong Glumm, when *Nasgig* told me, no one could endure my Weight so long a Flight. But what charmed me most was, the lovely *Youwarkee* offered to carry me herself if she could; and if I can't hold out, says she, my Dear, we can but at last drop both together. I kiss'd the charming Creature with Tears in my Eyes, but declined the Experiment.

I told *Nasgig* I wanted to divide my Weight between two or four Glumms, which, I believed I could easily do; and asked if each could hold out with a fourth Part of my Weight. He told me there was no doubt of that; but he was afraid I should drop between their Graundees, he imagining I intended to lie along on their Backs, Part of me on each of them, or should bear so much on them as to prevent their Flight. I told him, I did not purpose to dispose of myself in the manner he presumed; but, if two or four could undoubtedly bear my Weight so long a Flight; I would order myself without any other Inconvenience to my Bearers than their Burthen. He made light of my Weight between four, as a Trifle; and said, he would be one with all his Heart. Nay, says I, if four cannot hold out, can eight? He plainly told me, as he knew not what I meant he could say nothing to it; nor could imagine how I could divide so small a Body as mine, into eight different Weights; for it seemed impossible he said to him; but if I would shew him my Method, he would then give me his Opinion.

I then leaving him, took out my Tools; I pitched upon a strong broad Board my Wife had sent me from the Ship, about twelve Feet long, and a Foot and half broad:[1] Upon the Middle of which, I nailed down one of my Chairs. Then I took one Cord of about thirty-four Feet long, making Handloops at each End, and nailed it down in the Middle to the under Side of my Board, as near as I could to the fore End of it; and I took another Cord of the same Length and Make, and this, I nailed within three Feet of the further End of my

Board. I then took a Cord of about twenty Feet long, and nailed about three Feet behind the foremost, and a fourth of the same Length, at the further End of my Board; by which Means, the first and third Ropes being the longest, and at such a Distance from the short Ropes, the Glumms who held them, would fly so much higher and forwarder than the short Rope ones, that they and their Ropes would be quite out of the others way; which would not have happened, if either the Ropes had been all of one Length, or nearer to, or farther from one another: And then considering that if I should receive a sudden Jerk or Twitch, I might possibly be shook off my Chair, I took a smaller Rope to tie myself with fast to the Chair; and then I was sure if I fell into the Sea, I should at least have the Board and Chair with me, which might possibly buoy me up, till the Glumms could descend to my Assistance.

Having carried the Machine down to the Level with the Help of two of *Nasgig*'s Men, he being out on a Walk, and having never seen it; I ordered one of the Men to sit upon the Chair, and eight more to hold by the Loops, and rise with him; but, as I found it difficult at their first rising, not being able to mount all equally, to carry the Board up even, and the back part rising first, the Front pitched against the Ground and threw the Fellow out of the Chair. I therefore bad them stop, and ordering eight others to me; said I, hold each of you one of these Ropes as high as you can over your Heads; then, says I, to the eight Bearers, mount on your Graundees, and come round behind him in the Chair gently, two and two, and take each of you a Loop, and hover with it till you are all ready, and then rise together; keeping your Eye on the Board that it rises neither higher at one End, or one Side, than the other; and see you all feel your Weight alike, then fly cross the Lake and back again. They did so, and with as much ease they told me, as if they had nothing in their Hands; and the Man rode with so much State and Composure, he said, that I longed to try it myself: So shifting Places with the Glumm, I mounted the Chair, and tying myself round, I asked if any one knew

s

which way *Nasgig* walked. One of them pointing to where he saw him just before in the Wood; I ordered them to take me up as before, and go that way.

Upon coming to the Place where I expected *Nasgig* was, I hallow'd and called him, who, knowing my Voice, ran to the Skirt of the Wood; and seeing me mounted in my flying Chair, I jokingly told him I was going, if he had any Commands; but he mounting immediately came up to me, and viewing me round, and seeing the Pleasure the Men seemed to carry me with; says he, are you all sure you can carry him safe to *Battingdrigg*? They all replied, yes, with ease. This then, says he, is your Doom; If you perform it not, every one shall be slit; but, if you carry the Deliverer safe, you are Filgays every Man of you, he verily thinking I was then going off; but I undeceived him, by ordering them to turn about, and set me down where I was taken up.

Nasgig alighting, and viewing my Contrivance; This, *Peter*, says he, is but a very plain thing. It is so, says I, but it is as far as my Ingenuity could reach. Ah! *Peter*, says he, say not so, for if the greatest Difficulties, as I and all my Nation thought it would be to convey you to them, are so plain and easy to you, what must lesser things be? No, *Peter*, I did not call it plain, because it might be easily done when it was seen; but in respect to the Head that formed it; for the nearest way to attain one's End is always the best, and attended for the most part with fewest Inconveniencies; and I verily think, *Peter*, tho' we believe the Rise or Fall of our State wholly depends on you, you must have stayed at *Grandevolet*, but for your own Ingenuity. Well, and when shall we set out, says he? I told him it would take up some time to settle the Affairs of my Family, and to consider what I had best take with me; and required at least three Days, being as little as I could have I told him for that Purpose.

Nasgig, who, as he was an honest Man, and for making the best for his Patrons, was sorry it was so long, tho' he imagining at the same time it was short enough for one who was to go on such an Enterprize, was glad it was no longer; and immediately dispatched a Trumpet Express with Notice, that on the fourth Day he should be at the Height of *Battingdrigg*; and that having myself formed a Machine for that Purpose, I would accompany him.

I began next to consider what part I had to act at *Doorpt Swangeanti*, for I neither could, or would call it by any other Name, when I came thither; and what it was they expected from me. I am, says I, to kill a Traitor; good, that may be, but then I must take a Gun and Ammunition; and why not some Pistols and Cutlasses? If I can't use them all, I can teach others who may; I'll take several of them, and all my Guns but two, and I'll leave a Pair of Pistols; I may return and want them. I'll take my two best Suits of Cloaths and other things suitable; for, if I am to perform things according to this Prediction, it may be a long time before I get back again. Thinks I, *Youwarkee* shall stay here with the Children; and if I like my Settlement, I can send for her at any time. I then began to see the Necessity of making at least one more Machine to carry my Goods on; and, says I, as they will be very weighty, I must have more Lasks to shift in carrying them; for I will retain sixteen for my own Body-machine, in order to relieve each other; and as the Distance is so great, I will not be stinted for want of fresh Hands.

Being come to this Resolution I called *Nasgig*, and ordered eight fresh Lasks to attend my Baggage: These, he soon singled out; so having settled all Matters with my Wife, and taken Leave of her and the Children, I charged them not to stir out of the Grotto till I was gone; and leaving them all in Tears, I set out with a heavy Heart for the Level; where the whole Convoy and my two Machines waited for me.

WHEN we came to the Level, I desired *Nasgig* to draw all
his Men into a Circle as near as they could stand; I then asked
them who would undertake to carry me? When not a Man but
proffered his Service, and desired to have the Post of Honour
as they called it. I told them my Question was only in Case of
Necessity, to know whom I might depend upon; for my
Bearers were already provided, saving Accidents. But, my
Friends, says I, as you are equally deserving for the offered
Service, as if you were accepted, are any of you desirous of
becoming Filgays? They all answering together, I, I, I. *Nasgig*,
says I, you and I must come to a Capitulation before I go, and
your Honour must be pledged for Performance of Articles.

I began with telling them what an Enemy I was to Slavery;
and, says I, to *Nasgig*, as I am about to undertake what no
Man upon Earth ever did before; to quit my Country, my
Family, my every other Conveniency of Life, for I know
not what, I know not where; and from whence I shall never
return: I must be indulged, if I am ever so fortunate as to
arrive safe in your Country, in the Satisfaction of seeing all
these my Fellow-Travellers as happy as myself; for which
reason, I must insist upon every Man present alighting with
me in Safety, being made free the Moment we touch the
Ground: And unless you will engage your Honour for this,
I will not stir a Step further.

Nasgig paused for an Answer; for tho' my Bearers were his
own Lasks, and he could dispose of them at pleasure, yet, as
the rest were the Kings, he knew not how far he might venture
to promise for them; but being desirous to get me over the
Rock, fearing I might still retract my Purpose, he engaged to

procure their Freedom of the King: And this, I thought, would make the Men more zealous in my Service.

I then permitting them to take me up, we were over the Rock as quick as Thought, and when I had a little experienced the Flight, I perceived I had nothing to fear; for they were so dextrous on the Graundee, that I received not the least Shock all the way, or scarce a wry Position, tho' every Quarter of an Inch at hand made a considerable Deflection from the Perpendicular. We shifted but twice till we came to *Battingdrigg*; the manner of which I directed as I sat in my Chair: For I ordered the new Man to hover over him he was to relieve, and reaching down his Hand to meet the others which was held up with the Rope, the old Bearer sunk beneath the Chair, and the Reliever took his Course. This we did one by one, till all were changed; but there was one, a stout young Fellow, at the first short Rope on my Right-hand, who observing me to eye him more than the rest, in a Bravadoe would not be relieved before we arrived at *Battingdrigg* Arkoe; and I afterwards took him into my Family.

As it was now somewhat advanced into the light Season, I had hopes of a tolerable good Prospect; but had it been quite light, I should have been never the better for it. I had been upon very high Mountains in the inland Parts of *Africa*; but was never too high to see what was below me before, tho' very much contracted; but here, in the highest of our Flight, you could not distinguish the Globe of the Earth but by a sort of Mist, for every way looked alike to me; then sometimes on a Cue given, from an inexpressible Height my Bearers would dart as it were sloping like a shooting Star, for an incredible Distance almost to the very Surface of the Sea, still keeping me as upright as a Spaniard on my Seat. I asked them the Reason of their so vast Descent, when I perceived the Labour they had afterwards to attain the same Height again. They told me, they not only eased their Graundees by that Descent, but could fly half as far again in a Day, as by direct, they meant horizontal, Flight; for tho' it seemed laborious to mount so excessive high, yet they went on at the same time at a great

Rate; but when they came to descend again, there was no Comparison in their Speed. And on my Conscience, I believe they spoke true, for in their Descents, I think, no Arrow could have reached us.

In about sixteen Hours, for I took my Watch with me, we alighted on the Height of *Battingdrigg*; when I thought I had returned to my own Arkoe it was so like it, but much larger. Here, we rested four Hours; I opened my Chest, and gave each of my Bearers a Drop of Brandy, *Nasgig* and I also just wetted our Mouths, and eat a Piece of Preserve to moisten us; the rest of the Lasks sitting down, and feeding upon what they had brought with them in their Colapets; for their Method is, when they take long Flights, to carry a Number of hard round Fruits, flat like my Cream-cheeses, but much less, which containing a sort of Flower they eat dry; then drinking, that swells, and fills them as much as a good Meal of any thing else would. Here, we met with abundance of delightful Pools of Water on the vast Flat of the Rocks. They told me, in that Arkoe the young Glumms and Gawreys came in vast Flights seperately, to divert themselves on the fine Lake of Waters, and from thence, went sometimes as far as my Arkoe for that Purpose; but that was but seldom.

When we had sufficiently rested, they shut their Colapets, which sometimes hung down from their Necks, and were sometimes swung round to their Backs, and crossing the Arkoe and another large Sea, but nothing comparable to the first, we arrived in about six Hours more, to the Height of the white Mountains, which *Nasgig* told me were the Confines of *Georigetti*'s Territories; but, thinks I, it may belong to whom it will for the Value of it; for nothing could be more barren than all the Top of it was; but the Inside of it made amends for that, by the prodigious tall and large Trees it abounded with, full of the strangest Kinds of Fruits I had ever seen: And these Trees, most of them seemed to grow out of the very Stone itself, not a Peck of Dirt being to be collected near them. Without-side of these Mountains, it was scarce darker than at my Arkoe; for I made all the Observation my time would allow me; when spying at a vast Distance several Lights, which were unusual things to me in that Country; they told me, the largest was the Burning-mountain *Alkoe*, this I remembered to have heard the Name of upon some former Occasion, tho' I could not recollect what; and that the rest were of the same sort, but smaller. I asked if they were in *Georigetti*'s Territories? They said no, they belonged to another King formerly, whose Subjects were as fond of Fire, as *Georigetti*'s were of avoiding it; and that many of them worked with it always before them, and made an insufferable Noise by it.

At hearing the above Relation, an Impression struck my Fancy, that they might be a sort of Smiths or Workers in Iron, or other Metals; and I wished myself with them, for I had a mighty Notion of that Work, having been frequently at a neighbouring Forge when a Boy, and knew all their Tools, and resolved to get all the Information I could of that Country some other time; for our Company drawing to their Posts, and preparing to set forward again, I could have no more Talk now; and you must know, I had observed so many idle Rascals before I left *England*, who could neither strike a Stroke, or stir a Foot, whilst you talked with them; that I feared if I asked Questions by the way, they should in answering me neglect their Duty, and let me drop.

When we came near our Journey's End, *Nasgig* asked me where I would please to alight. I told him, I thought at my Father's; for tho' I came on a Visit to the King, it would not shew Respect to go before him just off a Journey. But, I might have spared me the Trouble of settling that Point; for we were not gone far from the Black-mountain, it going by that Name within side, tho' it is called the White without, before we heard the Gripsacks, and a sort of squeaking or screaming Musick very loud. *Nasgig* told me the King was in flight. I asked him, how he knew that, for I could see no body. He knew it, he said, by the Gripsack and the other Musick, which never played but on that Occasion; and presently after, I thought the whole Kingdom were on the Graundee, and was going to order my Bearers back to the Mountain, for fear of the Concourse. Thinks I, they will jostle me down out of Civility, and I shall break my Neck to gratify their Curiosity. So, I told *Nasgig*, if he did not somehow stop the Multitude, I would turn back for the Mountain, for I would never venture into that Croud of People.

Nasgig sprung away to the King, and informed him; but the King fearing the People should be disgusted at his sending them back, gave Orders for the whole Body to file off to the Right and Left, and taking a vast Sweep each way, to fall in behind me; but upon no Account to come near me, for fear of Mischief. This was no sooner said than done, and all spreading into two vast Semicircles, met in a Train just behind my Chair.

Nasgig had also persuaded the King to retreat back to the Palace, telling him, it was not with me as with them, who could help themselves in case of Accident; but, as I was under the Guidance of others, and on a Foundation he should scarce, in my Condition, have ventured upon, he was sure, I should be better satisfied with his intended Respect only, than to receive it there: But, says he, that your Majesty may see his Contrivance, I will cause him to alight in the Palace-Garden, where you may have the Pleasure of viewing him in his Machine.

The King returning, ordered all the *Colambs*, who waited my Arrival, to assemble in Council again; and as I went over the City, I was surprized to see all the Rock of which it consisted quite covered with People, besides prodigious Numbers in the Air, all shouting out Peels of Welcome to me; and as we were then but little above their Heads, every one had something to say of me; one wondring what I had got on, another swearing he saw Hair on my Face as long as his Arm; and in general, every one calling upon the Image for my Safety.

The King was present when I alighted in the Garden; and himself taking me from my Chair, I bent on one Knee to kiss his Hand, but he took me in his Arms, called me his Father, and told me, he hoped I would make his Days equal in Glory to his great Ancestor *Begsurbeck*. We complimented sometime, before he took me into a small Refectory in the Garden, and gave me some of his Sort of Wine; which I found was loaded[1] with Ramshorn, and some dried and moist Sweetmeats. He then told me, I had a Piece of Ceremony to go thro', after which, he hoped to have me to himself. I told him, whatever Forms of State were customary, they become necessary, and I should obey him.

His Majesty then called one of the Persons in waiting, and telling him he was going to the Room of Audience, ordered him to conduct me thither forthwith.

Following my Guide, after a long Walk thro' a sort of Piazza, we entred under a stately Arch curiously carved, into a very spacious Room, lighted with infinite Numbers of Globe-lamps; where he desired me to sit down on a round Stone Pedestal covered with Leaves, and all round the Sides of it were running Foliages exquisitely wrought; on the Walls were carved Figures of Glumms in several Actions, but chiefly in Battle, or other warlike Exercises, in *alto-relievo*,[2] very bold; with other Devices interspersed. I sat down, having first paid my Submission to the Throne, and to the several *Colambs* who sat on the King's Right and Left, down the Sides of the Room.

The Person then who introduced me, going into the Middle of the Room, spoke to this Effect: 'Mighty King, and you honourable Lords his *Colambs*, here is present the Glumm *Peter* of *Grandevolet*; I wait your Commands, where to dispose him.'

Then the King, and all the *Colambs* arising, another Person stepped forth, and looking at me, for I was standing; Glumm *Peter* of *Grandevolet*, says he, I am to signify to you, that the mighty King *Georigetti*, and all his honourable *Colambs*, congratulate your Arrival in *Norrunbdsgrsutt*, and have commanded me to give you Rank according to your Merit. Then the King and *Colambs* sat down, and I was led to the King's Right-hand, and placed on the same Stone with, but at some small Distance from, his Majesty.

The King then told me the great Pleasure I had done him and the *Colambs*, in my so speedy Arrival upon their Message; but said, he would give me no further Trouble now, than to know how I chose to be served; and desired me to give Orders to a Bash, he would send to me, for whatever I wanted; and then giving Orders to a Bash to shew me my Lodgings, I was permitted to retire to refresh myself.

I was then conducted to my Appartment, up a sloping Flight of Stone, very long, with a vast Arch over my Head; I believe it might be fifty Paces long at least, but being a very broad easy Assent, and smooth, it was not in the least fatiguing. All the way I went, were the same sort of Globe-lights as in the Audience-Room. The Stair-case, if I may call it so, it answering the same Purpose, was most beautifully carved, both Sides and Top; at length I came into a very large Gallery, at least fourscore Paces long, and about twenty broad; on each Side of which, hung the same Globes. At the further End of this Gallery I entered by an Arch, very narrow, but most neatly wrought into an oval Room; in the Middle of this Room, on the right Hand, was another small neat Arch-way; entring thro' which about ten Paces, there were two smaller Arches to the Right and Left, and within them, with an easy Ascent of about three Paces, you came to a flat Trough of Stone, six or seven Feet long, and about the same width; these, I understood by my Bash, were the Beds to lie on. I asked him, if they were used to lie on the bare Stone. He told me, some did; but he had Orders to lay me on Dossee [Softs]; and presently up came four Fellows with great Mats, as I took them for by my Globe-light, full of something, which by their so easily carrying so great Bulk, I perceived was very light. They pitched it down upon my Stone-bedstead, and first with great Sticks, and then with small Switches having beat it soundly, retired.

Whilst I was looking about at the Oddity of the Place, I found my Bash was gone too. So, says I, all gone? I suppose they intend I shall now go to Bed. I then went into my Bed-chamber, for there were Globe-lights there too, and observing my Bed lay full four Feet above the Stone, and sloping higher to the Sides and Head, I went to feel what it was; but laying my Hand upon it, it was so soft, I could feel no Resistance till I had pressed it some way; and it lay so light, that a Fly must have sunk upon it. Well, thinks I, what if I never lay thus before, I believe I have lain as bad.

I then took a Turn into my oval Room again, and observed the Floor, Sides, and all was Stone, as smooth as possible, but not polished; and the Walls, and Ceiling, and in short every Place, where they could be ornamental, were well adorned with Carvings, as can be conceived.

Tho' no body came near me yet, I did not care to be too inquisitive all at once, but I longed to know what they burnt in the Globes, which gave so steady a Light, and yet seemed to be inclosed quite round, Top and Sides, without any Vent-hole for the Smoak to evaporate. Surely, thinks I, they are a dullish Glass, for they hung almost above my Touch, and must be exceeding hot with the Fire so inclosed, and have some small Vent-hole, tho' I can't see it. Then standing on tip-toe to feel, it struck quite cold to my Finger; but I could only reach to touch that, or any of the rest, being all of one Height.

Whilst I was musing thus, I heard the Sound of Voices coming along the Gallery; and presently came a Train of Servants, with as much Victuals as an hundred Men could eat, and Wines proportionable; they set it down at the upper End of the oval Room, on a Flat of Stone, which on making the Room had been left in the upper Bend of the Oval quite cross it, about Table high, for that Purpose. These Eatables, such as were liquid, or had Sauces to them, were served up in a sort of grey Stone-bowls; but the dry were brought in neat wooden Baskets of Twig-work.

The Servants all retiring into the Gallery, except my Bash, I asked him, if any Body was to eat with me; he told me no. I wonder, says I, they should send me so much then. He replied, it was the Allowance of my Appartment, by his Majesty's Orders; which silenced me.

I believe there were twenty different things on the Table, insomuch, that I did not know where to begin, and heartily wished for an Excuse to get rid of my Bash, who stood close at my Elbow, that I might have smelt, and tasted, before I helped myself to any thing; for I knew not what any one thing was.

In this Perplexity, I asked my Bash, what Post he was in under his Majesty? He said, one of the fifty Bashes, appointed to be near the King's Favourites when at Court. And pray, said I, are you the Person to attend me? He was, he said, the Principal to wait on my Person; but there were at least sixty others, who had different Offices in this Appartment. I would be glad, said I, to know your Name, that I may the more readily speak to you. He told me, his Name was *Quilly*. Then, pray *Quilly*, says I, do you know what is become of my Baggage and my Chair? I found, tho' he guest at my Baggage, he was puzzled at the Name of Chair; my Seat, says I? O, I understand you, says he. Then pray, will you go bring me word of them, and see them brought safe up into the Gallery. He tripped away on my Errand. So, thinks I, now I am fairly rid of you; but I had scarce turned any of my Viands over, before I found he had but stepped into the Gallery, to send some of the idle Fellows in waiting there; and this putting me to a Nonplus, *Quilly*, says I, you know I am a Stranger here; and as different Countries have different Ways and Customs, as well of dressing their Eatables as other things, and these Dishes being dressed contrary to my Custom; I shall be glad if you will name some of them to me, that I may know them when I see them again.

Quilly began with this, and run on to that, which was a fine Dish; and the other, few but the King have at their Tables; and here, says he, is a Dish of Padsi; and there—Hold, hold, says I, *Quilly*, let's try these first, before you proceed; for I remembered, at my Grotto they all eat my Fish for Padsi, and I cut a Slice of it, for I always carried my Clasp-knife in my Pocket, and they had no such thing there, and laying it on a round Cake I took for my Trencher, I tasted it, and

found it so, to my Apprehension, in the Palate; but it did not
look or flake like Fish, as I observed by the Slices they had
cut it into; for all the Victuals was in long Slices ready to bite
at. I asked him, if these things were not all cut, and with what?
for I understood they had no Knives, shewing him mine. He
said, the Cook cut it with a sharp Stone. I then asked him the
Names of several other things, and at last he came to Crullmott;
which having heard of before, I now tasted, and could have
sworn it had been a hashed Fowl. I asked him, if Crullmotts
were very common? He told me, yes, towards the Bottoms of
the Mountains there were abundance of Crullmott-Trees.
No, no, says I, not Trees; I mean Fowls, Birds. I don't know
what they are, said he, but these Crullmotts grow on very
large Trees. Indeed, I did not know yet, what I was at; but,
says I, if your Fowls do, sure your Fish don't grow on Trees
too. We have none of them, says he, in this Country. Why,
says I, it is but this Moment I tasted one. I don't know then,
said he, where the Cook got it. Why here, says I, what you
call Padsi, I call Fish. Ay, Padsi, says he, grows upon a Bush
in the same Woods. Well done, says I, this is the first Country
I was ever in, where the Fish and Fowl grew on Trees; 'tis
ten to one, but I meet with an Ox growing on some Tree by
the Tail, before I leave you.

I had by this time, out of these two and some other Pickings, made up a very good Meal; and putting my Knife into
my Pocket, desired something to drink. My Bash asked me,
what I pleased to have. I told him, any thing to take a good
Draught of. Then he filled me a Bot [Shell] of Wine, very well
tasted, tho' too sweet for Meals; but putting some Water to
it, it did very well.

My Messengers being returned, and having set all my
things in the Gallery; I desired *Quilly* to let the Victuals be
taken away. Upon which, there came more Servants than
Dishes, who took all at once; but some Wine and Water
I desired might remain.

I told *Quilly*, I saw there were two Beds, who are they for?
says I. One for you, and one for me, says he; for we Bashes,

never leave the King's Favourites. Pray *Quilly*, says I, what is the Meaning that to the several Rooms I have been in there is never a Door? Door! says he, I don't know that. What, says I, don't you shut your Rooms at Night? No, no; shut at Night! I never heard of that. I believe, says I, *Quilly*, it is almost Bed-time, is it not? No, no, says *Quilly*, the Gripsack has not sounded. How do you know, says I, in this Country, when you should lie down, and when rise? For my Wife has told me, you have no Clocks. No, no Clocks, says he. Then, says I, does every one rise and lie down when they please? or do you all lie down, and all rise together about the same time? O, says *Quilly*, you will hear the Gripsack presently; there are several Glumms, who take it by Turns to sound it for Rest; and then we know it is time to lie down; and when they sound it again, we know it is time to rise: And afterwards I found these People guessed the time, being twelve Hours between Sound and Sound, so well, that there was but few Minutes Variation at any time, between them and my Watch; and I set my Watch to go from their Soundings at six o'Clock.

I found myself pretty much fatigued after my Journey; for tho' I had only to sit still, yet the excessive Velocity of such an unusual Motion strained every Muscle as much as the hardest Labour: For you may imagine, I could not at first be without my Fears upon ever so small a Variation of my Chair; which, tho' I could not possibly by my own Inclination one way or other rectify; yet a natural Propensity to a perpendicular Station, involuntarily byasses one to incline this or that way in order to preserve it: And then, at first, my Breath being ready to fail me in Proportion to the Celerity of the Flight, and to my own Apprehensions; and being upon that Exercise near thirty Hours, and without Sleep for almost forty, you may judge I wanted Rest: So I told *Quilly*, I would lie down, and ordered him not to disturb me, till I waked of myself.

I could not prevent the Officiousness of my Valet, to put me to Bed, and cover me with the Down, or whatever it was; for having no Sheets, I pulled off nothing but my Coat, Wig, and Shoes, and putting on my Flannel Night-cap, I laid me down.

CHAPTER X

*The King's Apartments described; is introduced to
the King; a Moucheratt called; his Discourse with
the King about Religion*

I HAVE known some Travellers so peculiar in their Taste,
as not to be able to sleep in a strange Lodging; but, thanks to
my kind Stars, that did not prove my Case; for having looked
on my Watch when I went to Bed, as I call it, and finding it
was down, I wound it up, and observed it began to go at
about three o'Clock, whether Day or Night matters not; and
when I waked it was past nine, so that I know I had slept
eighteen Hours; and finding that a very reasonable Refreshment, and myself very hungry, I called *Quilly* to get me my
Breakfast.

Quilly told me his Majesty had been to visit me, but would
not have me disturbed. I begging him to dispatch my Breakfast as soon as possible, and let me have some Water for my
Hands, he ordered the Gallery-Waiters, and every thing came
immediately.

My Breakfast was a brown Liquid, with a sort of Seeds or
Grain in it, very sweet and good; but the Fear of the King's
Return, before I was ready for him, prevented my inquiring
into what it was: So having finished it, and washed my Hands,
Quilly presented me a Towel, which looked like an unbleached
coarse Linen, but was very soft and spongy; and I found
afterwards was made of Threads of Bark, stripped from some
Tree. I put on my brown Suit, Sword, and long Wig, and sent
Quilly to know when it was his Majesty's Pleasure I should
wait upon him.

I had been so much used to Lamp-light in my Grotto, that
the Lights of this gloomy Mansion did not seem so unusual
a thing to me, as they would have done to a Stranger. The King
sent me Word he would admit me immediately, and *Quilly*
was my Conductor to his Majesty's Apartment.

We passed through the Gallery, at the further End of which was a very beautiful Arch, even with the Stair-case, through which *Quilly* led me into a large Guard-Room, wherein were above an hundred Glumms posted in Ranks, with their Pikes in hand, some headed with sharp-pointed Stone, others with multangular Stone, and others with Stone Globes. Passing through these, we entred another Gallery as long as that to my Apartment; then under another Arch we came into a small square Room, carved exceeding fine; on the Right and Left of which were two other Arch-ways, leading into most noble Rooms, but we only saw them, passing quite cross the little Room through an Arch that fronted us, into a small Gallery of prodigious Height; at the further End of which *Quilly* turning aside a Mat, introduced and left me in the most beautiful Place in the Universe; where neither seeing or hearing any body stir, I employed myself in examining the Magnificence of the Place, and could, as I then thought, have feasted my Eye with Variety for a Twelve-month. I paced it over one hundred and thirty of my Paces long, and ninety-six broad; there were Arches in the Middle of each Side, and in the Middle of each End: The Arch-Ceiling could not be less than the Breadth of the Room, and covered with the most delightful Carvings, from whence hung Globe-lights innumerable, but seemingly without Order, which I thought appeared the more beautiful on that account. In the Center of the Room hung a prodigious Cluster of the same Lights, so disposed as to represent one vast Light; and there were several Rows of the same Lights hung round the Room, one Row above another at proper Distances; these Lights represented to me the Stars, with the Moon in the Middle of them; and after I came to be better acquainted with the Country, I perceived the Lights were to represent the southern Constellations. The Archways were carved with the finest Devices imaginable, gigantick Glumms supporting on each side the Pediments. At every ten Paces, all along the Sides and Ends, arose Columns, each upon a broad square Base, admirably carved; these reached to the Cornice, or Base of the arched Ceiling, quite round the Room. On the

Pannels between each Column were carved the different
Battles, and most remarkable Achivements of *Begsurbeck* himself. Over the Arch I entred at was the Statue of *Begsurbeck*,
and over the opposite Arch the old prophetick Ragam. In the
Middle of the Room stood a long Stone Table lengthways,
most exquisitely carved, almost the Length of the Room,
except where it was divided in the Middle, about the Breadth
of the Arch-ways, in order for a Passage from one Arch to the
other. In short, to describe this one Room particularly, would
make a Volume of itself.

I staid here a full Hour and half, wondring why no body
came to me; at length turning myself about, I saw two Glumms
coming towards me, and having received their Compliments,
they desired me to walk in to the King. We passed through
another middling Room, and taking up a Mat at the further
side of it, I was conducted in where his Majesty was sitting
with another Glumm. They both arose at my Entrance, and
calling me their Father, and leading me, one by each Hand,
obliged me to sit down between them.

After some Compliments about my Journey, and Accommodation since, the King told me I had not waited so long
without, but he had some urgent Dispatches to make, and
as he chose to have me in private with him, he imagined, he
said, I would be able to divert myself in the Boske [great
Hall or Saloon]. I declared I had never seen any thing like
it for Grandeur and Magnificence before; but the Beauty of
the Sculpture, and Disposition of the Lights, were most
exquisite.

All this while I felt the other Glumm handling my long
Wig, and feeling whether it grew to my Head, or what it was;
for he had, by this time, got his Finger under the Caul,[1] and
was pulling my Hair down: When I turning about my Head,
Glumm *Peter*, says the King, don't be uneasy, the Ragam will
do you no hurt, it is only to satisfy his Curiosity; and I chose
to have the Ragam here, that we may more leisurely advise
with you what Course to take in the present Exigencies of my
State. I have fully heard the Story of your Travels from my

T

Colambs, and we have returned thanks to the great Image for bringing you, after so many Hazards and Deliverances, safe to my Dominions for our Defence.

The Ragam desired to know whether all that Hair, meaning my Wig, grew upon my Head, or not. I told him no, it was a Covering only, to put on occasionally; but that Hair did grow on my Head, and pulling off my Wig, I shewed them. The Ragam then asked me if I had Hair of my own growing under that too, meaning my Beard, which he then had in his Hand, for their Glumms have no Beards; but I told him that grew there of itself. O parly Puly! [sweet Image] says the Ragam, rising up and smiting his Hands together, it is he, it is he!

Pray, says I, Ragam, who is this Puly you speak of? It is the Image, says he, of the great Collwarr. Who is that, says I? Why, he that made the World, says he. And pray, says I, what did his Image make? O, says he, we made the Image. And pray, says I, can't you break it again? Yes, says he, if we had a mind to be struck dead we might; for that would be the immediate Consequence of such an Attempt, nay of but holding up a Finger against it in Contempt. Pray, says I, did ever any body die that way? No, says he, no one ever durst presume to do it. Then perhaps, said I, upon Trial, the Punishment you speak of might not be the Consequence of such an Attempt. Pray, says I, what makes Collwarr have so great a Kindness for that Image? Because, says he, it is his very Likeness, and he gives him all he asks for us; for we only ask him. Why, says he, it is the Image that has brought you amongst us.

I did not then think it a proper time to advance the contrary to the Person I then had to do with, as I was sure it would have done no good; for a Priest is only to be convinced by the strongest Party: So I deferred my Argument on that Head to a fitter Opportunity.

Most admirable *Peter*, says the King, you, you are the Glumm we depend upon to fullfil an ancient Prediction delivered by a venerable Ragam. If you will, Ragam I. O. shall repeat it to you, and therein you will be able to discern yourself, plainly described, in not only similar, but the express Words I myself, from your Story, should describe you in.

In good earnest, I had from divers Circumstances concluded, that I might be the Person; and resolved, as I thought I had the best Handle in the World for it from the Prediction, to do what I could in the Affair of Religion, by fair Means or Stratagem, for I was sensible my own single Force would not do it, before I began to shew myself in their Cause, or else to desert them; and having had a small Hint from *Nasgig* of what the old Ragam's Design was in part, and which I approved of, I purposed to add what else was necessary, as part of his Design, if his Proposals had been approved of.

I told the King I would excuse the Ragam the Repetition of the Prediction, as I had partly been informed of it by *Nasgig*; and that conceiving myself, as he did, to be the Person predicted of by the Ragam, I had the more readily set out on this Expedition, which nothing but the Hopes of performing so great a Good could have prevailed with me to undertake; and I did not doubt, with God's Blessing, to accomplish it.

The King grew exceeding joyous at what I said, and told me he would call a Moucheratt, at which all his *Colambs* should attend to have their Advice, and then we would proceed to Action; and ordered the Ragam to let it be for the sixth Day, and in the mean time that he and his Brethren should, Day and Night, implore the Image to guide their Deliberations.

The Ragam being gone, I told the King I had something to impart to him, in which it was my Duty to obtain his Majesty's Sentiments before I appeared publickly at the Moucheratt. He desiring me to proceed; I told him I had been some time considering the old Ragam's Prediction, with the Occasion of it; and, says I, it is plain to me, that all these Mischiefs have befallen you for neglect of the Ragam's Proposal concerning Religion; as I understand your great Ancestor would have come into it, and would have had his People done so too, but for the Ragams, who hindered it.

You find, says I, by your traditional History, that *Begsurbeck* lived long, and reigned gloriously; and I would aim at making you as prosperous as he was, and infinitely more happy, not only in outward Splendor here, but in great Glory hereafter.

Perceiving that my Discourse had quickened the King's Attention; says I, I must let your Majesty know it is the old Ragam's Plan I must proceed upon in every Branch of it. Why, says the King, he would have abolished our Worship of the Image. And so would I, says I; nay, not only would, but must and will, before I engage myself in your Deliverance; and then with the only Assistance of the great Collwarr, whom I adore, and whom you must too, if you expect any Service from me, I don't doubt to prevail.

Your Majesty sees, says I, in few Words, I have been very plain with you, and I desire you in as concise and plain a Manner to answer me, what are your Thoughts on this Head; for I can say no more till I hear them.

The King seeing me so peremptory; Glumm *Peter*, says he, looking about to see no one was near, I have too much Sense to imagine our Image can do either good or hurt; for if it could have done us good, why would it not, in our greatest Distress, now near two hundred Years past? For my own part I put no Trust in it, nor did my famous Ancestor the great *Begsurbeck*; but here is my Difficulty, where to chuse another Object of Worship; for I perceive by myself, Mankind must, through natural Impulse, look to somewhat still above them, as a Child does to his Father, from whom he hopes for, and expects Succour in his Difficulties; and tho' the Father be not able to assist him, still he looks to him: And therefore, I say, we must have another before we can part with this, or the People, instead of the Part who have been in the Defection, will all desert me; for they are easy now in hopes of Help from the Image, and every little Gleam of Success is attributed to it: But for the Disadvantages we receive, the Ragams charge them on the Peoples not praying, and paying sufficiently; which they, poor Souls! knowing in their Consciences to be true enough, are willing rather, as they are bid, to take the

Blame upon themselves, than to suffer the least to fall on the Image.

All this, says the King, I am sensible of; but should I tell them so, my Life must pay for it; for the Ragams would bring some Message from the Image against me, to desert or murder me; and then happy would be the first Man who could begin the Mischief, which the rest would soon follow.

This so frank and unexpected Declaration gave me great Confidence in the King; and I told him, if that was his Opinion, he might leave the rest to me, I would so manage it that the thing should be brought about by my means; and I would then satisfy all his Scruples, and make him a flourishing Prince. But I could not help reflecting with myself, how nearly this distant Prince, and his State, copied some of my Neighbours in *Europe*.

CHAPTER XI

Peter's *Reflections on what he was to perform; settles the Method of it; his Advice to his Son and Daughter; Globe-lights living Creatures; takes* Maleck *into his Service;* Nasgig *discovers to* Peter *a Plot at Court; Revolt of* Gauingrunt

HAVING now fully entred into the Spirit of the Business with my own good Liking, I was determined to push it vigorously, or perish in the Attempt. Have I, says I, so large a Field before me now to manifest my Maker in to a whole Nation, and under his own Call, and to fullfil their own Prediction too; and shall I shrink at the possible Danger? Or may there not rather be no probability of Danger in it? The Nation is in distress, the readier therefore to try any Remedy for help: Their Image has stood idle two hundred Years; there has been an old Prophecy, or at least if not true, as firmly believed to be true as if it was so; and this in regard to the People answers in all respects as well. But why should it not be true? It is better attested by the frequent Repetition, from the original Delivery to this time, than are many Traditions I have heard of amongst us Christians, which have come out spick and span new from the Repositories of the Learned, of twelve, or fifteen hundred Years old, little the worse for lying by; though they are not pretended to have seen Light all that time, and are undoubted Verities the Moment they receive the grand Sanction. Then, if any Means but Fraud or Force can gain so large a Territory to the Truth, and I am the only Person can introduce it, shall not I endeavour it? Yes, surely; but I am not excluded all Advantages neither, for all the Works of Providence are brought to pass by appointed Means: And indeed was it otherwise, what could we call Providence? For a peremptory Fiat, and it is over, may work a Miracle it is true, but will not exhibit the Proceedings of Providence. Therefore let me consider in a prudential way how to proceed to the Execution of what I am to set about; and guide me, Providence! I beseech you, to the End.

Upon the best Deliberation I could take, I came to the following Resolutions: First, to insist on the Abolition of the Image-Worship, and to introduce true Religion by the fittest Means I could find Opportunity for.

Secondly, as the Revolters had been one People with those I would serve, and had this Prediction amongst them too, and were interested in it, in hopes of its distant Accomplishment: So if they came properly to the Knowledge, that the Person predicted of had appeared, and was ready for Execution of his Purposes, it must stagger their Fidelity to their new Master; and therefore I would find Means to let them know it.

Thirdly, that I would not march till I was in Condition not easily to be repulsed; for that would break both the Hopes and Hearts of my Party, and destroy my religious Scheme; and therefore I would get some of my Cannon.

Fourthly, that I would go to the War in my flying Chair, and train up a Guard for my Person with Pistols and Cutlasses.

These Resolutions I kept to myself till the Moucheratt was over, to see first how Matters would turn out there.

Whilst I waited for the approaching Moucheratt, my Son *Tommy* and Daughter *Hallycarnie* paid their Duties to me. It is strange how soon young Minds are tainted by bad Company. I found them both very glad to see me, for every body, they said, told them I was to be their Deliverer. They had both got the Prophecy by heart, and mentioned the Image with all the Affection of natural Subjects. The Moment *Tommy* spoke of it to me; hold, says I, young Man, what's become of those good Principles I took so much pains to ground you in? Has all my Concern for your Salvation been thrown away upon you? Are you become a Reprobate? What! an Apostate from the Faith you inherited by Birth-right? Is the God, I have so often declared to you, a wooden one? Answer me, or never see my Face more.

The Child was extremely confounded to see me look so severe, and hear me speak so harsh to him. Indeed Father, says he, I did not willingly offend, or design to shew any particular Regard to the Image; for, thanks to you, I have none; but what I said was only common Discourse in every Body's Mouth; I meant neither good or harm by it.

Tommy, says I, it is a great Fault to run into an Error, though in Company of Multitudes; and where a Person's Principle is sound at bottom, and founded upon Reason, no Numbers ought to shake it. You are young, therefore hearken to me; and you, *Hallycarnie*, whatever you shall see done by the People of this Country, in the Worship of this Idol, don't you imitate it, don't you join in it. Keep the sound Lessons I have preached to you in mind; and upon every Attempt of the Ragams, or any other, to draw you aside to their Worship, or even to speak or act the least thing in praise of this Idol, think of me, and my Words; pay your Adoration to the Supreme Father of Spirits only, and to no Wooden, Stone, or Earthen Deity whatsoever.

The Children wept very heartily, and both promised me to remember and do as I had taught them.

Being now in my oval Chamber, and alone with my Children, I had a mind to be informed of some things I was almost ashamed to ask *Quilly*. *Tommy*, says I, what sort of Fire do they keep in these Globes? and what are they made of? Daddy, says he, yonder is the Man shifting them, you may go and see. Being very curious to see how he did it, I went to him; as I came near him, he seemed to have something all Fire on his Arm. What has the Man got there, says I? Only Sweecoes, says *Tommy*. By this time I came up to him; Friend, says I, what are you about? Shifting the Sweecoes, Sir, says he, to feed them. What Oil do you feed with, says I? Oil! says he, they won't eat Oil; that would kill them all. Why, says I, my Lamp is fed with Oil.

Tommy could scarce forbear laughing himself; but for fear the Servant should do so too, pulled me by the Sleeve, and desired me to say no more. So turning away with him; Daddy, says he, it is not Oil that gives this Light, but Sweecoes, a living Creature; he has got his Basket full, and is taking the old ones out to feed them, and putting new ones in; they shift them every half Day, and feed them. What, says I, are all those infinite Number of Globes I see living Creatures? No, says he, the Globes are only the transparent Shell of a Bot, like our Calibashes, the Light comes from the Sweecoe within. Has that Man, says I, got any of them? Yes, says he, you may see them; the King, and the *Colambs*, and indeed every Man of Note has a Place to breed and feed them in. Pray let us go see them, says I, for that is a Curiosity indeed.

Tommy desired the Man to shew me the Sweecoes; so he set down his Basket, which was a very beautiful Resemblance of a common Higler's Basket, with a Handle in the Middle, and a Division under it, with Flaps on each side to lift up and down. It was made of Straw-coloured small Twigs, neatly compacted, but so light as scarce to be of any Weight. Opening one of the Lids, I could make very little Distinction of Substances, the Bottom seeming all over of a quite white Colour. I looking surprized at the Light, the Man took out one, and would have put it into my Hand; but perceiving me shy of it, he assured me it was one of the most innocent things in the World: I then took it, and surveying it, it felt to my Touch as smooth and cold as a Piece of Ice. It was about as long as a large Lobworm, but much thicker. The Man seeing me admire the Brightness of its Colour, told me that had done its Duty, and was going to be fed; but those which were going upon Duty were much clearer; and then opening the other Lid, those appeared far exceeding the others in Brightness, and Thickness too. I asked what he fed them with? He said Leaves and Fruit; but Grass, when he could get it, which was not often, they were very fond of.

Having dismissed my Children, I sent for *Nasgig* to gain some Intelligences I wanted to be informed of. The Moment I saw him it came into my Mind to inquire after my new Filgays. He said the King granted my Request at the first Word. I told him then he had saved his Honour with me, and I was obliged to him; but, says I, you told me my Bearers should be free too. They are so, says he. Then there is one thing I want, says I, and that is to see the second Bearer on my right Hand, who came through without shifting. I have a fancy for that Fellow, says I, to be about my Person: I like him, and if you can give him a good Word, I should be glad to treat with him about it.

My Friend *Peter*, says he, you are a Man of Penetration, though it ill becomes me to say so in regard of Persons; but I can say that for him, if he likes you as well as you seem to like him, he is the trustiest Fellow in the World; but as he knows his own Worth, he would not be so to every Body, I can tell you that. I don't fear his disliking me, says I, for I make it my Maxim to do as I would be done by; and if he is a Man of Honour, as you seem to say, he will do the same, and we shall be soon agreed. But, says *Nasgig*, it being now the fourth Day since he was freed, he may be gone home perhaps; for he is not of our Country, but of Mount *Alkoe*. If *Quilly* can find him he'll come; so he ordered *Quilly* to send for *Maleck* of Mount *Alkoe*, with Orders to come to me.

We descended from one Discourse to another, and at length

to King *Georigetti*'s Affairs; when *Nasgig* giving a Sigh, Ah, *Peter*, says he, we shall loiter away our time here till the Enemy are upon our Backs. There is Venom in the Grass; I wish my good Master is not betrayed. By whom? says I. By those he little suspects, says he. Why, says I, they tell me you are much in his Favour, if so why do you suffer it? I believe, says *Nasgig* I am in his Favour, and may continue in it, if I will join in Measures to ruin him, but else I shall soon be out of it. You tell me Riddles, says I. These things, says he, a Man talks, with his Head in his Teeth. There is Danger in them, *Peter*; there is Danger. You don't suspect me, says I, do you? No, says he, I know your Soul too well; but there are three Persons in these Dominions who will never let my Master rest till out of his Throne, or in Hoximo. I am but lately in Favour, but have made as many Observations perhaps as those who have been longer about the King.

Nasgig, says I, your Concern proceeds from an honest Heart; don't stifle what you have to say; if I can counsel you with Safety I'll do it, if not I'll tell you so.

Peter, says he, *Georigetti* was the only Son of a well-beloved Father, and ascended his Throne ten Years ago on his Decease; but *Harlokin*, the Prince of the Revolters, whose Head is never idle, finding that Whispers and base Stories spread about did not hurt *Georigetti*, or withdraw his Subjects Affections, has tried a Means to make him undo himself. As how? says I. Why, said he, by closely playing his Game he has got one of his Relations into the King's Service, than whom he could never have chosen a fitter Instrument. He by degrees feeding the King's Humour, and promising Mountains, has pushed into the best Places in the Kingdom: His Name is *Barbarsa*, a most insolent Man, who has had the Assurance to corrupt the King's Mistress, and has prevailed and brought her over to his Interest. O Perfidy! says I, is it possible? Yes, says he, and more than that has drawn in, till now, an honest Man, called *Nicor*; and it has been agreed between them to protract this War, till by their Stratagems in procuring the Revolt of *Gauingrunt*, a very large and populous Province, and now the

Barrier between us and the Rebels, and two or three more Places, they shall have persuaded *Georigetti* to fly; and then *Barbarsa* is to be King, and *Yaccombourse* his Queen. A Union is then to be struck between him and *Harlokin*, and Peace made, by restoring some of the surrendered Provinces. And upon the Death of the first of them, or their Issue, childless, the Survivor, or his Issue, is to take the whole. They laugh at your uniting the Dominions, and the old Prediction.

These, said I, *Nasgig* are serious things, and, as you say, are not lightly to be talked of; but *Nasgig* know this, he that conceals them is a Traitor. Can you prove this? I have heard them say so, says *Nasgig*. How, says I, and not discover it? I am as anxious for that as you can be, says he; but for me to be cashiered, slit, and sent to *Crashdoorpt*, only for meaning well, without Power to perfect my good Intentions, where will be the Benefit to my Master or me? When and where did you hear this? says I. Several, and several times, says he, in my own Bed. In your own Bed, says I? I'll tell you, says he, it so happens that when I rest at the Palace, as I am bound to do when on Duty, there is a particular Bed for me: Now as the whole Palace is cut out of one solid Rock, tho' *Yaccombourse*'s Apartment at the Entrance is at prodigious Distance from the Entrance to mine, yet my Bed, and one in an inner Apartment of hers, stand close together; the Partition indeed is Stone, but either from the Thinness of it, or some Flaw in it I have not yet discovered, I can plainly hear every Word that is spoken. And there it is, in their Hours of Dalliance, when they use this Bed, that I hear what I have now told you. Say nothing of it, says I, but leave the Issue to me.

By this time the Messenger returned with *Maleck*, and he and I soon agreeing, I took him into my Service.

I went to Bed as usual, but could get no Rest, *Nasgig*'s Story ingrossing my whole Attention. I was resolved however to be better informed, before I acquainted the King of it. But rising pretty early next Morning, the King came into my Chamber, leaning upon *Barbarsa*, to tell me he had received an Express that *Gauingrunt* had revolted. *Peter*, says he, behold a distressed Monarch, nay an undone Monarch. Great Sir, says *Barbarsa*, you afflict yourself too much; here is Mr. *Peter* come to assist you, and he will settle all your Concerns, never fear. I eyed the Man, and, tho' Prejudice may hang an honest Person, found him a Villain in his Heart; for even while he was forcing a feeling Tone of Affliction, he was staring at my laced Hat and Feather that lay on the Seat, by which I was sure nothing could be at a greater Distance than his Heart and Tongue. His sham Concern put me within a Moment of seizing him in the King's Presence; but his Majesty, at that Instant speaking, diverted me.

Before the King left me, I told him, having certain Propositions to make to the Moucheratt next Day, it was possible they might require Time to consider of them; wherefore it would be proper, at this critical Time, to let them meet every other Day, Business or none, till this Affair was over. The King ordered *Barbarsa* to see it was so, and then we parted.

CHAPTER XII

Hold a Moucheratt; Speeches of Ragams and
Colambs; Peter *settles Religion; informs the King*
of a Plot; sends Nasgig *to the Ship for Cannon*

ATTENDING at the Moucheratt Today, I happened to be seated within two Paces of the Idol. There was the most numerous Assembly that had ever been seen; and when all was quiet, the King opened with signifying the Revolt of *Gauingrunt*, the Approach of the Enemy, and no Forces in the Field to stop them. This, he set forth in Terms so moving, that the whole Assembly were melted into Sighs; till one of the *Colambs* rising up, says he, His Majesty has set forth the State of his Affairs in such a manner, and I am satisfied a true one, that it becomes us all to be vigilant. We all seem to have, and I believe have great Faith, in the Remedy this Day to be proposed to us, in answer to our ancient Prediction. And as I doubt not but Glumm *Peter* is the Man; so I doubt not, but thro' his Management, we shall still receive Help; but let us consider, if we might not have prevented these pressing Evils, and especially this last, by speedier Preparations against them. What Province, or Member of a State will not revolt to a numerous Host just ready to devour them, if they can receive no Assistance from their Head? for to my certain Knowledge, his Majesty had ordered this almost a Year ago, and not a Man gone yet. Can we expect *Peter* to go singly to fight an Army? Did your Prediction say he should go alone? No, he shall stay, that is, he and his Army; what is done by them, being always attributed to their General. Inquire therefore into your past Conduct, send *Peter* your General, and trust to the great Image.

His Majesty then said, if there had been any Remissness in executing his Commands, he believed it was done with a View to his Service; but a more proper Opportunity might be found for an Inquiry of that Nature. As for the present Moucheratt, it was called solely to propose to *Peter* the Execution of the remaining Part of the Prediction; or at least such part of it, as seems now, or never, to wait its Accomplishment.

Here, arose a Ragam, and told the Assembly in the Name of himself and Brethren, That the Prediction had never yet been applicable to any one Person, till Glumm *Peter* arrived; and that his Sagacity of itself was a sufficient Recommendation of him to the Guidance of the Enterprize; and requested, that Glumm *Peter* might forthwith be declared Protector of the Army, and set forward with it, that the State might receive Safety, and the great Image its proper Honour.

I could now hold out no longer, but standing up, made my Speech in the following manner, or very near it. 'Mighty King, you reverend Ragams, and honourable *Colambs*, with the good People of this august Assembly: I am come hither, led by the Force of your own Prediction, at the Request of his Majesty and the States, at the Peril of my Life, to accomplish things said to be predicted of me Glumm *Peter*. If then you have a Prediction; if then your Prediction describes me, and the Circumstances of these times; it consisting of several parts, they ought seriously to be weighed, that I may know when and where I am to begin my Operation; and when and where to leave off: For in Predictions, the whole is to be accomplished as much as any Member of it.

'It is said, I shall destroy the Traitor of the West; I am ready to enter upon it, settle the ancient Limits of your Monarchy; are you willing therefore that should be done? yea or nay?' Then every one answered yea. 'And by common Consent, establish what the old Ragam would have taught you.' Here the King rose up; but *Barbarsa* giving him a Touch, for every one waited to be guided by the Voice of the Ragams; he sat down again, and no one answering yea. I again put the same Question and told them, as it was their own Concern, I would have an Answer before I proceeded. One of the Ragams then rose and said, that part of the Prediction was too loose to be relied on; for it was to settle what he would have taught: Now who knows, says he, what he would have taught? The Assembly paused a considerable time; and just as I was opening my Mouth to speak, an ancient and venerable Ragam rose; says he, I am sorry at my Years to find the Truth wants an Advocate; my Age and Infirmities might well have excused me from speaking in this Assembly; so many of my Brethren being present, younger and better qualified for that Purpose than myself; but, as we are upon a sacred thing, and least, as I find none of them care to declare the Truth, I should also be thought to consent to its Suppression, if I sat silent and suffered it to be hid under a Quibble: I must beg to be heard a few Words. My Brother who spoke last says, the Words are too loose, which say, *and by common Consent establish what I would have taught*; but, I beg leave to think it far otherwise; for we all know what he would have taught, and the Memory of that hath been as exactly kept as the Prediction: For how could our Ancestors have opposed his Doctrine, but from hearing and disapproving it; And we all know, not only the

Prediction, but the Doctrine hath been punctually handed down to us; tho' wo be to us, we have not proclaimed it as we have the Prediction; and let me tell you, when you my Brethren severally come to my Years, and have but a single Step further to Hoximo, you will wish you had taught it, as I do; who do believe and approve it.

The poor old Man having spoke as long as his Breath and Spirits would permit him, sat down; and I again resumed the Question, as I now thought on a much better Foundation than before, and was immediately told by another Ragam, that there would be no End of the Assembly, if we considered every Point at once; for we might next go upon what Countries we should conquer, and of whom to demand Tribute; which would be debating about the Fruit, before the Seed was sown. But his Opinion was, to go on and quell the Rebellion, and restore the Monarchy, and then go upon the other Points.

I told them, if they made so light of the Prediction, as not to declare publickly, since they knew it, what the Ragam would have taught; it ill became me, to be more zealous in their own Concerns than they were themselves; and I should imagine there was very little Truth in any part of it, and would never hazard my Life for their sakes, who would not speak the Truth to save the Kingdom; and desired Leave of the States[1] for my Departure; for I was not a Person I told them, to be cajoled into any thing. I undertook it at first voluntarily; and no Man could, or should compel me to it; my Life they might take, but my Honour they should never stain; tho' I was assured I could easily with their Concurrence, compleat all that related to them.

The senior *Colamb* immediately rising, desired me to have a little Patience, and not to leave the Assembly, for I was going out, till I had heard him.

Here is, says he, this Day a thing started, which I think, every whit as much concerns us all, and the Body, and every Member of the People to know, as it does *Peter*; and I am surprized, unless the present Ragams believe what their Predecessor would have taught to be better than what they now teach, for nothing else can make us consent to it, that they should scruple to let us know it, and keep us ignorant, who are Worshippers as well as themselves, of any Matter which so nearly concerns us to know. I am for obliging the Ragams to declare the Truth. If this be a true Prediction, all the Relatives to it are true; and I insist that we hear it.

This Speech imboldened several others, and all the Populace, siding with the *Colambs* out of Curiosity, cryed out to know it.

Perceiving the Ragams still hush, I rose and beckoning the Populace to silence: 'Mighty King, you honourable *Colambs*, and you good People, says I, for it is to you I now speak, hear me with Attention. You think perhaps that the Suppression of the Truth by your Ragams, (charged to their Teeth by the most Reverend of their whole Body, whose Infirmities rendering him unable, tho' his Will is good, to declare this Secret to you) will prevent the Knowledge of that Truth your old Ragam would have taught; but you are mistaken, and that you may know I don't come here at a venture to try if I can relieve you, but with an Assurance of doing it if you consent: I must let you know, from me, what the Ragam would have taught. The Ragam would have demolished this trumpery Piece of Dirt, this Grimalken,[1] set out with horrid Face and Colour to fright Children; this, I say, he would have demolished, being assured it could neither do good or hurt, give Joy or Grief to any Man, or serve any other Purpose whatsoever, but to procure a Maintenance to a Set of Men, who know much better than they dare to tell you. Can any of you believe this stupid Piece of Earth hears me?' Some of the Ragams cried *Yes*. 'And that he can revenge any Affront I shall give him?' Again, *Yes to be sure*. 'Let him then if he dare, says I,' whipping out my Cutlass, and with the Backside of it striking its Head off. 'This, says I, O Glumms, is what the Ragam knew, and what I defy them to deny. Now, says I, I will further shew you, to whom the old Ragam would have taught you to make your Petitions, and pay your Adoration; and that is, to the Supreme Being, Maker of Heaven and

Earth, of us and all things; who provides for us Meat and Drink, and all things; by causing the Earth which he has made, to produce things necessary for our Use. That Being, whom you have heard of by the Name of *Collwarr*, and are taught, at present, to be afraid to speak to. And I appeal to your own Hearts, if many of you have ever thought of him. Again, says I, let any thing in the Shape of Man, that gives himself leave to consider at all, only tell me, if what he can make, and does make with his own Hands, hath not more Occasion to depend on him as its Maker, than he on that? Why then should not we depend upon, and pray to our Maker?

'You greatly mistake me, O Glumms, says I, if you imagine I would have all those reverend Men turned out of Imployment as useless. No, I find they know too much of what is valuable; and therefore those who are willing to continue in the Service of the Mouch, and faithfully to teach you the old Ragam's Doctrine, and such further Lights of the great Being as they shall hereafter receive, let them continue your Ragams still; and let others be chosen, and trained up in that Doctrine.'

Here, the poor old Man got up again with much Difficulty. Mr. *Peter*, says he, you are the Man predicted of, you have declared the old Ragam's Mind, and all my Brethren know it.

Finding I had the Populace on my side, for I did not doubt the King and the *Colambs*. I put the Question to the Ragams: 'Reverend, says I, you see your Prediction this Day about to be fulfilled; for if it is a true one, no Force of Man can withstand it. You see your Image disgraced; you see, and I appeal to you all for the Truth of it, that what the Ragam would have taught has, without your Assistance been disclosed. I therefore would have you the first to break the Bondage of Idolatry, and turn to the true *Collwarr*; as it will be so much Glory to you. Will you, and which of you, from henceforth serve *Collwarr*, and no longer worship an Idol? Such of you as will do so, let them continue in the Mouch: If none of you will, it shall be my Business to qualify a sufficient Number of true Ragams, to form a Succession for that Purpose. The Issue of

U

this great Affair, depends upon your Answers.' They waited sometime for a Spokesman to begin; and so soon as he was able to get up, the poor old Ragam said, I will continue in it, and do all the little good I can; and blessed be the Day this Prediction is fulfilled, to succeeding Generations. I have lived long enough to have seen this. Then the rest of the Ragams, one by one, followed his Example. And thus, with prodigious Acclamations both of the Ragams and People, ended the great Affair of Religion.

I now, more and more believed the Truth of the Prediction; and told them, I should have Occasion for seven hundred Men before I set out against the Rebels; and desired that they might be commanded by *Nasgig*. This was readily granted. I then told them, as I purposed to act nothing without their Concurrence, I desired the *Colambs* would remain in the City till I sat[1] out, that they might be readily called together.

I then desired I might be quite private from Company, till I departed.

I took *Nasgig* home with me, and when we came there; my dear Friend, says he, what have you done to Day! You have crushed a Power hitherto immoveable; and I shall never more think any thing too difficult for you to attempt. *Nasgig*, says I, I am glad it is over. And now, says I, you must enter on a new Imploy; but first, can you provide me fifty honest, faithful Glumms, for a particular Expedition? they must be sensible, close, and temporizing.[2] He said he would, and come to me again.

I then desired a private Audience of the King; who, on seeing me, began upon my Success at the Moucheratt. I told his Majesty, if I alone, and a Stranger, could gain such Influence there; I might have had much more, if he had joined me; especially as he had told me, he gave no Credit to the Image; and that I expected he would have appeared on my side. Ah! *Peter*, says he, Monarchs neither see, hear, or perceive with their own Eyes, Ears, or Understandings. I would willingly have done it; but *Barbarsa* prevented me, by assuring me it would be my Ruin; and as he is my Bosom Friend, what

Reproaches must I have suffered, if it had gone amiss? Nay, I will tell you; that he and *Nicor* are of Opinion, that your coming hither, which is looked upon by us all as such a Blessing, will one Day undo me: For, say they, tho' he may perform what you expect from him, it is not to be supposed he should suffer it to redound to you. No, say they, if he can do these great things, he can soon set you aside. Thus, tho' I have no doubt of you, is my Spirit wasting within me thro' perpetual Fears and Jealousies; and I can't get these Men, who knowing all my Secrets are feared by me, into my own way of thinking.

Mighty Sir, says I, don't think I came hither to possess, but redress a Kingdom. I lived far more to my Ease in my Grotto, than I can in this Palace; but I now desire you, drawing my Sword and putting it into his Hand, to pierce this Heart's Blood, and make yourself easy in my Death, rather than, suffering me to survive, live in distrust of me. No, great King, says I, it is not I that would injure you; but, tho' I have been so short a time in your Dominions, I find there are those, who would; and will too, unless you exert the Monarch and shake off those Harpies, which lying always at your Ear, are ever buzzing Disquiet and Mischief to you. *Peter*, says he, what do you mean? sure I have not more Traitors in my State? Your Majesty has, says I. How can you prove it? says he. But pray inform me who they are? I came not hither great King, says I, to turn Informer, but Reformer; and so far as that is necessary in order to this, I will give you Satisfaction. I only desire you will wholly guide yourself by my Direction for three Days; and you shall be able to help yourself to all the Information you can require, without my telling you. In the mean time, appear no more thoughtful than usual, or in any other way alter your accustomed Habits.

Nasgig having sent me the fifty Men, I asked them if they were to be trusted, and if they could carefully and artfully execute a Commission I had to charge them with. They assuring me they would, I told them I would let them into my Design, which would be the best Instructions I could give them, and let the Management alone to them.

My Confidence in them made them twice as diligent as all the particular Directions in the World would have done; so I only told them I had a mind the revolted Towns, and also the Enemy's Army, should know that the Person so long ago predicted of was now at *Brandleguarp*, and had, as the first Step towards reducing them, and killing the Traitor *Harlokin*, already altered their Religion to the old Ragam's Plan; and that they had nothing now to expect but Destruction to themselves, as soon as I appeared against them with my unknown Fire and Smoke, which I always had with me; and that the thing was looked upon to be as good as done already at *Brandleguarp*; and then to slip away again unperceived. They all promised me exact Performance, and went off.

Nasgig then coming in, I told him he was now under my Command, and must take six hundred Glums with him to *Graundevolet*; tell *Youwarkee* to shew him my Ship, and then he must bring me the things I had described to her by the Name of Cannon; he must bring them by Ropes, as I was brought; and bring Powder, which she would direct him to, and about fifty heavy Balls which lay in the Room with the Powder. I told him, if he thought he should not have Men enough, he must take more; and must be as expeditious as was consistent with Safety. I desired him to tell *Youwarkee* I hoped in a short time to send for her, and all the Family, over to me. And now *Nasgig*, says I, my Orders are finished; but, says I, the King! I must assist that good Man. I therefore want to know the particular Times *Barbarsa* and *Yaccombourse* usually meet. That, says he, is every Night when she is not with the King; for he is excessive fond of her, and seldom lies without her; but whenever he does, *Barbarsa* is admitted to her. And how can I know, says I, when she will, or will not lie with the King? When she is to lie with him, says he, the King never sups without her. Now, says I, you must shew me your Lodging, that I may find it in your Absence; and give Orders to the Guard to let me, and whoever comes with me, enter at any time. He then took me to his Chamber; but I passed thro' so many Rooms,

Galleries, and Passages, that I was sure I should never find it again, so I asked him if *Maleck* knew the way; and he assuring me he did, I took my Leave of him, and he set out for *Graundevolet*.

CHAPTER XIII

The King hears Barbarsa *and* Yaccombourse *discourse on the Plot; they are impeached by* Peter *at a* Moucheratt; *condemned and executed;* Nicor *submits, and is released*

I HAD now several important Irons in the Fire, and all to be struck whilst hot: There was the securing Religion, sowing Sedition amongst the Enemy, tripping up the Heels of two Ministers, and a She-Favourite, and transporting Artillery in the Air some hundred Leagues; either of which failing, might have been of exceeding bad Consequence; but as the Affair of the Ministers now lay next at hand, I entred upon that in the following Manner.

The King coming to me the next Day, as by Appointment; and having assured me he had hinted nothing to any one, no not to *Barbarsa*, or *Yaccombourse*, told me, that *Barbarsa* had given Orders for stopping *Nasgig* and his Men; and had per-suaded him not to be in such haste in suffering me to do as I pleased, but to shew his Authority, and keep me under. Says I, your Majesty's Safety is so near my Heart, that even Want of Confidence in me shall not make me decline my Endeavours to serve you. But have you suffered him to stop *Nasgig*? No, says he, *Nasgig* was gone some time before he sent. O! Sir, says I, you do not half know the Worth of that Man! but you shall hereafter, and will reward him accord-ingly: But now, Sir, says I, to what we meet upon; if you will, as I told you, but comply with me for three Days, without asking Questions, I will shew you the greatest Traitors in your Dominions, and put them into your Power too. He promised me again he would. Then, Sir, says I, you must not send to *Yaccombourse* to sup with you To-night. Nor lie with me? No, says I. Pray what Hurt can arise to my Affairs from her, says he? Sir, says I, you promised me to ask no Questions. Agreed, agreed, says he. Then, says I, please to meet me at *Nasgig*'s Lodgings without being perceived, if you can; at least without Notice taken. Good, says he; and when you are there, see or hear what you will you must not say a Word till you are retired again: All which the King engaging to perform, we parted till Evening.

I called *Maleck*, and asked if he knew the way to *Nasgig*'s Lodging. He told me very well; and the Time being come, he conducted me thither; where I had not waited long before the King came, most of the Court being in Bed. I desired the King to stay in the outer Room till I went into the Bed-chamber two or three times, and I thought we must have put it off till another Night: But listening once again, I found they were come; so I called the King, and led him to the Place; intreating him, whatever he heard to keep his Patience, or he would ruin all. We first heard much amorous Discourse between *Barbarsa* and *Yaccombourse*, and then the ensuing Dialogue.

Yac. My dearest *Barbarsa*, what was all that Uproar at the Moucheratt the other Day?

Bar. Nothing, my Love, but that mad Fellow *Peter*, who sets up for a Conjurer, and wants us all to dance to his Pipe.

Yac. I heard he overcame the Ragams at an Argument about the Image.

Bar. Why I don't know how that was; but it was the doating old Ragam did their Business; and truly the King's Fingers itched to be on *Peter*'s Side, but I gave him a judicious Nod, and you know he durst not displease so dear a Friend as I am, ha, ha, ha; am not I a sad Fellow, my Love, to talk so of my King?

Yac. He that wants but one Step to a Throne, is almost a King's Fellow.

Bar. And that but a short one too, my dear *Yaccee*; but

I must get rid of that *Nasgig*, tho' I think I have almost spoiled
him with the King too. I don't love your thinking Rascals;
that Fellow thinks more than I do, *Yaccee*.

Yac. He'll never think to so good Purpose, I believe; but
how goes Cousin *Harlokin* on, I find *Gauingrunt* is gone over.

Bar. And so shall *Bazin*, *Istell*, *Pezele*, and *Ginkatt* too,
my Dear, for I am at work there; and then good Night, my
poor King *Georigetti*; thou shalt be advised to fly, and I'll
keep the Throne warm for thee. I don't see but King *Barbarsa*,
and Queen *Yaccombourse*, sound much better than *Georigetti*.
Well, my Dear, whenever we come to Sovereignty, which now
can't be long, if *Nicor* has but play'd his Part well, for I have
not had an Account of his Success yet; I say, when we come
into Power, never let us be above minding our own Affairs,
or suffer ourselves to be led by the Nose, as this poor insignificant King does. For, in short, he may as well be a King of
Matts, as a King of Flesh, if he will not use his Faculties, but
suffer me to make a Fool of him thus; and I should be a Fool
indeed to neglect it, when he thinks it the greatest Piece of
Service I can do him.

Yac. Come, come, my Dear, let us enjoy ourselves like
King and Queen till we come to the Dignity.

Finding a Pause, the King, who had admirably kept his
Temper, even beyond Imagination, stole into the outer
Room. *Peter*, says he, I thank you, you have shewn me myself.
What Fools are we Kings! In endeavouring to make others
happy, how miserable do we make ourselves! How easily are
we deceived by the designing Flattery of those below us?
Ungrateful Villain! Degenerate Strumpet! I hate you both.
Peter, says he, give me your Sword; I'll destroy them both in
the very Act.

Hold, Sir, says I, your Majesty has heard sufficient to found
a true Judgment upon; but Kings should not be Executioners,
or act by Passion and Revenge; but as you would punish that
in others, so carefully avoid it yourself. You, who are in so
exalted a Station, as always to have it in your Power to punish
a known Crime in Individuals, have not that Necessity to

prompt you to a violent Act, that private Persons have; to whom, it may be difficult to obtain Justice. Therefore, my Advice is, that you summon the *Colambs* To-morrow; when *Barbarsa* and *Nicor* can't fail to attend; and I would also desire *Yaccombourse* to be there, you having great Proposals to make to the States which you shall want her to hear. I will in the mean time prepare the Servants under *Quilly*, and order *Maleck* with another Possee to attend, as by your Command, to execute your Orders given by me; and I myself will impeach those bad Persons in publick; and *Nicor*, if he will not ingenuously confess what Commission he was charged with from *Barbarsa*, shall be put to the Torture I direct, till he discovers it.

The King was very well pleased with this Method; so I ordered *Quilly*, as from the King, to bring all my Servants to the Assembly, appointing him his Place. And *Maleck*, to select me fifty stout Persons, and to wait to execute my Orders on a Signal given. So soon as the Assembly met, I told them, since I had concerned myself in their Affairs, I had made it my Business to search into the Cause of their Calamities; and finding some of the Traitors were now approached, not only near to, but even into the capital City; his Majesty had therefore ordered me to ask their Advice, what Punishment was adequate, in their Judgments, to the Crime of conspiring against him and the State, and holding treasonable Correspondence with his Enemies, under the shew of his greatest Friends.

I stopped; and looking at *Barbarsa*, he turned as pale as Ashes, and was rising to speak; when the senior *Colamb* declared, If any such thing could be made appear, the common Punishment of *Crashdoorpt* was too trivial; but they deserved to be dropt alive, either into *Hoximo*, or Mount *Alkoe*. The several *Colambs* all declaring the same to be their Judgment, and even those to be too mild for their Deserts, I then stept up to *Barbarsa*, who sat at the King's Left-hand, as did *Yaccombourse* at his Right; and telling them and *Nicor* they were all Prisoners of State; I delivered *Barbarsa* and

Yaccombourse in Custody to *Quilly* and his Men, and *Nicor*, to *Maleck* and his Men; ordering them into separate Appartments, with strict Commands that neither should speak to the other, upon pain of the last pronounced Judgment.

Barbarsa would have spoke, and called out to the King, begging him not to desert so faithful a Servant, for the Insinuations of so vile a Man as *Peter*: But the King only told him, the vile Man would be made appear presently, and he hoped would meet his Deserts.

I then stood up, and told the Assembly the whole of what we had heard, how it first came to be discovered, and that the King himself had been an Ear-witness of it; which the King confirming, the whole Assembly rang with Confusion; and Revenge and Indignation appeared in every Face.

I then proposed, as we yet knew not what that secret Commission was which *Nicor* was charged with, having enough against the rest, that *Nicor* might be brought forth; and, upon Refusal to answer, be put to the Torture.

Nicor appearing before the Assembly; I told him, I was commanded by the King, to ask him what Commission he was charged with by *Barbarsa*, and to whom. I told him, the safest way for his Life, his Honour, and his Country, was to make a true Confession at first; or, I had Authority to put him to the Torture: For, as for Slitting and Banishment, as they were too slight to atone for this Offence, he might rest satisfied, his would be of another sort, if he hesitated at delivering the thing in its full Truth.

My Prelude terrifying him; he openly confessed, that his last Commission was to several Towns, as from the King, and with his Gripsack, to order their Submission to *Harlokin*; the King not being in any Condition to relieve them; and that as soon as they had submitted, *Harlokin* would be let into this City, which could not stand against him.

He also declared, that it had been agreed, and the Boundaries settled, how far *Barbarsa*, who was to be declared King and marry *Yaccombourse*, should govern, and how far *Harlokin*. That *Barbarsa* was to be stiled King of the East, and *Harlokin*

King of the West, and that either of them, on the other's dying childless, was to inherit the whole Monarchy.

The King declaring this to be all true, and that by my Procurement he heard it all mentioned but the last Night, between *Barbarsa* and *Yaccombourse*, as they were solacing themselves in Bed; the whole Assembly ordered them to be brought out, carried with Cords about their Necks, and precipitated into Mount *Alkoe*.

I then begged they might be suffered to speak for themselves before Execution; and acquainting them severally with the Evidence; I first asked *Barbarsa*, what he had to say against his Sentence; he declared his Ambition, and the Easiness of his Master's Temper, had instigated him to attempt what had been charged upon him; having as he thought, a fair Opportunity of so doing. I then asked *Yaccombourse* the same Question; she answered me, her Ambition had been her sole Governour from a Child, and I had done my worst in preventing the Progress of that; and whatever else I could do, was not worth her Notice: But, to have reigned, says she, with some Emotion, was worth the Lives of Millions, and overbalanced every thing.

I pleaded hard for *Nicor*, as I perceived him to be only the Favourite's Favourite, and not in the Scrape for his own Views, more than what he might merit from his new Master: And, as he had declared the Truth, and I believed I might make further Use of him, I obtained that he might be only committed to me; and that I might have Liberty of pardoning or slitting, as I saw fit. And, as I expected, he afterwards proved very useful to me and my Designs, and I pardoned him.

Before the Assembly rose, a Party of the Natives of Mount *Alkoe*, were ordered to convey *Yaccombourse* and *Barbarsa* to the Mountain, slit their Graundees, and drop them there. And thus ended the Lives of these two aspiring Persons.

When I came home, I called *Nicor* before me. You know, says I, *Nicor*, you are obliged to me for this Moment of your Life; but I don't remind you of it for any return I want to myself; but, as you are sensible my Endeavours are to serve this State, I offer you Life and Freedom, upon Condition you employ your utmost Diligence to repair your past Conduct, by a free Declaration of every thing in your Power, that may be for the Benefit of the Kingdom; as you know the Springs, by which all these bad Movements have been set at work. And I desire your Opinion, how best to counteract the Schemes formed, and redress the Evils.

Nicor being fully convinced of his Error, and having lost his Patron, was very submissive; and declared, he believed none of the Provinces would have gone over to *Harlokin*, unless they had thought it was the King's Order *Barbarsa* had acted by; which by hearing his Gripsack, they made no doubt of. He advised to send Expresses with the King's Gripsack, to such Places as had lately submitted, and to such as were about it, to put a stop to them. I told him, I had done that; but not by the Gripsack, says he, and unless they see and hear that, they will give no Credit to the Message. He then gave me some particular Hints in other Affairs, of no mean Consequence: And seeing him truly under concern, and, to my thinking, sincere in what he said, I told him, I was an absolute Enemy to Confinement, and if any Person of Repute would engage he should be forthcoming upon all Occasions, that I might have Recourse to him, I would let him have his Liberty.

Poor *Nicor*, as it commonly happens to great Men in Disgrace, finding himself abandoned by all his Friends, after trying every body; dropping some Tears, told me next Morning, he was highly sensible of what a Dye his Offences had been; for that not one amongst all his former Friends would even look upon him in his present Circumstances; wherefore he must submit to Fate.

Nicor having borne a good Character before seduced by *Barbarsa*; and knowing that an obliged Enemy often becomes the sincerest Friend; I pressed him again to try his Friends. He told me, every body was shy of engaging in such an Affair; and that he had rather suffer himself, than meanly to intreat any one into an unwilling Compliance. Come, *Nicor*, says I, will you be your own Security to me? may I take your own Word? He said, he could not expect that; for as the Terror of slitting lay over him, and in my Hands too, he could not answer, but he might deceive me, in case he should conceive I had a Design against him; which I myself too might have from a mistaken Motive.

Why then, *Nicor*, says I, you are free; now use your own Discretion. I think, you will never cause my Judgment to be impeached for what I have done; but if you do, I can't condemn myself for it, and hope I shall have no reason to repent it.

Nicor fell at my Feet, embraced them, and was so overcome with my Generosity to him, that I could with Difficulty prevail on him to rise again; saying he was now, more than ever, ashamed to see my Face. I told him, I had not done with him; but would use him henceforth as my Friend; and ordered him to call upon me daily, for I might have several Occasions for him; and truly, next to *Nasgig*, he proved the usefullest Man in the Kingdom.

CHAPTER XIV

Nasgig *returns with the Cannon;* Peter *informs him of the Execution; appoints him a Guard; settles the Order of his March against* Harlokin; *Combat between* Nasgig *and the Rebel-General; the Battle;* Peter *returning with* Harlokin's *Head, is met by a* Sweecoan; *a public Festival; Slavery abolished*

THE tenth Day *Nasgig* arrived, whilst I happened to be in the King's Garden; and hearing the Trumpet coming before, I called out to him, to give *Nasgig* Notice where I was, and to desire him to alight there.

After Ceremonies past, and I had enquired after my Wife and Children, and his Answers had informed me of their Healths; Well, says *Nasgig*, my Friend, am I to live or die?

Explain yourself, says I. Nay, I only mean, says he, have you discovered me to the King? Pardon me, says I, dear *Nasgig*, I must own the Truth, I have. Then, says he, I suppose his Majesty has no more Commands for me. No, says I, it is not so bad as that neither. But pray, says he, what says *Barbarsa* to it? O! nothing at all, says I, quite quiet. Nor *Yaccombourse*; did you discover her Baseness to the King? Yes, says I; and the King behaved like a King upon the Occasion. And where are they now, says he? Only in Mount *Alkoe*, says I. Mount *Alkoe*! replies he; what do you mean by that? how can they be in Mount *Alkoe*? did they go of their own Accords? They fled off, I suppose, with Ropes about their Necks, says I, as your Criminals go to *Crashdoorpt*. Are they slit too, says he? No, says I, but slipt, I'll assure you. Come, my good Friend, I'll let you into the History of it; and then I told all that had happened, and the King's Satisfaction at the Judgment of the Moucheratt. And now, says I, *Nasgig*, you may call yourself the Favourite, I promise you; for his Majesty enjoys himself but to greet you on your Return: But have a care of Power; most grow giddy with it, and the next thing to that, is a Fall. Pray, says he, what is become of *Nicor*? is he under the same Condemnation? No, says I, *Nicor* is now by my Means absolutely free; and no two greater than he and I. I told him then my Proceedings with him: He was glad of it, for he said, *Nicor* he believed was honest at Bottom.

By this time up came the Cannon; and truly, had my Countrymen but the Graundee to convey their Cannon at so easy an Expence from place to place, the whole World would not stand before us. They brought me five Cannon, and three Swivel guns, and a larger Quantity of Ammunition than I had spoken for.

I introduced *Nasgig* to the King upon his Return, as the Person to whose Conduct the safe Arrival of my Cannon was owing. His Majesty embracing him, told him, the Service he had done him was so great in the Affair of *Barbarsa*, and his Management of it so prudent, he should from thenceforth take him into his peculiar Confidence and Esteem.

Nasgig thanked his Majesty for his Acceptance of that Act of his Duty; and desired to know when he pleased the Operations for the Campaign should begin. Ask my Father, says the King; do you conduct the War, and let him conduct you.

Then *Nasgig* desired to know, what Number of Troops would be requisite. I asked him, what Number the Enemy had; he said about thirty thousand. Then, says I, take you six only, besides the Bearers of me and the Artillery; and pick me out fifty of the best Men you have, as a Guard for my Person, and send them to me.

I shewed these Men my Cutlasses and Pistols, and shewed them the Use and Management of them; and says I, as our Enemies fight with Pikes, keep you at a Distance first; and when you would assault, toss by the Pike with your Hand, and closing in have at the Graundee; and this Edge, shewing them the Sharpness of it, will strip it down from Shoulder to Heel, you need strike but once for it; but be sure come near enough. Or, says I, if you find it difficult to turn aside the Pike, give it one smart Stroke with this, it will cut it in two, and then the Point being gone, it will be useless.

These Instructions, says I, if rightly observed, will make us Conquerors.

The next thing was, to settle the Order of my March, which I did in the following manner; and taking Leave of the King, I set out.

First, Ten Companies of one hundred Men, including Officers, with each a Gripsack, in ten double Lines, fifty a-breast.

Secondly, Four hundred Bearers of the Cannon, with two hundred to the right, the like to the left, as Relays.

Thirdly, Two hundred Men with the Ammunition, Stores, Hatchets, and other Implements.

Fourthly, Fifty Body-guards, in two Lines.

Fifthly, Myself borne by eight; with twelve on the right, and as many on the left, for Relays.

Sixthly, Two thousand Men in Columns, on each Side the Cannon, and me; fifty in a Line, double Lines.

Seventhly, One thousand Men in the Rear, fifty in a Line, double Lines.

I consulted with *Nasgig*, how *Harlokin*'s Army lay, that I might avoid the revolted Towns, rather chusing to take them in my Return; for my Design was to encounter *Harlokin* first; and I did not doubt if I conquered him, but the Towns would surrender of course.

When we arrived within a small Flight of his Army, I caused a Halt at a proper place for my Cannon; and having pitched them, which I did by several flat Stones one on another to a proper Elevation; I loaded them, and also my small Arms, consisting of six Muskets, and three Brace of Pistols; and placing my Army, two thousand just behind me, two thousand to my right, and the same Number to my left; I gave a strict Command for none of them to stir forwards without Orders; which *Nasgig* who stood just behind me, was to give. I then sent a Defiance to *Harlokin* by a Gripsack; who sent me word, he fought for a Kingdom, and would accept it; and, as I heard afterwards, he was glad I did; for since the Intelligence I had scattered in his Army, they had in great Numbers deserted him, and he was afraid it would have proved general. I then putting the End of a Match into a Pistol-pan with a little Powder, by flashing, lighted it; and this I put under my Chair, for I sat in that, with my Muskets three on each side, a Pistol in my Right-hand, and five more in my Girdle. In this manner I waited *Harlokin*'s coming, and in about an Hour we saw the Van of his Army, consisting of about five thousand Men, who flew in five Layers, one over another. I had not loaded my Cannon with Ball, but small sized Stones, about sixty in each; and seeing the Length of their Line, I spread my Cannons Mouths somewhat wider than their Breaches, and then taking my Observation by a bright Star, for there was a clear Dawn all round the Horizon, I observed, as I retired to my Chair, how that Star answered to the Elevation of my Cannon; and when the foremost Ranks, who, not seeing my Men stir, were approaching almost over me to fall on them, and had come to my Pitch; I fired two Pieces of my Ordnance at once, and so mauled them, that there dropped about ninety upon the first Discharge, together with their Commander; the rest, being in flight, and so close together, not being able to turn fast enough to fly, being stopped by those behind them, not only hindred those behind from turning about, but clogged up their own Passage: Seeing them in such a prodigious Cluster, I so successfully fired two more Pieces, that I brought down double the Number of the first Shot; and then giving the Word to fall on, my Cutlass-Guard, and the Pikemen, did prodigious Execution. But fearing the main Body should advance before we had got in Order again, I commanded them to fall back to their former Stations, and to let the Remainder of the Enemy go off.

This did me more good in the Event, than if I had killed twice as many; for they not only never returned themselves, but flying some to the right, some to the left, and passing by the two Wings of their own Army, consisting of six thousand Men each; they severally reported, that they were all that was left of the whole Van of the Army; and that the Prediction would certainly be fulfilled, for that their Companions had died by Fire and Smoak.—This Report struck such Terror into each Wing, that every one shifted for himself, and never appeared more.

The main Battle, consisting of about ten thousand Men, knowing nothing of what had happened to the Wings, for *Harlokin* had ordered the Wings to take a great Compass round to inclose us; hearing we were but an handful, advanced boldly; and as I had ordered my Men not to mount too high; the Enemy sunk to their Pitch. When they came nearer, I asked *Nasgig* who led them, and if it was *Harlokin*. He told me no, his General, but that he was behind; and, *Nasgig* begging me to let him try his Skill with the General, I consented; they not being yet come to the Pitch of my Cannon. *Nasgig* immediately took the Graundee, and advancing singly with one of my Cutlasses in his Hand, challenged the General to single Combat. He like a Man of Honour accepting it, ordered a Halt, and to it they went, each emulous of Glory,

and of taking all the Advantage he could, so that they did not suddenly strike or push; but sometimes one, then the other was uppermost, and whirling expeditiously round, met almost Breast to Breast; when the General, who had not a Pike, but a Pikestaff headed with a large Stone, gave *Nasgig* such a Stroke on his Head, that he reeled and sunk considerably; and I began to be in Pain for him, the General lowering after him. But *Nasgig* springing forward beneath him, and rising light as Air behind the General, had gained his Height again before the General could turn about to descern him; and then plunging forward, and receiving a Stroke a-cross his Left-arm; at the same time he gave the General such a Blow near the out-side of the Shoulder, as slit the Graundee almost down to his Hip, and took away part of the Flesh of the Left-arm; upon which the General fell fluttering down in vast Pain, very near me; but not before *Nasgig*, in his Fall, descending, had taken another severe cut at him.

Immediately upon this Defeat, *Nasgig* again took his place behind me. Our Army shouting to the Skies; but no sooner had the General dropt, but on came *Harlokin*, with Majesty and Terror mixt in his Looks; and seeming to disdain the Air he rode on, waved his Men to the Attack with his Hand. When he came near enough to hear me, I called him vile Traitor, to oppose the Army of his lawful Sovereign; telling him, if he would submit, he should be received to Mercy. Base creep-ing Insect, says *Harlokin*, if thou hast ought to say to me worth hearing, meet me in the Air? This Hand shall shew thee soon, who'll most want Mercy: And tho' I scorn to stoop to thee myself, this Messenger shall satisfy the World thou'rt an Impostor, and send thee lifeless back to the fond King that sent thee hither. With that, he hurled a Javelin pointed with Flint, sharp as a Needle at me; but I avoiding it: This then, says I, if Words won't do, shall justify the Truth of our Pre-diction: And then levelling a Musket at him, I shot him thro' the very Heart, that he fell dead within twenty Paces of me; but perceiving another to take his Room, notwithstanding the Confusion my Musket had made amongst them, I ran to my

X

Match, and giving fire to two more Pieces of Ordnance at the same time, they fell so thick about me, that I had enough to do to escape being crushed to Death by them, and the living Remainder separating, fled quite away, and put an End to the War. I waited in the Field three Days, to see if they would make Head again; but they were so far from it, that before I could return, as I found afterwards, most of the revolting Provinces had sent their Deputies, who themselves carried the first News of the Defeat, to beg to be received into Mercy; all of whom were detained there, till my Return with *Harlokin*'s Head.

At my Return to *Brandleguarp*, I was met by the King, the *Colambs*, and almost the whole Body of the People; every Man, Woman, and Child, with two Sweecoe Lights in their Hands; which unusual Sight in the Air, gave me great Alarm, till I inquired of *Nasgig* what it meant; who told me, it must certainly be a Sweecoan, or he knew not what it was. I asking again, what he meant by that; he told me, it was a particular Method of Rejoicing he had heard of, but never seen; wherein, if the King goes in Triumph, all the People of *Brandleguarp*, from fifteen to sixty, are obliged to attend him with Sweecoes. He said, it was reported amongst them, that in *Begsurbeck*'s time there were two of them, but there had been none since.

When we met them, I perceived they had opened into two Lines or Ranks of a prodigious Length; at the further End of which, was the King with innumerable Lights about him; the whole looked like a prodigious Avenue or Visto of Lights, bounded at the further End where the King was, with a Pyramid of Light. This had the most solemn and magnificent Effect on the Eye, that any thing of Light could possibly have; but as we passed thro' the Ranks, each of the Spectators having two Lights, one was given to each Soldier of the whole Army. And then to look backward, as well as forward, the Beauty of the Scene was inexpressible. We marched all the way amidst the Shouts of People, and the Sound of the Gripsacks, going very slowly between the Ranks; and at length arriving at the

Pyramid, where the King was; I heard abundance of sweet Voices, chaunting my Actions in triumphal Songs: But I could take little Notice of these, or of my Son with his Flagellet amongst them, for the extravagant Appearance of the Pyramid, which seem'd to reach the very Sky. For first, there was a long Line of a full half Mile, which hovered at even Height with the two side Ranks; in the Center of that, and over it, was the King single; over him, another Line, shorter than the first, and again over that, shorter and shorter Lines; till at a prodigious Height, it ended in one single Light. These all hovering, kept their Stations; while the King darted a little Space forward to meet me, and congratulate my Success; then turning, and preceding me, the whole Pyramid turned, and marched before us; singing all the way to the City; the Pyramid changing several times into divers Forms, as into Squares, Half-moons, with the Horns sometimes erect, and again reversed, and various other Figures; and yet amongst this infinite Number of Globes, there was not the least glaring or offensive Light; but only what was agreeable to the People themselves. As the Rear of the Army entred the Lines, they closed upon it, and followed us into *Brandleguarp*. While we passed the City to the Palace, the whole Body of People kept hovering, till the King and myself were alighted; and then every one alighted where he best could. All the Streets and Avenues to the Palace, were blocked up with People, crowding to receive the King's Beneficence; for he had proclaimed a Feast, and open House-keeping to the People for six Days. The King, the *Colambs*, *Ragams*, and great Officers of State, with myself, had a magnificent Entertainment prepared us in *Begsurbeck*'s great Room; and his Majesty after Supper, being very impatient to know how the Battle went, I told him, the only valourous Exploit was performed by my Friend *Nasgig*, who opened the way to Victory, by the Slaughter of *Harlokin*'s General. *Nasgig* then rose, desiring only that so much might be attributed to him, as Fortune had accidentally thrown into his Scale; for it might have been equally his Fate, as the General's, to have fallen; but except that Skirmish, says he, and some flying Cuts at the Van, we have had no Engagement at all; nor have we lost a single Man; *Peter* only sitting in his Chair, and commanding Victory: He spake aloud but thrice, and whispered once to them; but so powerfully, that having at the two first Words laid above three hundred of the Enemy at their Lengths, and brought *Harlokin* to his Feet, with a Whisper; at the third Word, he concluded the War. The whole time from the first Sight of the Enemy, to their total Defeat, took not up more space than one might fairly spend in traversing his Majesty's Garden. In short, Sir, says *Nasgig*, your Majesty needs no other Defence against public or private Enemies as I can see, than *Peter*; and my Profession, whilst he is with us, can be of little Use to the State.

After these Compliments from *Nasgig*, and separate ones from the King and the rest; I told them, it was the highest Felicity to me, to be made an Instrument by the great Collwarr, in freeing so mighty a Kingdom, and considerable a People, from the Misery of a tyrannical Power. You live, says I, so happily, under the mild Government of *Georigetti*, that it is shocking but to think into what a distressed State you must have fallen, under the Power of an Usurper; who claiming all as his own by way of Conquest, would have reduced you to a miserable Servitude. But, says I, there is, and I am sorry to see it, still amongst you, an Evil that you great ones feel not; and yet it cries for Redress. Are we not all, from the King to the meanest Wretch amongst us, formed with the same Members? do we not all breathe the same Air? inhabit the same Earth? are we not all subject to the same Disorders? and do we not all feel Pain and Oppression alike? have we not all the same Senses, the same Faculties? and in short, are we not all equally Creatures of, and Servants to the same Master, the great Collwarr? Would not the King have been a Slave, but for the Accident of being begotten by one who was a King? and would not the poorest Creature amongst us have been the King, had he been so begotten? Did you great Men, by any superior Merit before your Births, procure a Title to the high Stations in which you are plac'd? No, you did not. Therefore give me leave to tell you, what I would have done: As every Man has equal Right to the Protection of Collwarr, why when you have no Enemy to distress you, will you distress one another? Consider, you great ones, and act upon this disinterested Principle; do to another, what you, in his place, would have him do to you; dismiss your Slaves, let all Men be what Collwarr made them, free. But if this unequal Distinction amongst you, of Man and Man, is still retained; though you are at present free from the late Disaster, it shall be succeeded with more and heavier. And now, that you may know I would not have every Man a Lord, or every one a Beggar; remember, I would only have every serving Man at Liberty to chuse his own Master, and every Master his own Man: For he that has Property, and Benefits to bestow, will never want Dependants, for the sake of those Benefits, to serve him; as he that has them not, must serve for the sake of obtaining them. But then let it be done with Free-will; he that then serves you will have an Interest in it, and do it for his own sake with a willing Mind; and you, who are served, will be tenderer and kinder to a good Servant, as knowing by a contrary Usage you shall lose him. I desire this may now be declared to be so, or your Reasons, if any there are, against it.

One of the Ragams said, he thought I spoke what was very just, and would be highly acceptable to Collwarr.

Then two of the *Colambs* rose to speak together, and after a short Compliment who should begin; they both declared they only rose to testify their Consents.

The King referring it to me, and the *Colambs* consenting; I ordered Freedom to be proclaimed thro' the City; so that every one appeared at their usual Duties, to serve their own Masters for a Month; and then to be at Liberty to come to fresh Agreement with them, or who else they pleased.

This, Sir, says I, to the King, will now be a Day of Joy indeed, to those poor Hearts who would have been in no Fear of losing before, let who would have reigned; for can any Man believe a Slave cares who is uppermost; he is but a Slave still. But now, says I, those who were so before may by

Industry gain Property; and then their own Interest engages them to defend the State.

There is but one thing more I will trouble you with now; and that, says I, to the Ragams, is, that we all meet at the Mouch To-morrow, to render Collwarr Thanks for the late, and implore future, Favour. And this passed without any Contradiction.

When we met, the poor Ragams were at a great loss for want of their Image, not knowing what to do or say. For their Practice had been, to prostrate themselves on the Ground, making several odd Gestures; but whether they prayed or only seemed so to do, no one knew.

While the People were gathering, I called to a Ragam, seeing him out of Character; suppose, said I, for I see you want your Image, you and your Brethren had received a Favour of the King, and you was deputed by them to thank him, you would scarce be at a loss to express your Gratitude to him, and tell him how highly you all esteemed his Benefits, hoping you should retain a just Sense of them, and behave yourselves as dutiful Subjects for the future; and then desire him to keep you still in his Protection. And this, says I, as you believe in such a Being as Collwarr, who understands what you say, you may with equal Courage do to him; keeping but your Mind intent upon him, as if you saw him present. Indeed, says he, I believe you are right, we may so; but it is a new thing, and you must excuse us, if we do it not so well at first.

I found I had a very apt Scholar, for after he had begun, he made a most extraordinary Prayer in regular Order; the People standing very attentive. It was not long, but he justly observed the Points I hinted to him.

When he had done, another and another went on, till we had heard ten of them, and in every one something new, and very *a propos*; and several of them afterwards confessed, they never had the like Satisfaction in their Lives; for they had new Hearts, and New Thoughts, they said.

We spent the six Day Feast in every Gayety imaginable, and

especially in Dancing, of which they were very fond in their way; but it was not so agreeable to me, as my own Country way, there being too much antick in it. New Deputies daily arrived from the revolted Towns; and several little Republicks, not claimed by *Georigetti* before, begged to be taken under his Protection: so that in one Week, the King saw himself not only released from the Dread of being driven from his Throne, but courted by some, submitted to by others, and almost at the Summit of Glory a Sovereign can attain to.

CHAPTER XV

A Visitation of the revolted Provinces proposed by
Peter; *his new Name of the Country received;*
Religion settled in the West; Slavery abolished there;
Lasmeel *returns with* Peter; Peter *teaches him*
Letters; the King surprized at written Correspondence;
Peter *describes the Make of a Beast to the King*

THE Festival being over, the *Colambs* begged Leave to depart; but the King, who now did nothing without me, consulted with me, if it was yet proper. I told him, as things had so long been in Confusion in the West, that tho' the Provinces had made their Submission, yet the Necessity of their Circumstances, and the general Terror, might have caused them only to dissemble, till their Affairs were composed again; and that as it was more than probable, some Relations of the deceased *Harlokin*, or other popular Person, might engage them again in another Revolt; I thought it would not be improper, to advise with his *Colambs* about the Establishment of the present Tranquillity, and not by too great a Security give way to future Commotions; and as all the *Colambs* were then present, it might be proper to summons them once more.

When they were met, the King declared the more particular Satisfaction he took in that Meeting, than he had heretofore done, when they had been put to it for means to secure their Lives and Properties; for now, says he, our Deliberations must turn upon securing our new Acquisitions, and on settling those Provinces, which till now have never fallen under my Power. But, says he, I shall refer it to *Peter* to propose to you what at present seems most necessary for you to consider of; and that adjusted, shall dismiss you.

I told them, that as the too sudden healing of Wounds in the Body natural, before the Bottom was clean and uncorrupt, made them liable to break out again with greater Malignity; so Wounds in the Body political, if skinned over only, without probing and cleansing the Source and Spring from whence they arose, would rankle and fret within, till a proper Opportunity; and then burst forth again with redoubled Violence. I would therefore propose a Visitation of the several Provinces; an Inquiry into their Conduct; an Examination into the Lives and Principles of the *Colambs*, the inferior Officers, and Magistrates; and either to retain the old, or appoint new, as there should be Occasion. This Visitation I would have performed by his Majesty, and so many of you the honourable *Colambs*, says I, as he shall see fit should attend him in Royal State; that his new Subjects may see his Majesty, and hear his most gracious Words; and being sensible of his good Disposition towards them, may be won by his Equity and Justice, to a zealous Submission to his Government; which nothing but the Perception of their own Senses can establish in the Heart. This, I don't doubt, will answer the End I propose, and consolidate the Peace and Happiness of *Norm*, *Normus*, I must say *Doorpt Swangeanti*.

Hearing me hesitate at the Word *Normbdsgrsutt*, and call it *Doorpt Swangeanti*, the whole Assembly rang with *Doorpt Swangeanti*; and at last came to a Resolution, that the West being now united again to the East, the whole Dominions should be called *Sass Doorpt Swangeanti*, or the great Flight-Land.

They approved the Visitation, and all offered to go with the King; but insisted I should be of the Party: Which agreeing to do, I chose me out two of the most knowing Ragams, to teach the new Religion amongst them; for in every Project I had my View to advance Religion.

Some were for having the Deputies released, and dispatched with Notice of the King's Intentions; but I objecting, that they might disrelish their Confinement, and possibly raise Reports prejudicial to our Proceedings, it was thought better to take them with us, and go ourselves as soon as possible.

We set out with a prodigious Retinue, first to the right, in order to sweep round the whole Country, and take all the Towns in our way, and occasionally enter the middle parts as the Towns lay commodious.

We were met by the Magistrates and chief Officers of each District; at some distance from each City, with Strings about their Necks, and the Crashoe Instrument borne before them in much Humility. His Majesty said but little to them on the way; but ordered them to precede him to the City, and conduct him to the *Colamb*'s House; when he was commanded to surrender his Imployment to his Majesty; as did all the other Officers who held Posts under him. Then an Examination was taken of their Lives, Characters, and Behaviour in their Stations; and finding most of them had behaved well to the Government they had lived under, (for their Plea was, they had found things under an Usurpation, and being so, that Government was natural to them, having singly no Power to alter it;) upon their perfect Submission to the King, and solemn Engagement to advance and maintain his Right, they received their Commissions anew from his Majesty's own Mouth. But where any one had been cruel or oppressive to the Subjects, or committed any notorious Crime or Breach of Trust, for the meanest Persons had Liberty to complain, he was rejected, and for the most part sent to *Crashdoorpt*, to prevent the ill Effects of his Disgrace.

We having displaced but five *Colambs*, and a few inferior Officers; the Moderation and Justice of our Proceedings gave the utmost Satisfaction both to the Magistrates and People.

Having observed at *Brandleguarp* abundance of the small

Images my Wife had spoken of, and thinking this a proper Opportunity to shew my Resentment against them; I ordered several of the Ragams of the West before me, and asked what small Images they had amongst them. One, who spoke for the rest, told me, very few he believed; for he had scarce had any brought to him to be blessed. Where, says I, is your great Image? he told me at *Youk*. And have not the People here many small ones? Very few, says he, for they have not been forced upon us long. How forced upon you, says I, don't the People worship them? A small number now do, says he. Pray speak out, says I, when might you not worship them? Never, that I know of, says he, in our State, till about ten Years ago, when *Harlokin* obliged us to it. What, did you not worship them before, says I? No, says he, never since it has been a separate Kingdom; for we would follow the old Ragam's Advice of worshipping Collwarr; which they not admitting of, the State was divided between us who would, and they who would not come into the Ragam's Doctrine; and tho' *Harlokin* was a zealous Image-Worshipper, yet all he could do would not bring the People heartily into it; for Collwarr never wanted a great Majority. This pleased me prodigiously, being what was never hinted to me before; and I resolved not to let my Scheme be a loser by it.

As we were to visit *Youk* in about eight Days, I summoned the Ragams and People to meet at the Mouch: There recounting the great things done by Collwarr in all Nations; this I could make appear, says I, by many Examples; but as you have one even at your own Towns, I need go no farther.

I must begin in ancient times, when I presume you all worshipped an Idol; have you any Tradition before this? They said, no. This Image, says I, was worshipped in *Begsurbeck*'s Days, when an old Ragam, whose Mind Collwarr had enlightned with the Truth, would have withdrawn your Reverence from the Image, to the original Collwarr himself; you would not consent; he threatens you, but promises Success to *Begsurbeck*, who did consent; and he had it to an old Age. Then those who would also consent, were so far encouraged, as to be able to form an independant Kingdom. Could no body yet see the Cause? Was it not apparent Collwarr was angry with the East, that would not follow the old Ragam, and cherished the West who would? But to be short, let us apply the present Instance, and sure it will convince us, who is right who wrong.

So long as the West followed Collwarr, they flourished and the East declined; but no sooner had the West degenerated under the Command of *Harlokin*, and the East by my means had embraced Collwarr, but the Tables were turned; the East is found weighty, and the West kicks the Beam. These things whoso sees not, is blind indeed. Therefore let Publication be made, for the Destruction of all small Images; and let the Harbourers of them, contrary to this Order, be slit: And for myself, I'll destroy this Mother-Monster; take you, holy Ragams, care to destroy the Brood: And having said this, I hacked the new Idol to pieces.

I ordered Proclamation for abolishing Slavery, under the Restrictions used at *Brandleguarp*; and thus having composed the West, and given a general Satisfaction, we returned; almost the whole West accompanying us, till the East received us; and never was so happy a Union, or more present to testify it, since the Creation, I believe.

I ordered several of the principal Mens Sons to Court, in order for Imployments, and to furnish out future *Colambs*; and this I did, as knowing each Country will rather approve of a Member of their own Body for their Head, than a Stranger; and in my Opinion, it is the most natural Union. And then breeding them under the Eye of the King eight or ten Years or more, they are as it were naturalized to him too, and in better Capacity to serve both King and Country.

As my Head was constantly at work for the Good of this People, I turned the most trifling Incidents into some use or other; and made the narrowest Prospects extend to the vastest Distances. I shall here Instance in one only. There was at *Youk* a private Man's Son, who by mere Accident I happened to ask some slight Question; and he giving me, with a profound

Respect and graceful Assurance, a most pertinent Answer; that, and the manner of its Delivery, gave me a Pleasure, which upon further Discourse with him, was, contrary to Custom, very much increased; for I found in him an extensive Genius, and a Desire for my Conversation. I desired his Father to put him under my Care, which the old Man, as I was then in so great Repute, readily agreed to; and his Son desiring nothing more, I took him with me to *Brandleguarp*. I soon procured him a pretty Post of but small Duty, for I had purposed other Imployment for him, but of sufficient Significancy to procure him Respect. I took great Delight in talking with him on different Subjects, and observed by his Questions upon them, which often puzzled me, or his Answers to them, that he had a most pregnant Fancy and surprizing Solidity, joined to a continual and unweary'd Application. I frequently mentioning Books, Writing, and Letters to him, and telling him what great things might be attained that way; his inquisitive Temper, and the Schemes he had formed thereon, put me upon thinking of several things I should never have hit upon without him. I considered all the ways I could contrive, to teach him Letters; and letting him into my Design, he asked me how I did to make a Letter. I described a Pen to him, and told him I put a black Liquor into it, and as I drew that along upon a flat white thing we made use of, called Paper, it would make Marks which way ever I drew it, into what shape I pleased. Why then, says he, any thing that will make a Mark upon another thing as I please, will do. True, says I, but what shall we get that will make a black Mark? We were entring further into this Debate; but the King sending for me, I left him unsatisfied. I stayed late with the King that Night, so did not see *Lasmeel*, for that was his Name, till next Night, wondring what was become of him. I asked him then, where he had been all the Day? He told me, he had been looking for a Pen and Paper. I laughed, and asked him if he had found them? Yes, says he, or something that will do as well: So he opened one Side of his Graundee, and shewed me a large flat Leaf, smooth and pulpy, very long and wide, and about a Quarter of an Inch thick, almost like an *Indian* Fig-leaf. And what am I to do with this, says I? To mark it, says he, and see where you mark. With what, says I? With this, says he, putting his Hand again into his Graundee, and taking out three or four strong, sharp Prickles. I looked at them both, and clapping him on the Head, *Lasmeel*, says I, if you and I were in *England*, you should be made a Privy-Counsellor. What, won't it do then, says he? I told him we'd try. I thought, says he, it would have done very well; for I marked one all about, and tho' I could not see much at first, by that time I had made an End, that I did first, was quite of a different Colour from the Leaf, and I could see it as plain as could be. I told him, as he was of an Age to comprehend what I meant, I would take another Method with him than with a Child; so I reasoned from Sentences, backwards to Words, and from them to Syllables, and so to Letters. I then made one, the Vowel A, told him its Sound, and added a Consonant to it, and told him, that part of the Sound of each distinct Letter put together, as the two Letters themselves were, made another Sound, which I called a Syllable; and that joining two or more of them together made a Word, by putting the same Letters together as made the Sounds of those Syllables which made that Word. Then setting him a Copy of Letters, which with very little Difficulty were to be drawn upon the Leaf, and telling him their Sounds, I left him to himself; and when he had done, tho' I named them but twice over, his Memory was so strong as to retain the Sounds, as he called them, of every one, but F, L, and Q.

In two Months time, I made him Master of any thing I wrote to him; and, as he delighted in it, he wrote a great deal himself; so that we kept an epistolary Correspondence, and he would set down all the common Occurrences of the Day, as what he heard and saw, with his Remarks on divers things.

One Day, as the King and I were walking in the Gardens, and talking of the Customs of my Country, and about our Wars; telling him, how our Soldiers fought on Horse-back; the King could not conceive what I meant by an Horse. I told him, my Wife had said there were neither Beasts or Fishes in her Country; which I was very much surprized at, considering how we abounded with both; and therefore, says I, to tell your Majesty, that an Horse is a Creature with four Legs; you must naturally believe it to be somewhat like a Man with four Legs. Why truly, says he, I believe it is; but has it the Graundee? I could not forbear smiling, even at Majesty; and wanted to find some Similitude to compare it to, to carry the King's Mind that way; for else he would sooner, I thought, conceive it like a Tree or a Mountain, than what it really was; and as I was musing, it came into my Head, I had given *Lasmeel* a small Print of an Horse, which I found in one of the Captain's Pockets at *Grandevolet*, and believing it to be the Stamp of a Tobacco-paper, had kept it to please the Children with; so I told the King, I believed I could shew him the Figure of an Horse. He told me, it would much oblige him.

Seeing several of the Guards waiting at the Garden-Arch; I looked, and at last found one of *Lasmeel's* Leaves in the Garden; and cutting one of them up with my Knife, I took the Point of that, and wrote to *Lasmeel*, to send me by the Bearer the Picture of an Horse I gave him, that I might shew it the King. And calling one of the Guards, carry that to *Lasmeel*, says I, he is, I believe, in my Appartment, and bring me an Answer directly. Then falling into Discourse again with the King; and presently turning at the End of the Walk, I saw the same Guard again. Says I, you can't have brought me an Answer already. You have not told me, says he, what to bring you an Answer to. Nor shall I, says I; do as you are bid; for I perceived then what the Fellow stuck at. He walked off with the Leaf, but very discontentedly. The King said, he wondred how I could act such a Contradiction. This, Father, says he, is not what I expected from you; to order a Man to bring an Answer, without giving him a Message. I desired his Patience only till the Man came back. Presently, says the King, here he comes. Well, says he, what Answer? Sir, says the Fellow, I have only had the Walk for my Pains; for he sent it back again, and a little white thing with it. Ha, ha, says the

King, I thought so; come Father, own you have once been in the wrong; for I am sure you intended to give him a Message, but having forgot it, would not submit to be told of your Mistake by a Guard. I looked very grave, reading what *Lasmeel* had wrote; which was to tell me he had obeyed my Orders, by sending the Horse; for he was just then drawing it out upon a Leaf.

Come, come, says the King, give the Man his Message, Father, and let him go again. Sir, says I, there is no need of that; he has punctually obeyed me, and *Lasmeel* was then at the Table in my oval Chamber with a Leaf, and this Picture, in my Hand, before him.

The King was ready to sink when I said so, and shewed the Print. Truly Father, says he, I have been to blame to question you; for tho' these things are above my Comprehension, I am not to think any thing beyond your Skill. I made no Reply to it, but shewing the King the Picture, the Guard sneaked off, and glad he was, I believe, he could do so.

I went then upon the Explanation of my Horse, and answering fifty Questions about him; at last, he asked what his Inside was; exactly the same as your Majesty's, said I. And can he eat and breathe too, says he? just as you can, says I. Well, says he, I should never have believed there had been such a Creature; what would I give for one of them. I set forth the divers other Uses we put them to, besides the Wars; and by the Picture, with some supposed Alterations, I described a Cow, a Sheep, and numberless other Quadrupedes; my Account of which, gave him great Pleasure.

CHAPTER XVI

*Peter sends for his Family; a rising of former Slaves
on that Account; takes a View of the City; Description
of it, and of the Country; hot and cold Springs*

HAVING now some leisure-time on my Hands to consider
over my own Affairs; I had Thoughts of transporting my
Family, with all my Effects, to *Sass Doorpt Swangeanti*; but
yet, had no mind to relinquish all Thought of my Ship and
Cargoe; for the greatest part of this, was still remaining; I
having had but the Pickings thro' the Gulph. I had once a mind
to have gone myself, but considering the immense Distance over
Sea, though I had once come safe, I thought I ought not to tempt
Providence, where my Presence was not absolutely necessary.

Nasgig, to whose Care and Conduct any Enterprize might
be trusted, offered his Service to go, and execute any Commands I should give him. His only Difficulty, he said, was,
that it would be impossible for him to remember the different
Names of many things, which he had no Idea of to convey the
Knowledge of them to his Mind when he saw them; but
barring that, he doubted not to give me Satisfaction. I told
him, I would send an Assistant with him, who could remember
whatever I once told him; and that I might not burthen his
Memory with Names only, *Lasmeel* should carry his Memory
with him; and that he [*Nasgig*], should only have the execu-
tive part.

Lasmeel, who had sat waiting an Opportunity to put in for
a Share in the Adventure; having a longing Desire to see the
Ship, told *Nasgig*, he had a peculiar Art of Memory, so as to
remember whatever he would as long as he pleased; and that
if he carried that with him, they need fear no Mistakes.

The King having granted me as many of his Guards as I
pleased, for the Carriage of my things, we appointed them to be
ready on the fourth Day, when *Nasgig* and *Lasmeel* set out
with them.

I ordered *Lasmeel* however to be with me the next Morning, that we might set down proper Instructions; which I told him would be very long; and that he must bring a good Number of Leaves with him.

When *Lasmeel* entred my Chamber next Morning, he informed me, that the whole City was in an Uproar, especially those who had been freed by me. What? says I, have they so soon forgot their Subjection, to misapply their Liberty already? But step and bring me word what's the matter, and order some of the Ringleaders hither to me.

Lasmeel upon Inquiry found, that it had been given out I was going to leave the Country, and they all said wherever I went, they were determined to go and settle with me; for if I left them, they should be reduced to Slavery again. However, he brought some of them to me, and upon my telling them I thanked them for their Affection to me, but blamed them for shewing it in so tumultuous a manner; and that I was so far from intending to leave them, that I was sending for my Family and Effects, in order to settle amongst them; they rejoiced very much, and told me they would carry the good News to their Companions, and disperse immediately: But I was now in more Perplexity than before, for they having signified my Designs to the rest, they rushed into the Gallery in such Numbers, that they forced up to my very Chamber. I told them, this was an unprecedented manner of using a Person they pretended a Kindness for; and told them, if they made use of such Risings to express their Gratitude to me, it would be the direct means to oblige me to leave them: For, says I, do you think I can be safe in a Kingdom, where greater Deference is paid to me, than to the Crown? They begged my Pardon they said, and would obey me in any thing; but the present Trouble was, only to offer their Services to fetch my Family and Goods, or to do any thing else I should want them for; and if I would favour them in that, they would retire directly. I told them, when I had considered of it, they should hear from me; and this again quieted them.

This Disturbance not only took up much of my time, which

Y

I could have better imployed; but put me to a Nonplus, how
to come off with them; till I sent *Maleck* to tell them, tho'
I set a great Value upon their Esteem, yet, after what had
passed, it would be the most unadvisable thing in Nature for
me to accept their Kindness; for having before requested
a Body of Men of the King, as he had graciously granted
them, it would be preferring them to the King, should I now
relinquish his Grant, and make use of their Offer; and after
this I heard no more of it.

I had scarce met with a more difficult Task, than to fix exact
Rules for the Conduct of my present Undertaking; there being
so many things to be expressed, wherein the least Perplexity
arising, might have caused both Delay and Damage. For I
was not only forced to set down the things I would have
brought, but the Manner and Method of packing and securing
them; but, as *Lasmeel* could read my Writing, to *Pedro* at
home, and *Youwarkee* on board, it would be a means, tho' far
from an expeditious one, of bringing Matters into some
Order: And after I had done, as I thought, I could have
enumerated many more things, and was obliged to add an
et cetera to the End of my Catalogue; and while they were
ready for flight, I added divers other Particulars and Circumstances. Nay, when they were even upon the Graundee, I
recollected the most material thing of all; for my greatest concern was, having broke up so many of my Chests, to find
Package for the things; I say, even so late as that, I bethought
me of the several great Water-casks I had on board, that would
hold an infinite number of small things, and would be slung
easily; so I stopped them, and set down that; and they were
no sooner out of Sight and Hearing, but remembering twenty
more, I was then forced to trust them to my *et cetera*.

I had sent my own flying Chair to bring the Boys, who had
not the Graundee; with Orders for *Pedro* to sit tied in the
Chair, with *Dicky* tied in his Arms; *Jemmy* to sit tied to the
Board before the Chair, and *David* behind; so I hoped they
would come safe enough; and then my Wife and *Sary* were
able to help themselves.

Having dispatched my Caravan, and being all alone, I called *Quilly* the next Morning, and telling him, I had Thoughts of viewing the Country, I bad him prepare to go with me.

I had now been here above six Months, and yet upon coming to walk gravely about the City; I found myself as much a Stranger to the Knowledge of the place, as if that had been the first Day of my Arrival; tho' I had been over it several times in my Chair.

This City is not only one of, but actually the most curious Piece of Work in the World, and consists of one immense entire Stone of a considerable Height, and it may be seven Miles in Length, and near as broad as it is long. The Streets and habitable part of it, are scooped as it were out of the solid Stone, to the Level with the rest of the Country, very flat and smooth at Bottom, the Rock rising perpendicular from the Streets on each Side. The Figure of the City is a direct Square; each Side about six Miles long, with a large open Circle in the Center of the Square, about a Mile in Diameter; and from each of the Sides of the outer Streets to the opposite Side, runs another Street, cutting the Center of the Circle as in the Figure.

Along the whole Face of the Rock, bounding the Streets and the Circle; there are Arch-ways: Those in the Circle, and the four cross Streets, for the Gentry and better People;

and those in the outer Streets, for the meaner; and it is as easy to know as by a Sign, where a great Man lives, by the Grandeur of his Entrance, and lavish Distribution of the Pillars, Carving, and Statues about his Portico, within and without: For as they have no Doors, you may look in, and are not forbid Entrance; and tho' it should look odd to an *English* Reader, that an *English* Man should speak with Pleasure of a Land of Darkness, as that almost was; yet I am satisfied, whoever shall see it after me will be persuaded, that for the real Grandeur of their Entrances, and for the Magnificence of the Apartments and Sculpture, no Part of the Universe can produce the like; and tho' within Doors there is no other manner of Light than the Sweecoes, yet that, when you are once used to it, is so agreeable and free from all noisome Savour, that I never once regreted the loss of the Sun within Doors, tho' I often have when abroad; but then that would be injurious to the proper Inhabitants; tho' they can no more see in total Darkness than myself.

I have been over some of these private Houses, which contain, it may be, thirty Rooms great and small, some higher, some lower, full of Sweecoe-lights, and extremely well proportioned and beautiful.

The King's Palace, with all the Apartments, stands in, and takes up, one full fourth-part of the Square of the whole City, and is indeed of itself a perfect City.

There is no great Man's House without one or more long Galleries, for the Ladies to divert themselves at divers Sports in; particularly at one like our Bowls on a Bowling-green, and at somewhat like nine Holes; at which they play for Wines, and drink a great deal, for none of them will intoxicate.

In my Walk and Survey of the City, one of the *Colambs* being making a House to reside in when at *Brandleguarp*, I had the Curiosity to go in. I saw there abundance of Botts stand filled with a greenish Liquor, and asked *Quilly* what that was; he said, it was what the Stone-Men used in making the Houses. I proceeded further in, where I saw several Men at work, and stayed a good while to observe them. Each Man

had a Bott of this Liquor in his Left-hand, and stood before
a large Bank of Stone, it may be thirty Feet high, reaching
forward up to the Cieling of the place, and ascending by Steps
from Bottom to Top; the Workmen standing some on one
Step, some on another, pouring on this Liquor with their Left-
hands, and with their Right holding a wooden Tool, shaped
like a little Spadle;[1] I observed wherever they poured on this
Water, a Smoak arose for a little space of time; and then the
place turned white, which was scraped off like fine Powder
with the Spadle-hand; and then pouring new Liquor, he
scraped again, working all the while by Sweecoe-lights.

Having my Watch in my Pocket, I measured a Spot of
a Yard long, about a Foot high, and a Foot and half on the
upper Flat, to see how long he would be fetching down that
Piece; and he got it away in little above two Hours. By this
means I came to know how they made their Houses; for I had
neither seen any Tool I thought proper, or even Iron itself,
except my own, since I came into the Country. Upon Inquiry,
I found that the Scrapings of this Stone, and a Portion of common Earth, mixed with a Water they have, will cement like
Plaster; and they use it in the small ornamental Work of their
Buildings. I then went further into this House, where I saw
one making the Figure of a Glumm by the same Method; but
it standing upright in the solid Rock against the Wall, the
Workman held his Liquor in an open Shell, and dipping such
Stuff as my Bed was made of, bound up in short Rolls, some
larger, some less, into the Liquor, he touched the Figure, and
then scraped till he had reduced it into a perfect Piece.

'Tis impossible to imagine how this Work rids away;[2] for
in ten Months time after I saw it, this House was compleated,
having a great Number of fine, large, and lofty Rooms in it;
exquisitely carved to all Appearance.

My Wonder ceased as to the Palace, when I saw how easily
this Work was done; but sure there is no other such Room in
the World as *Begsurbeck*'s, that I described above.

The Palace, as I said before, taking up one Quarter of the
City, opens into four Streets by four different Arches; and

before one of the Sides, which I call the Front, is a large
Triangle, formed by the Entrance out of one of the cross
Streets, and the two Ends of the Front of the Palace. Along
the lower Front of it, all the way runs a Piazza of considerable
Height, supported by vast round Columns, which seemed to
bear up the whole Front of the Rock; over which was a Gallery
of equal Length, with Ballustrades along it, supported with
Pillars of a yet finer Make; and over that a Pediment, with
divers Figures, and other Work to the Top of the Rock; which
being there quite even for its whole Length, was inclosed with
Ballustrades between Pedestals all the way; on which stood
the Statues of their ancient Kings, so large as to appear equal
to the Life. The other two Sides of the Triangle, were Dwellings for divers Officers belonging to the Palace. Under the
middle Arch of the Piazza, was the way into the Palace, thro'
a long, spacious, arched Passage, whose further End opened
into a large Square; on each Side of this Passage were large
Stair-cases, if I may so call them, by which you ascend
gradually, and without Steps, into the upper Apartments.

The next Morning we took another Walk, for I told *Quilly*,
I had a mind to take a Prospect of the Country; we then went
out at the back Arch of the Palace, as we had the Day before
at one of the Sides; there being a like Passage thro' the Rock
from that we went out at, to an opposite Arch leading into
the Garden. I say, we went out at the Back-arch, and after
passing a large Quadrangle with Lodgings all round it, we
ascended thro' a cut in the Rock to a large Flat; where we
plainly saw the black Mountain with its Top in the very Sky,
the Sides of which afforded numberless Trees, tho' the Ground
within view afforded very little Verdure, or even Shrubs.
But the most beautiful Sight from the Rock was, to see the
People come home loaded from the Mountain, and from the
Woods, with, it may be, forty Pound weight each on their
Backs; and mounting over the Rock, to see them dart along
the Streets to their several Dwellings, over the Heads of
thousands of others walking in all parts of the Streets; whilst
others were flying other ways. It was very pleasant to see

a Man walking gravely in one Street, and as quick as Thought to see him over the Rock, settled in another, perhaps two Miles distant.

The near view of the Country seeming so barren, naturally led me to ask *Quilly*, from whence they got Provision for so many People as the City contained; which to be sure, could not be less than three hundred thousand. He told me, they had nothing but what came from the great Forest, or the Skirts of the Mountain. But for the Grain of it, and some few outward Marks, says I, I could have sworn I had eaten some of my Country Beef the other Day at the King's Table. I don't know what your Beef, as you call it, is, but I am sure we have nothing here, says he, but the Fruit of some Tree or Shrub, that ever I heard of. I wonder, says I, *Quilly*, how your Cooks dress their Victuals. I have eaten many things boiled, and otherwise drest hot; but have seen no Rivers or Water, since I came into this Country, except for drinking, or washing my Hands; and I don't know where that comes from. And another thing, says I, surprizes me; tho' I see no Sun as we have to warm the Air, you are very temperate in the Town, and it is seldom cold here; but I neither see Fire or Smoak. We have, says *Quilly*, several very good Springs under the Palace, both of hot Water and cold; and I don't know what we should do with Fires; we see the Dread of them sufficiently at Mount *Alkoe*. Our Cooks dress their Fruits at the hot Springs. That's a Fancy, says I, they can't boil them there. I'm sure we have no other dressing, says he. Well, *Quilly*, says I, we'll go home now the way you told me of, and To-morrow you shall show me the Springs; but pray, how come you to be so much afraid of Mount *Alkoe*? I suppose your Eyes won't bear the Light, is not that all? No, no, says *Quilly*, that is the Country of bad Men; some of us have flown over there accidentally, when the Mountain has been cool, as it is sometimes for a good while together; and have heard such Noises, as would frighten any honest Man out of his Senses; for there they beat and punish bad Men. I could not make much of his Story, nor did I inquire further; for I had before determined if possible, to get over thither. As we were now come into the Garden, I ordered *Quilly* to get ready my Dinner, and I would come in presently.

We went next Morning to view the Springs, and indeed it was a Sight well worth considering; we were in divers Offices under the Rock, (*Quilly* carrying two Globe-lights before me) in which were Springs of very clear Water, some of hot, and some of cold; rising within two or three Inches of the Surface of the Floor. We then went into the Kitchen, which was bigger than I ever saw one of our Churches; and where were a great number of these Springs, the hot all boiling full Speed Day and Night, and smoaking like a Caldron, the Water rising thro' very small Chinks in the Stone into Basons, some bigger, some less; and they had several deep Stone-jars to set any thing to boil in. But what was the most surprizing was, you should see a Spring of very cold Water, within a few Feet of one of hot, and they never rise higher, or sink lower than where they are. I talked with the Master-Cook, an ingenious Man, about them; and he told me, they lie in this manner all over the rocky Part of the Country; and that the first thing any one does in looking out for an House is, to see for the Water, whether both hot and cold may be found within the Compass he designs to make use of, and finding that, he goes on, or else searches another place. And he told me, where this Convenience was not in great Plenty, the People did not inhabit; which made the Towns all so very populous. He said too, that those warm Springs made the Air more wholesome about the Towns, than in other parts where there were none of them. I thanked him for his Information, which finished my Search for that time.

CHAPTER XVII

Peter sends for his Family; Pendlehamby *gives a
fabulous Account of the Peopling of that Country;
their Policy and Government;* Peter's *Discourse on
Trade;* Youwarkee *arrives; invites the King and
Nobles to a Treat; sends to* Grandevolet *for Fowls*

THE Days hanging heavy on my Hands till the Arrival of my
Family; I sent *Pendlehamby* word, that as I had sent for my
Family and Effects in order to settle in this Country, and
expected them very soon; I should be glad of his, my Brother
and Sister's Company, to welcome them on their Arrival.

My Father came alone, which gave me an Opportunity of
informing myself in the Rise and Policy of the State; as I purposed to take several further Steps in their Affairs, if they
might prove agreeable and consistent: For hitherto having
had only slight Sketches or Hints of things, I could form no
just Idea of the whole of their Laws, Customs, and Government. Explaining myself therefore to him, I begged his
Instruction in those Particulars.

Son *Peter*, says my Father, you have already done too much
in a short time, to leave any Room to think you can do no
more; and as you have hitherto directed your own Proceedings with such incredible Success, neither the King or *Colambs*
will interpose against your Inclination, but give you all the
Advices in our Powers; and I shall esteem your selecting me
for that Purpose, no small Honour.

Know then, that this State, by the Tradition of our Ragams,
has subsisted eleven thousand Years; for before that time, the
great Mountain *Emina*, then not far from the black Mountain,
but now fallen and sunk in the Sea, roaring and raging in its
own Bowels for many Ages; at last burst asunder with great
Violence, and threw up numberless unformed fleshy Masses
to the very Stars; two of which, happening in their Passage
to touch the Side of the black Mountain, for all the rest fell

into the Sea and were lost, lodged there, and lying close together as they grew, united to each other, till they were joined in one; and in process of time, by the Dews of Heaven, became a Glumm and a Gawrey; but being so linked together by the Adhesion of their Flesh, they were obliged both to move which way either would; living thus a long time in great Love and Fondness for each other, they had but one Inclination, lest both should be Sufferers upon the least Disagreement.

In process of time, they grew tired of each others constant Society, and one willing to go here, and the other there, bred perpetual Disorders between them; for Prevention whereof for the future, they agreed to cut themselves asunder with sharp Stones. The Pain indeed was intolerable during the Operation, but however they effected it; and the Wounds each received were very dangerous, and a long time before they were perfectly healed; but at length, sometimes agreeing, sometimes not, they begat a Son, whom they called *Perigenæ*, and a Daughter they called *Philella*. These two as they grew up, despising their Parents who lived on the Top of the Mountain, ventured to descend into the Plains, and living upon the Fruits they found there, sheltered themselves in this very Rock. Mean time, the old Glumm and Gawrey, having lived to a great Age, were so infirm, that neither of them was able to walk for a long time; till one Day, being near each other, and trying to rise by the Assistance of each other, they both got up, and leaning upon, and supporting each other, they also walked commodiously; this mutual Assistance kept them in good Humour a great while, till one Day, passing along near Hoximo, they both fell in.

Perigenæ and *Philella* had several Children in the Plains; who as they grew up, increasing, spread into remote Parts and peopled the Country; at last one of them, being a very passionate Man, at the Instigation of his Wife, became the first Murtherer by slaying his Father. This so enraged the People, that the Murtherer and his Wife, in Abhorrence of the Fact, were conveyed to Mount *Alkoe*, where was then only a very

narrow deep Pit, into which they were both thrown head-
long; but the Persons who carried them thither, had scarce
retired from the Mouth of the Pit, when it burst out with Fire,
raging prodigiously, and has kept burning ever since. *Arco*
and *Telamine*, the Murtherer and his Wife, lived seven
thousand Years in the Flames; till having with their Teeth
wrought a Passage thro' the Side of the Mountain, they begat
a new Generation about the Foot of the Mountain; and
having brought Fire with them, resolved to keep it burning
ever after in Memory of their Escape; and Power being given
them over bad Men, they and their Progeny are now wholly
imployed in beating and tormenting them.

A great while after *Arco* and *Telamine* were thus disposed
of, the People of this Country multiplying, it happened one
Year, that all the Fruits were so dry, that the People not able
to live any longer upon the Moisture of them only, as they
had always done before, and fearing all to be consumed with
Drought, one of their Ragams praying very much, and
promising to make an Image to Collwarr, and preserve it for
ever, if he would send them but Moisture; in one Night's
time, the Earth cast up such a Flood, that they were forced to
mount on the Rocks for fear of drowning. But the next Day
it all sunk away again, except several little Bubbles which
remained in many places for a long time, and the People lived
only on the Moisture they sucked from the Stone where those
Bubbles settled, for many Years; for they found that the
Water arose to the Height of the Surface, and no higher; and
where they found most of those Chinks and Bubbles, they
settled and formed Cities; living altogether in Holes of the
Rock: Till one *Lallio*, having found out the Art of crumbling
the Rock to Dust by a Liquor he got from the Trees, and working himself a noble House in the Rock, in the place where our
Palace now stands, he told them, if they would make him their
King, they should each have such an House as his own; to
this they agreed, and then he discovered the Secret to them.

This *Lallio* directed the cutting out this whole City, divided
the People into Colonies where the Waters were most plenty;

and while half the People worked at the Streets and Houses, the other half brought them Provisions. In short, he grew so powerful, that no one durst dispute his Commands; all which Authority he transmitted to his Successors, who finding by the Increase of the People, and the many Divisions of them, that they grew insolent and ungovernable, they appointed a *Colamb* in every Province, as a Vice-king, with absolute Authority over all Causes, except Murther and Treason, which are referred to the King and *Colambs* in Moucheratt.

As we had no want but of Victuals and Habitations; the King, when he gave a Colambat, gave also all the Lands and the Fruits thereof, together with all the hot and cold Springs to the *Colamb*; who, again distributed Parcels to the great Officers under him; and they part of theirs, to the meaner Officers under them, for their Subsistance; with such a number of the common People as was necessary, in respect to the Dignity of the Post each enjoyed; who for their Services, are fed by their Masters.

In all cases of War, the King lays before the Moucheratt the Number of his own Troops he designs to send; when each *Colamb*'s Quota being settled at such a Proportion of the whole, he forthwith sends his Number from out of his own Lasks, and also from the several Officers under him: So that every Man, let the Number be ever so great, can be at the Rendezvous in very few Days.

We have but three Professions, besides the Ragams and Soldiery, amongst us, and these are Cooks, House-makers, and Pike-makers; of which, every *Colamb* has several among his Lasks; and these, upon the new Regulation, will be the only Gainers, as they may work where they please, and according to their Skill will be their Provision; but how the poor Labourers will be the better for it, I can't see.

Dear Sir, says I, there are, you see, amongst Lasks, some of such Parts, that it is great Pity they should be confined from shewing them; and my Meaning in giving Liberty is, in order for what is to follow, that is, for the Introduction of Arts amongst you. Now, every Man who has natural Parts will exert them, when any Art is laid before him; and he will find so much Delight in making new Discoveries, that, did no Profit attend it, the Satisfaction of the Discovery to a prying Genius would compensate the Pains: But, I propose a Profit also to the Artificer. Why? what Profit, says my Father, can arise, but Food, and perhaps a Servant of their own to provide it for them?

Sir, says I, the Man who has nothing to hope, loses the use of one of his Faculties; and if I guess right, and you live ten Years longer, you shall see this State as much altered, as the Difference has been between a Lask and a Tree he feeds on. You shall all be possessed of that, which will bring you Fruits from the Woods without a Lask to fetch it. Those who were before your Slaves, shall then take it as an Honour to be imployed by you; and at the same time, shall imploy others dependant on them; so as the great and small shall be under mutual Obligations to each other, and both to the truly industrious Artificer, and yet every one content only with what he merits.

Dear Son, says my Father, these will be glorious Days indeed! But, come, come, you have play'd a good part already; don't, by attempting what you can't master, eclipse the Glory so justly due to you.

No, Sir, says I, nothing shall be attempted by me to my Dishonour, for I shall ever remember my Friend *Glaulepzie*. Sir, says I, see here, shewing him my Watch; why this, says he, hung by my Daughter's Side at *Graundevolet*. It did so, says I, and pray what did you take it for? A Bot, says he. I thought so, says I, but as you asked no Questions, I did not then force the Knowledge of it upon you. But put it to your Ear; he did so: what Noise is that, says he, is it alive? No, says I, it is not, but it is as significant. If I ask it what time of the Day it is, or how long I have been going from this place to that; I look but in its Face, and it tells me presently.

My Father looking upon it a good while, and perceiving that the Minute-hand had got further than it was at first;

was just dropping it out of his Hand, had I not caught it. Why, it is alive, says he, it moves. Sir, says I, if you had drop't it, you had done me an inexpressible Injury. O, ho, says he, I find now how you do your Wonders; it is something you have shut up here that assists you, it is an evil Spirit. I laughing heartily, he was sorry for what he had said, believing he had shewn some Ignorance. No, Sir, says I, it is no Spirit, good or evil, but a Machine made by some of my Countrymen, to measure time with. I have heard, says he, of measuring an Abb, or the Ground, or a Rock; but never yet heard of measuring time. Why Sir, says I, don't you say three Days hence I will do so; or such a one is three Years old? Is not that a measuring of time by so many Days or Years? Truly, says he, in one Sense I think it is. Now Sir, says I, how do you measure a Day? Why, by rising, and lying down, says he. But suppose I say, I will go now and come again, and have a particular time in my Head when I will return. How shall I do, to make you know that time? Why, that will be afterwards, another time, says he, or I can think how long it will be. But, says I, how can you make me know, when you think it will be. You must think too, says he. But then, says I, we may deceive each other by thinking differently. Now this will set us to rights; then I described the Figures to him, telling him, how many parts they divided the Day into, and that by looking on it, I could tell how many of such parts were passed; and that if he went from me, and said he would come one, or two, or three parts hence, I should know when to expect him. I then shewed him the Wheels, and explained where the Force lay, and why it went no faster or slower, as well as I could; and from my Desire of teaching, insensibly perfected myself more and more in it. So that beginning to have a little Idea of it, he wished he had one; and, says he, will you teach all our People to make such things? Then they would be disregarded Sir, says I. 'Tis impossible, says he. I'll tell you Sir, how I mean, said I. I can hereafter shew you an hundred things as useful as this; now if every body was to make these, how would other things be made? Besides, if every body made them, no body would want them: And then what would any body get by them, besides the pleasing their own Fancy? But if only twenty Men make them in one Town, all the rest must come to them; and they who make these, must go to one of twenty others, who make another thing that these Men want, and so on; by which means, every Man wanting something he does not make, it will be the better for every Maker of every thing.

Son, says my Father, excuse me; I am really ashamed, now you have better informed me, I asked so foolish a Question. I told him, we had a Saying in my Country, that every thing is easy when it is known.[1] I think, says he, a Man might find every thing in your Country.

Two Days after, my Wife and Daughter *Sally* came very early; but sure no Joy could be greater than ours at Sight of each other. I embraced them both over and over, as did my Father; especially *Sally*, who was a charming Child. They told me, I might expect every thing that Evening, for they left them alighting at the Height of *Battingdrigg*; for tho' they came out the last, yet the Body of the People with their Baggage, could not come so fast as they did. And little *Sally* said, we stayed and rested ourselves purely, Daddy, at *Battingdrigg*, before the Crowd came, but as soon as Mammy had seen all my Brothers safe, who came before the rest, and kissed *Dicky*, we set out again.

About seven Hours after, arrived the second Convoy from abroad, that ever entred that Country. I had too much to do with my Wife and Children that Night, to spare a Thought to my Cargoe; so I only set a Guard over them; for tho' I had now been married about sixteen Years, *Youwarkee* was ever new to me.

I was now obliged to the King again, for some additional Conveniencies to my former Apartment; and the young ones were mightily pleased, to have so much more Room than we had at home, and to see the Sweecoes; but finding themselves waited upon in so elegant a manner, and by so many Servants, for with our new Rooms, we had all the Servants belonging to them, they thought themselves in a Paradice to the Grotto; where all we wanted, we were forced to help ourselves to.

The next Day, *Tommy* came to see us, the King having given him a very pretty Post, since the Death of *Yaccombourse*; and *Hallycarnie*, with the Princess *Jahamel* her Mistress, who was mightily pleased to see *Youwarkee* in her *English* Dress, and invited her and the Children to her Apartment.

It was but a few Months since my Wife saw the Children; yet she scarce knew them, they were so altered; for the two Courtiers behaved with so much Politeness, that their Brothers and *Sally* looked but with an ill Eye upon them, finding all the fault, and dropping as many little invidious Expressions on them as possible. But I sharply rebuked them: We were all made chiefly, I told them, to please our Maker; and that could be done only by the Goodness of the Heart; and if their Hearts were more pure, they were the best Children; but if they liked their Brother and Sister's outward Behaviour better than their own, they might so far imitate them.

When we were settled in our new Apartment, I unpacked my Chairs and Table, and set out my Side-board, and made such a Figure, as had never before been seen in that Part of the World. I wanted now some Shoes for *Pedro*, his own being almost past wear, for the young ones never had worn any, but could find none; till applying to *Lasmeel*, and shewing him what I wanted, he pointed to one of the great Water-casks; but as there were eleven of them, big and little, I knew not where to begin; till having invited the King and several of the Ministers to dine with me, I was forced to look over my Goods for several other things I should want.

In my Search, I found half a Ream of Paper, a Leather Ink-bottle, but no Ink in it, some Quills, and Books of Accounts, and several other things relative to Writing. This Prize gave me Courage to attempt the other Casks; but I found little more that I immediately wanted. In the last Cask were several Books, two of them Romances, six Volumes of *English* Plays, two of Devotion, the next were either *Spanish* or *Portuguese*,

and the last looked like a Bible; but just opening it, and taking
it to be of the same Language, I put them all in again, thinking to divert myself with them some other time. I here found
some more Paper, and so many Shoes, as when I had fellowed
them, served me as long as I stayed in the Country.

Having as I said before, invited the King to eat with me,
I was sorry I had not ordered my Fowls to be brought; and
Youwarkee said, she thought to have done it, but I had not
wrote for them. I told her, I would send *Maleck* for some of
them I was resolved; for I should pique myself, on giving the
King a Dish he had never before tasted. So I called *Maleck*,
telling him, he must take thirty Men with him to *Graundevolet*;
and carry six empty Chests with you, says I, and put eight of
my Fowls in each Chest, and bring them with all Expedition.
Where do they lie, Sir, says he? You will find them at Roost,
says I, when it is dark. I never was there, says he, and don't
know the way. What, says I, never at *Graundevolet*? Yes, says
he, but not at Roost. I laughed, saying, *Maleck*, did not you
see Fowls when you was there? He said, he did not know,
what were they like? They are a Bird, says I. And what sort
of a thing is that, says he? *Youwee* hearing us in this Debate,
Maleck, says she, did not you see me toss down little Nuts to
something that you stared at, you saw them eat the Nuts.
O dear, says he, I know it very well, with two Legs and no
Arms. The same, says I, *Maleck*; do you go look for a little
House almost by my Grotto, and at Night you will find these
things stand on Sticks in that house. Take them down gently,
and come away with them in the Chests. *Maleck* performed his
Business to a Hair, but instead of forty-eight, brought me
sixty, telling me, he found the Chests would hold them very
well; and I kept them afterwards in the King's Garden.

z

CHAPTER XVIII

Peter *goes to his Father's; traverses the black*
Mountains; takes a Flight to Mount Alkoe*; gains the*
Miners; overcomes the Governour's Troops; proclaims
Georigetti *King; seizes the Governour; returns him*
the Government; Peter *makes Laws with the Consent*
of the People; and returns to Brandleguarp *with*
Deputies

No further Project being ripe for Execution, I took a Journey
home with my Father to *Arndruumstake*, and he would take
all the Children with him. *Youwarkee* and I stayed about six
Weeks, leaving all the Children with my Father.

Upon my Return, I frequently talked with *Maleck* about
his Country; who they originally were, and how long it had
been inhabited, and what other Countries border'd thereon,
and how they lay. He told me, his Countrymen looked upon
themselves to be very ancient, but they were not very
numerous; for the old Stock was almost worn out, by the
Hardships they had undergone; that about three hundred
Years before, he said, as he had it from good Report, there
were a People from beyond the Sea, or as they called themselves from the Little-lands, had strangely over-ran them;
and he had heard say, they would have over-run this Country
too, but they thought it would not answer. He said, when
those People first came, they began to turn up the Earth to
a prodigious Depth; and now, says he, bringing up some nasty
hard Earth, of several Sorts, they put it into great Fires till
it runs about like Water, and then beat it about with great
heavy Things into several Shapes; and some of it, Sir, says
he, looks just like that Stuff that lay at the Bottom of your
Ship, and some almost white, and some red; for when I was
a Boy I was to have been sent to work amongst them, as my
Father did; but it having killed him, I came hither, as many
more have done, to avoid it. And what do they do with it,

says I, when they have beat it about as you say? Then, says he, they carry it a long way to the Sea. What then, says I? Why then the Little-landers take it, and swim over the Sea with it. And what do they do with it, says I? Why, says he, there are other People who take it from them, and go away with it. Why do they let them take it, says I? Because, says he, they give them Cloaths for it. Do they want Cloaths, says I, more than you? He told me they had no Graundee. And what other Countries have you here about? There is one Country, says he, North of *Alkoe*, where they say, there is just such another People as the Little-landers, and they get some of the things from Mount *Alkoe*. What do they do with them, says I? I don't know, says he; they fetch a great deal; but they won't let any body come into their Country. Is there no body inhabits between the Mountain *Alkoe* and the Sea? He told me no, the Little-landers would not let them.

Having got what Information I could from *Maleck*, and also from a Countryman or two of his, he had brought to me; I considered it all over, and thinks I, if I could but get Mount *Alkoe* to submit, (for they had told me, they were only governed by a Deputy from the Little-lands,) to see the Work done, I might, by intercepting the Trade to the Sea, turn the Profit of the Country my own way; and make it pass thro' our Hands.

I next enquired of those who brought the Fruits from the great Forest, what sort of Land they had there; and found by their Description, it was a light Mould, and in many places well covered with Grass and Herbs; and, by all the Report I could hear, must be a fruitful Country well managed; and being a flat Country, and not encompassed on that side with the black Mountain, was much higher than *Doorpt Swangeanti*. This News put me upon searching the Truth of it; and I made the Tour of the black Mountain, and the great Forest; alighting often to make my Observations. The Forest is a little World of Wood without End, with here and there a fine Lawn very grassy; and indeed the Wood-grounds bear it very well, the Trees not standing in Crowds, but at a healthy Distance from each other. I went abundantly further than any one had ever before been, but no Variation in the woody Scene; and coming round westward home, I had a View of Hoximo; which is nothing but a narrow Cleft in the Earth, on the Top of the black Mountain, of a most extraordinary Depth; for upon dropping a Stone down, you shall hear it strike and hum for a long time before all is quiet again; and laying my Ear over the Cleft, whilst I ordered one of my Attendants to throw a large Stone down; after the usual thumps and humming, I imagined I heard it dash in Water, so that it is not impossible it may reach to the Sea; which is at least six or seven Miles below it. Into this Hole, all dead Bodies are precipitated, from the King to the Beggar; for four Glumms holding by the Ankles and Wrists of the Deceased, fly with them to Hoximo, and throw them down, whilst the Air is filled with the Lamentations of the Relations of the Deceased, and of such others as are induced to follow the Corps for the sake of the Wines, on such Occasions plentifully distributed to all Comers by the Gentry; and, in the best Proportion they are able, by even the meanest amongst them.

After a stay of about fourteen Days at home, I fixed my next Trip for Mount *Alkoe*; and having told *Maleck* my Design, he said, he would go with me with all his Heart; but feared I should get no *Brandleguarpine* to bear me: For he told me, they had an old Tradition, that *Mindrack* [the Devil] lived there, and would not go for all the World; which has been the greatest Security that Country has had, for this would have devoured them else, says he.

I spoke to the King, to *Nasgig*, the Ragams, and found them all unanimous, that the Mountain *Alkoe* was the Habitation of *Mindrack*, and that the Noises which had been heard there were his Servants beating bad Men. Says I to myself, here is one of the usefullest Projects upon Earth spoiled, by an unaccountable Prepossession; what must be done to overcome this Prejudice?

I told *Maleck*, I found what he said to be too true, as to the People of *Brandleguarp*; but, says I, are there not enough of your Countrymen here, to carry me thither; he believing there were, I ordered him to contract with them; but it vexed me very much, to be obliged to take these Men. However, tho' I resolved to go, yet I chose to reason the Ragams into the Project, if I could; thinking they would soon bring the People over.

I called several of the Ragams together, and said: Because you are a wiser and more thinking People than the Vulgar, I have applied myself to your Judgments, in the Affair of Mount *Alkoe*. Now consider with yourselves, whether you have any real Reason beyond a Prepossession, for thinking these People Fiends or Devils Servants, as you call them, without further Examination; for, according to my Comprehension, they only understanding the Nature of several sorts of Earth, reduce them by Labour and Fire to solid Substances, for the Use of Mankind; and the want of these things is the Reason of your living as you do, without an hundredth part of the Benefits of Life. These sort of People, these Noises, and these Operations, which you hear and see carried on at *Alkoe*, are to be heard and seen in my Country; and we deal and traffick with their Labours, from one End of the World to the other; and we who are with them the happiest, without them should be the most miserable of People. Did not some of you see at my Entertainment, what I called my Knives, and Forks, and Spoons, my Pistols, Cutlasses, and Silver Cup; all these, and infinitely more, are the Produce of these poor Mens Industry. Now, says I, if we settle a Communication with these People, your Dues will be all paid in these curious things; you will have your People imployed in working them, and have Strangers applying to you to serve them with what they want; who, in return, will give you what you want; and you will find yourselves known and respected in the World. Finding some of these Arguments, applied to the Men, had staggered them a little; I applied to their Senses. Says I, it still appears to me, that you have your Prejudices hanging on you; but what will you say, if I go thither, and return safe? will you be afraid to follow me another time? They persuaded me from it, as a dangerous Experiment; but said, if I did return, they would not think there was so much in it as they suspected.

Maleck having chosen me out fourscore of his Countrymen, in about a Month's time I trained them up to the Knowledge of my Pistols, and Cutlasses, and the Management of them; and taking a Chest with me for the Arms and other Necessaries, we sallied up to the black Mountain. I rested there, and there *Nasgig* and *Lasmeel* overtook me; saying, that when they found me obstinate to go, they could not in their Hearts leave me, happen what would. This put new Spirits into me, and we consulted how the Noises lay, and agreed to engage first upon the Skirts of them, where the Smoaks were most straggling. I charged six Guns, and all my Pistols, which I kept in my Chest, and ordered them to alight with me, about an hundred Paces from the first Smoak they saw; then ordered three of them to carry my Guns after me, and twelve of them to take Pistols and follow me; but not to fire till I gave Orders. The Remainder I left with the Baggage.

We marched up to the Smoak, which issued out of a low Arch-way just at the Foot of the Mountain. It was very light there with the Flames of the Vulcano, and entring the Arch, a Fellow ran at me with a red-hot Iron-bar; him I shot dead, and seeing two more and a Woman there, who stood with their Faces to the Wall of the Hut or Room, as unwilling to be seen; I ordered *Maleck* to speak to them in a known Tongue, and tell them we were no Enemies, nor intended them any Hurt; and that their Companion's Fate was owing to his own Rashness, in running first at me with the hot Bar; and that if they would shew themselves good-natured and civil to us, we would be so to them; but if they offered to resist openly, or use any manner of Treachery towards us, they might depend upon the same Fate their Companion had just suffered.

Upon hearing this, they approached us; and shewing great Tokens of Submission, I delivered my Gun to *Maleck*, and bad them go on with their Work, ordering all the Guns out of the Shop for fear of a Spark. I then perceived they were direct Forges, but made after another Manner from ours, their Wind being made by a great Wheel, like a Wheel of a Water-mill, which worked with the Fans or Wings in a large Trough, and caused a prodigious Issue of Air, thro' a small Hole in the Back of the Fire-place. They were then drawing out Iron-bars.

I gave each of these Men, and also to the Woman, a Dram of Brandy; which they swallowed down very greedily, and looked for more, and seemed very pleasant. I then inquired into the Trade; by whom, and how it was carried on? and they told me just as *Maleck* had done. I then asked where the Mines lay? and one of them looking full at me said, then you know what we are about. Yes, says I, very well; he told me, the Mine was, in his Language as *Maleck* interpreted it, about a Quarter of a Mile off, and directed me to it. I ordered them to go on with their Work, telling them, tho' I left a Guard over them, it was only that they might not raise their Neighbours to disturb me; tho' if they did, I should serve them all as I had done their Companion; and left four Men with Pistols at the Arch-way.

I proceeded to the Iron Mine, but supposed the Men were all within; for I saw no body, but there were many large Heaps of Ore lying, which I felt of, and, being vastly heavy, I supposed it might be rich in Metal.

I returned to my Men at the Arch, and asked them, what other Mines there might be in that Country, and of what other Metals; but *Maleck* not knowing the Metals themselves, was not able to interpret the Names they called them by. I then shewed them an *English* Half-penny, a *Portuguese* Piece of Silver Money, and my Gold Watch; and asking if they had any of those; they pointed to the Half-penny and Silver Piece, but shook their Heads at the Watch. I then shewed them a Musket-ball; and they said, they had a great deal of that.

I desired them to shew me the way to the Copper Mine, pointing my Finger to the Half-penny, and told them, if they would go with me, they should have some more, pointing to my Brandy; and they readily agreed, if I would stand by them for leaving their Work. I believe, it might be two Miles further on the right to the Copper Mine, and as these Men had the Graundee, I expected they would have flown by me; but I found they had a light Chain round their Graundee, which prevented them; so I walked too, and having made them my Friends, by being familiar with them, I desired they would go in, and let the Head-man of the Works know, that a Stranger desired to speak with him and view his Works; and to inform him how peaceable I was, if he used me civilly; but that I could strike him dead at once, if he did not.

I don't know how they managed, or what Report they made; but the Man came to me very courteously, and I bad *Maleck* ask if he came in Friendship, as I did to him; and he giving me that Assurance, I went in with him, taking *Nasgig* and *Maleck* with me, and leaving our Fire-arms without. I ordered them both, as I did myself, to carry their Cutlasses sheathed in their Hands, for fear of a Surprize. We saw a great Quantity of Copper Ore, and several melting Fats,[1] being just at the Mouth of the Mine; the Mine running horizontally into the Side of the Mountain; and, as they said, was very rich. I gave the Head-man a little Brandy, and two or three more of them, who had been industrious in shewing and explaining things to me.

I desired the Fore-man to walk out with me, and asking how long he had been in that Imploy; he told me, he was a Native of the *Born* Isles, and was brought thither young; where he first wrought in the Iron, then in the Silver, and now in this Mine. That he had been there twenty Years, and never expected to be delivered from his miserable Slavery; but as he was now Overseer of that Work, he did pretty well, tho' nothing like Freedom. He told me, they expected several new Slaves quickly; for the Mines killed those they did not agree with, so fast, they were very thinly wrought at present, and that the Governor was gone to the Isles to get more Men. I was glad to hear this: And pray, says I, where does the Governor reside? He, pointing to the place, told me. And what Guard, says I, may he keep? About four hundred Men, but no body durst molest him, says he, for he tortures them in such a manner, never killing them, that not the least thing can be done against his Will.

After we had talked a good while on the Misery of Slavery, and finding him a Man fit for my Purpose; I asked him, if he would go with me to *Brandleguarp*, for, said I, there are certainly good Mines in those Mountains; and if you will overlook them, you shall be free, and have whatever you desire. He shook his Head, saying, how could he expect to be free, where all the rest were Slaves; and besides, says he, they are in such Commotions among themselves, that it is said, the State will be torn to Pieces. You are mistaken, says I, very much; I myself have settled Peace amongst them, and killed the Usurper. Is it possible, says he, and are you the Man, it was said they expected to come out of the Sea? The very same, says I, and as to Slavery, there is not a Slave in the Kingdom, nor shall be here, if you will hearken to me. That would be a good time indeed, says he. Well, says I, my Friend, I promise you it shall be so; only observe this, that when I come to reduce the Governor, do none of you Miners assist him. He promised he would let the other Miners secretly know it, and all should be as I wished; but desired me to be expeditious, for the Governor was expected every Day.

I went from him to the other Mines, and my Guides with me; who seeing me so well received at the Copper Mine, and reporting it to the others, it caused my Proceedings to go on smoothly, and my Offers to be readily embraced wherever I came.

Having prepared Matters thus, I set *Maleck* and his Countrymen upon the Natives, to treat with them about Submission to *Georigetti*, on promise of Freedom; who being assured of what I had done at *Brandleguarp*, and in hopes of like Liberty, readily came into it; so that the only thing remaining was, before the Governor's Return, to attack the Soldiery. Having therefore renewed my Engagements with the Miners, and believing myself upon as good Terms with the Natives as I could wish; I was advised by *Nasgig* and

Lasmeel, to return for Cannon and a large Army, before
I attacked the Soldiery: But I, who had all my Life rode upon
the Spur, having considered that an Opportunity once lost is
never to be regained; and tho' I could have wished for some
Cannon, I valued the Men but for shew, I therefore formed
my Resolves to march with the Force I had next Morning,
and pitch upon a Plain just by the Governor's Garrison, in
order if I could to draw his Men out. I did so, and it answered;
for upon the first News of my coming, they appeared with
a sort of heavy headed Weapons; which hurling round, they
throw upwards aslope, in order to light upon the Backs of
their Enemies in flight, and beat them down; but they could
not throw them above thirty Paces.

I sat still in my Chair, with a Gun in my Hand, and *Maleck*
with another at my Elbow; with four more lying by me, ready
to be presented; *Lasmeel* standing by to charge again, as fast
as we fired. I ordered a Party of twenty of my Men with
Cutlasses, to attack the Van of the Enemy, by rushing
impetuously upon them, they coming but thin against me;
for I was not willing to imploy my Pieces, till I could do more
Execution. They began the Attack about an hundred Yards
before me, not very high in the Air; and my Cutlass-Men
having avoided the first Flight of their Weapons, fell upon
them with such Fury, that chopping here a Limb, and there
a Graundee, which disabling their Flight was equally pernicious, they fell by Scores before me: But I seeing those in the
Rear, which made a Body of near three hundred, coming very
swift and close in treble Ranks, one above the other, hoping
to bear down my Handful of Men with their Numbers;
I ordered my Men all to retire behind me, and not till the
Enemy were passed over my Head, to fall on them. *Maleck*
and I, as they came near, each firing a Piece together, and
whipping up another, and then another, in an Instant; they
fell round us, roaring, and making a horrid Yell. This, the
rest seeing, went over our Mens Heads, not without many
falling from the Cuts of my Men; and those who escaped
were never heard of more.

The Miners, who from their several Stations had beheld the Action, came singing and dancing from every Quarter round me; and if I had not drawn my Men close in a Circle about me, would probably out of Affection have done me more hurt, than two of the Governor's Armies; for against these, common Gratitude denied the use of Force, and they crowding every one but to touch me they said; for fear of being pressed to Death myself, as some of them almost were, I ordered them to be let in thro' my Men, at one Side of the Ring, and passing by, and touching me, to be let out on the other Side; and this quite quieted them, but kept me in Penance a long time.

We then marched in a Body all into the Town, where we were going to proclaim *Georigetti* King of Mount *Alkoe*; when a surly Fellow, much wiser than the rest, as he thought, being about to harangue the People, against being too hasty in it, was knocked down, and trod to Death for his Pains; and we went on with the Proclamation, giving general Liberty to all Persons without Exception.

The next thing to be considered was, how to oppose the Governor when he came; and for that Purpose, I inquired into the Manner of his coming, the Road he came, and his Attendants; and being informed, that an hundred of his Guards who had not the Graundee, waited for him at the Sea-side; and that he had no other Guard, except a few Friends and the Slaves he went for; and that the Slaves always came first, six in a Rank tied together, under Convoy of a few of his Guards; I went in Person to view the Rout he came, and seeing a very convenient Post in a thick Wood, thro' which they were to pass, from whence we might see them, before they came near us; I posted a Watch on the Sea-side of the Wood, and myself and Men lay on the hither Side of it, just where the Governor's Party must come out of it again: So that my Watch giving Notice of their Approach, we might be ready to fall on, at their coming out of our Side of the Wood.

When we had waited three Days, our Watch brought Word they were coming: So we kept as close as possible, letting the

Slaves and Guards march on, who came by about two Hours March before the Governor: But so soon as he approached, I drew up my Men on the Plain within the Wood, in Ranks; ordering them to lie close on their Bellies, till they saw me rise, and then to rise, follow me, and obey Orders.

Several of the first Ranks having passed the Wood; just as the Governor had entred the open Country, I rose, and bad *Maleck* call aloud, that if any of them stirred or lifted up a Weapon, he was a dead Man; and then seeing one of the foremost running, I fetched him down with a Musket-shot, bidding *Maleck* tell the rest, that if they submitted, and laid down their Weapons, they were safe; but if they refused, I would serve them all as I had done him who fled. This Speech, with the Terror of the Gun, fixed every Man to his place like a Statue.

I then went forward to the Governor, and by *Maleck* my Interpreter, asked him, who they all were with him; he told me, his Slaves. I then made him call every Man before him, and give him Freedom; which, finding no way to avoid, for I looked very stern, he did, and I had enough to do to quiet my new Freemen, who I thought would have devoured me for Joy. I asked whither he was going? He said to his Government. Under whom do you hold it, says I? Under the Zaps of the Isles, says he. I then told him, that whoever held that Government for the future must receive it from the Hands of *Georigetti*, the King of that Country, to whom all the Natives and Miners had already engaged their Fidelity. I told him, both Natives and Foreigners had been all declared free.

The Governor seemed much dejected, and told me, he hoped I would not use him or his Company ill. I told him, that depended intirely on his own and their good Behaviour. I asked who his Friends were that were with him, he said, they were some of the Zaps Relations, who were come to see the Methods of the Government, and inspect the Mines.

Ordering all the Governor's Guards and Friends to go before, and all my own but *Maleck*, to keep backwards some Paces; I entred into Discourse with him, about the State of the Isles, and the Country of *Alkoe*; and finding him a judicious Person, and not a Native of the Isles; I thought with some Management he might prove a useful Person to me, but did not like the Character I had heard of his Severity: So I plainly told him, that only one thing prevented my making him a greater Man than ever he was; which was I had been informed, he had a Roughness in his Nature, which drove him to Extremities with the poor Slaves; which I could not bear. Sir, says he, whatever a Man is in his natural Temper, where Slavery abounds, it is necessary to act, or at least be thought to do so, in a merciless Manner. I am intrusted with the Government of a Land of only Slaves; who have no more Love, nor are they capable of any, for me, than the Herbs of the Ground have. I am to render an Account to my Masters of their Labours; they work by Force, and would not stir a Step without it, or the Fear of Correction; for which Reason, the Rod must be ever held over them; and tho' I seldom let it fall, when I do, the Suffering of one is too long remembred, to permit others quickly to subject themselves to the like Punishment: And this Method, I judged to be the most mild; as the Death or Sufferings of one but seldom, must tho' ever so severe, be milder than the frequent Execution of Numbers. And as to my appearing severe to them, my Post required it; for Mercy to Slaves, being interpreted into Fear, arms them with Violence against you.

I could not gainsay this, especially as he told me he was glad I had freed them all; for no Man, says he, but if he were to chuse, would rather reign by Love, which he may in a free Country, but is impracticable in one of Slaves, rather than by Fear, which alone will keep the latter in Subjection.

I asked him, whether as he knew the Nature of the Country, and the Business of the Governour, he could become faithful to my Master *Georigetti*. He told me, he had ever been faithful to his Masters the Zaps; and would till he was sure, without suspecting in the least my Veracity, all was true that I was pleased to tell him; for nothing could satisfy his Conscience, but being an Eye-witness of it; and then being discharged from any further Capacity of serving them in an open way, he should be free to chuse his own Master; of all whom, *Georigetti* should to him, be most preferable; but begged me not to interpret his Desire of retaining Fidelity to his old Masters till he could no longer serve them, into an Implication of assisting them, by either open or concealed Practices; for wherever he engaged, he would be true to the utmost.

At the End of six Days, for I travelled on Foot with them, we arrived at the Governor's Palace, which we found without a Guard; and all the Slaves he had sent before him, at Liberty: So I ordered my Men to supply the usual Guard, and took my Lodging in the Governor's Apartment.

As *Gadsi*, for that was the Governor's Name, was not confined, or any of his Friends; he came into my Apartment, and told me, since he had found all things answered my Report; if I pleased, he would quit the Palace to me, and every thing belonging to the Government. I told him, he said well. He did so, taking with him only some few things his own Property. So soon as he was without the Territory of the Palace, I sent for him and his Friends back again; he could not help being dejected at his Return, fearing some Mischief. *Gadsi*, says I, this Palace, and this Country, which I now hold for my Master *Georigetti*, I deliver in Custody to you as his Governor; and now charge you to make Acknowledgement of your Fidelity to him. Then taking it from him in Terms of my own proposing, I delivered him the Regalia of his Government, charging him to maintain Freedom; but, says I, let no Man eat, who will not work, as the Country and the Produce is the King's.

I then summoned an Assembly of the People, and sent Notice to all the Miners to attend me. I told them, all that the King desired of them was, to make themselves happy; and as the Mines at present, says I, are the only Imployment of this Country, I would have it agreed by your own Consent, for I will force nothing upon you, that every Man amongst you, from sixteen to sixty, shall work every third Week at the Mines, and other Duties of the Government; and two Weeks out of three shall be your own, to provide in for your Families. And if I live to come back again, you shall each Man have so much Land of his own, as shall be sufficient for his Family; and I will make it my Business to see for Seeds, to improve it with. And this Week's Work in three, and if afterwards it can be done with less, in four, shall be an Acknowledgement to the King, for his Bounty to you. Do you agree to this? They all with one Voice cried out, *we do*. Then, says I, agree amongst yourselves, and part into proper Divisions for carrying on the Work; that is, into four parts, one for each Sort of Metal; and then again, each of those four into three parts; and on every seventh Day in the Morning, let those who are to begin, meet those who are leaving off Work; so that there be clear six Days Work, and one of going and returning. Do you all agree to this? All cried, *we do*. Then, says I, whoever neglects his Duty, unless thro' Sickness, or by Leave of the Governor, shall work a double Week. Do you agree to this? *We do*. Then all Matters of Difference between you shall be decided by the Governor; and in case of any Injury or Injustice, or wrong Judgment in the Governor, by *Georigetti*. Do you agree? *We do*. Then, says I, agree upon ten Men, two for the Natives, and two for each Mineral Work, to send with me to *Brandleguarp*, to petition *Georigetti* to confirm these Laws, till you shall make others yourselves; and to acknowledge his Sovereignity. Do you agree? *We do*.

I then told them, that as those who had been Slaves, were now free, they might if they pleased, return home; but, as I should make it my Endeavour to provide so well for them, in all the Comforts of Life, I believed most of them would be of Opinion, their Interest would keep them where they were. And above all things, recommending a hearty Union, between the new Freemen and the Natives, and to marry amongst each other, and to continue in Love amongst themselves, and Duty to the King and his Governor; and promising speedily to return, and settle what was wanting, I dismissed the Assembly, and set out for *Brandleguarp* with the ten Deputies: But I left *Lasmeel* behind with the Governor, and two Servants with him, to give me immediate Notice, in case any Disturbance should happen in my Absence.

CHAPTER XIX

Peter arrives with the Deputies; presents them to the King; they return; a Colony decreed to be sent thither; Nasgig *made Governor; manner of chusing the Colony; a Flight-race, and the Intent of it;* Walsi *wins the Prize, and is found to be a Gawrey*

As we alighted at the Palace late at Night, I kept the Deputies with me till next Morning; when I went to the King, desiring them to stay in my Apartment, till I had received his Majesty's Orders for their Admission.

The King was but just up when I came in; and seeing me, embraced me, saying, dear Father, I am glad to meet you again alive; your stay has given me the utmost Perplexity, and could I have prevailed with any of my Servants to have followed you, I had sent before this time to have known what was become of you.

I told his Majesty, the greatest Pleasure of my Life consisted in the Knowledge of his Majesty's Esteem for me; and he might depend upon it, I would take care of myself from a double Motive, whilst I was in his Dominions; the one, from the natural Obligation of my own Preservation, and the other, equally compulsive, of continuing serviceable to his Majesty, till I had made him more famous than his Ancestor, the great *Begsurbeck*.

I told his Majesty, as a small Token of my Duty and Affection to him, I was come to make him a Tender, of the additional Title of King of Mount *Alkoe*. Father, says he, we shall never be able to get a sufficient Number of my Subjects to go thither; for tho' your safe Return may be some Encouragement, yet whilst their old Apprehensions subsist, and I know not what will alter them, we can do no Good; and indeed were they free to go, and under no Suspicion of Danger, it would cost abundance of Men to conquer Mount *Alkoe*.

Great Sir, said I, you mistake me; I told you, I came to make you a Tender of it; I have proclaimed you King there, and Freedom to the People; I have held an Assembly of the Kingdom; placed a Governor; taken the Engagement of himself and Subjects to you; settled Laws amongst them for your Benefit, the full third part of all their Labour; have brought ten Deputies, two from each Denomination of People amongst them; and they only wait your Command to be admitted, to beg your Acceptance of their Submission, and pray your royal Protection.

Father, says the King, you amaze me! but as it is your doing, let them come in.

The Deputies being received, and heard, by *Maleck* their Interpreter, very graciously; the King told them, in a very favourable Speech, that whatever his Father had done, or should do, they might accept as done by himself; and commanded them to remind the Governor, for whom he had the highest Esteem, to observe the Laws, without the least Deviation, till his Father should make such further Additions, as were consistent with his own Honour, and their future Freedom; and having feasted them in a most magnificent Manner, they returned, highly satisfied with the Honours they had received.

This Transaction being immediately noised abroad; all the *Colambs* came themselves, and the great Cities by their Deputies, sent his Majesty their Compliments upon the Occasion; and there was nothing but Mirth and Rejoicing throughout the whole Kingdom. And those who had refused going with me, as *Maleck* told me, hung their Heads for Shame and Sorrow, that they had missed the Opportunity of bearing a part in the Expedition.

I demonstrated to the King, that the only way to preserve that Kingdom was, to settle a large Colony on the Plains,

A a

between the Mountain and the Sea, to intercept clandestine
Trade, and make a stand against any Force that might be sent
from the Little-lands, to recover the Mines. And I promised
to be present at the Settlement, and an Assistant in it.

Most of the *Colambs*, as I said, being at Court, upon this
complimentary Affair; the King summoned them, for their
Advice on my Proposals; and told them, he had ordered me
to lay before them my Thoughts on the Affairs of that Kingdom; and after many Compliments and Encomiums had
passed on me, I told them, the Necessity of the Colony, the
Commodity that would arise from it, how I intended to
manage it, and what Prospect I had of introducing amongst
them several extraordinary Conveniencies they had never
before had.

The *Colambs*, who for want of Practice this way, knew but
little of the Matter; thinking nevertheless, that in the general
Turn of things, they must somehow come in for a Share;
approved of all I said. I desired them then to settle, out of
what part of the People, and how to be nominated, such
Choice of the Colony should be made for the new Settlement;
but found them much at a loss to fix on any Method of doing
it: So I told them, I believed it would be the best way to issue
an Order, for such as would willingly go, to repair to a particular Rendezvous; and in case sufficient should not appear
voluntary, to issue another Order, that the *Colambs* out of
their several Districts, should compleat the Number; so as
to make a Body of 12000 Men of Arms, besides Women and
Children; and that such a Territory should be allotted to each,
with so much Wood-grounds, in common to all, as would
suffice for their Subsistence; all which passed the Vote.

I then told them, that this large People must have an Head
or Governor, to keep them to their Duties, and to determine
Matters of Property, and all Disputes amongst them. Here,
they one and all nominated me; but I told them, I apprehended
I could be more useful other ways, having too many things in
my Head for the general Good, to confine myself to any particular Province; but if they would excuse me, in presuming

to recommend a Person, it should be *Nasgig*. And immediately *Nasgig* being sent for, and accepting it, they conferred it upon him.

All things, as I judged, went on in so smooth a way in reference to the new Colony, that I was preparing with the Assistance of the proper Officer, Expresses to be sent with the King's Gripsacks, into the several Provinces, with Notice of these Orders, and an Appointment for a Rendezvous. But whilst this was doing, abundance of People came crowding about me, to be informed, whether I thought it safe for them to go; and, I believe, I had fully satisfied all their Scruples; when, by some Management of the Ragams, who, having so long declared Mount *Alkoe* to be inhabited by *Mindrack*, did not care the People should all of a sudden find out they had deceived them, there was a Report ran current, that tho' I, and my Bearers, who were all Mount *Alkoe* Men, returned safe; yet if any of the *Brandleguarpians* had gone, they would never have come back again. This Rumour coming to my Ears, and fearing whitherto it might grow, I had no small Prospect of a Disappointment: And I thereupon stopped issuing the Orders, till I had considered what further to do in the Affair; at length, being persuaded I had already satisfied abundance of their Scruples, and in order to dissipate the Doubts of others, and to familiarize them in some measure to the Country and People of Mount *Alkoe*; I proposed a Prize to be flown for, and gave notice of it for six Days all about the Country, both to those of Mount *Alkoe*, and those of *Sass Doorpt Swangeanti*: That whoever, except those who were with me in the late Expedition, should make the most speedy Flight to the Governor's of Mount *Alkoe*, to carry a Message, and bring me an Answer from *Lasmeel*, should have one of my Pistols, with a Quantity of Powder, and so many Balls; and the Person who should be second, should have a Cutlass and Belt. The time being fixed, very few had entred in the first two or three Days; but on the third Day came several over from *Alkoe* to enter; which the *Brandleguarpines* seeing, and having equal Inclination to the Prize;

after half a Dozen of them had entred on the fourth Morning, before Noon on the fifth I had near sixty of them on my List, besides the *Alkoe* Men; making in all about one hundred.

The time of starting was fixed for the sixth Morning, from off the Rock, on the back-side of the Palace; upon my firing a Pistol.

This unusual Diversion occasioned a prodigious Confluence of Spectators; for scarce a Person in *Brandleguarp*, except those who were either too young or too old for flight, but were upon one or other of the Rocks; even the King himself, and all his Court were there; with infinite Numbers from all distant Parts.

I had dispatched a Letter by one of my old Bearers to *Lasmeel* some Days before, to inform him of it, that he might get two Letters ready wrote, one to deliver to the first, and another to the second Messenger; but not to take further notice of the rest: Now my Flight-race being for the equal Benefit of both the Kingdoms, it happened, as I was in hopes it would, that so many of the Mount *Alkans* coming over to me to be entred, and staying with me till the Flight began; and such vast Numbers of Persons meeting of both Nations upon the black Mountains, to see them go and return; and several of the *Swangeantines* going, out of Bravado, quite thro' with the Flyers; the Intercourse of the two Nations was that Day so great, and the Discourse they had with the Natives and Miners, so stripped the *Swangeantines* of their old Apprehensions of Danger from Mount *Alkoe*; that in three Days after, the whole Dread of the Place was vanished, and he would then have been thought mad, who had attempted to revive it.

The time being come, I set my Flyers in a Row on the outer Edge of the Rock; and having given Notice, that no one should presume to rise till the Flyers were on the Graundee, and at such a Distance; I then let the Flyers know, I should soon give Fire; which I had no sooner done, but down they all dropt as one Man, as it were head-long from the Edge of the Mountain; and presently the whole Field were after them. They skimmed with incredible Swiftness cross the Face of the Plain, between the Rock and the Mountain; the Force of which Descent swung them as it were up the Mountain's Side, in an almost, upright Posture; till seeming to sweep the Edge of the Mountain with their Bellies, they slid o'er its Surface, till they were lost in the Body of the *Swangean*; our Rocks echoing the Shouts of the Mountaineers. I fired my Pistol by my Watch, at 9 o'Clock in the Morning; but had no occasion to inquire when it was thought they would return; for every one was passing his Opinion upon it. Some said it could not be till Midnight, or very near it; and others, that it would be almost next Morning. However, we went to Dinner, and coming again about six o'Clock, by my Watch, I was told by the People on the Rock, as the general Opinion, for it was then top-full, that they could not yet be expected a long time, and the major part concluded, they could not be near half way home yet; when on a sudden, we heard a pro-digious Shout from the Mountain; which growing nearer and nearer to us, and louder and louder; in a few Moments came a slim young Fellow, and nimbly alighting on the Rock, tripped briskly forward, as not able to stop himself at once, from the Violence of the Force he came with; and delivered me a Letter from *Lasmeel*, as I was sitting in my Chair. I gave him Joy of the Prize, and ordered him to come to my Apart-ment, so soon as I got home, and he should have it. I then asked him where he left the other Flyers; he told me, he knew nothing of them, since he came past the Forges in his Return; for there he met them going to *Lasmeel*. Why that, says I, must be a great way on this side the Governor's. He told me, about half an Hour's Flight. I then told him, as he must be strained with so hard a Flight, it would be better if he lay down, and call'd on me in the Morning. He thanked me, and after he had told me his Name was *Walsi*, he said he would take my Advice; and springing up as light as Air, went off: The Rock being quite thronged with those who had followed from the Mountain, to see the Victor.

When *Walsi* came in, it was just seven o'Clock by my

Watch; so that according to the best Computation by Miles, I could make from their Descriptions of things, I judged he had flown at little more or less, than at the Rate of a Mile a Minute.

I stayed till near nine o'Clock upon the Rock; where it being cold, and the time tedious, I was taking *Quilly* home with me, and designed that *Maleck* should wait for the coming of the second; but hearing again a Shout from the Mountain, I resolved to see the second come in myself. The Noise increasing, I presently saw the whole Air full of People, very near me, for I had retired near two hundred Paces from the Edge of the Rock, to give Room to the Flyers to alight, and expected nothing less than to be borne down by them; when I spied two Competitors, one just over the Back of the other; the uppermost bearing down upon the other's Graundee; their Heads being just equal: So that the under Man perceiving it impossible to sink lower for the Rock, or to mount higher for the Man above him; and as darting side-ways would lose time, and fearing to brush his Belly against the Rock, he slackned just to job[1] up his Head in his Antagonist's Stomach; which giving the upper Man a smart Check with the Pain; and the under one striking, at that Instant, one bold Stroke with his Graundee, he fell just with his Head at my Feet, and the other upon him, with his Head in the under Man's Neck.

Thus they lay for a considerable time breathless and motionless, save the working of their Lungs, and heaving of their Breasts; when each asked me, if he was not the first; and the under Man giving me a Letter; I told them no, *Walsi* had been in almost two Hours ago. They both said it was impossible; they were sure no Glumm in the *Doorpt* could out-flie either of them. I ordered them both to call on me in the Morning, and I would see they should have Right done to their Pretensions. The under Man had but just told me his Name was *Naggitt*; when another arrived, who seeing *Naggitt* before him, told me he was sure he was second; but on seeing the other also, he gave it up.

I would stay no longer, it being now so late; but the next Morning I was informed, that all the rest had stopped at the Mountain but two; who were obliged to give out before, being overstrained, and unable to hold it.

The next Morning, *Walsi* was the first at my Apartment, when I happened to be with the King; and speaking of his Business to *Quilly*, he ordered him to stay in my Gallery till I came back: And *Quilly* presently after seeing *Youwarkee*, told her, the Victor at the Flight-race was waiting for me in the Gallery. *Youwarkee*, who had great Curiosity to see him, having heard how long he came in before the rest; stepped into the Gallery, and taking a Turn or two there, fell into Discourse with him about his Flight. And as Women are very inquisitive, she distinguished by the Flyer's Answers, Speech, Shape, and manner of Address, that it was certainly a Gawrey she was talking with; tho' she had endeavoured to disguise herself, by rouling in her Hair, and tying it round her Head with a broad Chaplet like a Man; and by the Thinness of her Body, and Flatness of her Breasts, might fairly enough have pass'd for one, to a less penetrating Eye than *Youwarkee*'s. But *Youwarkee* putting some Questions to her, and saying she was more like a Gawrey than a Glumm; she put the poor Girl, for so it was, to the Blush, and at last she confessed the Deceit; but, upon her Knees, begged *Youwarkee* not to mention it, for it would be her Undoing.

This Confession, gave *Youwarkee* a fair Opportunity of asking, how she came to be an Adventurer for this sort of Prize. The Girl, finding there was no Remedy, frankly confessed, she had a strong Affection for a Glumm Boss, who was a very stout Glumm, she said, but somewhat too corpulent for speedy Flight; who ever since the Prize had been proposed, could rest neither Night nor Day, to think he was not so well qualified to put in for it as others; especially one *Naggitt*, who he well knew made his Addresses to her; and also was an Adventurer. Had it been a Matter of Strength, Valour, or Manhood, says he, I had had the best of Chances for it; but to be under a natural Incapacity of obtaining so glorious a Prize, as even the King himself is not Master of such another; I cannot bear it. She then said, he had told her, he was resolved to give in his Name, and do his utmost, tho' he died in the Flight. What? said he, shall I see *Naggitt* run away with it, and perhaps with you too; when he has that to lay at your Feet, which no Glumm else can boast of? No, I'll overcome, or never come home without it. I must confess Madam, says *Walsi*, as I knew his high Spirit could never bear to be vanquished, I was afraid he would be as good as his Word, and come to some unlucky End; and told him, that tho' he need not have fear'd being Conqueror in any thing else, had it been proposed; yet in Flight, there were so many, half Glumms as they were, who from their effeminate Make and Size, and little Value for any thing else, would certainly be in before him; that it was unworthy of a thorough Glumm, to contend with them, for what could be obtained only by those, who had no Right to, or Share in any thing more excellent; and that he must therefore not think of more than his Fatigue for his Pains. But as he had set his Heart so much upon it, I would enter, and try to get it for him; as from my Size and Make, I believed few would have a better Chance for it than myself. And thanks to Collwarr, Madam, says she, I hope to make him easy in it; if you will but please to conceal your Knowledge of who, and what I am.

Youwarkee was mightily pleased with her Story, and promised she would; but engaged her to come again to her Apartment, so soon as she was possessed of the Prize.

When I returned, hearing *Walsi* waited for me, I called him in, read the Letter he brought, and finding it *Lasmeel*'s, I looked over my List for *Walsi*'s Name; for I set them all down as they entred, and finding it the very last Name of all, and that it was entred but on the Morning the Race was flown: So, says I, *Walsi*, I find the last at entring is the first at returning; but I see you have been there, by what *Lasmeel* has sent me; tho' there were some last Night, who questioned it, by your so speedy Return. Here, says I, take the Prize, and see they are only used in the Service of your Country; and then I dismissed him.

My two Competitors appeared next, for the Cutlass; and had each of them many Arguments to prevail with me, in favour of him; but I told them, I must do Justice; and that, tho' the Difference was so small between them, yet, certainly *Naggitt* was the nearest me, at the time they both ceased Flight, his Face lying on my Foot; so that as they both complained of foul Play, and were therefore equal in that Respect; *Naggitt* in Justice must have it. And I gave it him with these Words however; take it *Naggitt*, as certainly yours by the Law of the Race; but with a Diffidence in myself, who best deserves it.

I own I pitied the other Man's Case very much; as I should *Naggitt*'s, had the other won it; but seeing the other turning away, and hearing him say, but by half a Head! when I had strove so hard! as in a sort of Dejection; I told them, they were both brave Glumms, and of intrepid Resolution; and gave him also one, with the like Instruction as to *Walsi*.

Walsi went from me, as she had promised to *Youwarkee*, who wanted more Discourse with her; for in an Affair of Love, her gentle Heart could have dwelt all Day, upon the Repetition of any Circumstances, which would create Delight in the enamoured. *Youwarkee* found *Walsi* sat on Thorns, wanting to be gone; but *Youwarkee* asking Question upon Question, *Walsi* got up, and begged she would excuse her, she would come and stay at any other time; but, says she, Madam, when the Man one loves is in Pain, for I am sure he is on the Rack, for fear of a Discovery, till he sees me; if you ever loved yourself, you can't blame me for pressing to relieve him.

When she was gone, *Youwarkee* finding me alone, was so full of *Walsi*'s Adventure, she could not be silent; but after twenty round-about Speeches, and Promises that I was to make not to be angry with any body, or undo any thing I had done that Day, and I know not what; out came the Story. I was prodigiously pleased with it, and wished I had taken more notice of her. Says *Youwarkee*, I endeavoured to keep her till you had done, that you might have seen her. And why did not you, says I? My Dear, says *Youwee*, had you seen the poor Creature's Uneasiness, till she got off with it, yourself could not have had the Heart to have deferred that Pleasure, you would have perceived she expected when she came home; nor could you in Conscience have detained her.

CHAPTER XX

The Race reconciles the two Kingdoms; the Colony proceeds; build a City; Peter views the Country at a Distance; hears of a Prophecy of the King of Norbon's *Daughter* Stygee; *goes thither; kills the King's Nephew; fulfils the Prophecy, by engaging* Stygee *to* Georigetti; *returns*

THIS Race, notwithstanding all that the Ragams could say to keep up their Credit, and to prevent the Peoples perceiving what Fools they had made of them; had so good and sudden an Effect on the Peoples Prejudices; that upon issuing the first Proclamation, there was no Occasion for the second; for at least twenty-five thousand Men appeared voluntary at the Rendezvous, of the old Slaves, whose Masters, tho' they were declared free, had used divers Devices to oppress them, and render even their Freedom a sort of Slavery, besides Women and Children: So that we had now only to pick and chuse those who would be likeliest to be of Service to the new Colony.

Nasgig and I differed now about the Choice of Persons; he as a Soldier, was for taking mostly single young Men, and I for taking whole Families; tho' some were either too old or too young for War; and upon further Consideration, he agreed with me; for I told him, young Men would leave a Father, Mother, or Mistress behind them, which would either cause a hankering after home, and consequently the bad Example of Desertion; or else create an uneasy Spirit, and perhaps a general Distaste to the Settlement; so we chose those

whole Families, where they offered, which had the most young
Men in them first; then others, in like Order; after that, Man
by Man, asking them severally, if any Woman they liked
would go with them; and if so, we took her, till we had about
thirteen thousand fighting Men, besides old Men, Women
and Children; and then marching by the Palace, the King
ordered ten Days Stores for every Mouth, and with this we
took our Flight: But as I was always fearful of a Concourse in
the Air, *Nasgig* led them, and I brought up the Rear.

Besides the above Number of People, I believe we could
not have less than ten thousand Volunteers to the black
Mountain; some to take Leave of their Friends, and others
out of Curiosity to see our Flight. I took three Pieces of
Cannon with me, and proper Stores.

Our first Stage, after a short Halt on the black Mountain,
was to the Governor's Palace; where *Gadsi* received us with
great Respect. I told him my Errand, which he approved; for,
says he, Countryman, it is now as much my Interest to keep
my old Masters out, as ever it was to serve them when in:
And you have taken the only Method in the World, to do it
effectually. I consulted him, where I should fix my Colony,
and by his Advice, fixed it on this Side the Wood, with some
scattering Habitations behind the Wood, as Watch-houses,
to give Notice of an Enemy; having the Wood for shelter,
before they could reach the Town, and at the worst, the Town
for a Retreat.

I found by *Gadsi*, that the Ships from the Little-lands were
soon expected; for that he said, the Zaps knew nothing yet of
the Change of Government, nor could, till the Ships returned;
he asked me, as there was now a good Lading, whether I
thought fit to let them have it upon proper Terms. I told
him, I would not hinder their having the Metals, or endeavour
to stop their Trade in the least; but should be glad to treat
with them about it myself.

I gave the Forge-men Descriptions, for making Shovels,
Spades, Pickaxes, Hammers, and abundance of other Iron
Implements, I should want in the Building the new Town;

all which we got ready, and carried with us. We then took Flight, and alighted on the Spot of our intended City; and having viewed the Ground some Miles each way, we drew the Out-lines, and set a great Number of Hands to cutting down Trees, digging Holes, and making Trenches for the Foundations. In short, we were all Hands at it, and the Women fetched the Provisions; but I was obliged to shew them every single Step they were to take, towards the new Erections: And I must say, it was with great Pleasure I did it, they seldom wanting to be told twice, having as quick an Apprehension of what they heard or saw, as any People I had ever met with.

The whole City, according to our Plan, was to consist of several long strait Streets, parallel to each other, with Gardens backwards, each way, and traverse Passages at proper Distances, to cross each Street, from one to the other, quite thro' the whole City.

While this Work was in hand, I took a Progress to view the other Country, *Maleck* had told me of. We had not taken a very long Flight, before we saw at a Distance, several Persons of that Country travelling to Mount *Alkoe* for Metals. I had a great mind to have some Talk with them about their Kingdom, and ordered my Bearers to go to them; they told me, they durst not, for one of them would kill ten Men. I did not chuse to force them to it, for fear of some Mischief; but observing which way they came, and that they came in several small Bodies, of six or eight together, and that there was a little Wood, and some Bushes between me and them; I ordered my Bearers to sink beneath the Trees out of their Sight, and to ground me just at the Foot of the Wood; for I resolved to know something more of them before we parted.

I lay perdue,[1] till they arrived within sixty Paces of me; then asking *Maleck* if he knew their Language, and he telling me he did, having often conversed with them at the Mines; I bid him greet them, and tell them I was a Friend, and be sure to stand by me. There were seven of them, and many more at

different Distances. I shewed myself, and *Maleck* spoke to
them, when two or three of the hindermost ran quite away;
one stood and looked very surly, but the rest who had stood
with him, turning to run; I bid *Maleck* tell him, if he did not
call them back, I would kill them. He that stood, then called
to them, but they mending their Pace upon it, I let fly, and
shot one in the Shoulder; who dropping, I was afraid I had
killed him. I then went up to the other, who had not stirred
even at the Report of the Gun; seeming quite terrified. I took
him by the Hand, and kissed it; which made him recover himself a little, and he took mine, and kissed it.

I bid *Maleck* tell him, I was a great Traveller, and only
wanted to talk with him; but seeing the Man I had shot stir,
I went to him, and by *Maleck* told him, I was sorry I had hurt
him; which I should not have attempted, had he not shewn
a Mistrust of me, by running away; for I could not bear that;
this I said, to keep the other with me. I saw I had hurt his
Shoulder, but being at a great Distance, the Ball had not
entred the Blade-bone, but stopping there, had fallen out; so
tying my Handkerchief over it, I told him, I hoped it would
soon be well.

I inquired into their Country, its Name, the Intent of their
Journey this way, their Trades, the Fruits, Birds, and Beasts
of the Country.

The Man I had shot, I found, was in Pain, which gave me
no little Concern; so I chiefly applied myself to the other,
who told me, the Name of his Country was *Norbon*, a large
Kingdom, and very populous, he said, in some Parts of it,
and was governed by *Oniwheske*, an old and good King. He
has only one Daughter, says he, named *Stygee*; so that I am
afraid when he dies, it will go to a good for nothing Nephew
of his, a desperate debauched Man; who will probably ruin
us, and destroy that Kingdom, which has been in the
Oniwheske Family these fifteen hundred Years. Won't his
Daughter have the Kingdom, says I, after his Death, or her
Children? Children, says he, no, that's the pity, all would be
well if she had but Children, and the State continue fifteen

hundred Years longer in the same good Family. How is it possible for any one to know that, says I? You may know how long it has, but how long it will last, is mere guess-work. No, says he, this very time, and the present Circumstances of our Kingdom, were foretold at the Birth of the first King we ever had; who was of the present Royal Family. How so, says I? Why, says he, before we had any King, we had a very good old Man, who lived retired in a Cave by the Sea; and to him, every body under their Difficulties, repaired for Advice. This old Man happening to be very ill, every body was under great Affliction for fear they should lose him; when flocking to his Assistance, he told them, they need not fear his Death, till the Birth of a King, who should reign fifteen hundred Years. At hearing this, all Persons then present, apprehended that his Disorder had turned his Brain; but he persisted in it, and recovered.

After a few Years, a great number of Persons being about him, he told them, he must now depart; for that their King was born, and pointed to a sucking Child a poor Woman had then in her Arms. It caused a great Wonder in his Audience, at the Thoughts of that poor Child's ever becoming a King; but he told them, it was so decreed; and further, that as he was to die the next Day, if they would gather all together, he would let them know what was to come in future times.

When they were met, the Woman and Child being amongst them, he told them, that Child was their King; and that his Loins, should produce them a Race of Kings for fifteen hundred Years; during which time, they should be happily governed: But then a Female Inhabitant of the Skies, should claim the Dominion; and together with the Kingdom, be utterly destroy'd; unless a Messenger from above, with a Crown in each Hand, should procure her a Male of her own kind; and then the Kingdom should remain for the like Number of Years to her Posterity. Now, says he, the time will expire very soon, and as no one has been, or its believed will ever come with such two Crowns; the Princess *Stygee*, tho' she undoubtedly will try for it, has little Hopes of succeed-

ing her Father; for her Cousin *Felbamko* pretends, as no
Woman ever reigned with us, he is the right Heir, and will
have the Kingdom. Pray, says I, what do you mean by an
Inhabitant of the Air? O, says he, she flies. And do most of
your Country-Folks fly, says I? for I perceive you don't. No,
says he, no one but the Princess *Stygee*. How comes that about,
says I? Her Mother, when she was with Child with her, says
he, being one Day in a Wood near the Palace, and having
straggled from her Company, was attacked by a Man with
a Graundee; who not knowing her, clasped her within his
Graundee, and would have debauched her; but perceiving
her Cries had brought some of her Servants to her Assistance,
he quitted her, and went off: This Accident threw her into
such a Fright, that it was a long time before she recovered;
and then was delivered of a Daughter with the Graundee.
My Friend, says I, your meeting with me will be a very happy
Affair for your Kingdom. I am the Man the Princess expects;
go back to the Princess, and let her and her Father know, I will
be with them in six Days, and establish his Dominions in the
Princess.

The Fellow looked at me, thinking I joked, but never
offered to stir a Foot. Why don't you go, says I? And for the
good News you bear to the Princess, I'll see you shall be made
one of the greatest Men in *Norbon*; the Man smiled still,
but could not conceive I was in earnest: I asked him then
how long he should be in going to the Palace, he said three
Days at soonest; deliver but your Message right, says I, and
I'll assure you it shall be the better for you. The Man seeing
me look serious, did at length believe me, and promised he
would obey me punctually; but he had not seen how I came
to the place he met me at, for I had ordered my Bearers into
the Wood with my Chair, before I shewed myself.

He arrived, as I afterwards found, at the Palace, the fourth
Morning very early, and passing the Guard in a great Heat;
with much ado, was introduced to the King, and discharged
himself of my Message. His Majesty giving no credit to him,
thought he had been mad; but he affirming it to be true, and

telling the King at what a Distance I had knocked down his
Companion, and made a great Hole in his Back, only with
holding up a thing I had in my Hand, which made a great
Noise; *Oniwheske* ordered his Daughter to come before him,
who having herself heard the Man's Report, and being very
willing to believe it, with the King's Leave, desired that the
Messenger might be detained till the appointed Day, and
taken care of; and that Preparation should be made for the
Reception of the Stranger, in case it should be true.

The Noise of my coming, and my Errand, excited every
one's Curiosity to see me arrive; and the Day being come,
I hovered over the City a considerable time, to be sure of
grounding right. The King and his Daughter, on the Rumour
of my appearing, came forth to view me, and receive me at
my alighting. The People were collected into a large Square,
on one Side of the Palace, and standing in several Clusters at
different places; I judged where the King might seem most
likely to be, and ordered my Bearers to alight there; but I
happened upon the most unlucky Post, as it might have
proved, and at the same time the most lucky, I could have
found there; for I had scarce raised myself from my Chair,
but *Felbamko* pushing up to me thro' the Throng, and lifting
up a large Club he held in his Hand, had certainly dispatched
me, if I had not, at the Instant, drawn a Pistol from my Girdle,
and shot him dead upon the Spot; insomuch, that the Club
which was then over my Head, fell gently down on my
Shoulder.

I did not then know who it was I had killed; but for fear
of a fresh Attempt, I drew out another Pistol, and my Cutlass,
and inquiring at which part of the Square the King was, I
walked directly up to him, he not as yet knowing what had
happened. His Majesty, and his Daughter met me, and
welcomed me into his Dominions. I fell at the King's Feet,
telling him I brought a Message, which I hoped would excuse
my entring his Majesty's Dominions, without the Formality
of obtaining his Leave.

When we came to the Palace, the King ordered some

Refreshments to be given me and my Servants; and then, that I should be conducted to the Room of Audience.

The Report of *Felbamko*'s Death had reached the Palace before us, and that it was by my Hand; this greatly surprized the whole Court, but proved agreeable News to *Stygee*.

At my Entrance into the Room of Audience, the King was sitting at the further End of it against the Wall, with his Daughter on his Right-hand; and a Seat was placed for me at his Left, but nearer to the middle of the Room side-ways, on which I was ordered to sit down; there were abundance of the Courtiers present, and above me was a Seat ordered for one of them, who I found afterwards was one of the religious.

His Majesty asked me, aloud, how it happened, that the first Moment of my entring his Dominions, I should dip my Hands in Blood, and that too, of one of his nearest Relations.

I then got up to make my Answer; but his Majesty ordering me to my Seat again, I told him, that as it was most certain, I knew no one Person in his Kingdom, so it could not be supposed I could have an ill Design against any one; especially against that Royal Blood, into whose Hands I then came to render myself; but the Truth was, that what I had done was in Preservation of my own Life; for that the Person slain had rushed thro' the Crowd upon me, with a great Club, intending to murther me; and that whilst the Blow was over my Head, I killed him in such Position, that by his Fall, the Club rested on my Shoulder, but was then too weak to hurt me.

The King asking if that was the real Case, several from the lower End of the Room said, they were informed it was; and one in particular said, he saw the Transaction, and I had declared it faithfully. Then says the King, you are acquitted. And now, what brings you hither? relate your Business.

'Great Sir, says I, it is my peculiar Happiness, to be appointed by Providence as the Proposer of a Marriage for the Princess *Stygee* your Daughter, with a potent neighbouring Monarch; having already been enabled to perform things past belief for his Honour. Know then, great Sir, I am a Native of the North, and thro' infinite Perils and Hardships, at last arrived in the Dominions of *Georigetti*, where I have given Peace to his State, by the Death of the Usurper *Harlokin*. I have just also conquered the Kingdom of Mount *Alkoe* for my Master, and am here come to make your Daughter an Offer of both Crowns, and also of all that is my Master's, with his Person in Marriage.'

The old Priest then rose, and said, 'May it please your Majesty, we are almost right; but what has always staggered me is, how the Person should come; for the Messenger to us on this Errand, is to come from above. Now this Person has not the Graundee, and therefore could not come from thence: As for the rest, I understand the Prince, from whom he brings this Offer to your Daughter, has the Graundee; and so is a Male of her own kind: And I understand the two Kingdoms in his Possession, to be the two Crowns in the Messenger's Hands; but I say, what I stick at is, his coming from above.'

What, says *Stygee*, did not you see him come? No, says he; O, says she, he came in the Air, and was a long time over the City, before he descended. That's impossible, says the old Priest, for he is smooth like us. Indeed Sir, says she, I saw him, and so did most of the Court. The King and Nobles, then attesting this Truth; Sir, says the Priest to the King, it is compleated, and your Majesty must do the rest.

I little expected, says the King, to see this Day; and now, Daughter, as this Message was designed for you, you only can answer it; but still I must say, it surpasses my Comprehension, that in the Decree of Providence, it should be so ordered, that the very Hand which brings the Accomplishment of what has been so long since foretold us, should, without Design, have first destroyed all that could have rendered the Marriage State uncomfortable to you.

Stygee then declared, she submitted to Fate, and her Father's Will.

I stayed here a Week, to view the Country and the Sea, which I heard was not far off. Here were many useful Beasts, for Food and Burthen, Fowles also in Plenty, and Fish near the Sea Coasts, and the People eat Flesh; so that I thought myself amongst Mankind again. I made all the Remarks the shortness of the time would allow, and then taking my Leave, departed.

I returned to the Colony, where I heard that the Little-landers had been on the Coast; but I not being there, or any Lading ready, they were gone away again. However, they had detained two of them. I was pleased with that, but sorry they were returned empty.

I examined the Prisoners, and by giving them Liberty and good Usage, they settled amongst us; and the next Fleet that came, the Sailors to a Man were all my own, the Moment they could get to Shoar; this, tho' I thought it would have spoilt our Trade at first, brought the Islanders and me to the following Compromise, and upon this Occasion. Their Ships, having lain on our Coasts one whole Season, for want of Hands to carry them back; I came to an Agreement with their Commanders, for they were all willing to return, that such a Number of them, should be left as Hostages with me, till the Return of a Number of my own Men, which I should lend them to navigate their Ships home; and I sent word to the Zaps, that as it might be beneficial to us both, to keep the Trade still on foot, to prevent the like Inconveniencies for the future, I would buy their Shipping, paying for them in Metals; and agree to furnish them yearly, with such a Quantity of my Goods, at a stated Price; and would send them by my own People; which they approving, the Trade went on in a very agreeable and profitable Manner; and we in time, built several new Vessels of our own, and imployed abundance of Hands in the Trade, and had Plenty of Handicrafts-men of different Occupations, each of whom I obliged to keep three Natives under him, to be trained up in his Business.

CHAPTER XXI

A Discourse on Marriage between Peter *and*
Georigetti; Peter *proposed* Stygee; *the King accepts
it; relates his Transactions at* Norbon; *the Marriage
is consummated; Account of the Marriage Ceremony;*
Peter *goes to* Norbon; *opens a free Trade to Mount*
Alkoe; *gets Traders to settle at* Norbon; *convoys
Cattle to Mount* Alkoe

AT my Return to *Sass Doorpt Swangeanti*, I went directly
to the King, and giving him an Account of the Settlement, and
my Proceedings thereon; he told me, his whole Kingdom
would not be an Equivalent for the Services I had done him.
I begged of him, to look on them in no other a light, than as
flowing from my Duty; but, if when I should be no more, he
or his Children would be gracious to my Family, it was all
I desired.

This Father, says the King, I can undertake for myself;
but who's to come after me, no body knows; for I shall never
marry, no, *Yaccombourse* has given me a Surfeit of Woman-
kind; and unless the States will settle the Kingdom on you,
to which I will consent, it will probably be torn to pieces
again, by different Competitors; for I am the last of the Line
of *Begsurbeck*, and of all the Blood Royal: And indeed, who
so proper to maintain it flourishing, as he who has brought it
to the present Perfection.

Great Sir, says I, my Ambition rises no higher, than to
abound in good Deeds whilst I live, and to perfect my Children in the same Principle; and this, I hope, will intitle them
to a Support, when I am gone: But, says I, why is your
Majesty so averse from Marriage, merely on account of a
Woman you could not expect to be true to you? Not expect
it, says he? what stronger Tie upon Earth could she have had
to be true, than my Affection, and all that my Kingdom could
afford her? Weak things all, Sir, says I. Why, what could she

have had, says he, in some Warmth? Honour, Sir, says I, and
Virtue, both which she abandoned to become yours; and
those once lost, how could you expect her to be true? You are
too hard for me, Father, says he; but they are all alike, and
I don't believe there's a Grain of Honour in any of them. In
any of them like *Yaccombourse*, I admit Sir, says I, but think
not so of others; for no part of our Species abounds more with
it, or is more tender of it, than a good Woman; and take my
word for it, Sir, there is more real Sincerity in an ordinary
Wife, than in the most extraordinary Mistress. We are all
biassed naturally by Interest; and as there can be but one real
Interest between the Man and Wife, so the Interest of a
Mistress is, and ever will be, only to accommodate herself;
for its all one to her with whom she engages, so she can raise
but the Market by a Change: Now, if your Majesty could
find an agreeable and virtuous Wife, one deserving of your
Royal Person and Bed, and perhaps with a Kingdom for her
Dowry; a Partner fit to share your Cares, as well as Glory;
would it not be a great Pleasure to you, to be possessed of
such a Mate? And to see Heirs arising under your Joint-
Tuition, to convey down your Royal Blood to the latest
Posterity? Would not this I say, be a grateful Reflection to
you, in your declining Years?

Truly Father, says the King, as you have painted it, the
Prospect could not fail to please; and under the Circumstances you have put it, it would meet my Approbation; but
where is such a thing, as a Woman of this Character to be
found? I fear only in the Imagination.

Sir, says I, after a seeming Muse for some time, what
should you think of *Oniwheske*, the King of *Norbon*'s Daughter; he has but that one Child I hear? Dear Father have done,
says his Majesty; to what Purpose should you mention her?
We but barely know there is such a State, we have never had
an Intercourse; and besides, as you say he has but one Child,
can you suppose she will ever marry, to leave so fine a Kingdom, and live here? But Sir, says I, now we are supposing,
suppose she should, with her Father's Consent, be willing to

marry you; would you have her for your Queen? To make any doubt of that Father, says he, is almost to suppose me a Fool. Then Sir, says I, her Father has consented, and she too; and if I durst have presumed so far, or had known your Mind sooner, she would, I believe, have ventured with me, to have become yours; but you might have slighted her, and crown'd Heads are not to be trifled with; but since you are pleased to shew your Approbation of it, I can assure you, Sir, her Person will yield to none in your Majesty's Dominions: For Sir, I have been there, and have seen her, and she is your own, and her Kingdom too, upon Demand.

Father, says the King, looking earnestly at me; I have been frequently, since I knew you first, in doubt of my own Existence; my Life seems a Dream to me; for if Existence is to be judged of by one's Faculties only, I have been in such a Delusion of them ever since, that as I find myself unable to judge with Certainty of any other thing, so I am subject to doubt, whether I really exist. Are these things possible that you tell me, Father?

I then told him the whole Affair, and advised him by all means to accept the Offer, and marry the Princess out of Hand.

His Majesty, when I had brought him thoroughly to believe me, was as eager to consummate the Marriage, as I was to have him: But then, whether he should go to her, or she come to him was the Question. I told him, it was a thing unusual, for a Sovereign to quit his own Dominions for a Wife; but would advise an Embassy to her Father, with Notice, that his Majesty would meet and espouse her, on the Frontiers of the two Kingdoms.

The Embassadors returning, with an Appointment of time and place; it was not above a Month, before I had settled *Stygee* on the Thrones of *Sass Doorpt Swangeanti* and Mount *Alkoe*, with the Reversion of the Kingdom of *Norbon*, without a Competitor.

I shall here give you an Account of the Marriage Ceremony. The King being arrived on the Borders; *Stygee*, who had

waited but a few Hours at the last Village in *Norbon*, advanced
to his Majesty on the very Division, as they called it, of the
two Kingdoms; a Line being drawn, to express the Bounds
of each. The King and *Stygee*, having talked apart from the
Company a little Space, each standing Hand in Hand, on
their own respective Ground: The chief Ragam advanced,
and began the Ceremony.

He first asked each Party aloud, if he and she were willing
to be united in Body and Affections, and would engage to
continue so their whole Lives; to which, each Party having
answered aloud in the Affirmative; shew me then a Token,
says he; and immediately each expanding the right Side of
their Graundees, laid it upon the other's left Side, so that they
appeared then but as one Body, standing Hand in Hand,
incased round with the Graundee. The Ragam then having
discanted upon the Duties of Marriage, concluded the Ceremony, with wishing them as Fruitful as *Perigene* and *Philella*.
So soon as it was over, and the Gripsacks and Voices had
finished an Epithalamium, the Bride and Bridegroom taking
Wing, were conducted to *Brandleguarp*, amidst the Acclamations of an infinite Number of *Georigetti*'s Subjects.

The King had made vast Preparations for the Reception of
the Princess *Stygee*, and nothing was to be heard or seen but
Feastings and Rejoicing for many Days; and his Majesty
afterwards assured me, of his intire Satisfaction in my Choice
of his Bride; without whom he confessed, that notwithstanding the many other Blessings I had procured him, his Happiness must have been incompleat.

Intending another Flight to *Norbon*, I was charged with the
King and Queen's Compliments to *Oniwheske*; which having
executed, I opened a free Trade to Mount *Alkoe*; and hearing
that small Vessels came frequently on the *Norbonese* Coast
to carry off the Iron, and other Metal from thence unwrought;
and paid part of their Return in wrought Metals: I ordered
some of the next that came, to be stopped, and brought to me;
and the Day before I had fixed for my Departure, Notice was
sent, that twelve of those Traders were stopped, and in

Custody at the Sea-side; I longed to see them, but then considering that it would take up more time to bring them to *Apsilo* the Capital, where I was, than I should take in going to them, and returning; I resolved to go and examine them myself.

They told me, they traded with small Vessels to *Norbon* for Metals; which they carried home, and wrought great part of it themselves, sending it to, and dispersing it in several Islands at a Distance; and also sold the unwrought to several People, who carried it they knew not whither, in great Ships. They said, they kept abundance of Hands at work in the Trade. I asked if their Artificers wrought it for their own Profit, or their Masters. They told me for Masters, themselves being all Slaves. And are you all Slaves, says I? They told me yes, all but one, pointing to him. I then ordered him to be secured and removed; and told them, if they would procure some Hands to settle at *Norbon* and Mount *Alkoe*, they should all be made free, have Lands assigned them, and have other great Privileges; and I did not doubt in time, would become the richest Men in the Country; for I understood by them, they were acquainted with the Use of Money. I asked them, what other Commodities they brought to *Norbon* in Exchange. They said, Cloaths for the People, both what they received in Exchange from others who bought their Iron, and some of a coarser sort of their own making. I found in my Discourse I had with them, that out of my eleven Men, there were Persons of four different Occupations; so I promised those who would stay with me, their Freedoms, good Houses, and other Rewards; and sending three Hands home with the Vessel, and a full Freight, according to the Value of the Cargoe they brought; I ordered them to engage as many as they could of their Countrymen of distinct Trades, to come and settle with me; and to be sure if they had any Grain, Corn, Roots, Plants, or Seeds, usually eaten for Food, to bring all they could get with them, and they should have good Returns for them; and as to those good Hands that settled here, they should be allowed all Materials, to work for their own Profit

the first Year; and after that, they should also work for themselves, allowing the King one tenth of the clear Profit.—
This took so far with them, that it was with the utmost Difficulty I got any of them to carry the Ship back, for fear they
should not be able to return.

Before I parted from them, I assigned the eight who were
left, all proper Conveniencies, and recommended them to the
King's Protection; and I ordered the Owner then in Custody,
to be conducted to Mount *Alkoe*, and from thence to *Brandleguarp*; where treating him kindly, and giving him Liberty,
I made my proper use of him.

The King having lent me a Convoy to conduct my Prisoner,
and given me a Licence for as many Cattle of the sorts I
chose, as I pleased to drive to *Georigetti*'s Dominions; I made
them drive a great Number of Sheep, of the finest Wool I ever
saw, and very large also; a great Number of Creatures not
unlike an Ass for Shape, but with two upright Horns and short
Ears, which gave abundance of rich Milk; and also some
Swine. All these were drove to, and distributed at my new
Colony; where I let them remain, till I had provided a proper
Receptacle for them at *Doorpt Swangeanti*, near the Woods;
when I brought many over the black Mountain, and distributed there, with Directions how to manage them; and in
about seven Years time, we held a little Beast Market 'near
Brandleguarp, twice a Year, where the spare Cattle were
brought up, and preserved in Salt till the next Market; for
I had some Years before, made large Salt Works near the Sea,
at Mount *Alkoe*; which imployed abundance of Hands, and
was now become a considerable Trade.

We had Iron, Copper, and Silver Money, which went very
current; and had Butter and Cheese from the Farms near the
Woods, as plenty as we had the Fruits before; great Numbers
of Families having settled there; and there was scarce a
Family but was of some Occupation or other.

By the Accounts I received from the Mines, from time to
time, it was prodigious to hear, what vast Quantities of Metals
were prepared in one Year now, by little above one third of the

Hands that were usually imployed in them before; for now the Mens Ambition was, to leave a good Week's Work done at their return, for an Example to those who were coming; and the Overseers told me, they would sing and work, with the greatest Delight imaginable, whilst they pleased themselves with telling one another, how they intended to spend the next fourteen Days.

CHAPTER XXII

Peter looking over his Books finds a Latin *Bible; sets about a Translation; teaches some of the Ragams Letters; sets up a Paper Manufacture; makes the Ragams read the Bible; the Ragams teach others to read and write; a Fair kept at the black Mountain;* Peter's *Reflection on the* Swangeantines

ALL things being now so settled, that they would go on of themselves; and having no further direct View in my Head, I spent some time with my Wife; and looking over my Books one Day to divert myself, with the greatest Joy imaginable, I found that the Bible I had taken to be in the *Portuguese* Tongue, was a *Latin* one. It was many Years since I had thought of that Language, but on this Occasion, by Force of Memory and Recollection, and with some Attention, Consideration, and Practice, I found it return to me in so plentiful a manner, that I fully resolved to translate my Bible into the *Swangeantine* Tongue.

I sent directly for *Lasmeel* to be my Amanuensis; and to work we went upon the Translation.

We began at the Creation, and descending to the Flood, went on to the *Jewish* Captivity in *Egypt*, and Deliverence by *Moses*; leaving out the Genealogies, and all the *Jewish* Ceremonies and Laws, except the ten Commandments. I translated the Books of *Samuel* and *Kings*, down to the *Babilonish*

Captivity. I then translated such parts of the Prophets, as were necessary to introduce the Messiah, and discover him; the Book of *Psalms*, *Job*, and the *Proverbs*, and with the utmost Impatience hasted to the New Testament. But then considering that when I had done, as only *Lasmeel* and myself could read it, in case of our Deaths, the Translation must die with us; I chose out six of the junior Ragams, and two of the elder, to learn Letters; and in less than twelve Months, I had brought them all to read mine and *Lasmeel*'s Writing perfectly well.

I instructed these Ragams at spare Hours, whilst I went on with my Translation, but finding my Paper grow low, having had a great Supply of coursish Linnen, and a sort of Callicoes from the Isles, in return for our Metals; I set up a Manufactory from that, and some Gums of the Trees, which we boiled with it to a Pulp in Iron Pans, and beating it to pieces, made a useful Paper, which would bear Ink tolerably. But I could find nothing to make Ink of, tho' I sent over all the Country, to search for every Herb and Fruit not commonly used; till at last I found an Herb and Flower on it, which if taken before the Flower faded, would by boiling thoroughly become blew; this, by still more boiling in a Copper Pan, till it was dry and burnt hard to the Bottom, in some measure answered my Purpose, and I fixed upon it, as the best I could obtain from all my Experiments.

When the Ragams were Masters of their Pens, I set six of them to copy what *Lasmeel* had finished, and the other two to teach their Brethren; and in two Years time, by a pretty constant Application, for I made them transcribe it perfectly fair and intelligible, we finished our Translation, and two fair Copies.

I then ordering the Ragams to read a Portion of it to the People constantly in the Mouch; they, from the Novelty of the Story, at first grew so exceeding fond of it, that upon the proper Expositions of it, I taught the Ragams afterwards to make, they began to apply it seriously to religious Purposes.

My writing Ragams were very fond of their Knowledge of

Letters; and Trade and Commerce now increasing, which put every one more or less in want of the same Knowledge; they made a great Profit of it, by instructing all who applied to them. This Increase of Writing, necessarily provided a Maintenance for several Persons who travelled to *Norbon* for Quills, and sold them to the *Swangeantines* at extravagant Rates; till the *Norbonese* hearing that, brought them themselves to the Foot of the Mountain, where the *Swangeantines* bought them, as they did several other Commodities, which one Country had, and the other wanted, especially Iron Wares of almost every Denomination; so that the Mountain being so excessive high, was the Barrier; for the *Norbonese* finding that Difficulty in ascending and descending, which the *Swangeantines* with their Graundees did not; there was a constant Market of Buyers and Sellers on the Mount *Alkoe* Side of the black Mountain; which by Degrees grew the general Mart of the three Kingdoms.

I have often reflected with myself, and have been amazed to think, that so ingenious and industrious a People, as the *Swangeantines* have since appeared to be; and who till I came amongst them, had nothing more than bare Food, and a Hole to lie in, in a barren rocky Country, and then seemed to desire only what they had; should in ten Years time, be supplied not only with the Conveniencies, but Superfluities of Life; and that they should then become so fond of them, as rather willingly to part with Life itself, than be reduced to the State I found them in. And I have as often on this Occasion reflected on the Goodness of Providence, in rendring one part of Mankind easy under the Absence of such Comforts, as others could not rest without; and have made it a great Argument for my Assent to well-attested Truths above my Comprehension. For, says I, to have affirmed at my first coming, either that these things could have been made at all, or when done could have been of any additional Benefit to these People, would have been so far beyond their Imaginations, that the Reporter of so plain a Truth, as they now find it, would have been looked upon as a Madman or an Imposter: But by opening their Views by little and little, and shewing them the Dependance of one thing upon another; he that should now affirm the Inutility of them, would be observed in a much worse Light. And yet, without any Imbellishments of Art, how did this so great a People live under the Protection of Providence? Let us first view them at a vast Distance from any sort of Sustenance, yet from the Help of the Graundee, that Distance was but a Step to them. They were forced to inhabit the Rocks, from an utter Incapacity of providing Shelter else where, having no Tool that would either cut down Timber for an Habitation, or dig up the Earth for a Fence, or Materials to make one: But they had a Liquor that would dissolve the Rock itself into Habitations. They had neither Beast or Fish, for Food or Burthen: But they had Fruits equivalent to both, of the same Relish, and as wholesome without shedding Blood. Their Fruits were dangerous, till they had fermented in a boiling Heat; and they had neither the Sun, or any Fire, or the Knowledge how to propagate or continue it. But they had their hot Springs always boiling, without their Care or Concern. They had neither the Skins of Beasts, the original Cloathing, or any other artificial Covering from the Weather; but they were born with that warm Cloathing the Graundee, which being of a considerable Density, and full of Veins flowing with warm Blood, not only defended their Flesh from all outward Injuries, but was a most soft, comely, and warm Dress to the Body. They lived mostly in the dark Rock, having less Difference of Light with the Change of Seasons, than other People have: But either by Custom or Make, more Light than what Providence has sent them in the Sweecoe, is disagreeable: So that where little is to be obtained, Providence by confining the Capacity, can give Content with that; and where apparent Wants are, we may see by these People, how careful Providence is to supply them; for neither the Graundee, the Sweecoes, or their Springs, are to be found where those Necessaries can be supplied by other means.

Amongst my other Considerations, I have often thought,

that if I had gone to the Top of the black Mountains North-ward of *Brandleguarp*, in the very lightest time, I might have seen the Sun; but these Mountains were so elevated, that our lightest time was only the gilded Glimmering of their Tops, having never seen so much Light on them, as totally to eclipse all the Stars; of which we had always the same in view, but in different Positions.

CHAPTER XXIII

Peter's Children provided for; Youwarkee's Death; how the King and Queen spend their time; Peter grows melancholy; wants to get to England; contrives Means; is taken up at Sea

I HAD now been at *Brandleguarp* ten Years, and my Children were all provided for by the King, but *Dickey*, as fast as they were qualified for Imployment; and such as were fit for it were married off to the best Alliances in the Country; so that I had only to sit down, and see every thing I had put my Hand to prosper, and not an evil Eye in the three Kingdoms cast at me: But about my eleventh or twelfth Year, my Wife fall-ing into a lingering Disorder, at the End of two Years, it carried her off. This was the first real Affliction I had suffered for many Years, and so soured my Temper, that I became fit for nothing, and it was painful to me even to think of Business.

The King's Marriage had produced four Children, three Sons and a Daughter; which he would frequently tell me were mine.

Old *Oniwheske* was dead, and the King and Queen divided their whole time equally, between *Brandleguarp* and *Apsilo*: But he was Building a Palace at my new Colony; which by this time was grown to a vast City, and was called *Stygena* in Compliment to the Queen; and this new Palace was designed to receive the Court one third of the Year, as it lay almost at equal Distance between both his other Palaces. This Method, which his Majesty took at my Persuasion on the Death of *Oniwheske*, tho' it went against the Grain at first, was now grown so habitual to him, and he saw his own Interest so much in it, in the Love and Esteem it procured him from the People, that at last he wanted no Spur to it.

My Melancholy for the Death of my Wife, which I hoped time would wear off, rather gained ground upon me; and tho' I was as much regarded as ever by the whole Court, yet it grew troublesome to me, even to be asked my Advice; and it not only surprized those about me, but even myself, to see the same Genius, without any visible natural Decay, in so short a time, from the most sprightly and enterprizing, become the most phlegmatick and unactive.

My Longings after my Native Country, ever since my Wife's Death, redoubled upon me; and I had formed several Schemes of getting thither; as first, I had formed a Project of going off by the Islands, as I had so many small Vessels at Command there, and to get into the main Ocean, and try my Fortune that way; but upon Inquiry, I found that my Vessels could not get to Sea or elsewhere, but to the Zaps Islands, by reason of the many Rocks and Sand-banks which would oppose me, unless I went thro' the Zaps Country; which in the Light they had reason to view me, I was afraid to do. Then I had Thoughts of going from the Coast of *Norbon*; but that must have been in one of the foreign Vessels, and they coming from a quite different Quarter than I must go, in all Probability if I had put to Sea any way they were unacquainted with, they having no Compass, we must have perished; for the more I grew by Degrees acquainted with the Situation of *Doorpt Swangeanti*, the stronger were my Conjectures, that my nearest Continent must be the Southern Coast of *America*; but still it was only Conjecture. At length being tired and uneasy, I resolved as I was accustomed to Flight, and loved it; I would take a Turn for some Days, carry me where it would, I should certainly light on some Land, whence at worst I could but come back again. I then went to see if my

Chair, Board, and Ropes were sound, for I had not used them for several Years past; but I found them all so crazy, I durst not venture in them; which Disappointment put off my Journey for some time. However, as I had still the Thought remaining, it put me on seeking some other Method to put it in Practice: So I contrived the Poles from which you took me, being a sort of hollow Cane the *Swangeantines* make their Spears of, but exceeding strong and springy; which interwoven with small Cords, were my Seat, and were much lighter than my Chair; and these buoyed me up when your Goodness relieved me. I had taken Mount *Alkoe* Bearers, as I knew I must come to a Country of more Light; and I now find, if I had not fallen, I must soon have reached Land, if we could have held out; for we were come too far to think of returning, without a resting place: And what will become of my poor Bearers, I dread to think, if they attempted to return, they must have dropt; for they had complained all the last Day and Night, and had shifted very often. If in your History you think fit to carry down the Life of a poor old Man any further, you will as well know what to say of me, as I can tell you; and I hope what I have hitherto said, will in some measure recompence both your Expence and Labour.

FINIS

A

T A B L E

OF THE

Names of Persons and Things,

Mentioned in the Two Volumes

A.

Abb,	A Room.
Apsillo,	Capital of *Norbon*.
Arco,	A Man who committed the first Murder.
Arndrumstake,	*Pendlehamby*'s Colambat.
Arkoe,	Water surrounded with Wood.

B.

Barbarsa,	*Georigetti*'s Favourite.
Barkatt,	A Husband.
Barras,	A Leathern Apron, or Flap behind.
Bash,	A Valet de Chambre.
Battingdrigg,	The Name of an Arkoe.
Begsurbeck,	An old King of *Sass Doorpt Swangeanti*.
Born Isles,	Islands to the right Hand.
Boskee,	A very grand Room, or Saloon.
Bott,	A Gourd.
Bougee,	Lie down.
Brandleguarp,	Chief City of *Sass Doorpt Swangeanti*.

C.

Calentar,	A Doctor, or Surgeon.
Cluff,	A Captain.
Colamb,	A Governor.

C c

Colambat,	A Government.
Colapet,	A Bag for Provision.
Collwarr,	God.
Coovett,	A Mansion-House, or Seat.
Crashdoorpt,	*Quangrallort's* Colambat, or Country of the Slit.
Crashee,	Slit.
Crullmott,	A Fruit tasting like a Fowl.

D.

David,	*Peter's* fourth Son.
Doorpt Swangeanti,	The Land of Flight.
Dorrs,	A sort of Apples.
Dossee,	A soft thing.

E.

Emina,	A Rock.

F.

Felbamko,	*Oniwheske's* Nephew.
Filgay,	A Freeman.
Filus,	A Rib of the Graundee.

G.

Gadsi,	Governor of Mount *Alkoe.*
Gauingrunt,	A revolted Town in the West.
Gawrey,	A Woman.
Georigetti,	King of *Sass Doorpt Swangeanti.*
Glaulepzee,	An *African* who escaped with *Peter.*
Glumm,	A Man.
Glumm Boss,	A young Man.
Goppo,	A Father in Law.
Gorpell,	An Ensign.
Gowren,	Women.
Graundee,	The Glumms Wings and Dress.
Gripsack,	A Trumpet.
Grandevolet,	*Peter's* Arkoe.
Gume,	The Leather between the Filus's of the Graundee.

H.

Hallycarnie,	*Youwarkee*'s Sister, also her second Daughter.
Harlokin,	Prince of the Rebels.
Hoximo,	A place to bury the Dead.
Hunkum,	Marriage.

I.

Jahamel,	The King's Sister.
Jemmy,	*Peter*'s second Son.
I. O,	The chief Ragam.

L.

Lallio,	First King of *Sass Doorpt Swangeanti*.
Lask,	A Slave.
Laskmett,	Slavery.
Lasmeel,	*Peter*'s Scholar.

M.

Maleck,	*Peter*'s Man from Mount *Alkoe*.
Mindrack,	The Devil.
Mouch,	A Church.
Moucheratt,	An Assembly of the States.
Mount Alkoe,	A Kingdom taking Name from a burning Mountain.

N.

Nasgig,	A common Soldier, made a General at the Request of *Peter*.
Nicor,	A Creature of *Barbarsa*, the King's Favourite.
Norbon,	The Name of the North Country.
Normnbdsgrsutt,	Ancient Name of *Youwarkee*'s Country.

O.

Oniwheske,	King of *Norbon*.
Ors clam gee,	Here am I.

P.

Padsi,	A Fruit tasting like Fish.
Palang,	A Town.

Parky,	Sweet.
Patty,	*Peter*'s eldest Daughter, also his first Wife.
Pedro,	*Peter*'s eldest Son.
Peter,	The Author.
Pendlehamby,	*Youwarkee*'s Father, the Colamb of *Arndrumstake*.
Perigene,	The first born Man.
Philella,	The first born Woman.
Puly,	An Image.
Praave,	Modest.

Q.

Quangrallort,	*Youwarkee*'s Brother, Colamb of *Crash-doorpt*.
Quilly,	*Peter*'s Bash.

R.

Ragam,	A Priest.
Razy,	Mighty.
Richard,	*Peter*'s fifth Son.
Roppin,	Marmalade.
Rossig,	*Quangrallort*'s Companion.

S.

Sarah,	*Peter*'s youngest Daughter.
Sass Doorpt Swangeanti,	*Peter*'s new Name given to *Georigetti*'s Dominions.
Slip the Graundee,	Drawing the Graundee tight to the Body, by a running Noose on a Line.
Stapps,	Minutes.
Stygee,	*Oniwheske*'s Daughter.
Sweecoe,	An Insect, giving a strong Light in the Dark.
Sweecoan,	A Flight with Sweecoes.
Swangean,	Flight.

T.

Telamine,	A Woman, whose Husband committed the first Murder.
Tommy,	*Peter*'s second Son.

Y.

Yaccombourse,	The King's Mistress.
Yacom,	A Man-child.
Youk,	Capital of the West.
Youwarkee,	*Peter*'s Wife.

Z.

Zaps,	Lords.

THE END

EXPLANATORY NOTES

ABBREVIATIONS

Astley   *A New General Collection of Voyages and Travels: . . . Comprehending every Thing remarkable in its Kind, in Europe, Asia, Africa, and America*, pub. Thomas Astley, 4 vols., 1745-7.

Robinson   Daniel Defoe, *The Life and Strange Surprizing Adventures of*
Crusoe   *Robinson Crusoe, of York, Mariner: . . . Written by Himself*,
            1719.

Title-page. R.S. a Passenger in the Hector: It has been suggested that these initials are 'a telonism of Peter Wilkins' (G. C. Boase and W. P. Courtney, *Bibliotheca Cornubiensis*, 1878, ii. 421) and that they are 'intended for the Richard Sympson who stood sponsor for Lemuel Gulliver' (W. Roberts, *The Bookworm . . .* , 3S., 1890, p. 199). As the introduction, by the same '*Passenger in the* Hector', is signed R.P., as is also the dedication, it seems probable that the reading on the title-page is a misprint.

Dedication. Elizabeth, Countess of Northumberland: Lady Elizabeth Seymour (1716-76). Her husband, Sir Hugh Smithson, became Earl of Northumberland on 7 February 1750, following the death of his father-in-law.

Introduction. Page 6. Flounce: splash.

   Page 7. he had been from England no less than thirty-five Years: cf. *Robinson Crusoe*, p. 330: 'I arriv'd in *England*, the Eleventh of *June*, in the Year 1687, having been thirty and five Years absent.'

VOLUME I

Page 15. Jefferys: George Jeffreys, first Baron Jeffreys of Wem (1648-89), held the 'bloody assize' in the west after the suppression of Monmouth's rebellion.

Page 18. (1) *double Pistole*: Spanish gold coin worth about £2.
   (2) *the Smoak of his Mother's Chimney*: see M. P. Tilley, *Dictionary of the Proverbs in England* (1950), S 572.

Page 19. (1) *Lubber*: big, stupid fellow.
   (2) *declining of Hæc Mulier*, etc.: learning elementary Latin grammar.

Page 23. tight: tidy, smart.

Page 27. *cocker'd up*: brought up indulgently.

Page 29. *bite*: deceive, overreach.

Page 32. (1) *operative*: active.

(2) *virtual*: effective, powerful.

Page 36. *bring to*: cause the ship to come to a standstill.

Page 37. (1) *Fusee*: light musket, firelock. Cf. *Robinson Crusoe*, p. 22: 'three Fuzees with Powder and Shot'.

(2) *apparently*: visibly.

Page 41. *flead*: flayed, skinned. Cf. p. 99: 'having flead him, and taken out the Guts and Intrails'.

Page 42. (1) *our Deliverers were Portuguese*: Both Crusoe (p. 36) and Gulliver (*Gulliver's Travels*, iv. 11) are rescued by Portuguese sailors.

(2) *Saint Salvadore*: Much of Paltock's information about Africa appears to come from Astley's *Collection of Voyages and Travels*; 'Mr. Robert Paltock, Attorney at Law, in Enfield' is among the subscribers whose names are printed in the first volume of this work. According to Astley, '*St. Salvador* . . . was once the Capital of *Kongo*, and Residence of the Kings' (iii. 247).

Page 43. (1) *Angola*: 'THE Kingdom of *Angola* is bounded on the North by *Kongo*, from whence it is separated by the River *Danda*, some say *Bengo*; on the East by the Kingdom of *Matamba*; on the South by *Benguela*; and on the West by the Ocean. It lies between seven Degrees thirty minutes and ten Degrees forty Minutes of South Latitude; and between thirty-two Degrees and forty-one Degrees twenty Minutes of Eastern Longitude: Being about five hundred and ten Miles long from West to East, and an hundred and ninety broad from North to South' (Astley, iii. 263).

(2) *Here we remained under Confinement*, etc.: Andrew Battel, an English sailor whose travels are related by Astley, is 'sent to *Angola* in *Africa*, . . . imprisoned, and after sent-up the River *Quansa* to a Garison Town' (iii. 137).

Page 44. *immediate Death, in the Attempt of Liberty*, etc.: cf. Astley, iii. 138: 'IN this Fort there were some *Egyptians* and *Moriscos* banished like himself. To one of these *Egyptians* Battel disclosed his Mind, telling him, it was better to venture their Lives for their Liberty, than continue in that miserable Place.'

Page 46. (1) *Congo*: '*KONGO* at large may be divided into four Parts or Kingdoms, namely, *Loango*, *Proper Kongo*, *Angola*, and *Benguela*. These Kingdoms lie from North to South' (Astley, iii. 212).

(2) *we saw a little Hovel*, etc.: 'throughout all the Kingdom, excepting in *St. Salvador*, there is never a Stone House, but only Straw and Stubble. The finest are built with Mud Walls, and thatched; most of them without Windows, the Door serving in their Stead' (Astley, iii. 147).

(3) *an old Man*, etc.: cf. Astley, iii. 138: 'On the third Day, they met an old Negro, who was travelling to *Mani Kabech*. Him they bound and made guide them the Way . . .'.

Page 47. (1) *Muletto*: young or small mule.

(2) *Loango*: '*Loango* . . . has *Gabon* to the North, to the East the Country of *Mokoko*, or *Anziko*; and on the South, the River *Zaire*, being about four hundred and thirty Miles long from West to East, and three hundred and twenty broad from North to South' (Astley, iii. 212).

Page 49. *Crocodile*: cf. Astley, iii. 138: 'THE fourth Day, at Night, they came to a River lying North, which they passed with great Danger, it being full of Crocodiles.'

Page 52. *a Lioness, and a small Whelp*, etc.: cf. Astley, iii. 149: 'ABOUT Midnight they were disturbed by a Lion and She-Tyger that came sporting towards their Huts . . . but the Blacks, after talking together a little, lighted a Fire, which made those Beasts fly towards the River.'

Page 53. (1) *Quamis*: cf. Astley, iii. 279: 'the Blacks of *Quisama*, residing on the South Side of the River *Quanza*'.

(2) *there came a Woman to it stark-naked*: cf. Astley, iii. 240: 'Within Doors they generally go stark-naked'; iii. 150: 'a handsome, young, black Woman stark naked'.

(3) *ringing for a Light*: 'a slip this, no doubt, of Peter's tongue' (*Retrospective Review*, vii, 1823, i. 156).

Page 54. *alternate*: reciprocal.

Page 57. *Factory*: merchant company's trading station.

Page 58. (1) *Gut*: sound, strait.

(2) *peremptory*: definite, actual.

Page 59. *stretch*: sail continuously in one direction. Cf. *Robinson Crusoe*, p. 165: 'the Boat began to stretch away'.

Page 62. (1) *bulging*: staving in.

(2) *by the Board*: by the ship's side, overboard. Cf. *Robinson Crusoe*, p. 11: 'Two Ships that rid near us we found had cut their Masts by the Board'.

Page 68. *primitive*: original.

Page 71. *Fluck*: fur.

Page 72. *main Ocean*: high sea.

Page 74. *Setts*: directions in which a current flows. Cf. *Robinson Crusoe*, p. 225: 'the Currents, or Sets of the Tide'.

Page 76. *Dismission*: liberation.

Page 78. *Higler*: itinerant dealer.

Page 83. *Lop-wood*: branches lopped from a tree.

Page 85. (1) *Truckle*: low-wheeled car, truck.
(2) *to seek*: at a loss.

Page 86. *Ell*: forty-five inches.

Page 88. (1) *Exoticks*: plants of foreign extraction.
(2) *blubber*: bubble.

Page 90. *Flower*: flour.

Page 93. *Languor*: faintness, softness.

Page 95. *Plat*: area, patch.

Page 97. *flacking*: flapping.

Page 99. *Sight*: pupil.

Page 103. *obnoxious*: liable, exposed.

Page 110. *salute*: kiss.

Page 129. (1) *delicately*: delightfully.
(2) *Rota*: round, routine. Cf. p. 154: 'a settled Rota of Action'.

Page 130. (1) *Ward*: small piece of enclosed pasture ground. Cf. p. 145: 'I had by this time cleared a Spot of Ground, on one side of my Grotto, by burning up the Timber and Underwood which had covered it; this I inclos'd, and within that Inclosure I raised my Aviary; and my Poultry thrived well there'.
(2) *America*: probably in mistake for Africa.

Page 131. *Vest*: garment.

Page 132. *admired*: wondered.

Page 133. *distract*: drive mad.

Page 139. *grisly*: gristly.

Page 140. *rigling*: wriggling.

Page 141. *factitious*: artificial.

Page 142. *Mantuamaking*: dressmaking.

Page 144. *familiar*: domesticated, tame.

Page 145. (1) *used*: accustomed.
(2) *Biddy*: sound used in calling chickens. Cf. Shakespeare, *Twelfth Night*, III. iv. 125-8: 'Why, how now, my bawcock! how dost thou, chuck? . . . Ay, "Biddy, come with me."'

Page 146. *Sorts*: species.

Page 152. *crazy*: unsound.

Page 156. *Doctor*: teacher.

Page 161. *Flota*: treasure fleet; the name given to the Spanish fleet which used to cross the Atlantic and bring back to Spain the products of America and the West Indies.

Page 164. *bulged*: with the bottom or sides stove in. Cf. *Robinson Crusoe*, p. 56: 'the Ship was bulg'd, and had a great deal of Water in her Hold'.

Page 165. (1) *Flagellet*: flageolet.

(2) *Terrella*: small artificial globe containing a magnet.

Page 189. *pulled off*: drank.

VOLUME II

Page 200. (1) *Point*: thread lace made wholly with the needle.

(2) *Bob-wigs*: wigs having the bottom locks turned up into 'bobs' or short curls.

Page 202. *drilling on*: protracting, lengthening out.

Page 203. *knocked . . . up*: dismayed, confounded.

Page 204. *Campain-wig*: plain, close-fitting wig introduced from France about 1712.

Page 206. *ungrateful*: distasteful, unpleasant.

Page 211. *caressed*: treated with kindness, favoured.

Page 219. (1) *Handy-cuffs*: blows.

(2) *come of*: extricate myself.

Page 221. (1) *Cod*: narrow closed part at the lower end of a fishing net.

(2) *Hale*: haul, draught of fish.

Page 222. *Drill's Mouth*: mouth of a rivulet or small stream. Cf. *Robinson Crusoe*, p. 173: 'two or three little Drills of fresh Water'.

Page 229. (1) *Shiver*: chip, splinter.

(2) *He stroaked his Chin*: cf. p. 177: 'thanked me by lifting his Hand to his Chin'. Cf. also *Robinson Crusoe*, p. 25: 'if you will not stroak your Face to be true to me, *that is, swear by* Mahomet *and his Father's Beard*'.

Page 248. *a Foot and half broad*: 'Since the board is so narrow as to make any voyage on it extremely hazardous, one wonders whether this detail is an oversight of Paltock or a mistake of his printers. Louis Pierre Boitard, who illustrated the original edition of the work, pictures a board considerably wider than a foot and a half' (A. N. Wilkins, 'Robert Paltock and the Bishop of Chester', *Notes and Queries*, cciii, 1958, 439).

Page 257. (1) *loaded*: made to appear full-bodied by adulteration.

(2) *alto-relievo*: high relief.

Page 265. *Caul*: netted substructure of a wig.

Page 279. *States*: parliament, constituted assembly.

Page 280. *Grimalken*: name often given to a witch's cat; here a contemptuous term suggesting childish superstition.

Page 282. (1) *sat*: started.
    (2) *temporizing*: adaptable.

Page 317. (1) *Spadle*: small spade.
    (2) *rids away*: is dispatched.

Page 327. *every thing is easy when it is known*: see M. P. Tilley, *Dictionary of the Proverbs in England* (1950), D 418; cf. Shakespeare, *Measure for Measure*, IV. ii. 221.

Page 336. *Fats*: vats.

Page 350. *job*: thrust, jab.

Page 356. *perdue*: hidden.